CRITICS RAVE ABOUT STOBIE PIEL!

THE RENEGADE'S HEART

"This tale is filled with humor, tenderness, introspection and plenty of passion. On a cold winter's night, *The Renegade's Heart* will warm you up."

—*Romantic Times*

RENEGADE

"Ms. Piel has written a love story filled with excellent characters... The hot, hot, hot love scenes add just the right amount of spice to a wonderful read!"

—*Romantic Times*

THE WHITE SUN

"Full of action, adventure, passion and romance.... Those who like some adventure with their romance will love this book."

—*Writers Write*

BLUE-EYED BANDIT

"Kudos to Ms. Piel for providing a love story with humor, passion and some whimsy. It's an all-around great read."

—*Romantic Times*

THE MIDNIGHT MOON

"Stobie Piel successfully brings to life another galaxy in a lively but realistic manner that will elate fans of the sub-genre and science fiction fans as well."

—*Affaire de Coeur*

THE DAWN STAR

"A refreshing story line that takes you to a distant planet.... Exciting and provocative."

—*Rendezvous*

A TASTE OF LOVE

"Our?" Eliana's face brightened and she clasped her hands in delight. "Then I am a Mage, too?"

He couldn't deceive her. "You are. As I said, we were trained together since childhood. It is part of what binds us, my dear, and it has always made us closer."

"Because we understand each other?"

Damir gazed into her eyes. "We do." That much, at least, was true. Yet somehow she had never seen how much she mattered to him, how much he cared what she thought and how she felt. He touched her cheek. "We are meant for each other. No one can understand you as I do."

She moved closer and his heart quickened. "Perhaps it is that power of mine which made me vulnerable to my current affliction."

He swallowed. "It's possible, yes." He drew her into his arms, and it felt natural, as if they had, indeed, done this a thousand times. She rested her head against his shoulder, and seemed comfortable when he held her.

She slid her arms around his waist and breathed deeply. With infinite tenderness, she pressed her lips against his neck, and a shudder of delight coursed through him. He had imagined her as a passionate lover, but he hadn't envisioned this sweetness. Eliana gazed up at him, her green eyes soft. She parted her lips to speak, and his breath caught in his throat....

Other books by Stobie Piel:

LORD OF THE DARK SUN
THE RENEGADE'S HEART
RENEGADE
MISTLETOE & MAGIC (Anthology)
BLUE-EYED BANDIT
FIVE GOLD RINGS (Anthology)
FREE FALLING
THE WHITE SUN
THE MAGIC OF CHRISTMAS (Anthology)
THE MIDNIGHT MOON
TRICK OR TREAT
MOLLY IN THE MIDDLE
THE DAWN STAR

STRANGE BREWS

STOBIE PIEL

LOVE SPELL NEW YORK CITY

To Chris De May,
for the sweetest & warmest energy...

LOVE SPELL®

November 2005

Published by

Dorchester Publishing Co., Inc.
200 Madison Avenue
New York, NY 10016

ISBN 0-505-52650-6

Printed in the United States of America.

Visit us on the web at www.dorchesterpub.com.

There was no fair fiend near him, not a sight
Or sound of awe but in his own deep mind...

—Alastor, *Percy Bysshe Shelley*

Chapter One

Mist filled the Vale of Amrodel, dew sparkled on the grass, and the leaves hung laden with moisture as Eliana Daere rode to the meeting. She journeyed deep into the heart of the Woodland realm, and the weight of impending glory rode with her. Her chubby brown mare plodded too slowly for Eliana's eagerness. "Move swiftly, Selsig! I must reach the glade before Damir, lest he lay a trap for me."

Selsig offered a brief trot, then slowed again to a walk. The path dipped low, then rose higher as they approached the Mage's Glade, the ancient meeting place of the greatest mystics the Woodland had ever known. Today, this legendary site would see the end of a battle between lifelong rivals, and the dawn of her own ascension.

Today, she would pour the Wine of Truce, and watch him drink.

Eliana's eyes narrowed and her lips curved upwards at the corners. Never had she reached this height of brilliance. Damir couldn't resist her offer of meeting. He couldn't resist learning her true intentions.

He would doubt her, of course, but she was prepared.

1

She had positioned herself in front of her polished looking glass and practiced her speech. She'd practiced looking innocent, guileless. She'd practiced a humble appearance.

A low, satisfied chuckle began in her throat as she anticipated her victory. She was the greatest herbalist that ever lived. Her talents with mystic brews surpassed even Madawc, the old mage who had apprenticed both Eliana and Damir.

Their competition had started in childhood. Damir was always a little ahead of her. When she was exploding mushrooms, he was making objects disappear. When she turned a horse's coat blue, he elevated Madawc's chair, and stole her glory. When she offered the Woodland king her wisdom concerning the Norsk threat, he chose Damir as Amrodel's defender, and ignored her. No one gave her the respect she was due. That would change. But not before she had eliminated the one person who always seemed to turn her plans upside down.

Today she had surpassed his greatest skills, and everything she had ever wanted would soon be hers for the taking.

Selsig picked her way toward the glade with exceeding care, avoiding a thorn bush on the right, and a jutting rock on the left. Eliana squeezed her legs against the mare's fat belly. "Move on, Selsig!"

She rode into the clearing, but too late. Damir sat there, astride a tall gray horse. Larger than any Woodland pony, the beast was heir to the great horses from the desert herds of Kora, a product of the magnificent stallion brought north by Damir's father. Dragonflies darted around the clearing and the filtered sunlight glinted on their delicate wings. The morning dew rose in a fine mist around his horse's strong legs, shrouding the Mage in an eerie light.

Damir exuded confidence and strength. He was too handsome and too powerful. He wore a satin tunic in

2

scarlet and indigo over ivory, the heraldic Beast of Amrodel emblazoned on his chest. Like most Woodland people, Damir rarely dressed in formal attire. But Eliana doubted that his choice of clothes was a gesture of respect. He had chosen this special garment to mock the formality of her invitation.

Each time she saw him, he seemed to have grown. And every time she saw him, the tingle in her fingers increased and her breath quickened. Eliana forcibly directed her vision from Damir to his horse. The beast champed at the bit and stomped, but Damir held it in place. Selsig jerked to a halt and started to back up.

How humiliating! Eliana kicked her heels into the mare's side. "Selsig! Proceed!"

The mare sidestepped around the edge of the glade. Seven upright stones marked the circle. The meeting rock sat in the center, placed there ages ago by the first Woodland Mages. Its surface was flat, and there were two smaller rocks set at the northern and southern points. Eliana had envisioned herself riding proudly to the rock. Instead, Selsig jigged sideways.

Eliana peeked at Damir. Yes. He was grinning. A blade of sunlight cut through the dawn mist and glinted on his black hair. The sun touched his face, and Eliana's heart took an odd bounce. In one miserable flash, she imagined herself in his arms, herself as the source of his renowned desire, herself lost in his passionate embrace.

It was a cruel fate, to desire one's enemy. But even the darkest fate could be overcome. It would be overcome with her wisdom and cleverness. She had arranged everything. Today, nothing would be denied her.

She glanced at him. He was smiling because Selsig was afraid of his overbearing horse. "That beast is frightening my mare!"

He stroked his horse's strong neck. "Llwyd hasn't

moved. The fear is in your mare's imagination." His voice was low, tinged with humor.

It was a fair point, so Eliana ignored it. "*Llwyd?* You named your horse *gray?*"

"It's accurate." Damir eyed Selsig, who balked at approaching the meeting stone. "*Selsig* means *sausage*. That also seems appropriate."

The morning wasn't going as she planned. Selsig flatly refused to move closer to Damir's horse, so Eliana was forced to dismount. She flung her leg forward over Selsig's neck, then hopped down. Damir dismounted with grace and ease, then tied Llwyd to a tree. Eliana led Selsig to the far side of the glen and hitched her to a shrub because the tree branches were too high for the pony.

Selsig forgot the threatening stallion and began stuffing herself on leaves. Eliana seized her pack, checked to be sure her decanter was still right side up, then turned to face Damir.

He wasn't carrying a pack, though a sword hung at his side in a jeweled scabbard. Damir had directed his skill at forging weapons with secret powers, and all blades created by his hand were immensely valuable, treasured by the King of Amrodel—and sought after by the king's enemies. Even Damir's simplest weapons sold for high prices in the port city of Amon-dhen. They were even more prized than the herbs and potions Eliana sold there herself.

But Damir's ability to create a protective shield of energy had become, in uncertain times, his most valuable creation. No invader could enter the realm of Amrodel while Damir's shield held, though nothing could protect its inhabitants from the dangers they carried within. With his power, he held together a land that had long ago lost its balance. In Eliana's view, this power kept Amrodel isolated, and in isolation, she saw doom.

Eliana hesitated, popped her lips like a bottle being uncorked, then approached the Mage's Rock. She set her pack casually down beside the rock, then clasped her hands before her body and bowed.

"I am deeply pleased and most honored that you consented to meet me here, Damir ap Kora."

Damir motioned outward with his hands and returned her bow. It wasn't sincere. "Could I deny such an unexpected invitation, Eliana? Your message spoke of truce and alliance. Yet what alliance can there be between us, who have so long been adversaries?"

The great bulk of Damir's power was in his voice, Eliana felt sure of it. It was low and curiously sensual, worming its way inside her and confusing her thoughts. His brown eyes betrayed nothing, but because her eyes were a misty green that revealed every thought, every scheme, she often had to avert them to disguise her intentions.

Now was such a time. She glanced around at the horses, then at the rock, then at a skylark as it flitted from the high chestnut branches.

Her gaze snapped back to Damir. "Let us put aside our past differences, Damir. They were small . . ."

"You tried to set me on fire."

". . . and best forgotten."

"I had almost no hair for a year after that."

"It grew back, didn't it?" She hadn't meant to snap. She caught herself and forced a smile. "Those tiresome, bleak days are gone. You and I have excelled at our craft. We are both gifted from birth, and well-skilled by learning. Surely we are better together than apart?"

"Are you offering marriage, Eliana?"

She cringed and shuddered, then sucked in air like a hiss. "Not in this lifetime!" He laughed, and she shook herself, fighting to remember her purpose. "I propose an alliance. We will combine our knowledge, and work together in the king's service."

"When Owain Daere made this same offer two years ago, you refused. You took the proposition of alliance with me as an insult," Damir's brow furrowed. "You flung grapes and apples at my head, called the king a snake, and—I'm certain—gave the king's wife a rash."

"I never did." She had. King Owain had insulted Eliana by denying her the position of honor she deserved—in favor of Damir. If the king had to sleep alone for a few days, or a week, it was as he deserved.

Damir nodded. "As you say, it is best forgotten. Come now, Eliana, what do you ask of me? It's well known to all that the Norsk chieftain, Bruin the Ruthless, threatens this land. It is known also that he bears a vial of your most deadly potion."

Eliana winced. This was a sore spot, and perhaps evidence that her uncle might be wise in refusing her a position in his service. "It's only deadly if used in full quantity. Its original purpose was to induce sleep."

His brow angled. "I doubt Bruin the Ruthless intended to combat sleeplessness. Nor is he likely to use your potion by the drop."

She couldn't allow herself to get angry or argue with him. "The potion was purchased in good faith." She paused, feeling small. "And once I learned it had fallen into the wrong hands, I immediately devised an antidote and gave it to the king. He is in no danger."

"Purchased, you say, but by whom?"

Eliana met his eyes and she did not waver. "This matter was discussed at Council. I see no need to revisit the matter here. It was resolved by my antidote."

"You gave no better answer there."

"And I never will!"

His smile had faded. "What allegiance do you bear the Norsk, Eliana? They are cruel, by all accounts, savage in battle, and nothing I have ever heard of them can be called admirable. Their whole culture, such that it is, is based on a love of warfare and mayhem."

"They fear us, too," she answered, but her jaw set firm. *I will say no more.*

He frowned. "From what I know of the race, the Norsk fear nothing, no one, though their might cannot rival the magic of the Wood. Yet." Eliana said nothing, but Damir's gaze seemed to bore into her, to penetrate her secret defenses. "You care for them," he said. "I see it in your eyes."

She averted her eyes. He saw too much. "That is none of your concern."

"There are some who say you have taken a Norsk lover."

She frowned and rolled her eyes. "There are some who are fools. Give me their names and I will deal with them accordingly."

"When you give me the name of your Norsk ally," he replied. "I know what 'accordingly' means to you, and I would not inflict it on another."

Eliana glared at him. "I care not what people say. You especially." This was not going as she had planned. She intended to disarm him with sweetness. Instead, she imagined a drawn bow clenched in her hands, and aimed at his heart. To her horror, she realized she was already adopting the stance, reaching back as if to draw an arrow, taking aim. . . . She snapped her hands to her sides and folded her hands together, tightly. Damir's brow elevated and a smile again flickered on his lips.

"Long have you counseled the king to lower our defenses, to negotiate with the Norsk," he said, ignoring her quickly resolved battle stance. "Until your motive is answered, I cannot imagine any alliance between us. By whatever means, you allowed a vial of deadly poison into the hands of Amrodel's most dangerous enemy. . . ."

"I have answered that!" She paused, but her teeth ground together until her jaw ached. "Bruin has no idea how to duplicate my poison—he only obtained a small vial."

"Enough, still, to kill a man?"

She paused. "Yes, if used in its entirety. But the antidote is simple to make from the herbs growing by the forest edge."

"By, of course, a method known only to you?"

Eliana fought anger and tried to remember her purpose. "It is for just this reason that I invited you to this meeting."

"You wish to share with me your secrets? In exchange for what?"

He sounded doubtful. If she betrayed her own intentions . . . Eliana turned aside, fighting to adopt the humble expression she had practiced in the mirror. Cheeks pursed slightly. Forehead puckered, chin flattened. It hurt, but she managed a semblance, anyway. She turned back. Damir's dark brow angled in obvious suspicion.

He motioned to the Mage's Rock. "Shall we sit?"

She straightened. The rock had seen many rituals, many great Mages in their most pivotal decisions. Today, it would see the resolution of a troublesome rivalry.

Eliana sat on the nearest rock before realizing her seat was lower than Damir's. The elevation served to heighten the disparity in their respective sizes. Damir started to sit, noticed her predicament, then rose again. He looked guileless. Innocent. Humble. "Shall we switch seats, Eliana?"

"No, thank you. This will be fine."

She had to perch on her knees to raise herself up. It was important to meet him eye to eye. A smile flickered on his lips as she adjusted herself.

"Tell me, Eliana, what have you to offer that might interest me? A tide of darkness encroaches on this land. All in Amrodel have sensed it, even the Mundanes. Its direction lies northeast of here—where the violent Norsk dwell. Among us, only you counsel on their behalf. If you have information concerning the Norsk plans, it would be wise to share it now."

"I have no such information, Damir. The Norsk are a mystery to me, as to everyone in Amrodel."

"But you do not fear them?"

"I fear nothing, and no one." *I fear you.*

"You have become a powerful Mage, Eliana. There are some who might say, too powerful."

"My strength pales in comparison to your own, Damir. Yet it might be that my own meager talents, combined in some measure with yours, would benefit this land we share, and forestall the darkness that we perceive." *Well done!* Perfect, how even her voice remained! She grew tired of living in a land where fate was determined by fear and by weakness, where her people had to be protected by this dark man's strength, and not her own.

"This should prove interesting," replied Damir. He was toying with her. Well, she was toying with him, too.

Her hair eased forward over her shoulder and escaped from beneath her sheer headdress. She pushed it back. "I will share with you the recipes for potions of both healing and . . . other uses."

"Would that include the concoction that made old Rhys the Bard believe himself to be a spider and take to weaving 'webs' around the Vale?"

"A shame it wore off." She paused, frowning. "The song he devised at my expense was most grating."

"Indeed? I rather enjoyed that one."

He would, considering it implied she harbored secret and intensely passionate feelings for Damir. Best to change the subject. "I will happily share with you all my potions."

His brow rose in surprise. "And what do you ask of me in return, my lady? The records of my own work, perhaps?"

Eliana ignored his reference to records, since he had

once caught her leaving his cottage with the entirety of his scrolls stuffed in a sack. "Only what might be useful in a combined effort at serving our land and our king, of course."

"Of course."

"I greatly admire your work, Damir. It is a product of your genius, a testament to the grandeur of your father's great culture."

"You flatter me, my lady."

"Yes, I might have been . . . overly zealous in my expression of that admiration, but all those secretive substances, books, curious objects . . ."

"It was too much for you to resist."

She tried to smile, but only one side of her mouth responded. "I am older now, and wise enough to know that no one Mage can possess every element of our craft. There will always be another who knows more about certain facets."

Damir didn't respond. He watched her, his face revealing nothing of his inner mind. His dark eyes took in all light, and every secret she possessed, yet yielded nothing in return. He was searching for deceit in her eyes. Eliana gathered every portion of her will and met his gaze.

She lasted a second only. His eyes saw too much. Rather than penetrate his dark soul, she studied his face. He had a broad, intelligent forehead, high cheekbones, a strong, angular chin. His lips were full and crafted, formed easily to a smile. A smile that always seemed to be laughing at her.

"In exchange for your potion lore, what you offer seems a fair trade. We might learn together what we never would apart."

"Quite so." She hadn't expected him to acquiesce so easily or so soon. But so much the better. "We would be far better allies than adversaries. If you agree . . ." She paused. Why was he agreeing this easily? "If you agree, we will meet again and begin the—gradual—opening of our records. That way, if anything should happen to one of us, the records of the other will be safe."

"It seems a reasonable suggestion." Damir started to rise, but slowly, as if teasing her. "Is that the end of our meeting, then?"

"Not quite." Eliana gulped and kept her eyes lowered. She felt sure she heard a low chuckle. A lavender dragonfly darted around the glade. It circled one way, then the other, then hovered. Eliana took the dragonfly's presence as a sign. The moment had come. She seized her pack and withdrew her decanter, then placed it on the rock between them. She set out two silver goblets, but Damir laughed.

"You don't expect me to drink that, do you?"

"This is only my Wine of Truce. We will drink to our alliance . . ." Damir interrupted her speech with another outburst of laughter. She frowned. "It shall be done as the greatest Elite Mages did of old. As ritual. Nothing more."

"My lady, you are queen of devilish brews. Dare I ask what you plan to do to me this time? Shrink me to the size of a newt, perhaps?"

Eliana clasped her hand to her breast. She had practiced this reaction over and over to get it right, and it came off perfectly. "Damir . . . I am deeply offended and most grievously shocked that you should doubt my sincerity." She allowed for a pause while he dried his eyes, then sniffed from his laughter. "I can understand you might have doubts, considering our past association."

"A few."

"But I assure you, my Wine of Truce poses no threat to your well-being. Here . . . I shall prove it to you." *Perfect.* Her voice was soothing, feminine, that of a woman to be trusted.

She poured the wine into his glass, then into her own. He would suspect the wine of carrying her concoction. What else? She held her glass to her lips and took a sip. Damir's eyes never left hers. Had she been so frivolous as to attempt to add her mixture now, he would have caught her.

Fortunately, she wasn't frivolous.

She showed him the half-empty goblet. "Do you see? I drank the wine from my goblet, and no ill has befallen me. Nor will it. Damir, you can trust me. I seek only to unite the two of us in an alliance that will benefit both. A truce." She paused as Damir idly fingered the rim of his goblet. "Drink!"

Sometimes, it was hard to contain her excitement, and her commanding nature. She quivered as he held his goblet to his lips. He paused, almost as if teasing her. He smiled. He looked young when he smiled.

"To our alliance, my lady Eliana. May it prove long and fruitful."

She seized her goblet and took a sip, watching him. He drank, and she struggled against a desire to cheer. "To our alliance . . ."

They set their goblets down at the same time. Eliana beamed, triumphant as she clapped her hands in delight. "How easily you fell for this trick, Damir! It was easier than I expected to defeat you."

He didn't look surprised, but then, he could have no idea of what she had done to him, no idea of the new depth of her power. "Is that so? And would you, dear lady, tell me what evil fate shall befall me thanks to your 'Wine of Truce?'"

"It will soon become apparent . . . or not."

Damir sighed. "Ah. Clever, you are. And is there an antidote to this particular potion?"

She lifted her chin, proud, but she felt a little dizzy. She had used a strong wine to disguise the taste of her potion. Perhaps too strong. "There is no antidote to this particular potion. I didn't have time to devise one."

Now, at last, he began to look concerned. "You would

give me no chance, then, to free myself from your spell? That isn't like you, Eliana."

"Fear not, Damir. My wine will cause you no physical harm." She leaned toward him, and her hair again came loose from its veil. She moved to push it back, but somehow, her hand missed its target and waved at thin air.

A soft cloud advanced through the trees to surround Damir. Fitting, yet odd. "The mist has returned to the glade. And at midday, too! How inconvenient!" She blinked, then shook her head. "I feel rather . . . light. I think I might float from this rock and peer down upon you as the Great Spirits do. That would be pleasing."

Damir's brow furrowed as he examined her expression. "Are you well, Eliana? Your face appears pale."

She shook herself and puffed a breath to clear her senses. "I'm perfectly fine." She started to stand, then swayed. "It's yourself you should worry about. You haven't much time . . ." Her voice sounded odd, high and faraway, as if spoken from a distant part of herself.

"Maybe you should rest a moment . . ." he advised.

Eliana rose up from her rock seat, but her knees went weak, and her legs threatened to betray her. "Damir ap Kora, you are mine!" As she spoke, the mist engulfed not Damir, but herself instead, and Eliana felt herself dissolving into it.

The first time he trusted Eliana Daere, she would be buried beneath the ground, flowers growing over her. Damir jumped up to catch her, but too late. Eliana fell flat on her face and lay there unmoving. Damir knelt beside her. Her breath came even and deep, and he drew a breath of relief. A pale purple dragonfly hovered over the Mage's Rock, its wings gossamer in the filtered morning light. Then it darted away and disappeared.

Damir turned his attention almost reluctantly back to

Eliana. Asleep, she was an exquisite sight, untarnished and beautiful. Asleep, she was just a woman. Not the rival who had tormented him since childhood.

Nothing Eliana did would ever surprise him. He had known her all his life. She had been, and still was, the Woodland king's favorite niece, while Damir was the only son of a Desert prince in exile. Damir had no memory of his father's homeland. His memory began with Eliana, a sprite peering at him through green-leaved trees in a deep forest.

No matter how different their heritage might be, they were two of a kind. They had both been orphaned young, and both had been determined not to show fear. Maybe that explained their competition over Madawc's attention, and why their power meant so much to both—it was all they had that protected them from an uncertain world.

Or maybe they just liked tormenting each other. As a small child, gifted in Magery, she had sat across from him while Madawc instructed them. Her bright green eyes would glitter with mischief as she directed her early efforts his way. He might find a snake in his shirt, a spider in his hair. He might find mud instead of wine in his cup.

In response, he put all his energy into staying one step ahead of her. She strove to best him, and her efforts kept him in prime form. If she succeeded, he had to better her. He loved seeing her angry. He'd spent countless hours thinking of ways to provoke her.

They drove each other crazy, and he had loved every minute.

Until they matured. Until she became a woman of such surpassing loveliness that she stole his breath each time he saw her. That sweet, devious face, those sparkling eyes—her proud, smug expressions and her rapid, melodious speech never failed to hold his fascination, and fuel his fantasies.

Eliana had directed all her power to defeating him in a

battle she brought on herself. He didn't want to feel sorry for her, but she had looked so proud as she waited for him to fall under her spell, even as her concoction stole its way through her instead.

"Eliana Daere, what have you done to yourself?"

Whatever she had done, it had been meant for him. She had plotted and schemed to lure him to this place. She'd thought of everything, but he knew her mind too well. She had poisoned not the wine, but his goblet instead, coating it with an unseen dust that blended with the wine she poured.

He'd watched her face, and she'd watched his. If she had attempted to put anything in his glass, he would have seen her. But because her attention was pinned on his face, she didn't notice him switching his goblet for hers. She drank from his goblet. He drank from hers.

And Eliana Daere lay on the ground.

Damir touched her hair and eased her disheveled headdress aside. Without thinking, he bent and kissed her forehead. Her skin was soft and warm. His heart constricted in his chest, and he knew the hold she had over him was stronger than any potion she could devise.

He picked her up and laid her over her fat mare's back, then mounted his horse. The mare laid her ears flat back in a gesture meant to intimidate the larger horse. Llwyd ignored her, though Damir detected a faint sigh within the horse's deep chest. Damir patted his neck.

"This one is too much like her master, my friend. Best to move on, and don't look back." He paused. "Advice best taken by myself, as well."

It might be wiser, after all, to return her to her cottage, or perhaps bring her to the elder Mage, Madawc, for whatever healing the old man could offer her.

Damir glanced back at Eliana. She hung limp over the felt pad she used as a saddle. The sunlight through the leaves illuminated golden lights on the waves of her dark hair. The outline of her lithe but shapely body caught his attention, and his gaze lingered on the pleasant curve of her backside. Eliana would not have approved the pose, but he could find no fault in it. He wondered how she had intended to move him, had their places been reversed.

A long, coiled rope caught his eye, and he frowned as he envisioned her plan. She would have tied him to her round mare, then dragged him through the woods to her small cottage south of the glade. Damir remembered a particularly bumpy and winding pathway, uphill, crossed with tree roots and thorny brambles, the culmination of which involved the crossing of an icy, swift stream. He imagined himself dragged along that path by his delicate but merciless captor, and his doubts concerning her fate abated.

He left the glade, leading the mare behind Llwyd. Though the pony remained leery of the larger horse, she seemed aware of her sleeping mistress's welfare, and she picked her path carefully as she walked alongside. Eliana made no sound, nor gave any indication of discomfort, though Damir checked her condition often along the ride. A small smile remained on her face throughout, and as Damir turned onto the stone pathway leading to his cottage, he wondered if, despite their relative positions, she still held the advantage over him.

The mare perked her ears as they entered the wide clearing in front of Damir's cottage. Apparently, she had spied Llwyd's pasture and liked the sight of sun-splashed grass. Only rare spots in the forest gave way to open grass. As a reminder of his native homeland, where no trees grew, Damir had chosen this spot to build his home when the Woodland king made him the realm's protector. Though Eliana lived deep in the forest, in a cottage that blended almost perfectly with the surrounding trees, she had coveted Damir's home—perhaps because it was a gift in honor of his elevated status, but also because the land itself gave way to a glorious vista of the meadows beyond the forest.

Damir dismounted, leaving Eliana affixed to her mare, and released Llwyd to the pasture, where the horse immediately began grazing. He chomped grass with an unusual delight, then glanced toward the little mare. Damir's brow rose. *As if teasing her with his good fortune . . .*

A boy crashed through the woods, running on foot as if chased by demons. Damir recognized Elphin, the young servant of the Woodland king's horse master. The boy stopped short, gasping as he stared first at Eliana's draped form, then at Damir, then back at Eliana.

"At it again, are you, sir?"

"This encounter was less of my own making, but the Lady Eliana and I have, it might be said, met in battle."

"Looks like you won this time, sir."

"It would appear so, for now. As with all things pertaining to Eliana, nothing is certain."

Elphin approached Eliana's mare, who seemed to recognize the boy's gentle manner and love of horses. He patted the mare's neck, then bent down to peer into Eliana's upside-down face. "Not dead, is she, sir?"

"Of course not." Damir paused. "She attempted to administer one of her devious potions upon me, and infected herself instead."

Elphin straightened. "Then it is as she deserves." He frowned and his mouth twisted to one side. Eliana hadn't endeared herself to the Mundane people of Amrodel—and even her fellow Mages feared her for her impulsive nature and unpredictable decisions. The matter of her rumored allegiance with the dreaded Norsk had solidified their doubt, and despite her beauty and talent, Eliana was no longer popular in the Woodland.

Elphin eyed her more closely, affording himself the opportunity to gaze at her rare beauty up close, but then he shook his head. "The lady is a fiend. The worst fiend in the Wood. Chased me with a herd of dragonflies once, she did, for getting too close to her herb garden."

Damir glanced at Eliana. "That doesn't sound so bad, Elphin. She's certainly done worse than that. Better dragonflies than wolves."

Elphin eyed Damir doubtfully. "Never been chased by the beasts, have you, sir?"

"Not exactly, though she managed to direct a hive of bees my way when we were children."

"That's nothing compared with dragonflies," said Elphin. "They *know*."

Damir shook his head. She'd certainly convinced Elphin of that, at least, though what the boy imagined the dragonflies *knew*, he couldn't guess. "The Lady Eliana is incapacitated, and I'm bringing her to my cottage for . . . safekeeping. When your current errand is done, would you fetch a few of her things and bring them back here?"

"My errand is done, sir. Just coming to check on you. Heard you had a meeting with The Fiend, and wanted to be sure you came out in one piece." Elphin tapped Eliana's shoulder but she gave no response. "Guess she isn't faking. You never know with this one." He paused and glanced at Damir. "You sure you want to keep her with you? Can't imagine the damage she could do if you let her in there."

"In this condition, she's not likely to do damage," said Damir. "And for once, her fate will be in my hands."

"Can't argue with that. I'll fetch her things. Want any of her potions?"

"Perhaps later. I wouldn't want to be the one to test them."

"True enough. Think I can use the pony?"

Damir pulled Eliana from her mare's back and cradled her in his arms. She didn't react or move, but felt warm and soft against his chest. He sighed. "Eliana Daere, what have you done to yourself?"

Elphin mounted the mare, but his young face puckered with doubt as he looked thoughtfully back at Damir. "Whatever she's done, sir, it was meant for you. I'm thinking you'd be wise to remember that."

"I will never forget." Damir hesitated. "It might prove interesting to see what fate she had planned for me this time."

Elphin huffed, shook his head, and turned the mare toward the path to Eliana's cottage. "She'll probably be spitting up toads by nightfall."

Evening came after tedious hours of waiting, and nothing had changed. Eliana still slept, peaceful and serene, lying on his bed with her soft hair coiled over her shoulders. Damir's patience neared its end. If the woman had devised a potion to put him to sleep for endless days, her scheming had indeed reached new lows.

He went outside to his well, filled a pitcher of water, then returned to her. He stood looking down at her sleeping face for a moment, anger warring with concern. Her lips curled in a slight smile, as if even in the far reaches of dreams, she felt pleased with herself, probably at his expense.

Damir emptied the pitcher over her head.

She squealed and jerked upright, a satisfying response. Her green eyes were wide, and she sputtered from the shock of cold water. Her startled gaze moved to him and she stared.

And stared.

"I thought you'd slept long enough."

She was trembling. Her eyes darted from side to side as if she'd never seen his cottage before. "Where am I?"

She couldn't have forgotten. She'd snuck into his home often enough. "You're in my cottage." She was trembling. "Eliana, are you ill?"

Her gaze shifted to him. "What did you call me?"

19

"Eliana." Damir sat down beside her, searching her face for guile. He saw only fear. "It's your name. Don't you know?"

She squeezed her eyes shut, then choked on a sob. "I don't remember anything."

The nature of her potion made itself known. Eliana truly didn't know who she was, where she was. "I am lost." She looked at him, desperate and young, and so beautiful that the sight of her pierced his heart. "Who . . . who are you?"

Vengeance was his. She'd handed it to him in a silver goblet. "I am Damir ap Kora." He paused and took her hand. "Your husband."

Chapter Two

"My husband . . ." Eliana stared down at the dark hand holding hers. For a moment, the words made no sense. Nothing made sense. "Husband . . ." Thoughts slowly took shape in her mind, like the shadows of trees at nightfall. "I know what that means . . ."

She looked up at the man, her husband. "But I do not know you." She squeezed her eyes shut, trying to force the shadowy images into shapes she recognized. "I know the shapes, but not my place within them."

He looked confused, his brow furrowed as if gauging the nature of her mood. She wrapped her fingers tighter around his to steady herself. "I am sorry. I don't understand why my thoughts evade me this way. What happened to me?"

"What happened . . ." He hesitated and cleared his throat and his gaze shifted to the left as if searching his memory. He looked around briefly, then back to her as if he had made a decision. "You fell. On our way home. Off your pony."

"I have a pony?"

"A mare. Very fat. Her name is Selsig."

"It means *sausage*. That is her name?"

He shrugged. "A food she resembles all too closely."

Eliana peered up into his face. It was a beautiful face, filled with mysteries, even beyond the loss of her memory. "You told me your name. Damir. I know what a sausage is, but I do not remember the pony. I know what *husband* means, but I do not know you."

He squeezed her hand. "You know me, Eliana. We have known each other all our lives."

This sounded promising. "That reassures me, somehow."

"We have been the best of friends, you and I. Always close, always together."

"So we wed because we were . . . friends?"

His eyes darkened. "More than that, my dear. Friendship developed into something deeper, more beautiful." He smiled and her heart fluttered.

"Have we been long wed?"

Again, his gaze shifted left. She glanced up to see what caught his eye, but there were only richly carved beams supporting a sloped ceiling. "Oh, a while," he said, his voice casual. "Not long. But we have been together for . . . a good while."

Eliana touched her hair. It was wet, like her gown—and the bed beside her. She glanced at Damir. "What is this?"

He looked uncomfortable. "I had to wake you."

A pitcher by her bed caught her eye. "With a whole pitcher of water?"

"I was terrified. You had slept overlong." He took her hand again and kissed it. She liked the touch of his mouth, but her gaze shifted again to the pitcher.

"I think a smaller amount would have woken me just as well."

He nodded. "Quite possibly. Forgive me, my dear. I was extremely distraught. You looked so pale. I could think of nothing else."

Eliana maneuvered herself away from the damp spot on the bed. Recognizing her discomfort, Damir covered the area with a square towel. "But you are well now," he said, almost as if to distract her from his overzealousness in waking her. "Yet you have no memory . . ."

"It must have been a bad fall, but I feel no pain in my head, nor anywhere on my body." She paused and adjusted her position. "Actually, my back is rather stiff."

Damir looked tense. "You were jarred, quickly, in the fall from your mare. Not enough to cause injury, perhaps, but enough to . . . dislodge your thoughts."

She wasn't certain this made sense, but her mind was clouded. Her thoughts felt heavy, her limbs tired and weak. "Then it will clear soon." She looked up at him. "This must be hard for you as well."

He smiled, but he still appeared tense. "As long as you are uninjured, here with me, my relief is endless."

"It is as if I remember the world, but not myself. Or you. I see a forest, but do not know the trees within. Except that there are trees."

"You speak like Madawc," he said. "Thoughtful, and given to metaphor."

"Who?"

"Our teacher."

"Did I not speak this way before?"

"No. Yes! At times . . ." He paused and coughed, and Eliana knit her brow in confusion.

"Do I seem much changed?"

He studied her face and chewed the side of his lip. "I'm not sure."

"Well, then, tell me of myself before."

Again, he gazed upward toward the ceiling. "You were an angel, kind, gentle, peaceful. A most agreeable nature . . . yes."

This sounded positive, but Eliana felt herself sigh. "I lacked spirit, then?"

"Oh, no . . . I wouldn't say that. No lack of spirit. But your spirit was directed toward . . . more pleasurable things." Damir paused again. "Toward me."

"But what was my skill?"

Now he looked uneasy. "You had some skill with . . . herbs . . ."

"Herbs . . . plants? What did I do with them?"

"Medicine. Food. You were an excellent cook."

"Was I?" Her heart fell distinctly this time. "I feel no affinity to that."

He grasped her hand. "You will."

"I hope I recall the methods."

"I will instruct you, and you will learn again."

"Nothing more interesting than that? What if I don't remember anything? What use will I be?"

Damir tightened his grip on her hand. "Your use wasn't in your arts, Eliana, but in your loveliness, your tenderness. As my wife."

"I sound impossibly dull!" She had no idea where this outburst came from, except that it was genuine, and within her by nature.

Damir seemed to recognize this and a quick frown altered his sweet mouth. "Not at all dull, I assure you, my dear. You were—are—an exceptional . . . lover." He stopped, gulped audibly, then waited for her response.

"In what way?"

"You are wildly imaginative."

"In the act of love?" She paused, her eyes narrow. "I know what this is. I can imagine it, yes, but I do not recall it. I cannot picture myself engaged in this activity. Yet it must be familiar to me . . ." She kept her gaze pinned on his face. This man was a stranger, and yet, she knew him. Their bodies had blended, no doubt many times before, and they had been entwined. Yet it still seemed strange to her. What if he demanded this act now, when he was strange to her?

"You are pleasing to look upon," she began carefully. "I can find no hesitation in facing you. But I do not know you."

He seemed to sense what was bothering her. "You have nothing to fear, my dear. It is enough that I have you with me, and that you are in my care."

"I can see you are a kind man." *And beautiful.* His skin was darker than hers, as if the sun sought him out and graced him with a rare tint. Black hair fell around his face in slight disarray, and she saw both innocence and wisdom in his dark brown eyes. His lips were full and sensual, a gift to tempt any woman who caught sight of him.

He was looking back at her with a strange expression, of both wonder and recognition of her sensual mood. He must guess that she assessed him favorably, but why that would surprise him, Eliana didn't know. Maybe they had become accustomed to each other over time, and this wonder she now felt had been removed to the past.

But wonder now filled her at the sight of him, and at his nearness. She reached to touch the slight cleft in his chin, then ran her finger along his face. Very gently, she touched his mouth, and she felt him tremble as he drew a quick breath.

"You are a beautiful man." Her voice came low and huskier than when she had spoken before. Eliana liked the sound, and Damir's eyes widened. "I will learn of you again. I think it will be the same path."

"I hope not . . ." He stopped himself and looked as if he hadn't meant to speak at all, but uneasiness grew in her. He clasped both her hands in his and drew them against his chest. "I mean, I hope we reach each other sooner . . . In less time. Fewer years."

"Our courtship was long, then?" she asked.

His gaze wandered. "Well, we were young. It took a while for friendship to blossom into love."

"Had we many obstacles?"

"No." He hesitated. "A few." He squeezed her hands. "Nothing the power of our love couldn't conquer."

She looked down at their clasped hands. "Then love will conquer now."

She heard him swallow, but he didn't answer. She looked around the room, and saw nothing that looked familiar. "Where are my things?"

"Your things?" For a flash, he looked almost panicked.

"Yes. My clothing and such." She tugged at her damp dress. "This is wet."

"Yes. Your things. Of course." He rubbed his chin. "Your things are . . . elsewhere. In a small room made just for . . . your things." He coughed, then offered a reassuring smile. "But you must rest now."

"I'm not sleepy."

"You may not feel the need of rest, but you have been through a great trauma."

"I suppose you're right." She fingered her damp dress. "Have I something else to wear?"

He looked around, then seized a long white shirt off a low bench and pressed it into her hands. "Wear this. It is comfortable for bed rest."

She examined the garment. "This is yours, I think."

"Yes . . ." He chewed his lip. "But you often wear it, when nights are cool."

"What do I wear when they are warm?"

His dark eyes glittered and he smiled. "Nothing."

Eliana's face warmed, and she touched her cheek. "Why do I feel this shyness? It is strange, when I know it should not be so."

"It is unlike you." His smile remained, but he sighed. "There is sweetness in your mood, Eliana. It does not displease me."

Eliana yawned, and the mists that she had left behind when she woke seemed to rise up again to claim her. "I feel as if I have floated upward from deep water, and now must return." She fought to hold her senses. "But when I wake, maybe my memory will wake with me."

He smiled, but he seemed a little strained. "Let us hope so, my dear."

Eliana fiddled with the shirt he had given her. He must have seen her unclothed many times, but she still felt awkward and unsure. He seemed to guess her mood. "Sleep now, Eliana," he said. "I have a few . . . errands, duties . . . things to do, but I will try not to disturb your rest."

Her eyelids drifted shut. "It is good to know you will be near." The soft mist enveloped her, and she felt herself fading. Fading from what she had been, once, beyond memory, into . . . him.

Damir stood outside his door and glared at the Woodland path, willing Elphin to hurry his task. Llwyd grazed in the paddock as the final rays of the sun glanced back eastward through the trees. Between the tall trees, Damir caught a last glimpse of the vast, open meadows beyond the forest before the light faded into the gray of night. There, the Woodland reached its ending, down over steep hillsides, coursed by swift forest streams. Like a golden haze, the unclaimed grassland lay beyond, stretching north and east, until finally, far beyond his sight, the plains gave way to the frozen northland long claimed by the Norsk tribes.

For long years, the Norsk had threatened only each other, their tribes warring for supremacy, with no civilized progress to show for their battles. Only the last generation had seen their tribes united beneath a single chieftain, and even still, many factions remained within their race.

Yet ever they sought to move outward and, unlike the Woodland people, the Norsk had many children, for the unpleasant purpose of replenishing their warriors, who often died young in battle. Not only fierce warriors, they were ruthless and avid traders, too. They simultaneously battled with and traded with the stout Guerdians, a solitary race who lived in the spiraling pinnacles of the eastern mountains. Of late, the Norsk traders were seen even in the city of Amon-dhen, once a Woodland outpost built by the Central Sea, a port city where Damir's father had fled when escaping the wrath of his brother. Few Woodland people remained in Amon-dhen now. Most Mages had returned to the Woodland's secret hamlets deep in the forest, though a few Mundane remained running the shops and taverns.

Only Eliana seemed to have any contact with the outside now. Damir paced back and forth across his stone walkway. Maybe it wasn't so strange that Eliana would be attracted to the violent Norsk. She might have the face and body of a Woodland sprite, but her spirit had at least as much fire as a Norsk warrior. Maybe their primitive culture drew her, and seduced her with its primal power.

He didn't want to care where her heart might lie, or what kind of man attracted her. She had tormented him too often about her secretive dalliances and ravaged his thoughts with images of her in another man's embrace. She had placed subtle hints as to the passions she shared with others, a word or a look that told him no other woman he bedded would compare to her, while making it absolutely clear that she was a treasure he would never sample.

Eliana had given herself to him this time, whether she intended to or not. It was a fair trade for all he had suffered. He would make love to her so sweetly and so perfectly that all other lovers would pale in his shadow. Her memory would return, eventually, but while the spell held, he would make the most of having this wife.

Elphin arrived on Eliana's pony carrying a sack of items. The boy's eyes were wide, and he was out of breath.

"Sir . . . what did you do to the lady's cottage? I know you're at odds, and I know she deserves a lot . . ."

Damir went to him and took the mare's reins as Elphin dismounted. "What are you talking about? I haven't been to Eliana's cottage . . ." He paused. "Well, not in several months, and then only to leave a note on her door saying I was sorry I'd missed her." That sort of thing drove her crazy, that he could so easily find his way to her hidden domain, and that he would be brazen enough to leave a note.

Elphin hauled a large sack off the pony and dropped it on the ground. "You can trust me, sir. I wouldn't tell anyone, but what a mess!"

"I wasn't there, Elphin. What happened?"

Elphin studied Damir's face and seemed to trust what he saw. "If you didn't, someone nigh onto destroyed the place. Maybe she did it herself."

A chill wound its way around Damir's heart. "Eliana loves her home. She wouldn't cause it damage. What did you see there?"

"By the stars, sir! Potions everywhere, cast about the floor, broken and shattered all over. Her dresses were ripped out of cabinets. Nothing she had was in its place. I didn't think you could have done that. I felt . . . anger, even rage, as if a madman had rampaged through there." Elphin paused. "Of course, after what she's done to you in the past, you couldn't be blamed for a bit of anger."

"I would never harm Eliana." He would tease her, torment her senses, drive her crazy, but he wouldn't hurt her for any reason. "No, someone was looking for something. One of her potions, most likely."

"Maybe . . . looking for *her*," said Elphin.

Damir glanced back at the cottage. "That also is possible." He paused to consider the matter. "It may have something to do with our encounter this morning, or the timing might, indeed, be coincidental. And possibly fortu-

29

itous for Eliana. Had she been at home when this oc-curred, her fate might be worse than what she's done to herself . . ."

"If she's in trouble, you can count on this—she brought it on herself," said Elphin.

"That may be. But an intruder who was willing to leave her cottage in shambles must have been desperate for something. Desperation drives dangerous acts."

Damir went to the pasture gate and summoned Llwyd, who apparently had enough of grazing and was again ea-ger for an evening ride. "Here, take my horse and bring this news to Madawc. Tell him also that the Lady Eliana has effectively erased her memory and knows nothing of herself . . ."

Elphin interrupted with a choking gasp. "Is that what she did, sir?" He paused. "What did you tell her she is? A little chattering squirrel, I hope?"

Damir shifted his weight and tried to appear casual. "My wife."

Elphin laughed, then shook his head. "Did she fall for it?"

"She did." Damir felt the boy's penetrating gaze, but he didn't explain the situation further.

Elphin smacked his lips. "Well, well, well! This should prove interesting. Think I'd better tell Madawc that part, sir?"

Damir hesitated. "I suppose it's necessary, but remind him it is my right in vengeance for her attempt against me. Tell him also that she is safe with me, but the news con-cerning her cottage should be brought to the king."

"Well, no one will ever think to look for her here, that's for sure," said Elphin. "I know I wouldn't."

"Go now, before total darkness makes the ride impossi-ble. The journey is long, an hour in the dark, but Madawc will let you spend the night at his home."

Elphin whistled, thrilled with his new assignment. "A night in the palace of the wizard! I will do that, sir! Thank you!"

"It is hardly a palace, Elphin." The old Mage lived in a stone building set into the north side of the same ridge where Damir's clearing lay, and only a trained eye could find the entrance. But many mysterious rooms lay beyond that door, rooms Damir and Eliana would know in the dark, but which a Mundane youth like Elphin would consider fascinating beyond measure.

Elphin sighed heavily. "I wish I'd been born with the Mage-gift, sir."

Damir patted Llwyd's neck and helped Elphin up onto the horse's back. Like all the Woodland people, the boy rode with only a felt pad in place of a heavier saddle, much to the comfort of the ponies they usually rode. "You have other gifts, Elphin. And sometimes, the gift of the Mage has been deemed a curse."

"After seeing what The Fiend has done to herself this time, I'm thinking you may be right," said Elphin. He cast a pertinent glance at Damir which suggested Damir had brought on his own troubles by taking "The Fiend" captive, but the boy said no more as he turned the horse and galloped away.

Darkness descended over the forest, and in the distance, Damir heard Llwyd's hoofbeats slow to a walk. As the sun disappeared, tall, crystal lamps glowed to life. They were an invention of the Madawc in his youth, and one that lent great beauty to the Woodland.

She was safe, for now. But who would dare ransack Eliana's cottage? Few even knew its location. It was no wonder Elphin suspected him. Perhaps one of the Norsk had plundered her home, but Damir's shield cloaked the forest in protective energy—a rampaging Norsk warrior would find it impossible to enter. If Eliana had a Norsk lover, however, surely he knew the location of her cottage, and obviously, they had found secrecy enough to meet before now.

Maybe this man she had chosen wasn't to be trusted with her safety. That came as no surprise to Damir—the Norsk were notorious in their disregard for others, taking women as slaves and concubines, treating sexual conquest as sport, nothing more than the spoils of battle.

A divergent thought rose in Damir's mind. Had it not been sport to him as well? He had dallied with many women, but never to the degree of permanence. He had never taken a woman against her will, never lied about his intentions. The only relationship he had that bordered on battle was with Eliana, and that hadn't been sexual.

Damir's gaze shifted to his bedroom window. If he made love to her, touched her with sweet eroticism, would the memory linger in her mind once her potion wore away? And if their passion were great enough, would she not long to hold onto it, despite her inevitable fury? Would it not be all the sweeter then? He imagined her, furious when she finally escaped from her self-induced confusion, dizzied with the memory of lovemaking in his bed. He could imagine her as desire filled her again . . .

His blood heated at the thought, and he could find no real fault in the image. Stars knew what she had meant for him. Had their places been exchanged as she had intended, he would probably be scrubbing her floors as an erstwhile servant, or washing her little feet.

He wouldn't force her. He would be gentle. It would be a sweet seduction so that when her memory returned, she would have to admit it as her desire, too. She had brought it on herself, after all. Fired by this image, Damir returned to his cottage and illuminated the front room with smaller crystal lamps. He emptied the sack Elphin had delivered and examined the contents.

Elphin had brought an extremely impractical red velvet gown, with jewels sewn into the fabric. Eliana had worn it once at the Palace of Amrodel, and she had stolen Damir's breath with her loveliness. He fingered it now, and remembered how she'd looked across the room at him, her eyes bright with challenge, as if daring him not to want her.

Damir fished around, and found a sheer muslin gown, an undergarment that might serve well enough for a bed-dress. He held it up to the light, and saw the trees through it. Too easily, he imagined Eliana's soft skin revealed just as clearly. He pulled out a third gown, much simpler than the first, the hue of a soft spring leaf throughout. It was a dress he hadn't seen before, yet the material was faded. It must have been favored attire for the young Mage.

A strange artifact clasped the throat of the green dress, and Damir held it closer to the light to examine it. He recognized the pale amber prized by the ruthless Norsk. The handiwork could only have come from their northern mines. A delicate shape had been carved into the golden stone—a dragonfly. It was a beautiful pin, primitive in design, and yet intricately carved, and it suited Eliana perfectly. Someone knew her well.

Damir's heart sank, though he had long suspected her allegiance was more personal than political in nature. Perhaps he hadn't fully believed it, though he had teased her with the rumors of her Norsk lover. Eliana had kept the Norsk gift to herself, wearing it only in secret, revealing a side of her that was both intimate and feminine. A side he had never known firsthand.

He laid the garments on his table and bowed his head. She had erased her mysterious Norskman from her memory, along with everyone else she had ever known. All in pursuit of her vengeance against Damir. Why? She had never sought outright power, except over him. He had known her since they were children. His mind warred with the evidence and the rumors, and perhaps, his own jealousy.

His bedchamber door opened and Eliana peeked out. Their gazes met, and the ache in Damir's heart intensified. She looked so innocent with her long dark hair falling around her face, like a Woodland faery peering out at him from ancient times.

"I thought you were sleeping," he said.

"I slept a little while. But I thought I heard you talking to someone outside."

She couldn't have heard the words spoken—he had been too far away. But Damir still felt nervous. "I sent an errand-runner to tell the elder Mage about your predicament."

"Do you think this elder Mage can help me?"

No other Mage could undo the spell she had wrought herself, but Damir could think of no better explanation. "It is possible."

Eliana nodded at the dresses on the table. "Are those my things?"

Damir edged the sack onto the floor. "I brought a few of your gowns . . . from your . . . closet . . ."

She came to the table and examined the red velvet dress, then eyed him skeptically. "This doesn't seem quite suitable, though it's pretty. Do I normally dress in such extravagant clothing?"

"No . . . It looked different in the dark of the closet." A good tale. As long as she didn't ask to inspect the closet before he had a chance to place her other garments there.

"Where is the closet? Maybe I can find something else. . . ."

As if she read his thoughts . . . "How about this?" He held up the green dress, with the pin still attached.

Eliana touched the dress. "It looks well worn and practical, a looser fit than the other." She noticed the clasp and her face softened as she gently fingered it.

"What is this? It's beautiful." A soft smile crossed her lips. "I think . . . I have memory of this. Did you give it to me?"

Damir's throat clenched. He had never seen such tenderness on her face. Yet it had been won, he imagined, by the most brutal of men, warriors who ravaged over icy plains and snow-laden hills. "Yes. . . ." He nearly choked on the lie. "It was a gift."

She smiled and looked shy. "It must have been special." She closed her eyes. "I can see my fingers around it, and I am crying, alone." She looked at him again. "Why did I cry?"

"It was the day . . ." He fumbled for an explanation as his thoughts whirled and the dark ache in his heart threatened to overwhelm him. "It must have been the day I asked you to marry me."

Color rose in her cheeks, and she looked beautiful. Sweet and young, she was the image of feminine grace. But her expression waned, and her confusion returned. "Yet the wisp of memory I have is of sadness, and not joy. I sense fear . . . as if . . . as if I believed the one who gave it to me would face terrible danger, and not return. As if something truly good—even great—might be lost."

He detected a rare emotion in Eliana's memory. *Love.* He had harbored the suspicion of a lover, but even so, it hadn't really occurred to him that she might truly love this man. "I was sent on a mission against the Woodland's greatest enemies—the Norsk." He paused, awaiting some recognition, but Eliana gave none. "There was danger involved." This much was true. He had gone, alone, to the forest's edge to drive away a band of rogue Norsk, warriors the king believed had been sent as a scouting party. Eliana had been against the mission from the beginning.

"But you came back, and we married," she said, her voice soft and still bearing traces of confusion. Perhaps the hidden part of her mind rebelled against his misdirection of her heart.

He couldn't meet her eyes. "Yes."

She ran her delicate fingers over the brooch. "It is good to have this. It is a connection to my past that I feel. I wonder why so small a thing would have such a great meaning, yet I do not recall your face?"

"I cannot explain it, my dear. But perhaps objects inhabit a different part of the mind than faces."

Something on the floor caught Eliana's eye, and she bent to retrieve it, then held up a parchment that must have been among the items Elphin recovered. "What is this?"

Damir recognized one of Eliana's own scrolls. He took it from her and his eyes widened. A rare find, it appeared to indicate her method of distilling herbs into potions. Fine drawings indicated the sun, which must be part of her process. It looked amazingly simple, not at all what he expected. He smiled when he saw that she had drawn a little face on the sun, and that it resembled herself.

"It is . . . my work," he said. "Just a parchment. I must have dropped it."

She eyed the scroll with obvious curiosity, but Damir rolled it up quickly and stuffed it in a cabinet filled with his own records. Eliana watched him, curious, but she didn't attempt to investigate the cabinet further. "What is your work?" she asked.

"I am an Elite Mage, the Mage Protector of the Woodland realm."

"What does that mean?"

He wasn't sure what she would remember of these terms, so he answered carefully. "Most people of the Woodland, like the lands beyond, are Mundane. Their personal energy, which we call *ki*, is limited to themselves, meant for creating their lives. Each being has its own

36

unique *ki,* but a rare few are born Mages, who have the ability to reach deeper into the *mana* of all. Our *ki* is wider, broader, stronger, and can be manifested to creations beyond ourselves."

"Our?" Her face brightened and her hands clasped together in delight. "Then I am a Mage, too?"

He couldn't deceive her about this. "You are. As I said, we were trained together since childhood."

"So I have a strong energy, like you?"

"Yes."

Eliana looked proud and her back straightened. He saw the old eagerness in her eyes, the delight in her own power. What if their history repeated itself, and with it, their competition and strife? "I am pleased to be a Mage. How wonderful!"

"It is part of what bonds us, my dear, and it has always made us closer."

"Because we understand each other?"

Damir gazed into her eyes. "We do." That much, at least, was true. Yet somehow she had never seen how much she mattered to him, how much he cared what she thought and how she felt. He touched her cheek. "We are meant for each other. No one can understand you as I do."

She moved closer to him and his heart quickened. "Perhaps it is the power I own that made me vulnerable to my current affliction."

He swallowed. "It's possible, yes." He drew her into his arms, and it felt natural, as if they had, indeed, done this a thousand times. She rested her head against his shoulder, and seemed comfortable when he held her.

She slid her arms around his waist and breathed deeply. With infinite tenderness, she pressed her lips against his neck, and a shudder of delight coursed through him. He had imagined her as a passionate lover, but he hadn't envisioned this sweetness. Eliana gazed up at him, her green eyes soft. She parted her lips to speak, and his breath held in his throat as he awaited her words.

"I'm hungry."

Chapter Three

She wanted to kiss him. Eliana eased out of Damir's arms, surprised by the intensity of her feelings. She bit her lip, her gaze still fixed on his mouth. A slow smile crossed his perfect lips and a shiver ran down her spine. He knew what she felt, because he knew her—better than she knew herself now.

"This affliction puts me at a disadvantage with you," she said. "I do not know what is normal between us."

His smile grew. "Don't worry about what is normal, Eliana. Go beyond thought to what you feel. You mentioned a desire for . . . food." He was teasing her.

She smiled. "I find it an appealing thought." She was teasing back. She turned away and surveyed the room. Large windows faced a wide lawn, and outside, she saw glimmering lights. Indeed, it was a magical effect, a fitting home for an Elite Mage. Rows of books and parchments lined the rear wall, with two doors and a low, arched hallway. "What is down that hall?"

"Various chambers," he answered. "Some for my work, and for study. In there . . ." He gestured to the door nearest the bedroom. "There is a fine bath, which you always coveted . . . enjoyed . . ." He coughed, then pointed to another room off the front. "There is my . . . our sitting room, where in the morning we have breakfast and look out over the trees to the great meadows beyond."

Eliana looked in that direction, but saw only night. "It sounds beautiful."

"It is." He paused. "That direction has beauty, but also danger. In attack, the Norsk come across those fields."

She glanced at him. "You mentioned the Norsk earlier. What are they?"

"People of the vast northern tribes. They are ruthless and savage warriors, with no magic but powerful nonetheless. Over the last generation, they have expanded and now seek control over the Woodland."

"Why?"

"None of us are entirely sure what use this forest would be to them. Perhaps the rumors of the Mages' power intrigues them. Few now have contact with them at all, and fewer still understand their purposes."

"If they are so many, and so brutal, how do we withstand them?"

"One Mage holds this land against them." Damir looked proud and sure of himself as he awaited her obvious next question, but Eliana nodded.

"You?"

"Me."

"Why is your power alone sufficient?" she asked. And why didn't she share that power?

"My *ki* is different from the Woodland folk, for I am not of this race. Or, at least, my father wasn't. He escaped persecution in his land, a desert realm far to the south of here, and took a Woodland Mage for a wife. The power I inherited from them gave me unique capabilities."

"Such as what?"

"The most useful to the Woodland now is my ability to

shield an area. With ritual and focus of *ki,* I can, in essence, bless an area and keep it from harm. This cottage, for instance, is impenetrable to attack. I have shielded the king's domicile, and the forest at large."

"So none of these Norsk warriors can enter while you shield the land?"

He paused as if something struck him, but he didn't share his thought. "No invader can enter. . . . Yet I cannot prevent single acts directed from one person to another. I can prevent overt attacks, but should an invader use guile, win the trust of his target first . . . A man could abduct a woman and take her from this land, if he chose."

Eliana's brow furrowed. "Why do you say that?"

He fiddled with something on the table. "Such an incident might have happened recently, though it was prevented."

"By you?"

"Well, in a way . . ." He glanced around the room. "I'd nearly forgotten your intense hunger." Eliana blushed.

"I suppose it still gnaws at me."

He drew a quick breath. "Then we will dine together."

He led her down the hall, past several closed doors, and into a wider, open room with a low fireplace in the corner. A black kettle hung over a smoldering fire, and a pleasant aroma wafted in the steam. He stirred the pot with a large wooden spoon and Eliana peeked over his shoulder. "It looks good," she said, and her stomach rumbled.

Damir tasted the stew, and shrugged. "It's all right. It could use something more." He offered her a small taste.

Eliana considered the bite in her mouth, then looked around the room. Canisters of loose herbs drew her attention. She moved closer to them, drawn as if to a familiar person. As her gaze shifted from one to the next, she felt an odd pang at the base of her throat. She drew a small jar from the shelf and passed it to Damir. "Try this."

He eyed her doubtfully, but he sprinkled some of the

purple herb into the stew, then stirred it. He waited a moment, then tasted it again, his face ripe with misgivings. His expression quickly altered and he looked at her in surprise. "That's perfect . . . how did you know?"

Eliana hesitated. "I didn't know. I *felt* it."

Damir studied her face as if assessing an old mystery. "I've always wondered how you selected your plants and herbs. I assumed there was some logic behind it, though I've never seen any evidence of logic in you. Even when we were children, you just seemed to know which herbs to use, which to mix together, and which to avoid. I knew Madawc didn't teach you, because your skill surpassed his in this area even then."

"You've never asked me about this before?"

Damir turned his attention back to the stew and began ladling it into two round stone bowls. "I guess it never occurred to me to ask."

For all the closeness he spoke of between them, this seemed odd to Eliana, but she said nothing further on the subject. It made her uncomfortable. Damir glanced back at her, his face thoughtful. "I wonder what else you might sense in this manner? What, exactly, did you feel when your attention fell on that herb?"

"A sensation in my throat that seemed to answer what was missing."

"We will test this later, tomorrow, and perhaps you will regain something of what you knew before."

Damir brought the steaming bowls back into his front room, and they sat opposite each other at his table. She tasted the stew and liked the improvement, then dove into it with an aggression she didn't realize she possessed. Damir watched her and smiled.

"One thing, at least, hasn't changed. Your appetite. I always wondered how one so slight of build could consume so much."

She cringed, but didn't slow her pace. "Perhaps," she

said thickly, speaking around a mouthful of food, "it is the nature of my *ki* to require much sustenance."

"Most likely." He ate, but his gaze remained on her, as if the nature of her appetite pleased him on some other level, too. "It will take much to satisfy you, I think." His voice came husky, as if that also intrigued him.

Eliana wasn't sure what he meant at first, but then she blushed. "Only if I am too long denied." This sounded worse, and her blush intensified. Eliana swallowed too fast and she coughed. "Tell me . . . tell me of this world. Why is this land so weak, if it has such magic within, that the northern people threaten us at all?"

He smiled, no doubt guessing why she had changed the subject. "There are some who feel the balance of this world was lost generations ago, when the elite Mages drove the dark Mages from their hold in the eastern mountains. A great battle was fought at that time, and in it, most of the Elite Mages were lost, including the queen of the Woodland, the greatest of the Elites at that time. In fact, you are descended from her, and if the stories are true, you share both her power and her beauty."

The tale intrigued Eliana enough so that she set aside her spoon to listen. "She died?"

"She was taken captive by the Arch Mage, the leader of the dark forces. Rather than submit to him as he desired, she released her life and died there, lost to her people and her land. It was a sad tale, for some believe she loved him once. The Arch Mage had the greatest power ever known on this world, and his pride was boundless. He might have done good, if not for that pride, but instead, he turned to darkness, and his power drew others of like mind, and like weakness, to his domain, which turned from a place of great beauty to one of even greater dread. But the Woodland folk hold that the love they held for the queen proved stronger than the dark fire of the Arch Mage, and in the end, the Elites proved victorious. But the

43

mountains themselves are lifeless now—no one, even the Guerdians who live closest, dare go there."

Eliana sighed, then took a wistful bite of stew. "I have forgotten so much!"

"It was long ago. And for many years after that war, this land knew peace. At that time, the Norsk were only a primitive people, divided into countless tribes that battled each other over their frozen land. Neither the dark Mages nor those of the Woodland had paid them any heed. They are hardly less primitive now, but they have multiplied, while the people of the Woodland have diminished. When my father fled north, the previous Woodland king learned of his shielding power, and enlisted him as protector. But my father died young, and I was his only child. I was sent to Madawc, and found that my skill surpassed even my father's. My mother was also a Mage, though she died before attaining the level of Elite."

Eliana took another bite of stew. "Why was your father in exile?"

"He was the younger brother of a proud man, the heir to the desert realm, though my father was more beloved by their people. When it appeared the people would reject my uncle in favor of my father, my uncle trapped him with deceit, and had him driven from the land."

Eliana gazed at him, admiring the heritage that gave him his dark good looks and a mysterious aura that graced him with uncommon beauty. "He must have been a lot like you."

"In some ways, perhaps. But he held to the traditions and the old ways of his people, and he remained closed to all else, though he was wise. When he died, he and I were already at odds."

"What of the dark Mages? Are they gone entirely now?"

"No one knows for sure, though some at the Council have suggested their energy might somehow be inspiring the Norsk."

"If the Norsk are as vicious as you say, they seem a likely target for dark magic," said Eliana. "How was the Arch Mage defeated, if he was so powerful?"

"The fate of the Arch Mage is known. Rather than face defeat or submit to death, he chose to bury himself in a binding spell that can only be released by some secret measure unknown to others. At the time, he believed one of his followers would soon release him, but they were all destroyed in the battle, leaving him locked forever in a spell of his own making."

"I suppose great power often bears its own demise," said Eliana, and Damir looked at her in surprise.

"Why do you say that?"

"It would seem that a person carries the seeds of their own destruction within, as well as the hope for their future."

Damir's mouth slid open. "That is true . . . for all of us."

Eliana sighed. "I guess it depends on which side we nurture, and where we feed our energy."

"It is said in the Woodland that the reward of the dark *ki* is quickest, but of the light, the most lasting. It is a struggle for us all, Mundane and Mage alike."

Damir resumed his meal but Eliana watched him for a while, then sighed. "I know why I loved you."

He stopped chewing and looked up as if astonished. He swallowed hard and seemed to be collecting himself. "What?"

"Why I fell in love with you . . ."

"Why?" His voice came small, almost shy.

"Because you share yourself with me. Not just your body and your heart, but your thoughts, your feelings, your soul. I am, I think, a very fortunate woman."

Emotion seemed to hold him silent for a moment. "That is what I have always wanted . . ." He paused. "What we have always had together."

Something in his response troubled her. Something was

off in his expression and the way he had assured her it had always been so. She felt a deep connection to him, she felt that they were truly joined. And yet, some space remained between them. At first, she had believed it stemmed from her memory loss. But what if it was more?

"We were happy, weren't we?" she asked, though she wasn't sure what she expected him to say.

He smiled, almost too easily and too quickly. "Of course." He reached across the table and squeezed her hand. "Our happiness together is complete."

She smiled, too, but the uneasiness in her heart remained. "Whatever happens, I would regain that."

Damir nodded. "We will build upon it, and together, our lives will be better even than before."

He definitely sought more than they'd had together, though perhaps he hadn't meant it to sound that way. Eliana decided not to press the matter. She would learn more of their relationship over the next days, and more still in his arms. She returned to her stew and finished it, then rose to clear the table. He watched her in surprise, but she smiled and took his bowl back to the kitchen. He followed her and they cleaned the dishes together, in silence.

As they worked, his shoulder brushed hers, and they stopped to look at each other. Something in the silence grew, and Eliana knew what it was. Desire.

"What do we do in the evenings, usually, when our work is done and we are fed?" she asked.

He didn't answer at first, but then a slow smile crossed his face and his dark eyes glittered. "We love."

He was living a dream. Eliana, his wife, stood facing him in his kitchen, her face aglow as he spoke softly of a night spent together. Damir tried to steady his emotion, and failed. He wanted this. He wanted her. The Fiend of his past was forgotten, and in her place stood a woman of such sweetness that no other would ever compare. No desire to defeat him sparkled in her eyes. Instead, he saw a new depth to her femininity, as if her potion had exchanged maturity for her lost past.

He knew what the "Wine of Truce" had done to her. He hadn't guessed what it might do to him. He had Eliana now, as he had always wanted her, bright and inquisitive as she had always been, but instead of the suspicion he had seen for so long in her eyes, he saw the curiosity of love shining there. Here, she was willing to love him. A small voice in his mind whispered that she loved him now only because he had told her it was so, but the dream outweighed his reason.

He took her in his arms and she yielded without hesitation. His gaze shifted to her mouth, and she followed the same path to his. She drew a soft breath and her lips parted in the faintest of smiles. He had kissed her once before, on the night before they left Madawc's school to head off on their own. It had not been romantic. It had been a challenge. They had both had too much wine to drink. One kiss, and it had lingered in his mind when all other women, actual lovers, were forgotten.

She had kissed him then angrily, the same way he had kissed her. She had grabbed his hair, and he pulled her close, and they melted into each other for a brief instant of perfect bliss. He remembered the feel of her lips, her warmth. He remembered the way she snapped away from him in fury, green eyes blazing, her hair wild around her face. He remembered that they both accused each other and stormed away from each other, still rivals.

And that he hadn't slept a wink that night.

Neither he nor Eliana had never mentioned that kiss again, though whenever he saw her, he thought of it, and it filled his fantasies. Most often, he had dreamed he would conquer her, and she would yield, at last admitting that she desired him, maybe whispering that she had always loved him. The dream blurred his reality, and Damir bent now to kiss her.

Eliana accepted his kiss without anger this time. Her lips parted as she tentatively answered, then more eagerly as she played against his mouth. This was the woman he wanted, curious and able to answer, as the real Eliana never had been. Damir felt the touch of her tongue, and he deepened the kiss.

Passion went beyond reason. He had this moment, a living fantasy, and if it was to be soon lost, so be it. He felt her hands on his waist, sliding around to his back as she moved closer into his arms. He slipped his tongue between her lips and she sucked gently. His whole body hardened, his thoughts fled. He forgot that this was vengeance between them, he forgot it had been a game. It became the only thing he wanted, and desire consumed him.

He lifted her off her feet and her breath caught on a gasp, but she didn't stop kissing him as he carried her to his bedroom. She kissed his neck and tangled her fingers in his hair. This was the Eliana he had dreamt of—alive with desire, free from all doubt. His to love.

He stopped at his bed and released her. Her green eyes darkened to slate and her lips were full and moist from his kiss. "I remember this," she said, her tone soft and husky.

"You do?" He tried not to sound anxious.

"This feeling."

Damir tried to smile, but his face felt tight. *Not with him, she didn't.* "What do you feel, my dear?"

She smiled, too, and she looked shy. "That I want you."

He liked this better. He would have to remind her of this when she emerged from her forgetfulness. "I want you, too, Eliana."

Her gaze drifted to the side and she bit her lip. "What do we do now?"

"Hm . . ." Damir eased her dress from her shoulder,

then pressed his lips against her skin. She shivered, and he knew she liked his seduction. "I kiss you . . . here . . ." He kissed her neck, then slid her gown lower. "And here . . ." He kissed her other shoulder, then edged the dress lower. "And here . . ." He ran his fingertips along her lowered neckline. Eliana caught her breath and held it, waiting. Damir teased her, then drew his mouth over the soft swell of her breast.

A twinge of guilt caught him off guard, and he hesitated before lowering her gown further. "What do I do?" she asked.

"What do you want to do?"

"I want to kiss you likewise, and feel your skin beneath my fingers." She spoke eagerly, and Damir's hesitation fled. He pulled off his over-tunic and tossed it aside. She reached tentatively to touch him, then untied his white shirt, and she pressed her lips against his chest. He felt the tip of her tongue against his skin and his blood leapt to fire.

He pushed her dress down to her waist, closed his eyes for a moment, then allowed himself to see her. The vision of her unclothed body defied his most vivid imaginings. Her skin was the color of new cream, her breasts small but rounded, with peaks like delicate rosebuds. Her chest rose and fell with swift breaths, but she didn't move to cover herself.

"You are beautiful, Eliana, the most beautiful thing I've ever seen."

"Am I?" Her voice quavered, but she looked happy.

"Yes . . ." His own had become a growl. "And you are sweet, and so rare . . ." He drew a line with his fingertips along her collarbone, then in a downward arch, just grazing the swell of her breasts, then lower. She held herself immobile, waiting, but he looked into her eyes and lightly brushed his thumbs over the tip of her breasts. Her eyes closed and her head tipped back. Damir bent and kissed her neck and he felt her pulse race beneath his lips.

He cupped her breasts in his hands, and he bent to take a rosy peak between his lips. She caught her breath, then uttered a soft moan when he laved his tongue across the tip. Eliana put her hands on his shoulders and braced herself as if she felt dizzy.

"Are you sure?" he whispered. "You have not fully recovered from your . . . fall."

Eliana nodded vigorously, breathless. "I am sure. I like this . . . very much." She fumbled with her dress, then pushed it impatiently to the floor. She stood before him naked, and Damir stared. His gaze shifted guiltily from her breasts to her soft stomach, and the perfect triangle of dark hair that crowned her womanhood. She moved to seat herself on his bed, and his gaze fixed on her firm backside, which had captured his attention on countless occasions even when concealed by her clothing. He ached at the sight now.

She sat with one leg curled beneath her, her breasts soft in the warm light of his room. "Are you going to take off your clothes, too?" She sounded so innocent, but eager. The combination overtook his senses.

"Do you wish it?" he asked. Best to make sure it was her request, so he could remind her of that later, too.

Eliana smiled. "I do."

Damir arched his brow and edged his shirt apart. "Like this?"

She bit her lip, but her eyes glittered. "More, I think."

Damir removed his shirt, slowly, letting her savor each revelation of his body. And he knew she savored him—she dampened her lips with a quick dart of her tongue, and her breath came swift. Damir held up his shirt, and she placed her hand on his chest, over his heart. "You are very, very beautiful."

"What else?" he asked. He liked teasing her. By the curve of her lovely mouth, he guessed she liked it, too.

She pointed at his leggings. "Those."

Damir offered his most seductive smile and he held her gaze while she waited. He untied the belt of his leggings, then delayed. Her little toes curled and she clasped her hands together. She looked a little worried. "They do come off, don't they?"

"Do you want them off?"

A muted laugh escaped her and she touched her mouth, embarrassed. "Yes."

He edged his leggings lower, and he relished every expression that crossed her face—shyness, curiosity, and then, what he wanted most—desire. He lingered, then slid them over his hips, and stepped out of them—slowly. He liked being naked—he felt comfortable in his own skin, and for that reason among others, he had been adored and prized as a lover. Only Eliana had scoffed at his sensual appeal, and disparaged those women who pursued him. Now she sat before him like a maiden who looked upon a god, and it was everything he had dreamed.

Her eyes widened in surprise and her gaze fixed on his arousal. She puffed a quick breath, and must have told herself it was something she had seen before. A surge of pride welled in Damir's chest. Perhaps her Norsk lover wasn't so generously endowed, and even without access to her memories, she realized the advantage to Damir's physique. The thought came from vanity—he knew it, but he had fully surrendered to his fantasies.

She leaned toward him and placed her palm on his stomach. "It feels like a dream," she said, echoing his thoughts. "One I have had before."

This was unexpected, but not unwelcome. He took her hand in his and kissed it. "One we have both had many times."

He knelt on the bed beside her, and she pressed her lips against his chest. She looked up and he cupped her face in his hands as he bent to kiss her again. She wrapped her arms around his neck and drew him lower against her, un-

51

til he could feel the warmth of her body against his arousal.

Eliana murmured against his lips, and he felt the sensual tension building inside her. Desire consumed him, obliterating all else in its path as he lowered her beneath him. He had longed for this, fantasized about it for years. She had brought it on herself. Without memory of their conflict, she was as drawn to him as he had been to her. It was fair that he take her.

He slid his knee between her legs, and she welcomed him. His kiss intensified, their tongues mingling in a dance that mimicked what would come between them. Nothing held him back, nothing stopped him. She wanted him. He ached for her, and it was so easy.

". . . the reward of the dark ki is quickest, but of the light, the most lasting. It is a struggle for us all . . ."

No . . . He didn't care. Let it be darkness. Let darkness take him. This was too strong for any man to resist. His arousal burned against the softness of her inner thigh. She murmured a sensual whisper and moved herself closer.

"Ah, Damir, be with me." Her voice quavered with passion, with desire. "Then I will be what I was, and remember."

He paused only a second, but her words cast another vision, and his dream took a darker, more erotic turn. He would make love to her, drive himself deep inside, bring her to the very edge of bliss, and she would quake beneath him. Let her memories return then, let her feel him inside her as her true identity returned to her. Let her resist as desire blazed between them.

A great darkness rose and surrounded him as he pictured her fury amid her lust, as her body gave way to its passion, as his poured into her. His release threatened at the thought. . . .

He rose above her and looked into her eyes. "Do you want this, Eliana? Do you want me?"

She looked a little confused, but she nodded, breathless. "I want you."

She had said it—it was all he needed to hear. Let her deny it now . . .

No Norsk warrior ravaging in conquest could be darker than Damir felt at this moment. Even the darkness of Arch Mage when he captured the Woodland queen wasn't beyond Damir now.

Eliana arched her back beneath him, and he felt the soft dew of her femininity against the hard end of his arousal. *I will make you want me.* It was a vow uttered in passion, throbbing in darkness. He edged into her soft, warm opening, and she moaned with pleasure. Nothing would stop him . . .

She clutched his shoulders to steady herself for his entrance. Her legs wrapped around his. His whole body quivered as he pressed inward. Her warmth teased him and invited him in, and he moved himself against her, teasing her small woman's bud until she writhed beneath him. Alive with desire, she kissed his chest, then nipped.

"I will have you," he whispered. . . . *The reward of the dark ki is quickest* . . . He pressed his length inward and her legs tightened around him. An inner threshold barred his entrance, one he did not expect, and one he had rarely, if ever, encountered in a woman. Damir froze, then moved again. The barrier remained. His heart clenched in a flash of light.

This woman had known no other lover. Eliana was a virgin.

Chapter Four

He stopped. Eliana's senses reeled and she squirmed beneath her husband's motionless body. She felt the wild rush of his pulse, matching the power of her own, but he moved no further. He was so close, almost fully inside her.

"Is something wrong?" she asked, breathless.

He snapped away from her, his breath hoarse and ragged. "This isn't right . . . the right time. Eliana . . ."

She saw longing in his eyes, but she didn't understand. "There is nothing to worry about, Damir. I am fine." She paused to catch her breath. "Did I do something wrong?"

His mood softened at once and he touched her face. "No. No . . . it's just . . ." His gaze shifted. "I have been thoughtless. You are not recovered, however it seems."

"I think I am."

"But . . . in this state, without your memory . . . if we do this . . . we could conceive a child." He paused as if he hoped this were reason enough to explain his sudden withdrawal.

"I would like a baby," she said, and she meant it. "Didn't we want to have children when we married?"

"Of course. Yes. But just now . . . while you are recovering, and we don't know the depth of your affliction . . . it would seem unwise. Don't you agree?"

"No." Eliana caught herself and smiled. "I am sorry. You are right, I suppose." She paused. "But what if my memory never returns?"

He didn't look as concerned about this as she felt. "When we are sure your health is intact . . . Don't worry, my dear. I should have controlled myself. I did not expect the darkness . . ." He stopped short and her eyes narrowed.

"Darkness?"

He drew a shuddering breath. "Not darkness . . . But the blur of my thoughts where you are concerned. I gave way to . . . my emotion and my desire for you, without thinking of your welfare."

Eliana felt cold and she sighed heavily. "That is good of you." Her body ached. Satisfaction had been bare moments away—she could still feel it just beyond her reach.

Damir rolled over onto his back beside her and he folded his hands on his chest. His breath still came swift, and he seemed to be steadying himself. He had wanted her, too—of that, Eliana felt sure. She lay on her side watching him. He looked as if something had surprised him, as if he hadn't expected what happened between them. Yet in marriage, could there have been any doubt where their encounter was leading?

She had wanted more than sex. She had wanted to sink into him, as if to do that would somehow restore her to what she had been, and what she had forgotten. As she lay watching him, she knew he was all she had of herself, all that remained from a lifetime she no longer recalled. He was the sanity she might have lost, and the solid place where she stood, when the rest of the world was in fog to her.

His withdrawal triggered more than disappointment. It shadowed doubt and fear, and a sudden, intense loneliness. All her life now was walking in darkness, trying to find spots of light, a place to ground herself.

"You are right, after all," she said quietly. "I am not yet myself. I don't know what I am, really. It is wrong to try to find that in you."

He looked over at her and she saw pain in his eyes. "You seek only to ease your fear, Eliana. But it is my error, not yours. I wanted to make you mine . . . again . . . too soon."

Again, his words disquieted her. Had she not been "his" before? But weariness laid an impenetrable claim over her and she closed her eyes. "Maybe tomorrow, things will be clearer between us. Maybe tomorrow, I will remember everything I forgot, and all will be well." Her voice faded as she spoke, but as she drifted toward sleep, she heard, or imagined she heard, a breath or a whisper, *"I hope not."*

Eliana woke early, as the first rays of the sun slanted through the window. She remembered nothing more than she had the night before, and her heart fell as she realized nothing had changed. Damir lay quietly beside her, still on his back, his breath even and deep. She rose quietly and found the green dress he had shown her the evening before. She put it on and fastened the open neckline with the amber clasp. The pin gave her comfort and strength and she held her hand over it for a moment.

"This is real," she said. "This jewel binds me to that other life I have forgotten, to my real self."

Eliana found her way to the bathing facility, and discovered an elaborate system of delivering water into various basins. To her delight, a portion of it was already heated. She bathed and washed her hair, and found a small brush to clean her teeth. It had been laid out for her, though she saw little evidence of other feminine items. As she had been the night before, she found herself drawn to a pot of mixed herbs, and with those, she cleaned her mouth.

She examined her hair in a mirror and wondered how she normally wore it, then left it loose around her shoulders. She fiddled with the amber clasp again as if to draw strength, but instead, loneliness filled her, and disappointment. No portion of her memory had returned overnight, and alone in a strange room, she felt odd and unprotected, with a sense of guilt she couldn't explain. *It is as if I don't belong here, as if I'm an intruder . . .*

Eliana wandered around the front room, touching furniture she must have passed a thousand times. Everything she saw reminded her of Damir, but in no way did she sense herself. *It is the nature of my affliction, nothing more.*

She went to the largest window, which looked out on a wide swath of clipped grass, and beyond to a small pasture where a pony grazed that must be Selsig, she thought. She pushed open the heavy wooden door and went outside. Warm, clean air touched her face and the sun slanted warm from the eastern sky.

Eliana went to the pasture's fence, and Selsig perked up, then came to her. The small mare touched her nose to Eliana's shoulder and pushed gently, as if expecting something Eliana had no idea what, and the mare appeared disappointed, even a little hurt. Eliana looked around, seized a large, flowery plant and passed it to the mare, who appeared grateful but not entirely satisfied as she edged back to grazing.

The mare, at least, knew her, and Eliana's mood lightened. She gazed across the pasture to where the tree line parted, revealing a triangular view of a great, wide land beyond. Far, far in the east, she could make out the dark blue of a mountain range. Her gaze shifted to the north, and her sadness returned, coupled with a feeling of imminent loss and of tragedy on that white horizon.

Eliana turned away. The dark woods to the south and east of the cottage triggered a different emotion—warm and comforting. A broader path lay to the south, obviously much traveled, and most likely the main entrance to their cottage. A smaller path to the west, barely discernable, drew her attention. She walked beneath the threshold of the trees and looked up through tall branches filled with dark green leaves, illuminated by the cool morning sun. She closed her eyes and breathed and caught a soft scent that almost reached her like a voice. *Here.*

Eliana looked down, spotted a green herb with a yellowish tinge on its edges, then bent to pluck it. She held it against her nose and found the scent settling to her nerves. She looked around and plucked more, then walked farther into the woods. Other herbs caught her attention, small sprigs of twiggy green with tiny white flowers, soft purple plants that grew straight and looked both strong and delicate. She gathered them all, and found the act comforting, though she had no idea what she might do with them.

Eliana walked along the footpath westward, and it wound uphill, over tree roots and around sharp corners. She wondered where it led—it seemed mostly overgrown, but still used occasionally, not on horseback since the overhanging branches were too low. She liked the path, and walked on until she found a patch of dark green plants on a small hill. She closed her eyes, and saw herself drinking warm, flavored liquid. Then she climbed up the hill and picked the whole bunch of plants.

"Eliana!" Damir burst through the trees behind her, stumbled, then clambered up the small hill. He caught up to her, gasping. "What are you doing out here?" He paused, but before she could speak, he looked closely at her face. "Are you . . . all right?"

Eliana sighed. "If you mean, have I regained my memory, no."

He drew a distinct breath of relief, and her eyes narrowed in suspicion, which he apparently noticed. "But you're . . . all right. I can see that." He looked around. "What are you doing out here?"

"Just walking. I found some herbs that might be useful, though I'm not sure of their uses yet."

He glanced at her collection. "Those, we use to make tea. The others, I'm not sure. One there, lavender, is often used to scent homes and soaps, that sort of thing, though you used it to good effect in my stew last night. It may have other uses as well. You also have gorse, though I don't know what it's used for."

Eliana picked her way back onto the forest path, and Damir edged her back toward the cottage. "You must not go far from my cottage, Eliana. I have shielded this area, but I don't want you to get lost."

Her brow angled. "You mean, more lost than I am now?"

He took her hand and squeezed it. "You are not lost when you are with me."

"My memory has not returned, but last night I had a strange dream."

"What was it?" he asked, and he seemed both curious and nervous.

"I dreamt that a dark man was calling me—he wanted to devour me. I felt he was evil, and I was terrified. But I escaped him to fall at your feet, and you picked me up."

His eyes widened at this, and he looked a little guilty. "I cannot explain it, my dear. Though it is interesting."

"The dream faded, and then resumed. I saw a woman behind me, almost like a shadow. She tried to tell me something, but I couldn't hear her. But I knew she was afraid of something, and she wanted me to help her. And then she disappeared into darkness."

"I suppose that is your memory trying to restore itself."

"So it seemed to me, too. But in the darkness that seemed to swallow me, there was a strange light, and when I got closer, I saw it was a boy with pale blond hair and an angel's face. He glowed with a strange power but when I drew near, I saw tears on his cheek. I tried to reach him, to help him, but then he faded back into the light and disappeared."

"The mind plays strange tricks in sleep, Eliana. For a Mage, and perhaps for all, there is always a struggle between darkness and light, a struggle for balance. Perhaps the evil man and the angelic boy represented that conflict."

"Perhaps. But they seemed so real, like people I should know, people I would remember if only my memory would return."

Damir kissed her hand gently and held it against his cheek. "Dreams are always that way, my dear. The brain invents people as if we know them, but they are nothing more than phantoms of our own hopes and fears. Think no more of it."

"I suppose you are right. And it is balance I seek. I feel that, too."

"We will find it together."

"I hope so." She held his hand as they walked back to his garden in silence. Eliana looked around at the flowers that lined the entrance to the cottage. "These plants are pretty, but why haven't I planted herbs here, too, for my Mage work?"

He hesitated. "You like to find them as they grow in the wild. That enhances their power."

"They must grow naturally, then?" she asked.

"I believe so, yes."

Eliana pointed toward the eastern clearing as the sun rose higher over the distant plains. "What lies that way?"

"The unclaimed lands beyond the Woodland, as I mentioned last night. Far beyond live the Norsk, though of late they build their hamlets ever closer to our borders."

Eliana gazed over the still horizon. "It makes me sad. I don't know why." She glanced at Damir. "Do you?"

"No. That land had no particular interest to you before."

Eliana recognized a strange set to Damir's proud jaw, a stance that seemed almost defiant. "It is a place of sorrow, and of growing unrest. I see it as if a storm cloud hangs above it, a portent of dark tides coming."

Damir shrugged. "A storm cloud probably does hang above that land. It snows often there, and even the summers are cool. You would think the Norsk might favor warmer climes, but they are not a sensitive race."

He was trying to evade her and diminish what she sensed. "It is not weather I feel. It is a state of being and an emotion."

"Then perhaps they are at war again. Not long ago, the Norsk united, more or less, under a single chieftain, but it is bound to be unstable."

"Have you known the Norsk people personally?" she asked.

"I've had encounters with a few."

Eliana puffed an impatient breath. "In some way other than with a sword!"

"I've seen them in the port city of Amon-dhen, where traders and rogues gather. Uniformly, they were drunk, boisterous and dangerous, especially to women." He added this part pointedly and glanced at Eliana.

"What do they look like?"

"Large-boned, fairly tall . . ."

"As tall as you?" she asked.

"Some, perhaps. But bigger. They are light-skinned, with light hair, usually blond, sometimes red. Most have beards, and they are generally unkempt and ill-mannered."

"But they are impressive warriors, I gather."

"They certainly fight with abandon. They carry broadswords and axes, and fight as if they have no value on their lives. For that reason, they are deadly."

"Then they are unskilled with weaponry?"

"Those I've dealt with are savage and untrained, though I will say they usually find their mark. Many have perished under those rough axes."

"Then you fear them?"

He huffed. "I do not." He paused. "Were I not armed with a greater power, that of my *ki* which I invest in the weapons I make, I might learn to be wary of them, however. Most Woodland folk flee them, that is certain."

"Had I experience with the Norsk?"

"I don't know. No. Only what is typical for most Woodland folk."

"What did I think of them?"

"I don't know!"

Eliana stepped back at his outburst. "I pester you with questions. Forgive me."

He drew a taut breath, then took her hand again. "No, no. It is I who am sorry. It is only that . . . that I have been concerned also about the Norsk threat of late. They are a danger to us. To us all, of the Woodland realm."

"I see."

He started to speak again, but the sound of horses interrupted them, and two men rode into the clearing. They spotted Eliana and Damir, then stopped, and they stared. The younger man leaned over and spoke to a much older man who sat astride a heavyset bay horse, but the old man just gaped.

Damir gulped audibly, then hurried forward to greet them. Curious, Eliana followed. The old man stared at her, mouth still agape, and the boy looked wary.

"Madawc," said Damir, somewhat breathless. "You surprise me with this visit."

Madawc kept his astonished gaze on Eliana. "What has happened to her?"

Damir cast a quick glance at the boy. "Didn't Elphin give you the details? Eliana, *my wife*, has fallen from her mare, injured herself slightly, and has lost her memory."

Madawc nodded. "The boy told me, all right. Thought I'd best see it with my own eyes." He waved his hand at the boy. "Assist me here, boy!"

The boy jumped off the other horse, which seemed too tall for him, and raced around to help the old man, who dismounted as if his joints pained him. The old man shook himself, seized a heavy wooden cane from his saddle, then propelled himself over to Eliana and peered deep into her eyes.

Eliana stood still as he scrutinized her. He stared first at her face, then her stance, and then he circled around her as if checking for peculiar growths. She didn't dare look to see his reaction. He came around to the front of her and again stared.

The old man's eyes were a bright blue that seemed almost unnaturally vivid and his face, though aged, had a liveliness of expression that gave him a look of perpetual youth and amazement, equal to the boy who accompanied him.

"So, forgotten everything, have you, girl?"

"It would seem so," she answered, but his bright eyes narrowed to slits.

"Or is that what you want the lad to think?" He spoke triumphantly, then awaited her response.

She glanced at Damir, whose brow knit in sudden suspicion, as if the old man had intimated an all-too-likely scenario.

"Why would I want him to think that?" Why, indeed? Eliana's chest constricted. Clearly, there was more at work in her marriage than Damir had indicated. "What kind of wife would deceive her husband into thinking she had no memory?"

Madawc jabbed his cane into the soil, then popped it up again. "A devious one!"

Unexpected tears welled in Eliana's eyes. "Was I devious?"

Damir hurried to her side and placed his arm over her shoulder. "Of course not, my dear. Madawc is always suspicious—of everyone." He shot the old man a distinctly forbidding look, but Madawc didn't appear appeased.

"What are those herbs clutched in her little hands, then? She's chosen a right good lot of them, for a Mage who has no memory!"

"Eliana senses herbs and their uses, Madawc. That is her method, and one she retains despite her memory loss."

"Oh, bother this!" Madawc cupped Eliana's chin in his broad hand and gazed into her eyes. Eliana bit her lip to keep from crying, but she met his gaze straight on. He searched for a long while, and apparently found nothing. He released her, then stood back. "Forgive me, my dear. It is as the boy said. You recall nothing."

She didn't answer, but Damir took her hand. "She is still weak from her . . . experience yesterday, and needs to rest. Eliana, take the plants you found and put them in the house. Your method was to dry them—you can put them on the counter in the kitchen."

Both Madawc and the boy, Elphin, waited expectantly, as if they expected her to argue. She hesitated, then nodded once. "As you wish." She started to turn away, then went back to Madawc and handed him a sprig of the gorse. "Here, sir. As I hold this herb, I feel an ache in my knees and elbows. I believe it will aid your pains, perhaps in a tea."

Madawc took the plant and nodded thoughtfully. "Same as she's given me afore now. Works, too. You can take the brain out of the Mage, but not the Mage out of the brain."

"What have you done to her?" Madawc's voice was raised well above what Damir considered necessary. He winced

64

and looked sharply around to be certain Eliana had entered the cottage.

"Keep your voice down! And I didn't do anything to her. As I'm sure Elphin reported, she did this to herself."

"Didn't bring herself here and posture herself as your wife!"

Damir shifted his weight. "That was my vengeance, to which I'm fully entitled."

"Have you any idea what could come of this?"

"Eliana will no doubt be angered, if she regains her memory."

"*If!* You can't be thinking of keeping her like this."

Damir drew a patient breath. "In the first place, I have no say in when—or if—she regains her memory. Only Eliana can do that, and as she told me at our meeting, for this particular potion, there is no antidote."

"Meeting? What did you go meeting with her for, anyway?" asked Madawc, suspicion ripe in his bright eyes.

"Her purposes intrigued me."

"It was the lass who intrigued you, lad. As always."

"I thought she might be ready to reveal her knowledge of the Norsk threat."

Madawc waved his hand dismissively. "That girl has no knowledge of the Norsk, leastways not what you're thinking. There's only one male who's ever interested her, and as it looks to me, she's got him right where she wants him."

Elphin looked back and forth between them as if awaiting the revelation of a mystery. "Figuring this was The Fiend's way of capturing Damir ap Kora at last, sir?"

Madawc frowned and cast a dark glance at the boy. "The Mundane are always so dramatic. I'm saying just what I'm saying—the lass has him where she wants him."

Damir frowned, too. "That hardly seems likely. I can think of nowhere she'd rather be less than with me." He paused, and lowered his voice. "Do you doubt her memory loss still?"

Madawc glanced toward the cottage. "There was no lie in Eliana's eyes, and I know her deceits better than anyone." A fond smile crossed his aged lips. "She could cause a sea of mischief, she could, but she couldn't tell a lie to save herself."

"You missed her performance in the glade yesterday, surely, as she attempted to entice me with her 'Wine of Truce.'"

"Not a lie . . . that was a method. Bright lass, she is. Always was." Madawc turned to Elphin. "You, boy, take the horses for a drink. Damir and I must speak alone."

Elphin sighed miserably, but did as he was told. Madawc motioned Damir toward a bench near the forest's edge. They sat together, but Damir glanced nervously toward the cottage. "Why does this conversation require privacy, Madawc?"

"The boy, Elphin, is too young to hear much of what I have to say to you. Also, there are matters which shouldn't reach Mundane ears."

"Elphin is a trustworthy boy."

Madawc snorted. "I can see that! My years have given me greater wisdom than any elite Mage, including yourself. It's those as may listen to the boy that concern me."

"I take it he told you about Eliana's cottage."

"He did. Said it was ransacked, apparently with evil intent."

"I hope you're not suspecting me in this," said Damir.

Madawc smiled. "I know you better than that, lad. As well as I know her. But I can't put my mind to anyone who would dare pillage Eliana's property, let alone leave it a shambles."

"Nor can I."

They looked at each other, and Madawc nodded. "Except the Norsk. But wouldn't your shield bar their entrance or leave them wallowing in confusion?"

Damir hesitated. "It should. But apparently someone got through. Had I held no suspicion of Eliana and the Norsk, my inclination would be to suspect someone within the realm itself, someone who gives no sign of danger, and who walks free in our realm."

"That is my suspicion also, and that's why we needed to speak in private." Madawc lowered his voice as if even the trees might have ears. "A shadow of a thought has been growing in my mind, a disquiet, and as I spoke of it to the other Mages, they have sensed the same. A darkness comes, its tendrils reach into the Wood—or maybe arise from within it."

"I would have thought it came from Eliana herself," said Damir.

"Ah, lad . . . Eliana is the heart of this realm. Didn't you know that?"

"She is an emotional creature, and too sensitive."

Madawc laughed. "You are both sensitive, and no one knows better than I. You have more in common than you realize. When you were children, you even had the same nightmares. But you never told her that, did you?"

Damir didn't answer. He remembered waking to the sound of Eliana's cries late at night, years ago. He remembered sneaking down the hall to listen as Madawc reassured her. He had known her nightmares came from the loss of her parents—because his were the same. She had spotted him standing by the doorway and reacted with fury, probably because she imagined he had witnessed her weakness and that he would tease her. But later that night, he had crept back into her room and sat on the edge of her bed as she slept. He had wanted, desperately, to wake her, to tell her he had the same dream, but he never did.

Instead, they both clung to the power of their *ki*, too

afraid of each other to accept what they shared. "Sometimes, I wanted to," Damir said quietly, and Madawc nodded, then patted Damir's knee.

"I know that, lad. And there's still time to do it, once she regains herself. No point telling this new Eliana."

"She is the same person, Madawc."

"Without her memories, she's barely a person at all."

Damir frowned. "You are wrong. She has many of the same qualities, but no longer infected by pride or anger."

"It wasn't Eliana's pride—or anger—that defined her, lad. It was her heart and her emotion—and too often, that emotion was fear."

Damir eyed him with misgivings. "You have always been blind to her faults."

"Not blind, lad. Never blind. But maybe I don't see them as faults."

"Be that as it may, it is possible that Eliana herself is in danger, and most likely she's brought it on herself through her allegiance with the Norsk. But Eliana is not without enemies even in the Wood."

"Not a one would dare cross her, save yourself," said Madawc. "Wonder what the intruder was after. The lass kept much to herself. Too much. She didn't trust others with her secrets, even me."

"You don't understand her mysterious defense of the Norsk, either?"

Madawc shook his head. "No, except that it is genuine. When she first came out on their behalf, I suspected . . ." His voice trailed.

"Suspected what?"

"Oh, that she was trying to stir you up. What else? And it worked well enough, too."

Damir frowned. He had wasted far too much time considering Eliana's possible relationship with a Norskman, but it irritated him to know his thoughts were read by the old Mage. "What changed your mind?"

"I watched her, listened to her. I saw she's been keeping something to herself, something she holds dear, and not part of her scheming, either. She has some reason to believe the Norsk can be treated with a different way."

"Or she's in love with one of them."

Madawc's brow elevated. "As I said, the matter has certainly stirred you up. But I know her heart better than that." He paused. "It's you I'm worrying about."

Damir eyed him doubtfully. "Why?"

"Just how far do you intend to take this 'wedding of vengeance?' "

"Only as far as need be to ensure Eliana's fury, of course."

"Lad. I saw how she was looking at you. And I see how you look at her. It's not Eliana you're seeing—it's the woman you think she should have been."

"If you mean a woman of gentleness and pleasant manner, that does have some merit," said Damir, but the old Mage's words went too close to the truth. "I cannot find this a change for the worse."

"And if this 'new' Eliana bears a child?"

Damir winced. "That is not going to happen."

"Well, there would be worse things for the Wood than a child born of the two of you. But there are better ways of reaching the same point, lad, *though that other road may be longer*. . . ." Madawc added that last part pointedly, and paused, while Damir wondered if the old man knew how much of the dark *ki* he had already engaged.

Damir shot him a dark glance. "Eliana remains . . . intact."

"For how long?"

Damir stood up and turned in a circle, then faced the old Mage. "Is *nothing* sacred in this Wood, nothing even remotely private?"

Madawc leaned back on the bench and looked comfortable. "Of course, it's sacred, boy! That's why we pry into it so much! Just you remember that she'll have your head and entrails, too, if you get her with child afore she's ready."

There was no point in arguing. Damir stifled his annoyance and offered a curt nod. "I wouldn't think of it."

"You've thought of it."

Damir faced Madawc and his jaw clenched tight. "It won't happen."

Madawc stood up and stretched. "Good. See that it doesn't." He paused and sighed. "Still . . . a shame not to have a little one from the two of you . . ."

"You just said . . ." He stopped and shook his head, but Madawc didn't seem to notice the inequity of his sentiment.

"Ah, well! What the lass has done can't be undone, at least, not unless by herself somehow, and I'll not be knowing the method there. But maybe Fate is guiding her, as it often does. She's safe here, more or less, and it's best she stay put for the time being, just so long as you be remembering yourself."

Damir glanced toward Elphin. "Can we trust the boy to say nothing?"

Madawc smiled, looking wily. "He won't say a thing. Taken him in, I have. A good lad. Shame he's a Mundane, but I can still teach him a thing or two. And keep him out of trouble."

"Is the king aware of our situation?"

"I'll tell him later," said Madawc, and he waved his hand dismissively. "He won't take kindly to your claiming Eliana as your wife, not without the proper ceremony and ritual."

"Tell him I will keep her safe."

"From everything but yourself," added Madawc.

"From everything, including myself."

Madawc arched his brow, but he didn't press the matter, much to Damir's relief. Madawc waved to Elphin. "You, boy, bring my horse!"

Elphin helped the old man mount, and Damir remembered when he and Eliana had fought over who would serve the great Mage. Maybe the old man had a scheme worth remembering. Elphin looked eagerly between them. "Did you decide what to do about The Fiend, sir?"

"She stays with me," replied Damir.

Elphin glanced toward the cottage and sighed. "Almost seems like two different people, doesn't she? I wasn't afraid of her for a second there." He turned to Madawc. "Do you think the good one could be here to stay, sir?"

Madawc scoffed, but Damir couldn't restrain a faint smile, which the old Mage noticed at once.

"She'll be back to her old self in no time," said Madawc with a glance of dark warning toward Damir. "Until then, keep her safe, and keep her presence here a secret."

"I will do that," said Damir, but he couldn't abandon the idea of Eliana, this way, forever. After all, she had said herself there was no antidote to this potion. "She is happy now, and I will see that our days here are peaceful."

Elphin mounted behind Madawc, and they turned toward the southern pathway. The boy shook his head. He didn't look back, but Damir heard the boy's skeptical tone. "Unless The Fiend returns. Then there'll be hell to pay, sir. This won't sit well with her at all."

They rode away, and Damir sighed. This woman was truly beginning to seem like two different people in his mind: His Eliana, who looked at him with trust—and desire, and The Fiend, a woman he had never been able to reach or win, no matter how he tried. If The Fiend returned, she would steal the Eliana whose eyes already glittered with love.

Maybe Madawc was wrong—he had never understood the depth and power of Eliana's concoctions, so he would have no way of knowing she had at last created one that couldn't be cured. Maybe he didn't have to lose his Eliana, after all.

Damir turned back to the cottage, then stopped short. She stood by the doorway, her face knit in doubt and confusion. Her eyes narrowed and her lovely head tilted to one side. He held his breath in fear for what she might have heard.

"Eliana?"

"Who is 'The Fiend?'"

Chapter Five

Damir's face drained of color at Eliana's question, and for a moment, he didn't speak. He just stared at her, aghast. When he spoke, his voice came small and weak. "What?"

"'The Fiend.' I heard the boy speak of someone's return—I am under the impression it was a woman. Who is she?"

He just stared, but she could see his mind racing. He drew a quick breath, then came to her and edged her back into the cottage. All the while, she could see him struggling for an explanation.

"The Fiend . . . The Fiend is another Mage. Yes, a woman . . ."

"Why is she known by such a negative term?"

Damir huffed. "She has earned the title, I assure you."

"Then she is your enemy?"

Damir hesitated, and a look crossed his face that troubled Eliana's heart, though she wasn't sure why. "Enemy is a strong word." He paused again. "She is a troublesome woman, and it is true that we are often at odds."

"Where has she gone? Is she the person you spoke of earlier, who was in some kind of danger?"

His eyes shifted to one side. "Yes." But then he waved his hand dismissively. "The Fiend often comes and goes this way. No one is ever sure of her purposes."

"The boy said '*This won't sit well with her at all.*' What did he mean?"

Damir seemed at a loss, but then his eyes brightened as if an idea struck him, and he took her hand. "She is jealous of you, because of your power, because you are well loved among the Woodland people, and because together, we have much influence with the Woodland king, Owain Daere."

"Or is she jealous of me because I am your wife?"

His dark eyes widened and he hesitated before answering. "I'm sure that has no part in it."

"Then what does she want?"

A faint, almost fond smile began on his lips. "I'm not sure anyone has ever known that."

"You speak of this woman in a strange way, first as an enemy and someone to be feared, and yet I see that you admire her in some way."

He glanced at her sharply, surprised. "She is a powerful Mage. That is all I admire about her."

"Do I know this woman, too? We are not friends, I gather."

"You know her, yes . . ." He cleared his throat. "Not friends, exactly, no . . . We were at the School of Mages, all of us, together."

"She was orphaned also?"

He hesitated. "Yes."

"It seems many children have lost parents in this realm."

Damir sighed. "That was true in those years, sadly. A deadly illness overtook many in the Woodland, troubling both Mages and Mundanes alike. The Mages were few even then, and the loss left Amrodel without much of its former power. Many died, including our parents. The greatest herbalists among the Mages were able to find a cure at last, but not before our parents were lost."

"Maybe this loss explains The Fiend's temperament. Anger is closely akin to fear, I think," said Eliana. Damir stared at her in astonishment.

"I believe that is true in her case, yes. Those of us born with great power are too likely to rely on the strength of our *ki*, and not on each other." He took Eliana's hand and held it between both of his. "But you and I were different. We found strength together."

"I am sorry for her, for The Fiend, if she has faced this life alone," said Eliana. "We must be alike in some way, if we were both born Mages."

"Oh, no . . . no, no . . . she is nothing like you. The Fiend is filled with ambition and pride, she is vain, unreasonable, and dangerous when angered. Her temper flares without reason, and she has a penchant for mischief."

Eliana frowned. "At least she sounds interesting."

"Enough about The Fiend. I promise you, my dear, she isn't important to us now. I would not have thoughts of her trouble you in any way."

Clearly, there was something strange, even amiss, in Damir's relationship with this woman known as "The Fiend." And he didn't want to discuss her with Eliana. She felt tired—there was too much she didn't know, and too much that swirled around her, making no sense.

Eliana gazed out the window as the morning sun crossed the clearing outside Damir's cottage. "I hope my memory returns soon. Did you ask the Elder Mage about it?" She glanced over her shoulder at Damir and saw that he looked uncomfortable. "About a cure?"

He moved beside her and placed his hand on the small of her back. "I did, of course. Unfortunately, it seems this affliction must wear off on its own."

Eliana eyed the forest's northern edge. "Or perhaps I could cure it myself, if my skill was as great as you say."

Now he looked nervous. "But you have forgotten your former methods, and I never knew them well enough to repeat."

Eliana's gaze fixed on the low plants that grew in the shadows of the trees. "I don't need to know my methods. I feel their uses, as I did earlier with the gorse."

"That is possible, yes. An extraordinarily good idea. Later, we will walk along the Woodland paths together, and you can gather the herbs that seem right to you. But though my knowledge of your craft is minimal, I am quite certain most must be gathered at dawn or dusk, and not when the sun is shining full, as it is now."

"But some call to me in the dark of night." She closed her eyes. "And one at the full of the moon." The one she needed most . . .

He breathed a muted sigh. "The moon is waning now. It will be nigh onto a month before it reaches fullness again."

"A month . . ." Eliana gathered her courage. "Then so be it. My heart tells me this is the herb I need, but I will only know it when the moon shines full on a cloudless night."

"Given the changes of weather experienced in the Woodland, it may be many moons," said Damir. Eliana glanced at him—his tone sounded almost hopeful. He offered a weak smile. "But we will not give up hope."

She held his gaze intently. "I will not. I must know who I truly am."

He eased her into his arms. "You know who you are, Eliana. It is in your heart, and that is what matters."

She lifted her chin. "Yes. That is true. My mind is clouded, but my heart is clear. I know that because of what I feel when I look at you."

For a brief flash, she saw sorrow in Damir's eyes, as if

he wished what she said were true, but didn't believe it. Eliana touched his face. "You can trust this much: Trust my heart. *Trust us.*"

He closed his eyes and kissed her palm. "Trust does not come as easily as it once did," he said quietly. "But while I have you, I will hold to it."

"It is all we have, in the end—to trust those who live in our hearts, to know they are real, and their hearts are true."

He nodded, but he seemed tense. "Of course."

"If I must wait for a month, or more, to get this herb, then I would make myself useful in the time being. What duties do I normally perform?"

Damir looked completely blank.

"Do I make potions?" she asked, and he nodded.

"Yes . . ."

"Well, do I have records, so that I might relearn some of my work?"

His gaze wandered to one side. "You didn't keep records, as such . . . Unfortunately, most of it was in your head and in your instinct for the task."

"I see. Perhaps I can help you at your task!"

He hesitated and cleared his throat, then shrugged. "I suppose you could. It might be interesting . . . I have been working on a project that might interest you. Or would have, before your injury."

"What is it?" Eliana felt a new excitement, like a child about to see a long awaited secret revealed.

Damir smiled as if he recognized her mood and liked it. "Come this way."

She followed him through the rear hallway, and out a small door in the back of his cottage. They crossed a small, round clearing overhung with massive tree branches. Moss covered the lawn and swaying ferns lined a stone path indicating that full sun never reached this spot. As she walked, red and green dragonflies swirled and darted over the ground, their delicate wings catching the light as they moved. A lavender dragonfly flew among them, larger than the rest, and Eliana stopped to watch it.

Damir saw it, too, and glanced at her with a trace of suspicion in his eyes. "I've never seen one so large before."

"She is beautiful," said Eliana, but her voice faded as the insect darted toward her, then circled over her head.

"How do you know it's female?" asked Damir.

"It just seems female." Eliana smiled. "Maybe it's their queen."

As she spoke, the lavender dragonfly flew around her, then in a reverse circle around Damir. "This is odd," he said. "It is almost as if it's communicating with us."

They looked at each other. "What would it want?" asked Eliana.

Damir studied the creature as it darted around. "Legends tell of the Great Spirits of Mages past who may take the form of animals. I imagined Woodland cats or falcons, but I suppose an insect is possible."

"Maybe it's trying to tell us something!" Eliana clapped her hands and leaned toward the dragonfly, but instead it flew upwards. It seemed to be waiting for something.

Damir shrugged. "Or it could be an ordinary bug. Come, let me show you my work."

Beyond the clearing, large rocks lay strewn against a steep mountainside. Damir led her through the rocks on a narrow path that wound upward and cut into the sheer face of the mountain. As they climbed, Eliana noticed a single white flower growing by the path, and her fingers tingled with an icy thrill. Transfixed, she paused to pick it, but Damir didn't notice as he climbed on ahead.

They reached a stony plateau, and Damir pointed down the hill to their cottage, visible through the dark trees below. Eliana squeezed her hands together in excitement. "This is a very interesting spot."

"And one you have never seen before."

"Truly? Why not?"

He shifted his weight. "Well . . . you didn't like the climb, I guess." He motioned around a rock, and she followed him into a shallow cave. It had been hollowed out by hand, and the air felt hot as she entered. Inside, a low fire burned in small pit, and as her eyes became accustomed to the dark, she saw many rows of weaponry, swords and shields, all in various stages of completion.

Damir smiled as she looked around. "This is my study and the craft I enjoy most. No other Mage, ever, has matched my skill at making swords."

"How is this the work of a Mage?"

His smile grew, and her heart moved at his pride as he drew a sword from the rack. "I put my craft into each weapon, and each is unique. For some, those that are made most easily, the craft is simple, and will keep the sword from injury during battle. But for others, the craft is subtler. This one instills fear in one's opponent, another, despair." He put the sword back, and drew another. "This one affects its bearer, giving a surge of confidence and power to the will. Still others grant benefits such as indicating when danger is near."

"That would be useful." Eliana spotted a long sword that seemed in its earliest stages. Its blade was a lighter silver than the others, and the end of the hilt was incomplete. "What is that one?"

Damir sighed. "That is my latest creation, though it's not finished, and perhaps not likely to be."

"Why not?"

He shrugged. "I'm at a loss as to its use and its power, though like you, I sense something beyond explanation."

"What did you intend it to do?"

He gazed thoughtfully at the sword. "It is to hold against darkness, but I cannot find the method of completion."

Eliana stared at the sword. "It needs . . . more."

"Yes. But what?" Damir lowered the long blade into the

fire. As the blade heated, it glowed, not red, but white. He held his hand over it, and Eliana felt the energy that grew inside him. It reached to her, and she fixed her gaze on the blade.

She watched her hand move as if it wasn't a part of her, and she saw herself drop the white flower she had picked on the mountainside onto the molten sword. It flickered, then disappeared into the blade.

Damir looked at her in surprise, but his eyes were shining. "That helped, but there is more."

Eliana's heart throbbed with excitement, though she wasn't fully sure why. Something formed and grew between them, as if their energy were attempting to blend, above them and beyond them. Their gazes met and together they held their palms over the blade. The silver turned to white. Eliana felt her energy, more sure and more powerful than what she had sensed before. It grew from deep inside her core, the very center of her being, and spread outward to blend with Damir.

She could almost see their energy meet and blend, but it was a feeling and a sense rather than an actual vision. Two currents of raw power came from each of them, then entwined as if somehow joined at the same source originally and now yearning to restore that bond. Their energy coiled together, and from it, a tendril fixed its power toward that unfinished sword. She heard Damir's swift breath, and knew he felt it, too. A voice in her head that was not quite her own whispered, *We are one*.

A tiny noise distracted Eliana from her trance, and she glanced over her shoulder, then gasped. "Look! It's the dragonfly!"

Damir turned in amazement as the insect entered the cave. Eliana's spine tingled, and she knew he felt the same awe. From the light of the entrance, the dragonfly came, and this time, it didn't dart or flit as was typical for the species. It came straight, and then circled first around

Eliana, then in reverse around Damir. It hovered nearly motionless over the blade of the sword, then without warning, but with obvious purpose, the dragonfly dove into the blade.

Eliana cried out in shock, but the dragonfly dissolved into the white blade and disappeared. Damir stood transfixed, but a tear ran down Eliana's cheek as she looked at him. "Why would it do that?"

"Moths will fly into a flame."

"She did it deliberately."

He nodded. "It seemed so, yes." He turned his attention back to the sword and again closed his eyes. "It is nearly complete." He put a heavy glove over his hand and drew the sword from the flames. In the red light of the fire, Eliana saw the faint outline of a dragonfly in the blade—not as it had fallen and sizzled in its demise, but pure and untarnished as if the creature still lived in the fate it had chosen.

"I know what it needs," she said quietly.

Damir watched in astonishment as Eliana unfastened the clasp at her throat and held the amber stone in her hands. Their eyes met, but Damir didn't speak as she pressed the brooch onto the open end of the hilt. It embedded as if designed to decorate a weapon, and not a woman's garb. It required no adjustment or binds as it adhered to the hilt.

Damir held up the sword and carried it out of the cave to the sunlight. For an instant, it glowed with a white light, and the light grew so that it enveloped Damir. It shimmered around him, and within that light, Eliana knew he was safe.

Damir lowered the sword and the light faded around him. He looked to Eliana, and her eyes glittered with admiration and awe. His heart felt swollen with happiness. "This is it—this is what I have been trying to create. This sword gives more than power, and more than safety. It has the power of . . . of something I do not fully understand." He looked into her beautiful eyes. "And we made it together."

"What of the dragonfly? What did that mean?" Eliana had always been tenderhearted with animals, if not with Damir himself. But the creature's strange passing had affected him, too.

"I'm not sure. Perhaps it was a blessing from the Great Spirit Mages."

"It felt more . . . individual to me," said Eliana.

"Perhaps the blessing of a single Mage. A female."

"Could it be the woman you told me about, the queen who died rather than submit to the Arch Mage?"

A tingle ran along his spine as she spoke, and he knew Eliana felt the same. "I thought of her also."

"Why would she come to us now?"

"Perhaps as a warning against darkness." Damir stopped. Was it darkness from the world beyond, or within his own heart, that the great queen warned against?

Eliana looked at the sword. "A tide of darkness is coming. I feel it. And you will be called to stand against it, Damir. But the light remains, though all may think it lost." Her voice came low and strange and Damir's breath held.

"You are her heir," he said quietly. "It may be that you hear her voice."

Eliana moved closer to him and laid her hand on his arm. "Damir . . . If darkness is coming, what does that mean?"

"That I do not know, but the elder Mages have sensed its wave approaching, like the precursor to a great storm. Many believe it comes from the Norsk, though they do not have our power, and all are Mundane."

"All we know of," she added, and Damir looked at her quickly, then at the hilt of his sword.

"This jewel is of Norsk origin," he said. "And it is embedded with the image of a dragonfly."

Eliana touched the hilt. "It seems odd that you gave me a Norsk gift. Where did you find it?"

And why had this item so much power, if only the rough handiwork of a barbaric race? "Norsk items aren't uncommon." He hadn't answered her question, but too many of his own remained unsolved. Damir returned to the cave and selected a sheath for the sword.

"What are you going to do with it?" Eliana asked. "Is it a gift for the king?"

"This is a gift for a warrior, not a king," said Damir. "If any hand but that of a Mage should touch this sword, it would burn, and destroy anyone who sought to wield it. Even a Mage would be at peril, unless his *ki* be strong enough to balance this sword's power."

"Could I wield it?"

Damir smiled. "If your arms were strong enough, yes. Your power is equal to mine, though you've never directed its force at weaponry before. But to wield it, you would have to add much mass to your body—and I'm not sure that would be appealing, to either of us."

Eliana flexed her arm, then furrowed her brow. "I am not very muscular. Perhaps I could use a little more bulk . . ."

"You have other gifts, my dear."

"So this sword would 'sear' even the king?"

"Quickly, I'm afraid. Though descended from the great Mages of old, Owain Daere is by nature a Mundane, and his *ki* even lighter than usual for the Woodlanders. But I have given him other weapons of protection and strength of will, which he values greatly."

"Is Magery not passed from parents to children, then?"

"It is, and it is not," answered Damir. "It is more likely that Mage parents draw the souls of Mage children, but in many cases, a Mage is born to Mundanes, or to those like the king, who despite their heritage, have a very limited *ki*. The king's youngest daughter has the *ki* of a Mage, but she is only twelve years old, and thus far, her gift appears to manifest with the bow and arrow. Energy usually directs itself toward particular strengths, such as my own skill with armory, and yours with herbs."

"It does not seem to me that the king wields much power in this land."

"In Amrodel, no, but in my father's land of Kora, the prince, the only title they bestow, perhaps held too much," said Damir. "In Amrodel, 'King' is best described as a ceremonial title, and in truth, Owain Daere isn't held up by any higher esteem than the tavern keeper, and less than the elder Mage, who is in many ways the true leader of the Woodland. But the king keeps alive the memory of the Woodland queen lost to Amrodel, and in ceremony is his real importance. Decisions are made at Council, where he presides, but it is a group of Mages and Mundanes who make the decisions."

"That sounds sensible enough," said Eliana. "What was my parentage?"

"You were a surprise," he said, and he smiled. "Your mother was the king's youngest sister, and like him, her *ki* was light. Your father was the palace horse master, and also Mundane. No one expected you to have the power you did. Perhaps that is why . . ." Damir stopped himself. It certainly explained why she had been spoiled by her adoring and amazed parents, and why Owain Daere set no limits on her behavior. "Why your skills are so unique."

Her eyes narrowed as if she knew he had changed his meaning, but her attention returned to his sword. "I believe this weapon is meant for you."

"For now, it is," he said. "But its fate may lie beyond

me, and in the hands of another. This also I feel to be true."

"It has a destination, doesn't it?" she asked, her voice soft and low. "I feel that, too. From you, to another, and then . . . to a fate I cannot see."

"It will fall into darkness," said Damir, and he closed his eyes with the vision, even as he resisted its force. But a tiny spark grew in his mind, deep from within the shadow and for an instant, he imagined the dragonfly emerging from its midst. "The essence of you and of me is in this sword. And out of darkness, there will come light."

She nodded, her eyes bright with understanding, as if she, too, shared the same vision. "Wherever its fate leads, that part of us stands with it. And when it faces darkness, it will be the only light."

Damir took her hand. This was the life he wanted. For the first time, he and Eliana had created something together, and its power was beyond anything he'd known before. She wrapped her fingers around his. "I feel powerful today, because I am with you. I don't remember what I have felt before, but somehow, I know this is new."

"It is new." He didn't want to explain, and he saw the doubt in her eyes, rational for a wife who had supposedly loved her husband for many years. "Maybe we have grown complacent together," he added. "We were . . . content with the lives we were leading, and didn't explore new possibilities."

"When old paths are erased, new ones are free to form," said Eliana, and Damir liked the thought. Their competitiveness had certainly been a long ingrained path, and he was glad to be rid of it, though a divergent thought reminded him that he had it easier because he determined the rules of their new relationship.

Damir touched her cheek. Her skin was even softer than he had imagined. He ran his finger along her cheek and down her neck, and she shivered as if the touch stirred her. He cupped her face in his hands and bent to kiss her.

A cold wind swept down the mountain, and they both startled at its force. It whipped around them, raising dust as it swirled. A puff of ash and smoke gushed from the cave of the forge. Eliana closed her eyes tight and hid her face. Damir stared up the mountain, suddenly enveloped in a cloud of ash. Eliana looked up at him, startled.

"What was that?" she asked, and she moved closer to him. Damir put his arm over her shoulder, but he shook his head.

"I don't know." He watched the ashen cloud as it rose, then dissipated. He drew a taut breath. "More than the wind's changing temperament, I think."

She nodded. "A breath of darkness."

"It is this energy, a dark *ki*, that the elder Mages have reported at odd whiles in the Wood, but ever-increasing in intensity and growing more frequent as fall gives way to winter."

Eliana shuddered. "It's cold."

Damir took her hand and without saying a word they walked back down the path to his cottage. The wind had come when he meant to kiss her. This time, he didn't sense a warning or a reminder of his deception. Instead, he sensed anger, as if some force of energy raged against the union he and Eliana had formed, and against the power in the sword they made together.

They reached the shelter of the trees behind his cottage, and Damir relaxed. *Just an odd trick of the wind, nothing more.* As they reached the stone path, his back door opened and a small black-haired girl peeked out. Her eyes widened when she spotted Eliana at Damir's side, and her gaze fixed on their clasped hands. Her mouth slid slowly open, then snapped shut as she readied herself for some outburst that would surely destroy everything Damir had won.

"Cahira!" He jumped forward, gave the child a quick hug, then eased her back into the cottage. Her little body remained stiff and firm, and she wedged herself around him to stare at Eliana.

"What are you doing with *The . . . ?*"

Damir coughed, spun the little girl around and issued the darkest warning look he could muster. "My *wife* and I were at work, Cahira, up at the forge on the mountain."

Cahira's face didn't alter. Only her eyes shifted as she looked from Eliana to Damir. Odd that a child so young could summon such a telling expression.

She opened her mouth to speak, then closed it again. Panic froze Damir's thoughts as he sought a way to silence her, but Cahira just nodded. "I *see.*"

Eliana came up beside him and smiled at the child. "Hello, little person," she said, her voice soft and kind. "I had an accident which affected my memory, so I'm afraid I don't recognize you as I should."

Cahira's brow arched and she glanced at Damir, her little face too knowing as she clearly assumed he was responsible for Eliana's affliction. "I'm sorry to hear that, Lady . . ." She paused as if wondering if Damir had changed Eliana's name as well as her marital status.

"Lady *Eliana* is otherwise unafflicted by the *accident*, so there's no need to worry, Cahira."

Now Eliana herself eyed him suspiciously and Damir cringed. He had drawn out those words in a too obvious fashion. Cahira shook her head as if dealing with simpletons, then turned around and marched back into the cottage. Damir offered a weak smile, and he and Eliana followed the child into the front room.

Cahira turned to face them, her hands on her hips. "So, do I have my lessons with both of you this time?"

Eliana beamed. "Were we instructing you?" she asked, both eager and happy.

Cahira maintained a practical and somewhat shrewd expression on her small face. "You were, Lady, but until today, my lessons have been held separately."

So, the little rascal had been studying with Eliana, too. . . . Cahira caught Damir's eye and issued a small smile. Damir couldn't help but admire her.

"Allow me to introduce, again, Princess Cahira, daughter of Owain Daere, a cousin of yours. She is the child I mentioned who has the *ki* of a Mage, and, so far, has been most adept at channeling her energy into her bow."

As Damir spoke, Cahira seized a small but supple bow from where it was propped by the front door and displayed it for Eliana, who stepped forward to admire it.

"I made it myself," said Cahira, and she passed the weapon to Eliana. Clearly, the child had admired The Fiend, because unlike the boy Elphin, Cahira showed no hesitation in her presence.

"It is quite magnificent," said Eliana as she tried the string with her fingers. "Did Damir help you?"

"He did, yes." Cahira paused. "But you helped, too, Lady, with the string in particular. You gave me many herbs for its strength, and you even suggested that I make longer strings at the same time for when I grow bigger."

It wasn't easy to picture Eliana instructing a child. Damir watched her face, and realized there was much he didn't know about her life, despite the close eye he'd kept on her over the years. "How else did she help you, Cahira?"

Cahira's eyes glinted. "In *secret* ways, that I promised not to tell."

Wise child. And honorable.

Eliana smiled and returned the bow to Cahira, who gripped it with pride. "I hope you remember those secrets, for I do not," she said. "One day, I will remember, and we will do more together."

Cahira glanced at Damir. "I hope so." She didn't let Damir interrupt, as he was about to do. She noticed the sheathed weapon at his side. "Did you finish your sword? I thought you had given up on it."

"I did, yes." He paused to allow a surge of happiness. "Eliana helped me."

"With herbs?" asked Cahira.

"A small white flower," replied Eliana. "I'm not sure what it signified, but it seemed to work. But an odd thing happened, too. A large, purple dragonfly flew into the forge and embedded itself in the blade."

Cahira shuddered. "To die?"

"It must have died, yes," said Eliana, "but that seemed to be its intent."

"Dragonflies always follow you, Lady," said Cahira. "Even you didn't seem to know why."

Eliana sighed. "I am sorry such a beautiful one followed me to its death."

Cahira's face knit in contemplation. "As I was riding to your cottage, Damir—by the way, I put my pony out with your horse and Selsig . . . I noticed something strange on the mountainside. A dark cloud was rising from the mountain, though the sky was blue and air warm before that."

"A gust of wind blew up ash and smoke from my forge," said Damir. "That is all it was."

"No, Damir," replied the child. "I saw it above the mountain first, and then it disappeared before rising again. I do not believe it came from your forge. There was thought behind it, and purpose. It was an angry cloud."

Damir touched Cahira's head. "I forget you have the insight of a Mage. You are right, I think. But I don't know the purpose of the cloud, or the darkness."

"I have seen it before," she said quietly, and she looked out the window toward the east. "It comes from the Norskland."

"The Norsk do not possess enough *ki* to direct the wind. They are primitive, and violent, but their energy is weak."

"There are some who say the Norsk are dangerous," said Cahira. She glanced at Eliana. "But others remind us that they are living creatures, too, and individual. I do not believe they are all bad."

So, Eliana had been instructing the child in more than herbs. Jealousy rose in Damir. "Yet if there is a wave of darkness, it would find a quick home among the Norsk."

Cahira shook her head. "If their *ki* is weak, then who summons that darkness, who directs it? Only a Mage can do that."

Damir didn't answer, but Eliana looked between them as if the answer were obvious. "We must have a traitor in our midst." She spoke the words no other Mage had yet dared say. "The Fiend."

Chapter Six

The little dark-haired girl stared at Eliana, her small mouth agape, and Damir's face paled. "Well, who else?" asked Eliana. "I have heard you speak of this woman as both a mischief maker and possibly an ally of the Norsk. Is she not likely to seek power from dark energy, too?"

Cahira bowed her head, then shook it slowly. "I do not believe she would do that."

Eliana eyed the child, then Damir. "The Fiend inspires strange loyalty, it seems. Why, if she is as devious as you say?"

Cahira looked between them. "My father says that *some* people who seem to dislike her are really *in love* with her. . . ." She paused and cast a meaningful glance at Damir. "I thought he was wrong, but now I'm not so sure."

Damir seized the little girl and directed her to the door. "I think you should run along now, Cahira, and tell both Madawc and your father about the cloud you saw."

"Why?" asked Cahira. "They must have seen it, too."

He puffed an impatient breath. "But they don't know

that it occurred just as Eliana and I completed this sword. That may have some significance. Also, ask both your father and Madawc about dragonflies, and be sure to tell them about the one that dove into the molten steel."

"Should I tell them it was purple?"

"More lavender, really," said Eliana. "Light purple."

Cahira fixed her bright gaze on Damir. "So you want me to go now? Without my lesson?"

He chewed his lip in obvious agitation. "Well, I had intended to show you the workings of the forge today, but the wind has killed the fire, and it will take some time to clean it up." He paused. "Unless you would like to help me at that task?"

She shook her head quickly. "No, I will bring your report to my father, and visit Madawc. I have a few things to talk to them about." She peeked at Eliana. "I suppose they already know . . . ?"

He cut her off. "Yes, they know about Eliana's accident, and her affliction."

"Is there a cure?" asked Cahira, almost as if teasing her mentor. "I mean, will she get her memory back?"

"Of course," answered Damir, too quickly. "Any time now."

Cahira smacked her lips. "That should be interesting." Damir's eyes narrowed, but she went to the door and looked back over her shoulder. "Very interesting!"

She departed before Damir could comment further, and he turned, too idly, to smile at Eliana. "She's a precocious child. Very bright."

"I saw that," said Eliana. "And she knows more than she says."

"All children seem that way. But I was not in the mood for teaching today."

Eliana smiled. "The excitement from our creation has left me . . . alive," she said. "Tingling."

He looked a little weak. "Is that so?" He paused, and smiled, too. "For me, also."

Eliana's pulse quickened. "I liked blending with you. It was . . . erotic."

His eyes closed. "Yes."

She waited no longer. Eliana rose up on her tiptoes, seized his black hair in her fingers, and kissed his mouth. He caught her in his arms and kissed her back, and her body filled with molten fire. His beautiful mouth opened against hers and she slid her tongue over his. *Please don't stop this time. . . .*

Eliana wrapped her arms around his neck, and he kissed her face, her mouth, her neck. He picked her up without warning and carried her to their bedroom, then laid her down upon the bed. She looked up at him, her heart racing, and saw the wild power in his dark eyes. "Is it all right this time?" she asked, her voice small and weak. "For us to be together?"

He stared down at her and seemed to be warring inwardly with himself. He caught a quick breath and she saw his frustration and his desire. Something held him back, and Eliana's heart ached. "Please, don't deny me this time."

"I would not, for the world," he answered. The frustration in his expression gave way to a darkly sensual warmth, as if he had come to some sort of decision concerning their lovemaking.

With his dark gaze fixed on her, Damir stripped away his white shirt and dropped it beside the bed. Eliana caught her lip between her teeth and held her breath. He was too beautiful and too strong, and she trembled at the sight of him. He knelt beside her on the bed. His gaze flicked over her body and lingered where her chest rose and fell with swift breaths. He smiled.

"No, not for the world would I deny you, Eliana." His

voice came low and husky and she felt weak at the sound. What could he do to her, and what did he know that she couldn't remember? From the look in his brown eyes, she guessed it was much.

With one finger, he eased apart the bodice of her dress, still looking into her eyes, teasing her with what he knew of their shared pleasures. "You are beautiful," he said, "every part of you." He ran his finger along her collar bone, then lower to the swell of her breast. "And you are soft, here."

He leaned down to kiss her, but not deeply as she wished. Instead, he moved lower and kissed her neck, then the hollow of the throat. He tasted her skin with a flick of his tongue and she shuddered. She felt his hand near her breast, but not touching, and she shifted herself to draw him closer. He laughed low in his throat and brushed his palm over the peak of her breast. It hardened beneath her dress, but his touch skimmed by and left her with a growing ache deep inside.

She wanted him to tear away her dress, but instead, he played with the fabric and teased it against her skin. "Are you warm, Eliana?"

She nodded, but couldn't speak beyond a small gasp.

He eased the dress aside, still not over her breast, and he pressed his lips against her chest. She felt her own heart pounding at his touch, but her breath held as he traced a line lower. He cupped her breast in his hand and dragged his lips over the tip. Eliana's teeth sunk into her lower lip as she fought to hold herself still. He tasted her through the cloth and her will crumpled.

Eliana clasped her fingers on his wide shoulders to steady herself, and instead slid her hands along his strong arms as she relished the feel of him. He caught the small peak of her breast between his teeth with impossible gentleness and laved his tongue back and forth. The damp cloth clung to her skin, and he sucked and licked until her breath came in hoarse gasps. Damir peeled aside the dress and exposed her skin fully to the cool air as the late afternoon sun cast amber shadows through the bedroom and across their bed.

He moved his attention to her other breast, still teasing the first with his hand, and she lay beneath him, disheveled and desperate as he played with her. They must have done this many times before, but it felt new. How slowly he moved, how well he knew her, as if he had planned every touch for years beyond count, and perfected each kiss.

He teased her until she writhed, until she thought she could stand no more without screaming or attacking him with wanton lust. But instead, he moved lower as he pulled apart her dress and spread it like wings beside her. She watched him in surprise as he kissed her stomach, now taut with anticipation, then rested his cheek for a moment against her skin as if he wanted the moment to last.

Damir edged himself lower, and Eliana's fingers tightened on his shoulders. He looked up at her and smiled, his eyelids heavy as desire soaked through him so strongly that she felt it like her own. "What are you doing?" she asked.

"I would satisfy you, my beautiful, sweet Eliana, as you have never been satisfied before."

Her gaze shifted to the side as she wondered what this might mean, but Damir maneuvered himself between her legs, and before her guess was complete, he kissed the soft skin of her inner thigh. Eliana gasped and struggled, but he cupped her hips in a firm grip, then flicked his tongue over her tiny, feminine bud. A spasm of pleasure shot through her and her legs stiffened, then wrapped over his shoulders. In a dizzying haze, she wondered if this was the usual way they made love.

Her mind went blank as he teased her, and she gave herself over to an array of sensation so strong that nothing else mattered. She felt his tongue, his mouth. He held her fast as he sucked and teased, and her heart raced faster and wilder than she had ever imagined it could. Her back arched and twisted, and she heard him moan with his own desire.

Her energy reached toward him, just as it had done in the cave, but this time, he didn't meet her. Instead, he seemed to absorb her need, tease her with it, and hold himself back from the place she knew they should be together. Eliana gripped his black hair, desperate for him to join her, but still, he didn't yield. Instead, his tongue swirled around her most sensitive spot and her energy curled tight around itself, trapped and set to fire by his skill.

He teased her until she could endure no more, until frustration and desire and fire pooled inside her and seethed beyond endurance. Some part of her resisted this final surrender, but his tongue encircled her and teased her, and her resistance gave way to a furious pleasure. She cried out, and her body gave way, a willing defeat to a great conqueror. Wild currents swept through her and every nerve seemed to catch fire. She quivered and sighed, twisting beneath him as waves of rapture consumed her.

The moment held, and then slowly faded, and she lay still as he rested his cheek on her thigh. She felt satisfied beyond measure, and empty beyond description, and the deep core of her ached for something he had not given, though he had denied nothing. Eliana closed her eyes and heard her own heart pounding.

Damir slid up beside her, took her in his arms, and kissed her cheek. She felt his pulse racing—he had not satisfied himself while driving her pleasure, but he seemed happy. His breath came ragged and swift, but he made no move to resume their lovemaking. She moved to look into his face as the fading sun cast its golden light on his dark skin. He looked amazed and blissful, as if he had witnessed a great wonder.

He peeked down at her. "Did you like this, Eliana, what I have done to you just now?"

"Do you doubt?"

He laughed. "No . . . but I would hear you say it."

She squirmed around in his arms so that she looked down at him, and her hair fell forward like a curtain around them. She rested above him, and felt his body tighten with the feel of her skin against his. Very gently, she kissed him. "I liked it very, very much." She paused. "But I would return this sweetness to you, as well."

"You have given me more sweetness than you know, my dear. To see you this way, to feel you give yourself over to me . . . that is bliss beyond anything."

"Have I not done so before, many times?"

"Oh, yes," he answered. "But because of your condition, this time was as the first."

She nodded. "That is an exciting thought."

"So nothing came back to you, just now?" he asked.

Eliana hesitated, confused by his question. "No memory, if that's what you mean. Did you think it would?"

"Oh, one never knows about these things. I wondered if your ecstasy might trigger the return of memory, but apparently not." Oddly, Damir sounded both disappointed and relieved by this, though Eliana couldn't imagine why.

"When my thoughts gave way . . ." she paused and felt embarrassed, but Damir brightened.

"Yes? What then?"

"I had an odd feeling as if I resisted and fought against surrender, but could not."

His low moan interrupted her, but he nodded quickly and waved his hand. "Go on, please."

"I felt as if you had conquered me, as if I could do nothing to hold myself back."

His eyes closed and his whole body went tight. "That is good, exactly as I imagined it." He paused and caught himself. "A good way to feel . . ."

"I liked it." Eliana yawned and tucked herself in closer beside him. "I would like to make you feel the same way."

He sifted her hair through his fingers and sighed. "You do, my love, every day of your life. Every day."

". . . as if I resisted and fought against surrender, but could not." Eliana's confession echoed in Damir's mind as she lay sleeping beside him. They had watched the sunset in bed, her sated and happy, himself taut with lust but happy, too. Then they had risen, taken the evening meal together, and walked through the woods hand in hand. She had told him she trusted him even more since their encounter, and that she shared the same vision he had experienced at the mountain forge—that their energy was one.

All the while, even as she had sweetly declared her trust, even as she bent to pick new herbs and told him what she sensed about them, his mind had been fixed on those whispered words. *"As if I resisted . . . but could not."* Torture. His body burned with unabated desire, so strong that the shield of her virginity threatened to pose no obstacle when they again lay down together this night.

Eliana had preserved her innocence, and he couldn't take that from her, not completely. Part of him knew that to do so would simply be wrong. It was a matter of honor. But the other part, darker and wily, feared that in taking that innocence, his deceit would be revealed, and he would lose her. Besides, making love to Eliana could take other forms besides intercourse. The sweetness of her lingered in his memory, the sounds of her soft sighs, the intensity of her desire, the utter surrender of her ecstasy . . .

Damir rolled over onto his side and stared at her as she slept. The waning moon shone on her beautiful face and she looked peaceful beside him. Her lips were parted slightly, and he recalled the taste of her kiss. The moment of rapture hadn't restored her memory as he'd feared—or hoped. But then, he hadn't been inside her, either. If he had, if the desire throbbing inside him had blended with her own pulse, she might have regained that memory, woken, and indeed resisted . . . until he moved again, until that wild desire that he had long imagined she possessed took its hold over her. Even his innocent Eliana sensed that part of her true nature. "*And could not . . .*"

Damir turned onto his back and stared at the dark ceiling. His arousal burned, every pulse an erotic torment. He wanted her with a power exceeding anything he'd known, even from the fiery desire of his youth when he'd spent a night in wild fantasy after their first kiss.

His solution then had been somewhat primitive, but it had served its purpose. He closed his eyes, now, and considered sleep. But nothing drove away the fantasy of Eliana beneath him, awakening from her self-imposed slumber of memory, wild with fury, and even wilder with lust. She would struggle, her back would arch, her lithe body twist. Her white teeth would cut into her lip as she fought her release, and then, with those sweet, desperate moans and quick gasps, she would give herself over.

He sat up in bed and raked his hands through his hair. If he could explain her virginity, or distract her from its existence . . . But could he risk losing his new Eliana, the woman who loved him and trusted him? He felt as if he were in love with a cherished wife, yet tormented by an erotic mistress—The Fiend.

He had to relieve this tension, or give way to his own desire and take her, no matter the outcome. He slipped from the bed and left their bedroom, and for a moment, stood in the cool darkness of his front room. He couldn't see her face now, but the fantasy refused to relent. He glanced back at the bedroom, then went down the hallway to his study. He didn't shut the heavy door fully lest the sound of the latch wake her, but he closed it until darkness enveloped him.

Damir sank into his chair and tipped his head back, then drew a long breath. *She is driving me crazy.* The Fiend had become both a fantasy and a threat—she could destroy everything he had found with his new lover, and yet still had the power to set his blood to fire.

It was this energy, this fire between them, that he couldn't resist. He wanted her, both the sweet lover and the furious temptress, and for the moment, he could have neither. For a time, he tried to control his thoughts, to fight the fantasy of The Fiend's surrender, but her little face burned in his mind, desire written in every expression, the moment of rapture mere seconds away. If she responded so well to the touch of his lips and his tongue, her reaction to his actual lovemaking would exceed his wildest dreams.

He couldn't resist—there had to be satiation. His shirt felt damp and taut as he tore it open and leaned back in the deep chair. In darkness, he slid his hand down over his stomach and then gripped his full length. His flesh burned, desire racked through him. Darkness was calling him. Was it so powerful because his *ki* was so strong? Or was his lust itself a product of that darkness?

For the moment, Damir didn't care. He knew what would happen, to every breath and every sensation in his body. The fantasy took shape with no barrier of reality, and if it was dark, so be it. *She quivered beneath him as he slid his length along her warm, damp cleft. They kissed, and she sucked his tongue. He entered her slowly. She was warm and tight inside, and her hips arched to receive him. She hovered on the brink of rapture . . . Her eyes shot open and she stiffened as the flood of her memory returned.*

She screamed, furious, and her green eyes blazed. "You!"

He caught her wrists in his hands and kept her from moving. "You brought this on yourself, Eliana. Do you want me to stop? Say it, and I will." She squirmed in fury, but the action increased her pleasure, and she bit her lip hard as she resisted its hold. A low, ragged moan grew in her throat, and she dug her fingers into his back. Her hips rolled against hers even as she screamed her protest at her own body's weakness, but her body quivered as the first waves of rapture claimed her. . . .

A soft touch slid over his shoulders, soft but firm as Eliana bent to kiss his neck. Damir froze, his heart slamming, but she slid her hands down over his chest, and before he could react further, those hands replaced his own.

"You will not leave me to ache in darkness, my love," she whispered, "nor save this sweetness for yourself alone."

He couldn't breathe and he couldn't move, half in embarrassment that the sweet Eliana had caught him this way, and half in shock. She wrapped her fingers around his arousal and took him in a snug grip. Apparently she had seen enough despite the darkness to know what he liked, but her ministrations exceeded his own, for she possessed an eagerness and an adoration of his body that he couldn't muster half so well. She kissed his neck and licked and tasted, then found the corner of his mouth.

She kissed him, and made love to him with her delicate hand, and he answered her kiss with the most total surrender and weakness he'd ever known. When he thought he could take no more, she stopped, moved around him, and knelt on the floor in front of him. Damir stared at her in disbelief, but she smiled like a goddess.

"What are you doing to me?" he whispered. His voice was raw, ragged with need.

"Only what you have done to me, with no answer for yourself at all." As she spoke, her lips drew close to his arousal, and then she pressed her mouth against the blunt tip. A hoarse cry began in his throat, but stopped short when her mouth closed around him and her tongue swirled out to circle his length. She moved up and down upon him, her fingers still wrapped tight around his base, and she licked, and sucked, and brought him to a place where all light seemed to burst around him, and from within him.

The control he had never had was lost beyond recall. He gave himself over to her, as he had tried to do with his fantasy, as he dreamed she would do in surrender to him. He watched her beautiful face as she made love to him this way, and the sight defeated any vestige of restraint. His release came with overpowering force, and a shuddering moan ripped from his throat. When his rapture abated, she moved back, touched the side of her mouth, and smiled as her tongue swept idly over her lips. An aftershock of pleasure shot through him at the sight. Her eyelids were low and heavy, and her breath came in swift gasps. She liked what she had done.

Damir stared down at her, but she rose up and settled into his lap. She touched his face, then kissed his cheek. "You felt what I felt. I am pleased. You have held yourself back from this. It pleases me that I could make you surrender."

He wrapped his arms around her and leaned his head against her. She wanted his surrender, too. The Fiend was not lost, she was simply buried deep in the sweetest woman he had ever known. His pulse raced in the aftermath of his rapture, and his skin tingled.

"You are my gift, Eliana," he said quietly. "If only . . ." He stopped. *If only it would last.* She eyed him quizzically. "If only you were fully well, I mean."

She looked like she didn't quite believe him, but she didn't question his comment further. "I am well."

He smiled. "So it seems." He rose up, lifting her with

him, and he carried her back to his bedroom. "But tonight, I think we will both sleep in peace."

A loud, repeated rap on the door woke Damir from a blissful and sound sleep. He opened one eye, and Eliana stirred beside him. "What is the hour?" she asked, her voice sleepy and low.

"Too early," he replied. He rose from the bed and pulled on a shirt and his leggings. "Stay here, my love. I'll find out who it is, kill him, and return to you."

He marched to the door with that intent, yanked it open, and saw Elphin standing bright-eyed outside. "Good morning to you, sir!"

"Morning," began Damir in his darkest voice, "begins with the sunrise, boy, and not before."

Elphin glanced cheerfully at the eastern sky. "Getting light out, though, sir. Almost morning, I'd say."

"With the sunrise, Elphin. *Not before.*"

Elphin appeared undeterred by Damir's budding wrath. "Hope I didn't wake your *wife,* sir, but it's you they want to see."

"My wife is sleeping, or trying to . . ." He paused, trying to force his groggy mind to take in the boy's purpose. "Who are 'they' and what do they want with me at this hour?"

"Oh, yes, that . . ."

"*That.*"

"Well, it was Madawc who sent me to fetch you."

"I will kill *him* then." Probably done to interrupt any chance he might have of defiling Eliana.

Elphin ignored Damir's threat. "But it was the king's order, and he's the one as wants to see you, sir, though Madawc intends to meet you at the palace."

Damir sighed heavily. "Why? And why now?"

"They didn't tell me the particulars, but apparently it has something to do with what the young princess saw up on the mountainside. We all saw it, and there are other reports from those who saw it from a better viewpoint. They're acting awfully secretive up there at the palace. The elder Mage has told the king about you and The Fiend, of course."

Damir frowned. Owain Daere adored Eliana. If this morning's venture had more to do with her sanctity than a perceived threat, Madawc would indeed suffer, elder Mage or not. "Very well. I will go."

He went back inside. To his surprise, Eliana was again sleeping. Apparently, their passion had worn her out, too. Damir bent and kissed her forehead, then gathered his gear and his new sword, and went back outside. Elphin had already collected Llwyd and was saddling him, busy fingering the jewels on the tack brought from the land of Kora by Damir's father.

"There's not another saddle like this in the Woodland, sir! Beautiful."

Damir took Llwyd's reins, and the horse sighed heavily. "It's early yet, my friend, for both of us, but we'll make the ride quick."

Elphin went to his own horse, but Damir called to him. "If you don't mind, Elphin, please stay here with Eliana. There's no need for you to return to the palace with me now, and my ride will be quicker alone. My domain is shielded, but she might need help, and I won't be back until afternoon. She is sleeping now, so please tell her, carefully, where I have gone and when I will return."

Elphin's eyes widened into green pools of shock. "You want me to stay alone with The Fiend?" The boy gave every indication of a quick escape, but Damir patted his shoulder.

"I think you'll find The Fiend is no longer a threat, Elphin. You might find her company enjoyable. And apparently even before this, she had been tutoring young Cahira."

Elphin huffed. "Well, young Cahira is not too far off from The Fiend herself! Though she doesn't scare me half so much. Yet. But if you say the lady has changed, I suppose I can do as you ask."

Damir smiled, then mounted his horse. "It will impress the other lads, later, when you're able to tell the tale."

"That it will," agreed Elphin. "Might impress the king's older daughter, the friendly one, too!"

Damir laughed. Owain Daere had several daughters, all black haired and beautiful, and one was indeed Elphin's age. None had quite the grace and charm of Cahira, but she was a rare child, like Eliana had been, and it would take a rare young man to win her attention.

"I wish you well. See that Eliana is cared for while I'm away," said Damir. "She enjoys walking in the woods, if you care to go with her. She might find an herb or two that could help you in the quest for a princess's hand, anyway."

"A fine idea, sir! We'd best make use of The Fiend's talents while she's peaceful-like and calm. She'll be hellfire soon, and there won't be peace for days and days after she snaps out of this!"

Damir tried to smile, but as he rode away toward the Palace of Amrodel, his heart sunk in his chest. *I am in love with her.* Last night, his Eliana had blended with the Fiend. She had stolen into his fantasy and given it new life, and he no longer wished to simply wake his old nemesis into sexual ecstasy. He wanted to stay beside her, to love her at night, to hold her hand, to practice their craft together. *To be one.*

His dark fantasy had given way to a greater desire—Eliana's love. The Fiend's return could bring him no joy now, and the return of the battle would break his heart. The mistress of his dreams was now the greatest threat to the thing he treasured most—his "wife."

Chapter Seven

Eliana lay on her back, arms folded behind her head, her hair splayed across a large down-filled pillow. She was happy. She gazed at the ceiling and drew a deep, satisfied breath. Damir had made love to her. She had made love to him, too. Their bodies hadn't joined in the way she expected, but they had still joined.

She had dreamt again of the dark man summoning her, and again, of the woman who desperately tried to tell her something that Eliana couldn't hear. Again, she had seen a vision of the angelic, pale-haired boy, but Damir had held up his white sword and the dream turned to light. Morning sunlight slanted through their bedroom, and Eliana felt safe. Damir drove away darkness and fear, and he loved her. She thought of the taste of him, and remembered his ragged moans as she had made love to him, there in his dark study kneeling before him. A tingle raced through her body.

Eliana sighed and fiddled with her hair. A small, random tune emerged from her lips and she got up from bed humming. She found the green dress that Damir had stripped from her body, and wrapped it around herself. *I must have something else to wear.*

Damir had placed her other garments along a wide bureau on the rear of the bedroom. A touch of autumn's chill had entered the room overnight, so she chose the more elaborate red velvet gown. She examined herself in a standing looking glass, and she felt beautiful. She chose a long dark gray mantle from the pile of clothing, and carried it with her in case the chill increased.

Eliana checked her image in the mirror again, adjusted her hair to fall artfully around her face, then left the bedroom in search of Damir. Instead she found the young man she'd met the day before. He was sitting at the large table, but jumped when he saw her and leaped up from his seat. He bowed awkwardly, and appeared distinctly nervous.

Eliana bit her lip. "I'm sorry to have startled you— Elphin, wasn't it? Where is Damir?"

He gulped. She couldn't imagine why. "My lady," he began, and oddly bowed again. "Damir ap Kora was called to the king's palace early this morning. I brought the message. He asked that I stay behind to look after you, and told me to tell you he would return by midafternoon."

Eliana sighed. "Then he is gone." She offered the boy an embarrassed smile. "I should not be so silly, I know. It is strange to be without my husband, when I know nothing else of my life." She eyed the boy, who looked tense. "Thank you for staying with me." Eliana paused. "Would you like tea?"

His eyes widened. "A . . . potion?"

"Tea."

Now his eyes narrowed. "Can I watch you make it?"

Eliana shrugged. "As you wish." She led him to the kitchen and brought water to a boil, then made them both tea from the leaves she had chosen the previous day. Apparently, her method of preparation satisfied Elphin, because he returned with her to the main room, and sat down facing her at the table.

He tasted the brew as if it might be poison, but his expression changed and he nodded. "Very good, it is, Lady. Thank you."

"Damir says I am a good cook, though I do not recall it," she said.

Elphin's gaze shifted and he appeared to repress a laugh. "Did he, now? Well, well. But I wouldn't be knowing about that."

She rested her elbows on the table as she sipped her tea. "But you did know me, didn't you?"

"Yes . . ." He answered very slowly and his face seemed to redden a shade. "Not as well as some."

"I do not mean to press you, but I wish to learn of myself."

"Hasn't Damir told you about yourself, Lady?"

"He has, but a husband's memory can be biased. He says I was sweet, and that seems to me, quite frankly, bland to the point of dullness."

The boy's brow angled. "I wouldn't ever call you 'dull,' Lady. And neither would he, I'm sure."

"He didn't say that, of course, but his description of me seemed rather tedious. Rather passive, and predictable."

A slight smile softened Elphin's face. "You were absolutely none of those things, I swear."

Obviously, he didn't want to talk about her. But another matter still begged her curiosity. "Then tell me about The Fiend."

His face went white, then pink, and his voice came like a squeak. "The who?"

"The woman known as 'The Fiend.' Damir says she is another Mage who went to school with us, and who causes mischief. I heard you mention her yesterday, so you must know her. What is she like?"

His mouth opened, then closed as if he had no idea what to say. "Well, Lady, she's . . . she's certainly capable of mischief."

"That, I've heard already." Perhaps questions would help. "I take it she is about my age."

"Thereabouts . . ."

"And she is not well liked?"

Elphin chewed his lip and looked decidedly uncomfortable. "I'd say she's more feared than disliked ma'am." He shifted his weight in the seat as if considering some dire future possibility that might be linked to his words—or as if The Fiend herself might overhear him. "Now, *I* always respected the lady. Clever, she is, and beautiful."

Eliana's eyes narrowed. "She is beautiful?"

"No more than yourself," he added quickly. "But she's right pretty."

Eliana didn't like this, though it shouldn't be of concern now, not after the night she'd shared with Damir. "Has she a husband?"

"No . . ."

"A lover?"

Elphin twisted his hands together and pretended to examine them. "Now, that's not something I'd be knowing, ma'am."

"That *is* personal. I'm sorry. But Damir hinted that she might have some contact with the Norsk."

"Not anymore, Miss. I'm fairly certain of that."

"What sort of mischief did she cause?"

"I'm not quite knowing where to begin there, Lady. There was the time she gave a potion to Old Rhys the Bard and had him thinking he was a spider. You should have seen the webs he wove, all over Amrodel!"

Eliana smiled at the image, though she wasn't sure why it pleased her. "That is imaginative. I would have liked to see it." She paused. "Did I?"

Elphin cleared his throat. "If memory serves, you did, yes."

"What inspired her to do that to a bard?"

"He made up a song about her that she didn't much like."

"About what?" asked Eliana.

"Oh, well . . . I don't recall exactly. Implied she had fonder feelings for a certain man than she wanted folks to think."

Eliana's lips twisted to one side. And she had a fair idea who that man was, too. "What else did she do?"

Elphin took a sip of tea. "Oh, too many things to mention. Chased me with a whole herd of dragonflies . . ."

"Dragonflies?"

"She's got some peculiar connection to them—they do her bidding, it's said, and I believe it."

Eliana sat back in her seat. Could The Fiend have been responsible for the herd that followed her to the mountain? Were they her spies, and did she, after all, have some connection to the darkness that arose after Damir's sword reached completion? Cahira had said that it was Eliana who attracted dragonflies—but maybe, even then, they were doing the work of The Fiend.

"Has she done any mischief to Damir or myself?"

"To you, Lady, not that I know of. But to Damir ap Kora, the list of her crimes is endless."

"Indeed. Such as what?"

"It's said she set him on fire, supposedly by mistake, but it left him without much hair for a long while afterwards. I was too young to remember that, though."

"She set him on fire? That does sound dark, and quite dangerous."

"Damir says she was trying to turn him some funny color, but I've always wondered if she weren't just trying to kill him like it seemed."

Eliana tapped her lip as she considered this. "He made excuses for her, then?"

"He may have been right. Her potions didn't always work as she intended." Elphin fiddled with his sleeve. "*And that's a fact.*"

"She fixes her attention upon him overmuch, I think."

Elphin looked up at her in surprise. "Why do you say that, Lady?"

"I sense it. As a woman."

"Ah . . ." His gaze drifted, then eased back to her. "If you say so, Lady." He paused. "Some say she has fondness for him."

"I have guessed that." Eliana felt sullen. "It seems odd her wrath was not turned upon me." The boy remained silent, and Eliana leaned forward. "Or perhaps it was."

He sucked his teeth and fidgeted. "What do you mean?"

"My affliction." Eliana sat back and watched his expression change from discomfort to astonishment. "Damir insists that my memory loss comes from a fall. But is it not possible that this woman, apparently well-versed with potions, somehow, in secret, administered one of her brews upon me?"

Elphin puffed a quick breath. "Well, I . . . I suppose it's possible, ma'am. But wouldn't Damir tell you that himself?"

"If he knew. Or maybe he is trying to protect me. That could explain why he left you here to guard me."

"I'm here just to help you, Lady. The shield of Damir ap Kora is enough to protect you here."

"But maybe she found a way around it. Maybe I trusted her for some reason. Damir says that such relationships, secretly perverted from what they seem on the surface, are impossible to guard against."

"Well, ma'am . . . that's an interesting theory, but I can't think why The Fiend would want to hurt you."

Eliana issued an impatient sigh. "Because she is in love with Damir herself, and wants me out of the way! What else?"

Elphin placed his fingertips against his temples. "Maybe you should ask Damir about that."

"He is reluctant to discuss her."

"I'll bet." The boy spoke under his voice, but she heard his words.

"Is it me he is trying to protect, or the Fiend?"

Elphin looked up at her, confused. "Lady?"

Eliana rose and set her tea aside. "Never mind. My imagination plays tricks on me. But there is something strange about this woman. I keep thinking I knew it before this happened, but it is lost to me."

"I'm sure when you get your memory back . . . Well, you won't be wondering about The Fiend, anyway."

"Why not?"

He rubbed his head as if it pained him. "You'll know about her then, and won't have to wonder?" he asked, as if hoping she would accept his response without further questions.

Eliana sighed. "I'm sure that's true—if I get my memory back. I'm not sure, at this point, if that's what I want after all."

"I trust my niece is safe and untarnished in your care, Damir ap Kora." Owain Daere sat upon a regal seat with Cahira perched on the armrest beside him.

"She looked untarnished to me, Papa," said Cahira. "She looked very pretty. Damir was even holding her hand, so I'm sure he wouldn't hurt Eliana."

Her bright gaze flicked to Damir, and he saw glee in her eyes. Elphin was right—the child bore too close a resemblance to Eliana already. Stars help the Woodland when she grew to adulthood.

"I was assisting Lady Eliana down the mountainside."

"You were in the moss garden behind your cottage," she countered, and Damir frowned.

Owain Daere looked between them. "I realize Eliana has brought this fate upon herself, Damir, as Madawc has explained to me. And I understand the code of Mages that allows for just retribution. But see that it doesn't go too far."

Damir gazed around the room, annoyed and embarrassed. "The privacy granted Woodland citizenry leaves much to be desired. I am not sure the intense and personal scrutiny benefits us. *Any* of us." He added this part with emphasis, with the intent of reminding the king of his own dalliances. After his first wife, Cahira's mother, died, Owain had taken a second wife, but their union was formed in haste, and its passion had soon died. Since then, Owain had taken solace with an assortment of idle lovers, the mark of a bored man seeking to recapture lost youth and assuage an empty heart.

Apparently, Owain understood, because he cleared his throat and changed the subject. "As Madawc requested, and I agreed, no one knows of Eliana's affliction, nor that she has . . . taken up residence in your cottage."

"Well, *I* know, but I have told no one," added Cahira, and Owain patted her head.

"You are a good child," said the king. "But you must run along now. If you see Madawc, send him in."

Cahira elevated her bow. "I will resume my practice. When I left you, Damir, I spent time directing my *ki* at blowing leaves." She paused for effect. "I put an arrow through every one."

Damir smiled. "Your skill with the bow will soon be unmatched."

Cahira frowned in response. "My skill is already unmatched, Damir. But I will improve, and soon inspire awe, just as you do with your swords." She clutched her bow tight and pretended to take aim. "The Norsk will shriek with fear when I am near."

Owain shuddered and directed her from the Council Chamber. Madawc entered just as she left. They nodded at each other, but didn't speak, each intent on their respective tasks.

The old Mage took a seat at the Council table. His grim expression belied the lightness of the king's mood. "We may need even the bow of a child before this darkness lifts, my liege." His tone indicated a mood Damir had seldom seen in the old Mage, and he seated himself beside Madawc.

"You speak of the darkness that encroaches upon this land," said Damir. "I have felt it, too, and no more than today."

Owain looked between them, confused, but ready to hear their wisdom. "All the Mages speak of this, but I confess that I feel no darkness, nor any ill tide in the Wood."

"You feel it, my liege, whether you recognize it for what it is or not. It comes by way of the north," said Madawc. "It can best be explained as a current of negative energy, always in existence on a normal level, but in this case, increasing in force and intensity. It comes from the Norsk, though that may seem impossible. But there have been whispers that the tide may run deeper than we know."

"What do you mean?" asked Damir, but an odd sensation of doom penetrated his heart. He had felt the darkness, even inside himself.

Madawc met his gaze steadily, his blue eyes pale as the morning light shafted through the chamber windows. "The Norsk do not have the power to direct such energy, as we all know this is. Yet it comes from their land. Of that, I am now certain."

"What have you seen?" asked Damir.

"Today, when the Mage Child reported a dark cloud by your forge, Damir . . . I saw the same cloud, but earlier as it hovered—hovered as if waiting. It seeks you, and it seeks Eliana, though I do not know the reason. But you are the strongest among us, for I am old, and my powers wane. If you were removed, and Eliana, too, this land would indeed be vulnerable."

"But what of the other Mages?"

"You, Eliana, and myself are the only true Elites. The others are less in power, less in the strength of their *ki*. And only you and Eliana have any gift that could be useful in either defense or combat."

"Do you believe this explains why her cottage was ransacked?"

"Most likely, though I do not know how any force could get through your shield."

"Unless she trusted this invader," said Damir. *Or loved him*.

"It is possible," agreed Madawc. He turned to the king. "With your permission, my liege, I have summoned several Mages to this Council meeting. I asked that you, Damir, and I meet in private first, for I do not think it wise to allow even our brethren to know of Eliana's current condition, or her whereabouts. But many saw the dark cloud today, and some may have news to aid us."

"Before they enter . . ." Owain paused and bowed his head, then looked between Damir and Madawc. "I love my niece as a daughter, but I know how volatile she can be, and how proud." He paused as if the words pained him, and he was reluctant to speak at all. "Is there any chance Eliana herself is involved in this? Rumors of her alliance with an unknown Norskman have reached my ears, and I cannot forget how she defended them at the last Council meeting. There is no shame in taking a lover, but if she has involved herself with a Norskman . . ."

Damir shook his head. "I do not know the extent of Eliana's involvement with the Norsk, but I can swear she has taken no lover among them."

Madawc's eyes narrowed to slits. "How do you know that, boy?"

Damir met his gaze evenly. "I know."

Madawc grimaced and shook his head, but Owain seemed content to take Damir's word. "For myself, such a dalliance might be trivial," said the king. "But for Eliana, I think the heart is stronger than the satiation of desire. Can you also say that she has not given that much, at least, to our enemy?"

Damir didn't answer, but Madawc huffed. "Any fool can see her heart remains right here in Amrodel, and not with the Norsk. Mundanes, as I've said many a time, are so dramatic! Eliana has reason to believe there is good in the Norsk. Stars know what gave her that idea, and she won't tell—can't tell now, given what she's done to herself in an effort to get this young man under her control. But if you focus your attention on the most visible person, and that's always been Eliana, you will miss the real danger among us."

Owain's brow furrowed. "But if the darkness comes from the Norsk, why should we look in our own midst?"

"Because the Norsk are naught but primitive warriors, of course! If they've been aroused to this dark tide, it's not without the prompting of a Mage."

Damir considered this. "Could it be someone with connections in the seaport of Amon-dhen? Few Mages go there that I know of, but if they chose to venture forth in secrecy, none of us would know." He paused. "Unless, of course, they went there with a lover, and then all of Amrodel would be discussing it."

Owain chuckled, but Madawc's chin firmed. "Always starts with sex, boy. That's why we keep such a close eye on you! But at least you've got a heart, and despite yourself, you put that heart first. It's when a person abandons the heart, that's when you need to beware."

Owain scratched his forehead in exasperation. "What has the dark tide to do with sex?"

"Well, not much," said Madawc. "I was just making a point."

Damir sighed. "I wonder if the Norsk give this much heed to romantic pairings? Perhaps their 'straightforward' approach to the issue is what earned Eliana's respect."

Madawc chuckled. "It's possible. Folks have certainly gossiped enough about the two of you!"

"I can't imagine why," said Damir. "There has never been anything beyond rivalry between myself and Eliana." He paused. "Until now, of course, and no one knows about that."

Madawc held up his hand and squeezed his eyes shut. "Say no more about that! But it's the lack of 'anything,' as you say, that has people intrigued. How long it will last, when and how you'll give in . . . that sort of thing."

Damir groaned. "There is absolutely no privacy in Amrodel."

"The Mundanes who frequent The Hungry Cat tavern have been waging bets on it for years," added Madawc with pleasure. "I, myself, cast a wager on the outcome."

Damir glared. "What did you wager?"

"I'm not revealing that until the outcome is certain. Back to more important matters, lad."

Damir chewed the inside of his lip. "I hope you wagered on my victory, for it was Eliana . . ."

"She has to be in her right mind, boy. This trickery of yours is no surrender on her part. In fact, right now, I'm giving her the edge."

Owain shook his head. "Damir has a point. The matters of the flesh are of too much interest to the Woodland folk."

Madawc's eyes twinkled. "There's more than one wager going on at The Hungry Cat, Sire. Got another going on which maiden has grabbed your attention lately, and yet another still on how long it will last."

Owain clasped his hands over his eyes. "The king should be immune to this idle speculation."

"As should the Mage Protector," added Damir. "Gossip will be the downfall of us all."

"Not if I win big, it won't," said Madawc, and both Owain and Damir glared at him. "But back to matters at hand . . ."

The Chamber door opened and a woman entered. Damir recognized one of Owain's assistants, though he could never recall her name. She resembled a smaller, lesser Eliana, though her eyes were dark. She had dark hair forcibly waved, and a taste for long, green gowns with wide sleeves, almost as if the mimicry had been intentional. It wasn't hard to imagine why a woman would want to emulate such profound beauty, but Eliana's charm went far beyond her appearance, and this woman shared nothing of Eliana's wild personality.

Perhaps because of her effort to resemble Eliana, some had considered she bore the Mage *ki* as well. Presumably, she had thought so, too, because she had spent time with Madawc before her limited energy made itself known. She had moved on to the Mundane tasks, but she had gained favor with both Madawc and the king, and still held a position of prominence at the court.

As she entered, Owain and Madawc rose from their seats to greet her, Owain too quickly, and his chair tipped back. Damir's brow angled as he, too, rose dutifully. Owain rushed forward to greet her, and Damir contemplated a quick stop at The Hungry Cat to place a wager of his own.

Owain smiled, and she offered a diffident response. "My liege, the other Mages are assembled. Shall I direct them into the Council Chamber?" Her gaze shifted, beneath lowered lids, to Damir, and she smiled at him warmly. She was an attractive enough woman, and she had expressed shy interest in Damir on previous occasions, but despite her contrived resemblance to Eliana, Damir hadn't responded. Eliana had despised the friendlier Mundane—Damir had assumed it was because of the girl's pleasant demeanor. In contrast to Eliana, she was well liked by everyone. Damir had spoken up for the girl when Eliana had accused her of various misdeeds, but secretly, he had found her tiresome, too.

Owain went to her and she touched his arm in a friendly but intimate gesture, and Damir recalculated the size of his upcoming wager at The Hungry Cat. "You may do that, Shaen. Thank you."

Shaen . . . A name that never seemed to stick in Damir's memory. But for the sake of his wager, it was best he try to remember her this time.

Shaen went to the door, then turned back, her face knit with concern. "I know it's not my place, my liege . . ."

Owain appeared moved by her hesitancy and shyness, though Damir didn't think it seemed particularly genuine. "What is it, Shaen? You may speak freely here."

She cast a quick glance at Damir. "I am so worried about Lady Eliana."

"Why?" Damir posed the question before he thought better of it. The two women had hardly been friends, though he'd never heard Shaen speak ill of Eliana—unlike most women, who feared her and resented her independent nature.

Shaen pressed her lips together as if hesitant to speak. "I know she has been missing for several days. I know she has never been kind to you, Damir, and you have every right to dislike her, but I hate to think of her lost, or worse. You must try to be forgiving. I've been worried about her for some time—she has become reclusive over the past few years. Since we're the same age, I tried to befriend her, but she would have none of it." Shaen paused to sigh. "But I am still fond of her."

Owain stroked her arm affectionately, and Damir's upcoming wager increased. "Two beautiful women such as yourself and Eliana are bound to come into conflict. Think nothing of it, Shaen. But rest assured, Eliana is in safe hands."

Her gaze shot to Owain, but then she breathed a deep sigh of relief. "You know where she is, then?"

"We do, and you have nothing to worry about. Unfortunately, this matter must remain secret for now."

"I hope she isn't in danger?" said Shaen, her eyes wide.

"She is not," said Madawc. "At least, not in any serious fashion."

Shaen's expression lightened and grew flirtatious as she turned to Damir. "Well, I hope Damir doesn't know where she is! After the horrible things she's done to him, I can't imagine the temptation to be rid of her!"

"I have no idea of Eliana's whereabouts," said Damir. "But I trust the king and Madawc have her safely stashed away." His voice sounded a little testier than he'd intended. Eliana hadn't done anything that horrible, after all. Shaen made it seem as if Eliana had truly hated him. He refused to believe that. She hadn't meant to set him on fire—she had been trying to turn his skin bright green. And she hadn't known a certain mushroom would explode, nor that his pony had been particularly skittish . . . or that Woodland cats had little sympathy for boys trapped in their dens.

Maybe she has been trying to kill me. Damir's face knit in a dark frown. "Eliana's intentions have never been entirely clear."

Shaen laughed. "If you say so! It's a shame such a beautiful woman is so ambitious and so proud." She moved to touch Damir's arm and lowered her voice in a commiserating fashion. "She has denied herself her own femininity, and something far more special. The love of a man."

Owain eased Shaen from Damir's side and assisted her to the door. Madawc cast a knowing look his way and

Damir leaned closer to the old Mage. "I'm placing a wager at The Hungry Cat today."

"Not before I do, boy!"

Damir grinned. "This is one we'll win together."

Shaen stood back in the doorway and gestured for the other Mages to enter. Several were nearly as old as Madawc, though none as spry. Some few were younger than Damir and Eliana, green in their craft, but with wisdom inherent to their kind. Few remained of the generation of Damir's parents. One, Rodern ap Jarna, was a contemporary of Owain Daere, and the King's closest friend. Rodern occupied an old stone tower south of the tavern, and was responsible for the trade routes leading to the port city of Amon-dhen. Though Damir had little in common with the dour Rodern, he respected him because Rodern hadn't objected when Damir was chosen as the Mage Protector over his own greater experience. Rodern even praised the selection at Council—while Eliana herself had exploded in fury and administered fiendish potions upon all who approved the measure.

The Mages entered and took their seats around the Council Table, and Rodern sat nearest the King. Only Madawc remained standing. He wasted no time on preliminaries or introductions.

"As you are all aware, my brethren, a tide of darkness encroaches upon the Woodland, though it is not yet perceptible to the Mundanes. Earlier today, many of us saw a visible manifestation upon the mountainside."

A young woman, Serafina Modair, spoke up. "I, too, saw the sight of which you speak, and it filled me with a vision of doom while it lasted, though when it abated, I knew such a time has not yet come. What might this portend, Elder? Nothing like this has been seen since the dark time when the Arch Mage made war upon Amrodel."

Madawc nodded. "You are young, Serafina, so you

speak of the Arch Mage easily. For those of us whose elders remember that time, it is not so easily said."

"Forgive me," said Serafina. "But that is what came to my mind."

Madawc smiled. "There is no need for apology, my dear. For you speak what we all have felt—that this darkness is, in some way, connected to that time, to that power that was his."

Damir said nothing. It hadn't been the Arch Mage he and Eliana had thought of—it had been the Mage queen that the Arch Mage had desired, and lost.

Rodern turned to face Damir. "I, myself, did not see this cloud of which many have spoken already. But I am told it came from the direction above Damir's cottage. Surely he must have some explanation for this."

Damir didn't answer at once. Even here, he couldn't risk any mention of Eliana's presence at the forge. "It is true the cloud emanated from—or least, sought out—the area of my armory. And I believe I know something of the cause." He stood up and slowly drew his white sword from its sheath. A collective gasp rose from the Mages present as it glimmered beneath the crystal lights of the Council Chamber. "Yesterday I wrought this sword, and the cloud rose in response to its creation."

Rodern's eyes glinted at the sight. "It must have been great magic to create such a weapon. Even here, I feel its power."

"Its power isn't known fully, even to me," said Damir as he returned the sword to his side. "But I feel its fate."

Madawc looked proud and his bright eyes were shining as Damir resumed his seat. "None have ever matched your skill with the blade, Damir ap Kora. The Great Spirits must have aided you in its creation, but the method is yours alone." He paused and a smile flickered on his lips as if he knew Eliana, too, had some hand in its making.

Damir returned his smile, and the love he felt for her filled his heart.

"Even I would be hesitant to touch that weapon," said Rodern. "Were a lesser man to touch it, their fate would be dark indeed."

"Even a brief touch would sear the hand," said Damir. "For a Mundane to hold it, that would indeed mean death. With this sword, I can hold at bay the darkness, even as I shield Amrodel from invasion."

"Isn't it a strain to maintain your shield and wield such a weapon at the same time?" asked Rodern.

Damir couldn't restrain a surge of pride. "No enemy yet, in this land or any other, has had enough power to require the full focus of my *ki.*"

Madawc studied his face, then nodded slowly. "All men are tested, Damir ap Kora, and we all reach our limits sooner or later. There is something in you greater than your *ki,* and one day, you may need it."

"What is that?" asked Rodern in surprise.

Madawc placed his aged hand over his heart and he smiled, but he didn't answer. Damir said no more. As had happened often during his youth, Madawc had managed to deflate—somewhat—Damir's vanity and pride. He heard an echo of his own voice from the past: *"Everyone has a heart, Elder, even the Mundanes. It is my magnificent* ki *that makes me great!"* Before Madawc had been able to correct him, Eliana had launched her small body across their study table and attacked him. *"He is so vain! Elder, let me kill him this time!"*

"What of the Norsk?" asked Serafina. Her question snapped Damir's attention back to the present. "Their raiding parties come ever closer to the Wood, yet no one has spoken of any increase in their relative *ki* that I know of. How do they connect to this darkness? Is there any way they could have resurrected the energy of the Arch Mage, or have some hand in bringing it to the surface now?"

"That is the question, it seems to me, that plagues us most," added Rodern. "Can you stand against the entire force of ravaging Norsk warriors, Damir?"

"Stand against them?" said Damir. "I'm not sure. But I can prevent their entrance into the Wood. The question, for me, is why they would want this in the first place."

"Power is ever an alluring goal, lad," said Madawc. "But I sense more behind their threat than that. A lure of darkness." The old Mage paused, and his voice lowered. Even the light in the Chamber seemed to dim. "Have we not all felt its pull, in our hearts, in our most secret desires?"

Damir stared at him, then nodded. "I have felt it, Elder. I feel it still."

Madawc met his gaze and his smile was kind. "I know you have, lad, but it will not defeat you, not while you hold true to that great heart of yours, and fast to that sword."

"I have felt it, too," said Serafina. "I have found my thoughts wandering to conquests I'd never imagined, to power over others, to things I have never wanted before."

"Even I, a Mundane, know of what you speak, though I hadn't recognized it as such until hearing you speak of it," added the king. "Of late, I have found myself lured down darker paths—erotic exploration, black lust, desire . . . you might say." He stopped and coughed, but Madawc held up his hand.

"Say no more, my liege! We know of what you speak, and share in the strange lure of darkness. Even I, too old for such visions, have found myself tempted to inflict my will on others, to force fate's hand . . ." He glanced at Damir and he winked. "You are not alone."

"But at times," said the king with a deep sigh, "it feels more lonely than I can say."

Loneliness. Damir sighed, too. He had felt its bite, even as he lay in the arms of beautiful women and heard them whisper his praises. Only with Eliana had he found true comfort—and her love for him was founded in a lie.

"We see it," said Madawc, "because we are wise, and because Mages are most sensitive to energy, both dark and light. But it will infect all the Woodland soon, and the Mundanes as well."

"Another subject bears consideration," said Rodern. "Where is the Lady Eliana? Despite her . . . robust temperament, she has been present at every Council meeting, even after she openly defied the king's will concerning the Norsk. Why isn't she here?"

No one answered at once, though Madawc and Owain exchanged a look. Damir kept his expression blank, though he felt resentment that Eliana should fall under scrutiny—despite his own suspicions about her allegiance.

Owain answered carefully. "Eliana is safe, but it is the wisdom of Madawc that she, too, is in danger from this 'dark tide' that afflicts us."

"I have heard that her cottage was ransacked," said Rodern. "I was concerned for her welfare."

Serafina gasped. "Who would dare venture anywhere near Eliana's domain? If she found out . . ." She stopped to shudder. "I would not want to be that person."

Typical. Not worried about Eliana, but about her retribution. Of course, Damir had worried about the same thing, but it still annoyed him.

Rodern glanced between them, but Damir maintained his silence. "As long as she is safe, I am relieved."

"She is," said Owain. "My niece is strong-willed and perhaps volatile . . ." Serafina interrupted with a huff, which the king pretended not to notice. "But the fact that she was targeted by violence should indicate she is not responsible."

Serafina frowned. "Unless it was a ruse. Eliana is clever enough to act against her own interests for the purpose of confusing her adversaries."

Damir could stand no more. "In this case, Serafina, there is good reason to believe in Eliana's innocence."

The other Mages all looked at him in surprise, and Serafina gaped. "If you speak on her behalf, Damir, her innocence must be all but assured. I will take your word."

"I am surprised you know of this, of all people," added Rodern. "One might have guessed you yourself were responsible in your ongoing battle with Eliana."

"I have never caused her injury, nor destroyed anything belonging to Eliana," said Damir. "Our rivalry has been . . . intense, yes, but not harmful."

"Except when she set you on fire," said Rodern. "Though you seem to have recovered well enough."

"It was long ago," said Damir, annoyed.

Serafina sighed. "Among the women of the Woodland, it is said that Damir remains flawless, and certainly undamaged by any of Eliana's mischief."

Damir felt the heat rush to his face, but Rodern offered a smile that Damir considered condescending. "Eliana alone, it seems, has been unmoved by our handsome young Mage Protector. Damir, you have certainly fueled the fantasies of the ladies of the Wood."

Damir frowned. "Always back to sex. I had thought the Mages, at least, above such speculation."

"Ha!" Madawc leaned back in his seat, enjoying the moment. "The greater our *ki,* the greater our interest in energy's finest art, boy! Get used to it. After all, it was the lust of the Arch Mage, and the passion of our own queen, that first led to trouble in the dark times."

"He wanted power over all," Damir reminded him, but Madawc shook his head.

"He wanted her first."

Damir didn't argue. The suggestion came too close to his

own inner demons concerning Eliana. Did the Arch Mage abandon his heart in order to possess the lovely queen, or was the darkness always a part of his soul? And in truth, was darkness not an element in every being's soul?

"What is the purpose of this meeting?" asked Serafina. "What do we do?"

"For now, wait," said Madawc. "Damir protects the realm. Woodland spies keep watch over the Norsk movement, and report to the king. But we must be on our guard—not only against the enemies we know, but the enemies we do not." He paused, and his gaze flashed to Damir as if he read his thoughts. "Most of all, perhaps, against the enemy we carry within ourselves."

Chapter Eight

"Do you really think this here flower will make the king's friendly daughter take notice of me, ma'am?" Elphin spoke eagerly, his eyes bright. Eliana sighed.

"No, I do not. What it will do instead is more important. It will freshen your breath, clean your mouth—if used daily—and make you even more appealing."

Elphin eyed the bag of herbs they had gathered together on a long morning's walk. "Anything in there to, well, bulk up my muscles?"

"Of course not! We must never use herbs as shortcuts, Elphin. They are to aid us, to help us restore balance as ourselves—not some puffed up version such as we imagine we might want to be!"

He deflated even more, and his still-narrow shoulders slumped. "Oh."

Eliana patted his shoulder. "You are perfect as you are. No boy of sixteen is meant to look brawny and large. You are growing."

He eyed her doubtfully. "Alouard at The Hungry Cat is brawny, and he's my age."

"Then Alouard isn't growing as tall as you are going to be. One day, you will tower over him, and he will feel foolish." Eliana paused. "If he's very brawny now, chances are by the age of twenty-five, he will resemble a stuffed ham, and be just as unattractive to women."

Elphin smiled. "You got a point there, Lady. He has a tendency to hang about at the tavern, slogging ale to the customers, and he don't move much already."

"Doesn't," she corrected. "As well pleasant breath, it is important to speak correctly, for the most part. It will make you seem more thoughtful, especially to a princess. I take it there is no great distinction in this land between classes?"

"Not really, Lady, though the royal ones trace their lineage to ancient time. But we don't pick heirs as other lands might so if I can get her to fall for me, no one would be objecting."

"I would hope not, if you win her heart. How is a new leader chosen, then?"

"Well, first of all, they have to step up and want the task, and not many do, though you get to live in the palace and all. Too many more interesting things to be doing, I guess. But Amrodel keeps alive the descent from the legendary queen, who died rather than give herself up to the Arch Mage. Plenty of stories about her. So the king now gives big parties at the solstice times, but we don't pay him much mind, on the whole. Of the current royals, only Cahira has any skill at bossing, but she's more interested in fighting than ruling." He hesitated. "Most folks figured the rule would pass to one of two people."

"Who?"

"You or Damir ap Kora," he said, smiling. "Well, maybe at this point, it will be both of you."

"Really? Damir would be a good king, I think. I wonder how I would be as a queen, especially if I never regain my memory?"

"I'm thinking you'll do fine as is, ma'am." He almost made it seem as if her current state was preferable, and Eliana's doubt resurfaced.

They stood in the shadow of the trees, shaded from the midafternoon sun. Elphin looked relaxed and happy. As the day together progressed, he had changed dramatically from their first meeting, and seemed more comfortable in Eliana's presence. "I was a good person, before . . . wasn't I?" she asked in a small voice.

He blinked, but then he looked at her kindly. "Of course, you were, Lady. You couldn't be this good now without having been the same before, inside."

"That is not entirely comforting, Elphin."

He patted her shoulder awkwardly. "Don't you doubt it, Lady. I'm figuring you're just where you were meant to be now."

"I feel so uncertain at times. Thank you for staying with me today. I am troubled in sleep by strange dreams, and sometimes during the day, when I am alone, I feel afraid, though I'm not sure why."

"Damir ap Kora won't let anything happen to you, Lady. You can be sure of that."

Eliana smiled. "I am fortunate to have him. At times, he seems more real and solid than I do myself."

Elphin nodded and shrugged and shifted his weight from foot to foot. "Well, I suppose that's to be expected, given what's happened to you. But you'll do fine as is, ma'am. Take my word for it. Don't go pressing to get your memory back. Things are best as they are."

Eliana looked at him in surprise, but he seemed to realize he'd said too much and he ambled out into Damir's garden. The pony, Selsig, whinnied, and another horse answered her call from the southern path. Damir rode into the clearing and laughed as the little mare came eagerly to the fence.

Selsig had seemed uneasy about Damir's big horse when she first arrived. "It seems they've made friends,"

Damir said as he dismounted, but he looked to Eliana, and she saw sadness in his eyes.

Damir looked between Elphin and Eliana and spotted the bag of herbs in the boy's hands. "I take it you two have made good work of the day?"

"We have, at that, sir!" said Elphin. "Your Lady Wife has taken me all through the western path, and we found herbs as I didn't even know existed! Gave me these here for . . ." He cast a quick glance at Eliana and smiled, "for my various pursuits."

Eliana patted his arm. "May they serve you well, Elphin." She held up another small bag of herbs. "These I collected from what I sensed about them. With each plant, I felt an essence of myself. I believe when I gather one final plant, the one I mentioned to you earlier, I might prepare a mixture that could restore my memory. But I think it will require an art of processing that I don't recall. If only I had notes on my methods!"

"None that I know of," said Damir as he dismounted.

Elphin looked uncomfortable and again shifted his weight. He took Damir's horse and released him into the field, then gathered his own horse. "It's time I headed back to the palace of the Mage." He paused to sigh. "The old fellow has many tasks as need doing. Thought it might be more exciting to live there, but as it is, it's more work than I had with the horse master."

"But the benefits of Madawc's company are greater," said Damir. "By the way, if you're interested in a little extra gold, take the name 'Shaen' to The Hungry Cat tavern, and place your wager on the king's latest mistress. Just don't tell them the tip came from me."

"Thank you, sir! I've got a few bets placed already," added Elphin with a quick glance at Eliana. "Think I'm going to have to change one of them."

Damir frowned. "Or you might better spend your time cleaning out Madawc's back room . . ."

"Shaen, eh? Pretty woman, but I always thought she was friendlier with the Mage Rodern. Well, well." Elphin hopped astride his horse, then bowed to Eliana. "I thank you, Lady. Don't you be worrying about dark dreams and such. You're as safe as a cat in a cave here. Good day."

Damir went to her side. "What did that mean? Have you had more dreams, Eliana?"

"Last night, I dreamt of the shadow woman behind me, and the angelic boy, but also of an evil man who called to me." She gazed into his eyes and smiled. "But last night, my dreams were tempered by sweeter thoughts."

Damir caught her meaning and he smiled. "Mine, also."

"Elphin says you were called to the king's Council. Did you show them the sword?"

"I did, and there was much awe in response." He seemed proud, but the sorrow in his eyes remained.

"You look sad. What troubles you, Damir?"

Damir drew her into his arms and kissed her forehead. "I've missed you. But let's go inside and talk there. The clouds are moving in from the east, and it will rain tonight."

"I have made you dinner," said Eliana. "It is a stew, and it should be nearly ready now. Elphin and I made it together. I'm afraid I didn't sense the methods of meal preparation as I did with my selection of herbs and their uses, but he seemed to know a great deal about the art, and I think it will be a good meal."

Damir looked both surprised and happy as she led him into the cottage, then brought him a bowl of hot stew and loaf of warm bread. "Elphin taught me how to bake bread, though it took several efforts at first. But this seems right to me."

Damir broke off a piece of the bread and tasted it. "It is good," he said, but he still seemed surprised.

"Is it like the bread I made before?" she asked as she sat down opposite him.

Damir swallowed and took another piece, but he didn't meet her eyes. "Even better."

"I'm pleased you like it."

They ate together, and he told her of the Council meeting, though she felt he skimmed over much of the conversation. The afternoon sun faded beneath encroaching gray clouds, and a soft rain began outside. It pattered on the windows and Eliana yawned.

Damir rose from the table and took her hand. "Come, I keep a low fire burning in the east room. Let us sit there for awhile. It is pleasant when the rain falls."

They sat together on a low, soft couch and Eliana rested her head on his shoulder. Damir sifted her long hair through his fingers, and she felt content. "Have we spent many evenings this way?" she asked.

"Countless," he replied, and his eyes closed as he rested his head against hers. "This is bliss, Eliana, to be with you this way."

She snuggled closer to him and laid her hand on his wide chest. "I am happy."

For a long while, they sat together in silence and Eliana listened to his strong heartbeat and the sound of his breath. But the rain outside intensified, and the wind increased to a whispering, low howl. Damir must have noticed it, too, because he sighed and opened his eyes.

"Peace is always short-lived," he said, and he sighed again.

Eliana looked up at him. "Did you learn anything about the dark cloud we saw after we made the sword?"

"Not much more than we had already guessed. But there was much concern over the darkness we have felt. Madawc explained it as a current of negative energy, in greater substance than is normal, as if it seeks to disrupt the natural balance of dark and light. Several Mages likened it to the dark time, when the Arch Mage destroyed the balance of this land, and the queen was lost."

"Where does it come from?"

"Of that, no one is certain, though all have perceived a mysterious link with the Norsk."

She knew what was bothering her now, and it wasn't the threat of external darkness. It was herself. "But the darkness comes from within, too."

Damir looked at her in surprise. "Madawc said the same. But I'm surprised to hear it from you. I sense no darkness in you."

Eliana sat up and drew away from him. "There is darkness in me, Damir. I would not lie to you and have you think otherwise." She drew a deep breath, then turned to face him. "I am plagued by an inner darkness and negative imaginings that I do not understand."

His dark eyes widened but he gave no sign that he guessed her thoughts. "Such as what?"

Eliana bowed her head. "Jealousy."

He hesitated and scratched his neck. "Jealousy? Of me?"

Eliana peeked up at him. "No, not *of* you. But about you."

He seemed truly confused, and that was some relief. A man who had given his wife cause for jealousy would certainly guess its source when mentioned. "I don't understand."

"I am jealous . . ." She paused to swallow, then continued, "of The Fiend."

His eyes drifted to the side, then shifted back to her, and his brow furrowed. "Why?"

"I don't know why, exactly, except that I sense some bond between you and her."

"You do?"

"Yes. You speak of her in a strange way, and I have

wondered . . . I have wondered about your relationship to her, before I lost my memory."

"She had no part in that," he answered, his tone careful, and still confused.

"So you say, but is it unreasonable to assume a woman known for imaginative potions might have found one that erases memory?"

"I suppose not. But The Fiend had no reason to destroy your memory."

"No? What if she wanted me gone, to have you for herself?"

He peered at her from the corner of his eyes, then crossed and uncrossed his legs. "I don't think you understand what she felt for me."

"One of us doesn't. I think it's you." Exasperation grew in Eliana, though she struggled against it. "As I said, it is my darkness. Forgive me."

"There's no need to apologize, my dear." He hesitated. "This is simply—an unexpected confession on your part." He reached over and took her hand. "I assure you, my relationship with The Fiend was built on rivalry, and nothing more."

"Elphin says she is beautiful."

Damir said nothing, though he fidgeted uncomfortably. "Is she?"

He cleared his throat. "I suppose so."

"She is." Eliana's lips twisted to one side. "Elphin mentioned rumors indicating she held fondness for you."

Damir frowned. "Did he? Well, he's wrong. She held no affection for me, I'm sure. I was her rival, and her nemesis. Nothing more."

"Have you affection for her?"

Damir's answer wasn't immediate and Eliana stiffened. "She has done little to inspire affection," he said, "nor ever indicated she wanted it from me."

Eliana slipped her hand away from his, and her eyes narrowed. "You don't deny it."

"This is ridiculous. Eliana, it is you I love. You are sweet . . ."

" 'Sweet' is a very dull flavor, Damir. Not so exciting as spice, I think. The Fiend is spice."

Damir hesitated. "I prefer sweet."

"Even in bed?"

He gaped, but Eliana clamped her hand over her eyes. "I don't know what's wrong with me."

"The dark tide is affecting the thoughts and fears of all the Mages. Young Serafina, generally mild and somewhat confused, confessed to fantasies of conquest. But you've been under more strain than the rest, because of your affliction."

"Maybe that is it." Maybe the dark tide was affecting her more than she realized. Outside, the wind increased and the rain fell harder, and evening darkened to night. They sat stiffly, in silence, together, but the darkness refused to yield. "It seems to me that this woman is an obvious threat, and has perhaps even taken a lover from among the Norsk, but you defend her. Why?"

Damir seemed tense, but he answered evenly. "I don't believe she has a lover among the Norsk, no."

Eliana glared at him. "Perhaps because she has a lover here!"

Damir appeared utterly shocked by her accusation. "This is crazy. Please believe me—I have no other lover but you."

"How would I know that?" Tears stung Eliana's eyes, and she hated herself for her behavior, but somehow, she couldn't control it. She gathered her strength and looked into his eyes. "Can you tell me you're not in love with her or that you do not desire her?"

A moment's hesitation was too much. She shot up from the couch and backed away from him. Damir rose, too, but she moved beyond his reach. "Eliana, don't do this. There is no need for jealousy."

Her tears fell, though she wasn't sure why. "You do not answer me, because you cannot. Tell me, when I found you . . . alone with yourself . . ." She paused until he understood her meaning, and his face reddened a shade. "Was it me you saw in your fantasy, or was it The Fiend?"

His mouth slid open, but then he shook his head. "Eliana . . ."

"I knew it!"

"You don't understand . . ."

"Then tell me, truthfully, what are your feelings for The Fiend?"

A strange expression crossed his dark face, one she couldn't read. "My feelings for The Fiend have always been . . . complicated."

"Fine!" Eliana marched from the east room, went to the front door and yanked it open. He hurried after her, but she held up her hand. "I need to think."

"You can't go out there!"

"I can." Eliana bowed her head and her shoulders slumped. "I don't know what's wrong with me. I need time alone."

"It's raining and cold." He pulled a long, gray cape from a hook by the door, then placed it gently over her shoulders. He kissed her forehead, then took her chin in his hand. "Do not go far. My shield protects this area, but I don't want you to get lost." He didn't release her. "But please listen to me before you go. I love no other woman but you. You must believe that."

"There is something wrong between us, Damir. I feel it." He didn't respond and she nodded. "You feel it, too."

"No . . ."

"I need time to think, to face my own darkness. It is not up to you to assuage my fears. Please, let me go. I will not be long."

Damir hesitated, then moved back. "Very well. But when you come back, we will lie together and speak of this. I think I can convince you that your fears are misplaced."

"It is my battle, and my darkness, not yours. I must face it alone." With that, she stepped outside. He started to follow, but she saw that he held himself back. "I won't be long."

He nodded, but she saw the pain in his eyes, and her heart ached for causing it. Eliana let the door close behind her. When she looked back, she saw Damir standing by the window. The rain fell hard against her face. She pulled up her hood, then walked away.

Damir lasted a moment only before he grabbed his own cape and went out after Eliana. Her accusation concerning "The Fiend" had left him nearly speechless. Given the accuracy, yet utter inaccuracy, of her assessment, he hadn't been able to answer her convincingly. If he could get her back, hold her in his arms, then he could make her see that she had nothing to worry about. But how strange to see Eliana jealous of herself!

Damir headed out into the cold night. He had seen her take the southern path, which made sense given the rain, and it should be easy enough to overtake her. He hurried along, and his thoughts raced for a way to ease her doubt. Briefly, he considered telling her the truth, but he couldn't risk losing her. Eliana didn't seem to realize that she had plenty of "spice" left without her memories. After last night, his fantasies had taken a more romantic turn. No longer did he want to conquer his old rival. He just wanted to keep his "wife."

He nearly caught up with her where the southern path rose sharply uphill. Eliana had stopped near the hill's crest, and his heart lifted as she started to turn back. Her little shoulders squared and she nodded once, and even from a distance, he guessed she was ready to come back to him.

Damir called out to her, but the wind and rain drove his voice backwards, and she didn't notice him in the shadow of the path below. She started to come back down the hill, but something caught her attention in the other direction. A caped and hooded horseman rode onto the horizon, then stopped when he spotted Eliana.

Damir's heart froze. He didn't recognize the rider in darkness, but by the size of the horse, he knew it wasn't Madawc or Elphin. He hurried up the hill, but too late. With her voice broken by the wind, Damir heard Eliana greet the rider, and he heard a man's voice respond in surprise. Damir ran, but the wind itself seemed against him.

"Eliana? Is that you?" A familiar voice, but Damir couldn't place it at once. Damir pressed on up the hill, slipped on the wet ground, caught himself, and hurried forward.

"It is, yes . . ." She shielded her eyes against the rain and looked up. Damir's heart pounded.

"What in the name of all the Mages are you doing out here, and so far from home?" Damir recognized the man's voice now. It was Rodern, the Mage of Jarna.

Eliana appeared confused. "I am not so far from home," she replied.

"Or were you up to mischief at the home of Damir ap Kora?" asked Rodern with a laugh. "Many of us have worried about you. And you and I have some unfinished business to attend to."

"We do?" The confusion in her little voice tore at Damir's heart. But what business could she have with Rodern?

"Don't toy with me, Eliana. You know of what I speak. The matter of the Norsk, and a certain potion that fell into the wrong hands."

Damir caught his breath as Rodern's meaning became clear. If the Mage intended to accuse Eliana of betraying Amrodel, he would have Damir to deal with first.

"I don't know what you mean," she said.

Rodern caught sight of Damir, and Eliana turned, too. She breathed an audible sigh of relief when she saw Damir, and started toward him, but Rodern's sharp laugh stopped her. "Don't tell me the two of you are in league now! That explains your reticence at the Council, Damir."

"Leave her alone, Rodern. Eliana is coming with me."

Rodern laughed again, a harsh sound that blended with the howling wind and the driving rain. "What? Have you finally surrendered to your lust for this woman, Damir ap Kora? The Mundanes will be thrilled to hear it."

Eliana looked between them, desperate and shocked. "What are you talking about?"

"No?" said Rodern. "It was too ripe to imagine, I fear. Come with me, Eliana. I doubt very much you'll want to spend the night with your nemesis, unless much has changed between you."

Damir reeled, but Eliana shook her head and backed away. She turned to him, her face stricken, her shock palpable. "What is he talking about?"

"I can explain . . ."

"Yes, please do," added Rodern, and Damir recognized the condescending tone that so often infected the older Mage's voice. "Why should Eliana Daere go with the man who has caused her so much grief, or spend any time with her lifelong rival?"

Eliana trembled as she looked back and forth between them. "What do you want with me?" she asked Rodern, and again, he moved closer to her.

"Only to talk, my dear, and to bring you out of this cold night. Surely, you know better than to trust Damir ap Kora?"

"Eliana, no . . ." Damir's voice came hoarse and broken

as he fought to regain her trust. "Please, come with me. This is not as it seems."

The wind swirled and whipped around her. She stared at him and her breath came in short gasps as she shook her head in denial. "This cannot be. You aren't . . ."

Rodern uttered an impatient breath. "Come, Eliana. Whatever has passed between you and our 'Mage Protector,' don't make a greater fool of yourself over him now. He has bested you before, but whatever trickery he has performed this time is surely matched by your past efforts against him."

Damir's throat tightened, and he knew that she cried. "Don't go with him, Eliana. My shield will protect you as long as you refuse him."

"She needs no protection from a fellow Mage, Damir. Eliana and I have a private matter to discuss that does not include you, and given the nature of your past relationship, I doubt very much she will want to spend more time with you!"

Eliana swayed, and Damir thought she might faint, but Rodern reached down and grabbed her, then pulled her up onto his horse. Eliana didn't resist. Damir nearly fell to his knees in grief. "I can protect you if you let me. Eliana . . ."

Her voice came small, but it quavered with emotion. *"Protect me?* The only person I need protection from is you!"

Chapter Nine

"What were you doing with Damir ap Kora, anyway?" The Mage, Rodern, stood beside a roaring fire in a round hall of the dark stone tower where he had brought Eliana. The rooms all appeared small, with few windows. Books and parchments were stacked everywhere. Eliana sat in silence in a large wooden chair and stared at the flames. Clearly, this man had no idea of her memory loss, and what remained of her senses told her to keep it that way.

"That is my concern," she answered, her voice low.

Rodern stood before her, a tall and menacing presence, though he hadn't really threatened her. She refused to look at him. "If you and your handsome rival have finally given in to your passions, that is not my concern. But you hold information that is of interest to me, Eliana, and it is time you gave it over."

"I don't know what you mean."

"The Norsk, Eliana. Who is your ally among them? I have lost patience with your delays, and it is time for you to share what you know."

Eliana's thoughts reeled and spun. Damir had lied to her, and she was lost. *Not my husband . . . Who am I?* Without him, she was nothing, no one. She was lost in a mist, and it had all been a lie. Rodern bent down and gripped either side of her chair, then spoke in a dangerous voice. "Tell me his name."

Fear gave way to a strong, throbbing anger and she met the Mage's threatening gaze steadily. "Do what you will. I will tell you nothing."

Rodern snapped back, his lips drawn tight in fury. "You are a foolish woman. So you've bedded a Norskman? And now you threaten the very fiber of . . . of Amrodel."

Eliana didn't flinch nor betray fear. She didn't care what he did to her. She was alone, but she would not yield. "It seems to me that your interest is for something other than Amrodel. One would guess you had designs of your own."

Rodern leaned toward her again, his eyes blazing. "Is that so? You are no more loyal to Amrodel or our weak-willed king than I am, so don't whine to me about honor. I know what you tried to do, Eliana, with your 'Potion of Sleep.' But Bruin the Ruthless was duly warned, and your plot failed. But I will know the name of your lover, lest you hatch another such plot in this treacherous devil's embrace."

A Norsk lover . . . Eliana closed her eyes as she tried to make sense of Rodern's accusations. "There is no truth in what you say."

"You seek power, Eliana, as all Mages do, but you will never have what I will soon achieve. You seek it with your lovers, a Norskman, now Damir ap Kora. You have no idea what power is out there, available for those daring enough to seize it." He gripped her chin and she saw that he trembled with repressed emotion. "Can you imagine what we could have, if you join with me? What can Damir ap Kora give you? A night with a well-practiced lover? Ha! That is nothing he hasn't given to every other woman in Amrodel, Mage and Mundane alike. Would you lower yourself to that?"

Eliana's heart clenched. A well-practiced lover . . . Well, there was no denying his skill. Despite the ache that soaked her limbs with heaviness, she answered evenly. "What do you offer me, Mage?"

He smiled as if he recognized a like mind, and had expected her acquiescence all along. "There is an energy above us and around us. You feel it. We all do. But can you imagine what could be if we could harness it?"

"It seems to me someone already has."

"The Norsk?" Rodern paused to laugh. "They are but animals to serve a greater task, a greater leader."

"You are the traitor," she said calmly, "the one who has brought this darkness upon Amrodel."

He laughed. "One day, my power might elevate to that point, but this tide is yet beyond me. Oh, I won't deny I have a hand in its art, but I will say that a chance find by a most unexpected person has led to something far, far greater than any of the 'Elite Mages' have guessed." His eyes darkened, and the expression she saw in them woke her dormant fear. "I am but the servant of a greater master. . . ."

"I know of whom you speak," she said in a low voice. It was the evil, dark man in her dreams, the one who was calling her. "But he is long gone, buried deep in the darkness he created for himself."

"No *ki* as strong as the Arch Mage's is truly gone, Eliana," said Rodern.

"Do you think he drives this darkness?" she asked in amazement.

"Not yet. But we hear his voice—'*Wake me, serve me.*'" Rodern's voice altered, and Eliana wondered if he had lost his mind.

"It is the dark tide you hear, Rodern. I have heard such a voice, too, but not his."

"Whose?" He startled her with the intensity of his question, but Eliana shook her head.

"I don't know."

"You know." Rodern's eyes gleamed with an unnatural light. "It is *her*, the one he seeks, the one whose fall destroyed him."

"I suppose he wishes to rise only to regain the love of a woman who died ages ago?" Eliana couldn't restrain her sarcasm, but Rodern glowered.

"Love? Don't be a fool. But what is death but a transition to another form? When he returns, he will again claim what was rightfully his, and the power of their combined energy will be unstoppable. Then this land, and all others, will fall beneath his grip."

Eliana frowned. "So you think he wants order, lands united under one banner?"

"All energy will flow to him, and he will be as a god."

Eliana huffed. "Or very busy with the daily cares of his subjects."

"You jest, Eliana, but you have no idea how close we are now. The Norsk will serve us. Their energy is weak, but there are many, ruthless and without fear. With a Mage as their leader, directing them, they would soon take control of Amrodel—if Damir ap Kora is removed as its protector. Then we might venture onward to the land of his father, to the desert of Kora itself. There, unimaginable riches lie, and unimaginable power. Only the Arch Mage has the power to defeat them, and he will, if we bring him forth to serve us."

"What would he want with Kora?"

"The bulk of all its power. But that was his homeland." Rodern paused, confused. "Didn't you know?"

Eliana's mouth slid open. "He was of the same race as Damir?"

"Yes, though his blood was true."

"What do you want of me? More than information about the Norsk, I think."

"We need you to resurrect the Arch Mage."

Eliana just stared. *"What?"*

"You are her heir, like to the queen in both beauty and temperament. If we take you to the pit where he lies in darkness, your presence will wake him."

"But I am not her." Eliana stopped. The queen had been in that lavender dragonfly, but she couldn't let Rodern know that. "My spirit is not hers."

"It doesn't have to be. You share her blood. The only other is the king's daughter, Cahira, who has both heritage and the *ki* of a Mage, and she is too young for our uses."

"So, what do you plan? To toss me or this child into a pit in hopes of waking a long-dead Mage? That is crazy!"

Rodern smiled, but she felt sure now that he was insane. "There's no need to 'toss' you, Eliana. Just your presence in the cavern of the Mage will wake him, for that is the sign he waits for, the key to unlock the unnatural captivity in which he has so long endured."

"He is dead."

"His spirit is too great for death. He will rise again."

"Then he must work himself out of his own darkness! I have no intention of aiding his escape! Were he a truly great Mage, he would have done as the Queen did, and surrender his life and his power, then move on."

"You echo Madawc's prattle, but are you not beyond that now? Think! Would you not enjoy ultimate power? Think how you could humble Damir ap Kora."

Eliana lowered her eyes. "I have no wish to humble him."

Rodern laughed. "Then there has been a great change. But I don't believe you."

She didn't want to talk about Damir ap Kora. "How has the Dark Mage reached you?"

"With the energy that Madawc terms 'negative,' the Arch Mage learned even as a young man how to harness it, how to 'ride its waves,' if you will. Others, of like mind, are drawn to him—those of us who are strong."

"I would call it 'weak,' but go on."

"Even the Mundanes can feel its pull. Some few among them even reach for it, knowing it can give them all the power they lack."

"You mean, those who are evil seek power through darkness. But what you say is nothing new. In the end, the Arch Mage gave up himself and his heart in order to possess this current, and he lost the power of the light."

Rodern's eyes flashed with anger. "Despite your reclusive state, you still cling to the wisdom of an old man who has nothing better to do than place bets on the sexual escapades of others while loitering at The Hungry Cat!"

Eliana had no idea what he meant, but she recalled Damir telling Elphin to place a wager on someone named "Shaen," so it must be a common practice. "The elder Mage seems a wiser person to listen to than yourself. And perhaps those small events that give joy have more value than all the power you seek."

"I am surprised to hear you, of all people, speak this way," said Rodern, his expression ripe with suspicion. "What is wrong with you?"

"Is it not possible that I have changed?"

"No. Traits such as yours don't change overnight. What has Damir ap Kora done to you?"

What, indeed? "I do not speak for Damir," she answered. "I speak for myself, and for what I feel is right and true."

Rodern stood back. "I will give you the night to consider. By morning, I will have the name of your Norsk ally, or your fate may not seem so pleasant."

She frowned. "Obviously, you can't kill me, not if you intend to use me to resurrect the Arch Mage."

"Kill you? No . . . and Damir's shield makes that impossible, for now. I need you for a more important task. You know that now. But this Norsk ally threatens my plans in ways I don't intend to explain. I will have his name—or I might consider waiting for the young princess to come of age, after all . . ."

Rodern summoned two servants who looked more like guards, and directed them to take Eliana to a bedroom. Neither man spoke, and it seemed to Eliana that they weren't quite human. Their eyes were dull and they never looked at her. She sensed both were Mundanes, but rather than a light *ki,* they seemed to bear almost none at all. They had somehow released themselves, all bounds to their hearts, and given control over to Rodern—and the dark energy he served.

The guards led her up a steep, winding staircase and left her alone in a small room with one window facing east. The room was empty except for two narrow beds and a small table, but it wasn't uncomfortable. Eliana sat on the edge of the bed nearest the window. Loneliness bit into her, and she knew, even without memory, that she had suffered this pain before. Loneliness was familiar— far more so than the love she had imagined she shared with her "husband."

Tears stung Eliana's eyes, but she refused to cry. Even Rodern's menacing presence seemed preferable to this. The rain fell in dark sheets outside the window and no light came from either the sky or the darkened lamp. There had to be some light in the darkness. Damir's image arose in her thoughts, but she banished him. *I will not think of you . . .* But where was light? Whoever she had been, once she had known hope, she had found something of value, something good. Something gave her strength.

Who am I? What is my hope? Why am I so alone?

Eliana closed her eyes, and for a while, she saw nothing

but darkness within. It pulsed and moved in patterns, but without light as she tried to focus her inward mind. Then from the utter black void within, a tiny glimmer grew. As it shone, she saw a shape emerge from within. Warmth circled her heart as a figure emerged, and she recognized the angelic boy from her dreams. He held out his hand to her, till the black void closed in around him, and he disappeared into nothing.

That is my hope. But why?

Eliana opened her eyes. She could trust no one now, not even herself. But there was something—perhaps the boy represented the spirit of a long-past great Mage. He seemed more real, however, and more vulnerable, than any angelic messenger.

The wind blew hard against her window, and it cracked open, tossing her hair around her face as it swung wider. Cold rain whipped her face and she stood up on the bed to shut the pane again.

A dark hand grabbed the pane and Eliana choked back a scream. With a grunt, Damir hoisted himself up, then clambered through the window. Eliana fell back on the bed, her heart racing, as he extracted himself from the narrow window—not without effort, because his shoulders were broad, and the window barely gave room for him to squeeze in.

He looked at her, gasping, and paused to catch his breath before he lowered himself to the floor. "This is not an easy tower to scale."

She didn't answer, so shocked was she to see him. Damir sat on the other bed facing her. He wiped away a spattering of blood where he had scratched his arms on the tower walls. Eliana bit her lip hard, but her eyes filled with tears. "What are you doing here?"

"I've come," he began, still out of breath, "to get you out of here."

"How did you know there was danger?"

"I sensed a great upsurge in dark *ki,* and I knew it didn't come from you."

She bowed her head. "Are you so sure of that?"

"Yes."

"You lied to me."

He nodded. "Yes."

Her tears resumed as she watched him. The words came as if torn from her throat, from the very core of her being. "I . . . I was The Fiend."

He nodded, but he didn't speak.

"Why did you do this to me?" Her voice was ragged with pain, but she had to know.

"I didn't," he answered. She started to speak, but he stopped her. "You have no reason to believe me now, but it's true."

"What? I 'fell?' "

"No, you didn't fall. You drank a potion you had meant for me, and loss of memory was the result."

"I poisoned myself? That hardly seems likely!"

"That wasn't your intention." He paused. "I switched the goblets, and you drank the one you intended for me."

She chewed the inside of her lip as she considered this. "Do you mean to say that I intended to ravage your memory? Why should I believe that?"

"I'm not sure I can convince you, but it was not out of character for you."

Eliana stared at her hands. "I would doubt you, but what you say explains Elphin's manner, and other things." She looked up at him. "So you did this, lied to me and made me a fool . . . for vengeance?"

A faint smile formed on his beautiful mouth, but tears glittered in his eyes. "I told you once, my feelings for 'The Fiend' are complicated."

A soft river of tears coursed down her cheeks, but she

didn't try to brush them away. "It was vengeance—against The Fiend for her crimes against you."

He looked down, then back at her and he nodded. "At first, that was my purpose, yes."

"Is that why you didn't . . ." She paused, uncomfortable with the topic of intimacy which had, hours ago, been so easy, "why you didn't complete the marital act between us?"

Damir's brow arched, though the pain in his face remained. "I am not so noble a man, I'm afraid. I would have completed the act, as I have long desired to do."

She frowned. "What stopped you? Did you fear getting me with child?"

He looked into her eyes and she saw a depth of emotion she couldn't misread. "You are a virgin, Eliana. When I realized that, I found I couldn't . . . tarnish you, or take what you had preserved."

"Why did that surprise you?" She paused. "I suppose because I am rumored to have a Norsk lover?"

"Yes, that, but you had hinted at other lovers before the matter of the Norsk arose between us. I didn't expect your innocence."

Eliana sat back. "Perhaps I made love to them as I did with you." She paused, and rebellion surged within her. "With the mouth."

He winced and cringed at once, and Eliana felt satisfied. "It is possible." His tone gave every indication it was a possibility he didn't want to consider.

"It did come easily for me," she added. Anger grew inside her, and she liked its force. Damir seemed to shrink as he sat opposite her. "But since you are known as a 'well practiced' lover yourself, virginity should cause no hesitation."

He fidgeted, but he didn't argue.

"I suppose I was the only one left you hadn't bedded."

He glared and straightened. "There are many who haven't captured my attention, if you would know it." He paused and his expression softened. "You are special."

"You wanted to defeat me and conquer me, just like the Arch Mage—to whom, I have recently learned, you are no doubt related."

He looked surprised, but Eliana huffed. "Rodern says he was a Mage from Kora, like yourself. That is one part of history you left out."

"Actually, I'd forgotten. It was long ago. But I suppose we are akin, from afar, as he was of the royal lineage there, though not of the prince's house."

"And I am akin to the queen. How fitting! By the way, Rodern—and unnamed allies—seek to resurrect the Arch Mage himself by the daft means of offering me as some kind of sacrifice to him, which they imagine will bring him back to power."

His eyes widened. "That may not be so daft. You are her heir, and it is the return of her energy that he vowed would unlock his eternal prison."

"I do not have her 'energy.' I am not her."

"Still, it may be enough. I would imagine Rodern has researched this matter. He is well versed in the history of our craft, even if he isn't the best practitioner." Damir glanced at the window. "This is more dangerous than I'd imagined. I have to get you out of here, now."

"Why should I trust you?"

"Would you prefer to place your trust in him?"

Eliana hesitated. "He seems mad to me. I would guess studying the dark current too closely has poisoned his mind. You said other Mages, too, have felt this pull, and his words to me indicated he is not alone. He mentioned even Mundanes who have some part in this."

"We must warn Madawc, and the king. Please, Eliana, let us set aside our differences. I lied to you, yes, but I would not hurt you."

"I do not trust you. I think I will never trust again. But I want to be free of this place, and the people of Amrodel must be warned. I will go with you."

The door opened and Rodern stood in the threshold. "An interesting disclosure, Eliana. I'm pleased to see you've patched up your differences. Damir . . ." He paused and gave an exaggerated bow, then assessed Damir carefully. "I expected you sooner, but then, the walls of my tower hold are steep and offer little in the way of footholds. I'm impressed you made it up without falling."

Damir rose and faced the Mage. "You can do nothing against us, Rodern. My shield protects us, and I will let no harm come to Eliana now that I know your intentions."

Rodern laughed, and Eliana found herself rising to stand next to Damir. "Your shield, 'Mage Protector,' covers only that part of the realm which *accepts* its power. Has it occurred to you that I refused your will, even at the time of your shield's creation? Even the greatest gift can be rejected—and I saw fit to do so."

"That may be, but my *ki* is strong enough to protect Eliana and myself, too. You cannot harm us."

"I cannot stop you, but you overlook the power of my own *ki*," said Rodern. "I, too, have invested my energy in something akin to your shield. But the force I have woven doesn't keep danger out. It locks it in. I doubt very much you can protect yourself or the woman when this tower crumbles over your head." He offered a mocking glance at Eliana. "I'm sorry, my dear, but you have learned too much, and the benefits of your heritage are outweighed by this sudden, and unwise, burst of honor. I cannot leave either of you alive and maintain my place in the realm. So I have thought of another way to gain both ends—it may be that I will have to await the Mage Child's ascent into womanhood, or maybe the energy of her sacrifice will be enough. The matter will require further study. But for now, with you gone, I have all that I need with the power of the Norsk warriors behind me. I doubt very much your mysterious ally can stand alone against both Rodern ap Jarna and Bruin the Ruthless together."

"You will never get away with this madness, Rodern," said Damir, but his words seemed impotent to Eliana's ears.

"Won't I?" Rodern laughed. "When this tower crumbles, the innocent folk of the Wood will assume I was killed with it. There will be speculation as to where the two of you have gone, until your bodies are found. I wonder what wagers they'll place at The Hungry Cat over this?"

Rodern left the room and locked the door, but Damir headed for the window. "He has no power over us. We can escape. Come . . ."

As he spoke, the tower began to tremble and Eliana caught her breath. "There's no time. Even if we climb out, we will be killed in its collapse!"

Damir turned to her. "Then trust me. I will not fail you this time."

"I cannot trust you now . . ."

He gathered her into his arms and drew her down to the bed farthest from the window. "No harm will come to you, Eliana, I swear it."

She didn't trust him. She couldn't. But the warmth of his arms was her only strength, and she leaned against him. No matter what they had been to each other, she felt the same comfort when he held her, and she buried her face against his chest. The walls shook and stones fell outside the window, and Damir's arms tightened around her.

"Was I really evil?" she whispered.

The ceiling above broke asunder, and loud crashes rent the night. Damir kissed her head and held her close. "You were spice."

Damir lay in a field of white, and around him, nothing moved. From the core of the light, a shape seemed to emerge, and for an instant, he saw a lavender dragonfly above him. He wrapped his fingers tight around the hilt of his sword, and sat up.

Eliana lay beside him, awake, her green eyes wide with astonishment. "What happened?" she asked, and he helped her to sit up.

He held up the white sword and smiled. Eliana smiled, too. "But you didn't have it with you when you came into my room. How did you get it?"

"It was hidden beneath my cape, at my back," he responded as he adjusted the sheath to a more comfortable position at his side. "Rodern had no idea of its power."

The rain still fell, and the waning moon cut blue light through the mist. Eliana adjusted her hood over her head, then looked around at the rubble surrounding them. "Nor did I."

"The stones broke like waves around us. The others . . ." Damir saw one of Rodern's guards lying dead beneath a large stone slab. "They were not so fortunate, though had any kept a connection of light to their hearts, I believe my shield would have protected them, too."

"They were far gone," said Eliana. "Their eyes were dull and it almost seemed they were dead already."

Damir took her hand and led her from the rubble. The light of his sword abated, but the moonlight glistened on her disheveled hair. Eliana dusted herself off and looked around. "What happened to the Mage, do you think?"

"I'm sure he's long gone, probably off to his ally, Bruin the Ruthless."

"Damir, I think he will go after Cahira first."

"My shield will protect her."

"Unless she trusts him."

"I did not!" A small, bright voice startled them both, and Damir whirled around to see Cahira standing beyond the rubble, bow clutched in her small hand.

Eliana picked her way over the fallen stones to the child and hugged her. "Cahira! I am so happy to see you."

"As am I," said Damir. "How did you escape?"

"I woke and heard a man tell my father that I was in danger, that he must take me away. I felt the darkness all around me, and I knew he was right—but the danger was him. I took my bow and snuck out of the palace, meaning to come to your cottage, Damir, but when I heard the tower crumble, I came this way instead."

"How did Rodern get from here to the Palace so fast?" asked Eliana.

"It's only a short way," answered Cahira in surprise. "But you have forgotten that, too, I suppose." She paused. "It's lucky . . . I mean, unfortunate that the crash didn't jar your memory, Lady."

"It didn't," said Eliana, "but I know who I am now. I am The Fiend."

Cahira's mouth dropped open and she stared at Damir. "You *told* her?"

Damir cringed. As if things weren't strained enough between them. "I didn't get a chance."

Eliana frowned at him. "I figured it out on my own. Rodern's description of me left little question. As well, I know now that I am no one's wife."

Cahira exhaled miserably. "That's a shame, Lady. It's good to know the truth, but it was really nice to have you married to each other. My father says you would be, sooner or later, but it would have been so much easier to have my lessons in one place!"

Eliana turned to Damir. "If a potion afflicted me, there must be an antidote, as I sensed. Did you deceive me about that, too?"

"No, I did not," said Damir. "No other Mage can reverse the brew you administered, and as it was taking its effect over you, you informed me you hadn't taken the time to create an antidote."

"I must have been very eager."

"You were always impatient."

"Perhaps I considered the matter pressing."

"What? To eliminate my memory?"

Eliana lifted her chin. "I expect I had a good reason."

"And I'd hate to think what it was!"

As they spoke, Madawc arrived with Elphin at his side, and in unison, they looked from the crumbled tower to Eliana and Damir, then back to the tower again. Madawc rubbed his bearded chin, sighed, shook his head, then gazed up into the misty sky. "So this is it. The two of you are set on pulling down the Woodland, piece by piece."

Damir glared. "As it happens, Elder, Eliana and I barely escaped this catastrophe with our lives. You have Rodern to thank for this particular disaster."

"Why would Rodern pull down his own tower?"

"Now, that is a story . . ." said Damir, but Madawc held up his hand.

"Save it for The Hungry Cat, then. I have no wish to listen to a long tale out here in a cold, wet night."

Cahira looked thoughtful. "I could use an ale."

Madawc's eyes narrowed to slits. "You'll be drinking goat's milk, Mage Child!" He turned to Elphin. "While we head to the tavern, you take news of this to the king, and assure him his daughter is safe." Elphin looked disappointed, but he nodded. Madawc glanced at Damir. "I take it Rodern isn't to be trusted."

Damir cast a pertinent look at the rubble. "That would be my opinion." Damir paused. "What I don't understand is why none of us sensed the darkness of his *ki*."

"And there was plenty of it!" added Eliana.

"*Ki* can be masked," said Madawc, "if the subject is diligent. Eliana could mask her *ki*."

"Could I?"

Cahira nodded. "You could, Lady. You were teaching

me to do the same, but for some reason, you couldn't quite make out the shape of mine."

"Your *ki* is strange, Mage Child," agreed Madawc. "At times, it seems almost impossibly strong, and at others, simple as any other child's. But Eliana was gifted at the concealment of her energy, if only for short times."

Damir eyed Eliana. "I expect she masked it to sneak up on me, steal my records, and deliver potions into my meals."

Madawc looked between them and his brow arched in surprise. "So you told her. That was honorably done, lad."

Eliana huffed. "He did nothing of the kind. I found out myself, despite his efforts to deceive me."

Elphin eased back and appeared crestfallen at the news. "So she's back to her old ways, then?"

"My memory hasn't returned," she said. "Although I begin to sense what might have driven me to such distraction."

Madawc shifted his gaze up into the falling rain. "It was too good to last." He paused and shook his head, then looked at the rubble where the tower had stood. "But every wall crumbles eventually. I expect it will be the same with the one standing between the two of you."

Chapter Ten

A crowd had already gathered at The Hungry Cat tavern by the time Damir and Eliana arrived. Apparently, the Woodland people knew of the tower's collapse, and were waiting to hear further news. Cahira held Eliana's hand and talked happily about the tavern, which seemed to be the central point for all variety of rumor and gossip. Why the princess of Amrodel knew the establishment so well, Eliana couldn't imagine, but Cahira greeted all the patrons by name as they entered.

"That is Alouard, the barkeep," she said, and she pointed out a thick-limbed young man poised by a row of heavy, wooden kegs.

"Elphin spoke of him," said Eliana. "And I was right—he will resemble a stuffed ham, sooner than I guessed." The young man took a long swig of ale, then munched into a slab of roasted meat.

"One of my sisters likes Elphin," Cahira whispered in a conspiratorial tone. "But she and my other sisters live with our stepmother on the far side of the forest, so she doesn't see him often."

"Why don't they live at the palace?"

Cahira shrugged. "My father and stepmother didn't get along very well. She was our mother's closest friend, and my sisters say that she married my father out of grief when my mother died." She lowered her voice. "But the real reason they won't stay at the palace is Shaen."

"Who is Shaen?" asked Eliana.

"She's my father's assistant, though we think she is also his girlfriend," said Cahira in disgust.

Eliana looked around to see if any woman in particular resembled her image of a mistress. None did, as far as she could tell. "Is she here?"

"That's her, over there." Cahira pointed to a woman seated at a round table with a group of other women. She looked demure, and unlike the others who held large tankards of frothing ale, she sipped wine from a small goblet.

"She looks harmless enough," said Eliana. "Not what I imagine of a mistress." This woman wasn't buxom or gregarious, nor did she display the overt sensuality Eliana expected. "Are you sure?"

"No, I'm not sure. But we suspect."

"Is she unpleasant?" asked Eliana.

Cahira's small face twisted in a grimace. "Oh, no. She's very *nice*." Cahira made "nice" seem like a curse.

"Then why don't you like her?"

"She's *nice* to me." Cahira paused and her lips curled. "Too nice. She says I'm cute and precious. Sometimes, when her back is turned, I draw my bow and aim it at her."

Eliana smiled. "Were you and I friends, before?"

"You were a good teacher and I think you liked me. You seemed a little disappointed that I didn't take to herbs the way you did, but you helped with my archery, and taught me how to hide my *ki,* if I needed to. But I always planned on being like you. Though when I meet my true love, I'm going to be kind to him, and not set him on fire," added

Cahira thoughtfully. "Well, first I'm going to engage him in combat—so I can see if he's worth the effort. But then I'll be good to him."

"That seems like a good plan," agreed Eliana. She considered the matter. "Maybe that's what I was doing."

Cahira shook her head. "I thought so, and that's where I got the idea for myself. But Damir proved himself worthy over and over, and you still played tricks on him. No, I think you were just afraid, that's all." Cahira paused. "But I think he was afraid, too."

Damir entered the tavern with Madawc and came to stand beside Eliana. "We sent Elphin on to alert the King," he told her as he surveyed the crowd. "But we can get a meal here, and relax after our eventful evening."

Madawc pushed his way into the tavern and aimed at the bar. Alouard was already filling a large tankard, which the elder Mage seized. Cahira slipped off to join him, Madawc issued a dark looking of warning, and Alouard handed her a smaller tankard with a froth that resembled milk. Eliana smiled. "She is a very bright child."

Damir smiled, too. "She reminds me of you at times."

They looked at each other and Eliana's heart stirred. The wave of shock that had sickened her and left her numb began to abate in the face of reality. Already she felt a surge of hope. Maybe it wasn't such a disaster, now that there was truth between them.

The crowd took sudden and unanimous notice of Damir and Eliana standing together, and after a short collective gasp, everyone fell silent as they stared. A stout man wearing a dirty white apron approached them. "I'm hearing that you two took out the Tower of the Mage," he said. "I'd have expected it of The Fiend here, but not you, Damir ap Kora!"

Damir glared, then turned to Eliana. "This is Fareth, proprietor of The Hungry Cat."

Fareth snorted loudly. "Don't know why you're telling

161

her that! She knows the place as well as anyone—after she plopped one of her brews into my ale and . . ." The man paused as if the memory were almost too dark to repeat. "And had my customers chirping like little birds for a week. *Female* birds!"

Eliana peeked up at Damir. "Did I do that?"

He scratched his forehead. "I seem to remember something along those lines, yes. He's right, in that their voices weren't particularly masculine for a time."

Fareth leaned toward Eliana. "She knows!"

"Well, actually, she doesn't," said Damir. "If you must know—and I gather you must—the Lady Eliana and I had a brief . . . run-in . . . that resulted in the loss of her memory."

Those standing nearest overheard Damir. Several gasped, a few chuckled, and one or two backed up a step as if fearing Eliana's retribution. Eliana's face twisted as she began to sense the depth of her former "mischief." "You have nothing to worry about." She paused, liking their reaction too much to fully assuage it. *"For now.* Apparently, a plot of mine failed and there were unexpected consequences. But after what happened here tonight, I think there's something more important for you all to consider."

"What's that?" said Fareth.

"The Mage Rodern has betrayed Amrodel, harnessed the 'dark current,' and intends to enlist the Norsk legions against this land. That's a little more important than the threat of chirpy voices, I'd say."

The king's mistress, Shaen, got up and gently maneuvered through the crowd. Though she had been seated farther away, she had apparently been trying to overhear their conversation. "I am so relieved to see you, Eliana. We have all been so worried. But what are you doing here? I had thought you were in hiding."

162

"I was in the tower when Rodern caused it to collapse," said Eliana casually. "Damir's shield protected us."

Shaen looked between them. "What were you doing together?"

"Eliana has been staying with me since her cottage was ransacked," said Damir. "We considered it the last place anyone would look for her."

Eliana turned to him. "My cottage was ransacked?"

"I mentioned that before, I think. But I would guess that Rodern was the assailant then, too, and that is why my shield didn't protect your home. You had trusted him, so his arrival caused the area no disturbance. Fortunately, you had already left for your meeting with me."

Shaen moved closer to Damir. "I can't imagine why Rodern would want to enlist the Norsk hordes against us. And why would he attack Eliana?"

"Because he wanted to use me to resurrect the Arch Mage, that's why," said Eliana.

A collective gasp shuddered through the tavern, and the crowd gathered around to stare at Eliana. She glanced at them and shrugged. "That's what he said. I thought he was completely mad, though Damir says it might be possible, because I have both a Mage's *ki* and share the Woodland queen's blood. For this reason, Cahira is also in danger."

Shaen stared at her in astonishment. "Why would he want to resurrect such an evil and dangerous person? I don't understand."

Eliana resisted the impulse to add, *I'm not surprised*, though she wondered at her instant dislike of the meek Shaen. "To connect himself to ultimate power, one supposes. Somehow, he's enlisted the Norsk chieftain, Bruin the Ruthless, and intends to overtake Amrodel with their hordes."

"But Damir's shield will protect us," said Cahira. "Won't it?"

"It should," said Damir. "But as with all magic, my shield has weaknesses, and Rodern had found a way to exclude his tower without my awareness. It may be that he has come up with a way around this, too."

The tavern patrons stared at Eliana in astonishment, then turned to Damir. "What's The Fiend talking about?" asked Fareth.

"Apparently, that is Rodern's plan," said Damir. "He has some reason to believe he can resurrect the Arch Mage using Eliana's *ki* and her heritage from the Woodland queen."

Madawc shoved his way through the crowd, then swigged his ale. "It's possible," he said. "There was even a time when the Council considered killing all blood relatives of the queen to prevent that chance, but it was considered unnecessary since the lineage wasn't direct. I'd still doubt whether just a distant heir would do the trick, but maybe Rodern has reason to think otherwise."

Eliana grimaced. "You were going to *kill* us?"

"That was before my time, lass, and yours," said Madawc, "and wiser Mages prevailed when that suggestion was put out."

"Good. Such a scheme is darkness itself!"

Cahira looked between Damir and Eliana, then sighed and shook her head. "If this is true, then you both have just told everyone secrets that might be better kept to yourself."

Eliana winced. "She has a point, Damir."

Damir considered, but he didn't seem concerned. "What difference does it make now? Your memory condition changes nothing now. Rodern has fled—to Bruin's hold in the Norskland, no doubt. Whatever we do, they know we're aware of their intentions, and that we'll try to stop them any way we can. Sometimes, a battle placed before you is better than maneuverings in the dark."

"I like that," said Cahira. "Not to sneak, but to go forward. To fight!"

"So it comes down now . . . to battle?" asked Eliana.

"If Rodern is a fool, yes," answered Damir.

"This is terrible news," said Shaen, "if we can believe it. I can't imagine how Rodern could come up with such a horrible plan. He once mentioned to me that the Arch Mage, even in his frozen state, still seeks out the woman he lost in order to regain his great power. And we all know that Eliana resembles that queen."

Eliana frowned. "How would you know that, if it was an age ago?"

Shaen eyed her doubtfully. "There are many portraits of the queen in the palace, Lady Eliana. Surely you have seen them? She was a dark-haired woman with features similar to yours—though, of course, no portrait is that detailed."

Eliana's lips twisted in annoyance. "Well, that description fits you, too, so maybe Rodern ought to toss you into the Arch Mage's pit!"

"I wouldn't do, Eliana," said Shaen. "I do not have a Mage's *ki.*"

"I sensed that," said Eliana, and she began to understand why Cahira disliked the woman so much.

Shaen looked hurt, but she turned her attention to Damir. "If Rodern can truly muster the Norsk legions on his behalf, what can we do?"

Everyone in the tavern waited expectantly for Damir's answer, and to Eliana's surprise, he seemed to have one. "I have an idea, but it's risky."

"What is it?" asked Madawc. "You are the strongest among us, and the only warrior, besides Cahira. What would you have us do in the face of a Norsk invasion?"

Damir fingered the hilt of his sword, and for the first time, Eliana saw the light of a warrior in his eyes. "Go out and meet them."

"But we don't have an army," said Shaen. "The Norsk would overwhelm us—they are far more powerful, physically, than the people of the Woodland."

Cahira's eyes glowed as she set aside her milk, and her hand clenched around her bow. "I will go with you."

Damir touched her head. "Not yet, little one. You have much training to do, and raising an army isn't my plan. There are other ways to face an attack."

"How?" asked Madawc.

Damir smiled. "From within."

"You're going alone?" said Shaen, and she placed her hand on his arm. "You can't do that, Damir. Even you can't stand alone against the Norsk warriors. Even if you could defend yourself—and I'm sure you could—they would simply sweep around you, and come after us."

"That is true," he answered, while Eliana fought a desire to swat the woman's hand from his arm. *He is not my husband. I have no right.* "But we know little of the Norsk, save that their chieftain craves power, and is apparently vulnerable to manipulation."

"One person knew them," said Shaen, and she looked to Eliana. "Though I have kept it to myself, the king confessed to me his fears that Eliana was involved with a Norskman. I think it's time she tells us all she knows."

That's it. I kill her . . . Eliana took a step toward Shaen.

The woman eased closer to Damir's side. He did nothing in response, but a smile flickered on his lips. "Unfortunately, Eliana's affliction makes that impossible."

"What affliction?" asked Shaen, her face ripe with concern.

Fareth, the tavern keeper, shoved his way forward. "The Fiend has lost her memory, thanks to her own brew, apparently."

Shaen caught her breath and stared. "Why did you do that?"

Eliana rolled her eyes. "Now, how would I know that?"

"I think I can guess," said Shaen, and she spoke as if her insight grieved her. "It was meant for Damir." She paused and shook her head sadly, then stroked his arm. "She has put you through so much."

"I haven't even begun!" Eliana's voice quavered with fury, and Shaen shrank away from her.

"Are you sure she's forgotten everything?"

"That seems to be the case," said Damir. Eliana's anger soared and aimed itself at him even more than the cowering female at his side. After his myriad deceptions, it seemed only right that he should step forward and defend her now.

Eliana glared at him, then swept a threatening gaze over the crowd. "See here, all of you! I may not remember, exactly, who I was, or what I could do, but that doesn't mean I can't devise a potion that will have you all hopping like little toads!"

Apparently, her threat still had weight, because several bar patrons eased back, and a few even left the tavern. Eliana slapped her hands to her hips. "So you all believe I have some connection to the Norsk." She paused, but only a few dared nod. "*Fine*. Maybe it's true. I assume, by the level and range of your propensity for gossip, that you all assume I had a lover." She paused to glance at Damir. "*Of some sort*. I can't deny it, because I don't remember, but after the treachery I've witnessed among you people, I'll take my own part in this. Furthermore, from what Rodern told me before he collapsed his tower over my head . . ." She left out Damir on purpose. "I gather that the Norsk themselves aren't totally unified. Rodern desperately wanted the name of my 'ally,' which, of course, I wasn't able to provide, but it was obvious that I had refused him before, when still in my full capacity."

To her irritation, Damir was still smiling. He left Shaen's side and took his place beside Eliana. He placed his hand on her shoulder, though she stiffened. "Exactly my thought. It seems to me that is our only hope."

She glanced up at him, confused. "What hope?"

He looked down at her and his dark eyes gleamed. "You and I will go to the land of the Norsk, and find your ally, of course. What else?"

"Did I despise that wench before, too?" Eliana stood glaring at Shaen, her lips curled in a tight frown.

"You didn't like her much, as I recall," said Damir. "This isn't the first time you've threatened her."

"Cahira was right. She is 'nice' to the point of vomitous refuse."

Damir chuckled. "Oddly enough, those are exactly the words you chose after the last Council meeting, when Madawc tried to extol her virtues."

"My memory may be lost, but my instincts remain," said Eliana proudly.

"I see that." An unexpected thought formed in his mind. *I've missed you.* "Although I must confess regret that your sweetness has abated."

She huffed. "It has, and you won't be seeing it again." Damir sighed, but she turned to face him. "When do we start off? On our mission, I mean."

"We must gather gear first, enough for traveling, gold as seems necessary, weapons—and we might do well to visit your own cottage as well and see what we can find there that might be useful."

"You said my cottage was ransacked. What would be left if Rodern destroyed it?"

"Elphin says nothing appeared stolen, and my guess now is that Rodern had hoped to find either some sign of your Norsk friend's identity—or perhaps he meant to seize you as a lure for the Arch Mage. I'm not sure of his purposes, but we might still find items of value."

"I doubt very much I kept love letters!"

Damir looked into her eyes. "You kept something." He

168

GET UP TO
4 FREE BOOKS!

You can have the best romance delivered to your door for less than what you'd pay in a bookstore or online. Sign up for one of our book clubs today, and we'll send you **FREE* BOOKS** just for trying it out...**with no obligation to buy, ever!**

HISTORICAL ROMANCE BOOK CLUB

Travel from the Scottish Highlands to the American West, the decadent ballrooms of Regency England to Viking ships. Your shipments will include authors such as CONNIE MASON, SANDRA HILL, CASSIE EDWARDS, JENNIFER ASHLEY, LEIGH GREENWOOD, and many, many more.

LOVE SPELL BOOK CLUB

Bring a little magic into your life with the romances of Love Spell—fun contemporaries, paranormals, time-travels, futuristics, and more. Your shipments will include authors such as LYNSAY SANDS, CJ BARRY, COLLEEN THOMPSON, NINA BANGS, MARJORIE LIU and more.

As a book club member you also receive the following special benefits:

- **30% OFF all orders through our website & telecenter!**
- **Exclusive access to special discounts!**
- **Convenient home delivery and 10 day examination period to return any books you don't want to keep.**

There is no minimum number of books to buy, and you may cancel membership at any time. See back to sign up!

*Please include $2.00 for shipping and handling.

YES! ☐

Sign me up for the **Historical Romance Book Club** and send my TWO FREE BOOKS! If I choose to stay in the club, I will pay only $8.50* each month, a savings of $5.48!

YES! ☐

Sign me up for the **Love Spell Book Club** and send my TWO FREE BOOKS! If I choose to stay in the club, I will pay only $8.50* each month, a savings of $5.48!

NAME: _____

ADDRESS: _____

_____

TELEPHONE: _____

E-MAIL: _____

☐ I WANT TO PAY BY CREDIT CARD.

☐ VISA   ☐ MasterCard   ☐ DISCOVER

ACCOUNT #: _____

EXPIRATION DATE: _____

SIGNATURE: _____

Send this card along with $2.00 shipping & handling for each club you wish to join, to:

**Romance Book Clubs
20 Academy Street
Norwalk, CT 06850-4032**

Or fax (must include credit card information!) to: 610.995.9274.
You can also sign up online at www.dorchesterpub.com.

*Plus $2.00 for shipping. Offer open to residents of the U.S. and Canada only.
Canadian residents please call 1.800.481.9191 for pricing information.
If under 18, a parent or guardian must sign. Terms, prices and conditions subject to change. Subscription subject to acceptance. Dorchester Publishing reserves the right to reject any order or cancel any subscription.

JOIN NOW!

edged his sword partially from its sheath and indicated the Norsk brooch now embedded in its hilt. "I believe this was a gift, but not from me."

"Another lie." She frowned, but then her face softened. "Then it was him—this mysterious Norskman—who was dear to me, and not you."

Her words stabbed into him like daggers, and he couldn't respond without revealing his emotion. For a moment, he considered telling her the truth—that he cared, and had always cared what she thought and felt for him. But he looked into her bright eyes and he saw The Fiend there, just beyond her awareness. He wanted to cling to the new love he'd found. Instead, he felt himself slipping back into the old patterns between them—a guarded dance where the true pulse of his heart was concealed. He pushed the sword back, and nodded. "It would seem so."

Eliana shook her head. "To think, I was jealous of myself, and over you!" She uttered a disgusted sigh. "And I was about to head back and beg your forgiveness before Rodern stopped me. You certainly made me a fool."

"That wasn't my intention, Eliana."

She glanced up at him. "Wasn't it? I think that's exactly what you wanted when you told me I was your wife."

He hesitated. It had been his plan, at first, and it was hard to deny his motive. "It may be that I wasn't entirely sure what inspired that lie."

She leveled her brow and her lips curled in disgust. "I know. Your feelings are 'complicated.' How tiresome! No wonder I set you on fire!"

He felt hurt, but he didn't want her to know how much he cared now. "You were trying to turn me bright green."

Her mouth twitched at the corners as if she liked the idea. "I can see how that would have been pleasing. You would have resembled a cheerful leaf, or a bright shrubbery."

He frowned. "Or maybe you just meant to kill me."

Her eyes danced with an expression he knew all too well. "I hope the journey to the land of the Norsk isn't overlong. I think it's possible that I will have to devise another method of vengeance, if you irritate me too much along the way."

An old, too-familiar feeling surfaced. "I am armed, Eliana . . ."

Madawc interrupted them. "I see you're getting back to your old selves, lost memory or not," he said, and sighed with exaggerated heaviness. "See that you contain this nonsense—you've got work to do! And a good plan, it is, Damir, though I did think Eliana had been heading toward it before you broke in."

She wasn't, Damir felt sure. But she elevated her perfect little chin and looked proud. "That was exactly my intention. Though I'm not sure I need him to complete the task."

"You need me." Damir's teeth ground together until his jaw ached. "Unless you care to wield this sword yourself?"

"Since it is half of my making, it shouldn't be too difficult!"

"Fine!" He whipped it out of the sheath and jammed it into her little hands. She gripped the hilt, but the weight of the sword proved too much and it sunk to the floor. She struggled briefly to lift it, recognized her lack of strength, then quite obviously pretended she had meant to lean against it.

"I don't need a sword," she said, refusing to meet his eyes.

He offered his most grating smile, then took it from her, swung it easily around and returned it to its sheath. "I thought not."

Her breath came in short, tight puffs, but she turned away from him. Damir fought an unreasonable desire to pull her close and kiss her. Madawc clucked his tongue in disapproval. "I'm thinking I should send someone along with you two."

"Why?" asked Damir. "I don't see what good another person will do against the Norsk."

"Not about the Norsk, boy. But how will we know . . ."

Damir groaned. "Tell me this isn't about your latest wager!"

Madawc didn't answer, and Eliana looked at him suspiciously. "Are we the subject of a wager?"

"More than a few, lass," said Madawc, but he rubbed his chin. "This that's happened, though, it throws off my bet more than a little. I'll have to consider whether to raise, or change it."

Damir found himself surrounded by eager Woodland folk, many of whom had just entered the tavern. He had a dark sense that he knew what they were waiting for. "I'll make this brief. Gather around, all of you." He paused while the crowd pressed in, some with tankards poised at their lips. "As I told Fareth earlier, the Lady Eliana has, by mistake, ingested one of her potions, and has no memory of herself in the past. However, as you have seen, her temperament remains much as it was."

Several sighs of regret sounded at this, and Eliana stiffened, though she kept her chin high.

"That doesn't explain why you're standing there, side by side," said the young barkeep, Alouard.

"Or why she's been staying with you, of all people," added Shaen.

His lips twisted to one side. "In vengeance—my right— for what she tried to do to me, I told her she was my wife . . ." As he expected, the room erupted in hoarse laughter, though Shaen blanched.

"Your *wife?*" she asked after a shocked gasp.

"Yes, my wife." In the back of the room, he noticed several patrons exchanging small bags of gold. "In name only!" The bags were returned to their rightful owners and he shook his head.

"*Well* . . ." Eliana interrupted him, and he looked at her in surprise. She shrugged. "You did express a fairly romantic interest in me. I wouldn't say it was entirely 'in name only.'" Several bags were elevated again at this.

Fareth stepped forward, his own felt bag in hand. "Let's get this straightened up. An awful lot rides on this one . . ." He cast a quick glance at Shaen. "Though the other matter seems settled, and a heap of gold will go to young Elphin once he gets back from the palace, as well as to the Elder Mage, whose winning streak, incidentally, will be tough to match."

"What else do you need to know, Fareth?" said Damir in irritation.

"How far has it gone between you?"

Damir gazed at the ceiling in disbelief. "*That* is none of your concern."

"Quite far," said Eliana. "Although I am still a virgin."

Damir groaned and spun around. "The Fiend would not disclose these details!"

Her green eyes glittered and a little smile curved her devious mouth. "But *I* am the sweet one, remember?"

Fareth smacked his lips, then looked around at his patrons. "Did anyone have a bet on this?" No one responded, and all appeared disappointed. "Very well. We'll take some wagers on their future, then, and leave it at that." He turned back to Damir. "We'll be expecting your honesty in this, Damir ap Kora, and a full report once you get back from the Norskland—assuming you get back alive, that is."

"You'll have mine," said Eliana, and Damir fought a desire to kiss her. All that stopped him was the certain knowledge someone had wagered on him doing so.

"I suppose you'll be betting on whether we come back alive or dead," added Damir, but Fareth looked aghast.

"Of course, not, sir! Life and death, that's just a transition, and one we all must take. But this here, as occupies so much of your time . . ." He paused and smacked his lips. "Sex, now that's a sacred matter, and of concern to everyone."

"An interesting perspective," said Eliana. Her eyes glittered, and she eased away. "If you'll excuse me for a moment . . ." Damir watched as she picked her way to the bar and engaged a nervous Alouard in conversation.

Damir's eyes narrowed. "What is she up to?"

Cahira watched Eliana approvingly. "Lady Eliana is a good woman. I can't imagine why you find her difficult."

"Obviously, she never tried to set you on fire," said Damir, but Cahira eyed him doubtfully.

"She was just trying to turn you green."

Cahira seated herself with Madawc, and they drank from their respective tankards, though Cahira eyed his ale with a degree of longing. For a moment, Damir stood by himself, but Shaen came to his side and placed her hand gently on his arm.

"You must beware of Eliana, Damir," she said softly. "I'm afraid she will hurt you, and despite what little Cahira says . . ." Apparently she'd overheard their conversation. "Eliana hasn't changed, not really. I could see that in the way she looked at me. I know she never liked me, perhaps because I had gained favor with the elder Mage as well as the king. But I never gave her reason for spite."

Damir watched as Eliana wrote something on a small parchment, then gave it to Alouard. She glanced at him over her shoulder and her bright eyes gleamed with challenge. "You don't have to give her a reason. She comes equipped with her own."

Shaen didn't seem to understand his comment, but she offered a sympathetic smile. "I know you have feelings for her. I just want you to be careful."

Damir glanced at Shaen. "Elphin mentioned that you knew Rodern, perhaps, better than some."

No reaction showed on Shaen's face. "I did know him, yes. He had expressed interest in me on several occasions, but I told him I simply didn't share his feelings. He could be persistent, but I never imagined he had turned to such darkness. And the king cares for him so much."

Eliana headed back to Damir, but Shaen remained at his side despite the dark expression on Eliana's face. Eliana looked between them and issued an exaggerated sneer. "Don't tell me. You're warning him about me."

Shaen met her gaze evenly. "I was, Eliana. You have caused Damir so much hurt in the past, and I don't want to see it happen again."

"Well, if he can't survive me, I don't know how he'll stand up to the Norsk."

"The heart, Eliana, is so much more fragile, and even a warrior is vulnerable to its weakness."

"Then I'll remind my Norsk ally to aim for his heart!" Eliana took a step toward Shaen, but Shaen faced Damir, then kissed his cheek.

"If she hurts you, and I fear she will, I hope you remember that I am here." Shaen turned back to Eliana. "I've spoken up for you whenever others speak ill about you, Eliana, and I have tried to be your friend. But your allegiance with this mysterious Norskman, whether you remember him or not, is undoubtedly the reason behind all this trouble. The king has been very concerned about it, though he is desperate to trust you, because you are his niece."

Eliana made a fist. "It's Rodern, and his ally, Bruin the Ruthless, who you should fear, you sneaky little wench. Or are you too dull of wit to recognize the purpose of our journey? My ally, whoever he is, may be the only thing that can save us."

"If anything can," said Shaen. She took Damir's hand

and squeezed it. "Take care, Damir ap Kora. I will suffer sleepless nights until your return."

"I want to kill her." Eliana didn't lower her voice as Shaen returned to her group of friends, who seemed to commiserate with her. "Apparently, she isn't satisfied with just one illicit lover. Now she's after you."

Damir repressed a smile. "At least you're jealous of someone besides yourself this time."

Eliana's green eyes flickered with indignation. "I am not jealous! I am insulted and disgusted, yes, but not jealous. Who you bed is of no concern to me."

"Good, because it's none of your business." She was trembling with anger, and Damir enjoyed her response. "However, you might be relieved to learn that I have not found Shaen an attractive alternative to you, despite her attempts to resemble you."

"She looks nothing at all like me."

"Not up close, and not in the delicacy of her features, no. But she does a good imitation from a distance."

"I will kill her."

Damir kissed her forehead, though he hadn't intended to. "Calm yourself, if it's possible. You and I have other matters to attend." A group of tavern patrons scribbled down what appeared to be notes, and Damir groaned. "Mind your own business!" He glanced back at Eliana. "By the way, what were you doing with Alouard?"

She looked innocent. "Placing a bet, of course. What else?"

"On *us*?"

"Yes, of course."

"I suppose you bet on your own victory."

"To be more precise, it's which of us ultimately yields to the other, and yes, I bet that it would be you." She paused, eyes twinkling. "You're free to place your own wager, you know."

"I am above betting."

"You don't have much confidence, do you?"

Damir marched to the bar, yanked the parchment from Alouard, and wagered the gold he would have won on the king's relationship with Shaen. Eliana waited with her hands on her hips, and she beamed when he returned to her. "I can goad you into anything! No wonder The Fiend made such a pudding of you."

Damir closed his eyes to suppress fury. "You're the one without a memory, woman."

"True, you have me at a disadvantage. For now."

Damir rubbed his forehead. "You were so sweet, so loving . . . now this."

"That was before I knew you lied to me." Her teasing voice altered, and he sensed genuine emotion. "I trusted you. You were all that was real to me. But that is gone now. I have only myself, and the knowledge that I was strong when I was The Fiend. That is something you can't take from me."

"I'm sorry, Eliana. I didn't mean to hurt you. It was just a game, at first, and one we have played many ways before. But for a little while, it was real to me, and you were mine. Can you not understand that for a while, that was all I wanted?"

Her lip quivered, but she bit it hard. "I don't know what to think, or what I feel now."

Damir touched her chin and waited until she met his eyes. "Whatever you truly feel for me, please don't hate me." He felt weak for begging, but her expression turned to kindness, and gave him hope that the sweet Eliana wasn't completely lost.

"I do not think I could hate you, Damir ap Kora. I doubt very much that I ever did."

A boyish smile stole across his face, despite his efforts to contain it. "That has always been my hope."

She seemed suddenly shy and awkward, as if she sensed his feeling for her, and wasn't sure how to react. But if they were to journey to the Norskland together, he had time to regain her trust, and her affection.

Elphin burst into the tavern, his face white with shock. "Madawc," he said, gasping. "Where is the elder Mage?"

"I'm here," said Madawc, and he rose from his seat. "What's ailing you, lad?"

Elphin looked like he wanted to speak, but he saw Cahira, and instead, drew Madawc aside. As they spoke, with Elphin gesturing wildly, Madawc's own face turned ashen. After a moment, he directed Elphin to sit, and the boy sank into a chair with his head in his hands.

Madawc went to Damir, and there were tears in his eyes.

Damir gripped his arm to steady the old man. "What is it, Madawc? What has happened?"

"The king is dead."

Chapter Eleven

Damir's expression revealed all Eliana needed to know. Something dire had occurred, something worse than the betrayal of Rodern. Damir and Madawc made their way through the tavern crowd, and their faces were grim. Damir took Cahira's hand and knelt before her, but he glanced up at Eliana as if to draw courage. Madawc stood beside Eliana, and she saw the glitter of tears in his eyes.

"Something has happened at the palace, Cahira," said Damir, his voice quiet. Cahira's whole body stiffened but she said nothing. A small mustache of milk still dotted her upper lip, and Eliana's heart clenched for her innocence. "Your father has died." Damir's voice caught, and Eliana put her arm over the child's small shoulders. Cahira just stared, then looked from Damir to Madawc.

Despite her age, her voice came even and low. "What happened to him?"

Madawc touched her head in an awkward gesture. "We don't know that for sure."

"He was murdered," she said, her voice still unnaturally even. "By the one who came to take me."

Madawc drew an agonized breath. "That explains why Damir's shield failed. The king trusted Rodern—they had been friends since childhood."

Damir drew a long breath. "There is no magic that can defend against misplaced trust, unfortunately. It has always seemed strange to me that our greatest gift, that of trust, can be the one most easily turned against us." As he spoke, his gaze drifted to Eliana. "And the one too easily used against others, even those we love."

"It is not Damir's fault," said Cahira quietly. "It is mine." She paused, her little face grim and set. "If I had stayed . . ."

Damir squeezed her hand. "No, Cahira. It wasn't your fault. There was nothing you could have done."

Cahira stepped back and elevated her bow, her eyes glittering like fire reflected in a forest pool. "Nothing? I can shoot a nut from a tree, a leaf in the wind. Could I not defend my own father?" Now emotion rose like a great storm, but still, she didn't cry. "I am a warrior, Damir. I was born a warrior. But when my father . . ." Her voice broke, but she didn't stop. "When he needed me, I ran." She closed her eyes and swayed against Eliana. Eliana drew her carefully into her arms, then knelt beside her. Cahira's emotion burst and she flung her arms around Eliana's neck and cried, at last, like the child she was.

Eliana held her as she sobbed, and Eliana cried, too. But then she drew back and eased Cahira's black hair off the girl's face. "You cannot determine the fate of another, Cahira, no matter how painful it is to lose someone. No one can hurt him now."

"He is with my mother," said Cahira softly. "But I will never see him again."

Damir kissed her hand. "He is with you, and if you close your eyes, you will feel him near. Madawc told me this when my parents died, and when I finally dared try, it was true."

Madawc tried to speak, but the old Mage was crying and his voice came ragged with grief. "Damir is right, Mage Child. You are not alone. I will take you to your stepmother and sisters, and you will be safe with them."

Cahira straightened and met his eyes, then shook her head. "No, Elder. I will stay with you. The time of my training has come, my real training. My bow has been a game to me, and I have been playing. But I have a Mage's *ki,* and you must teach me to use it."

Madawc glanced at Damir, but then he nodded. "As you wish, Mage Child. Your *ki* has always been hard for me to read, and I have wondered at the reason. There is something about you that I do not understand, and in study, it will be a lesson for us both."

Shaen rose up from her seat, then swayed as if about to faint. Her friends gathered around her, supporting her as she made her way to Madawc. "Is it true? He is dead?"

"I'm sorry, my dear," said Madawc, and Shaen sank forward into his arms, weeping.

"I can't believe it. I just left him . . . not long ago, to come here with my friends. He was fine."

"Then you saw nothing?" asked Madawc, and Shaen shook her head.

"Nothing. I was getting ready to come here, dressing and fixing my hair . . ."

Eliana eyed her with distaste. "To come to a tavern?"

Shaen glanced at Eliana, stricken, but Eliana wasn't impressed. "I get out so seldom, you see, with so much work to do at the palace. My friends knew how much I needed to have some time for myself." She choked back a sob. "I should never have left him!"

Madawc steadied Shaen as sobs racked her body. "Calm down, my dear. Are you sure you saw nothing, not the Mage Rodern?"

"Rodern?" Shaen wiped away tears, and appeared to struggle with memory. "I might have heard his voice when

I was leaving. But when I came out of my room, I saw another figure, and it wasn't Rodern."

"Who was it?" asked Madawc.

"I didn't see his face, but there was one thing that struck me." She paused, eyes wide. "His hair was pale blond."

Madawc caught his breath. "A Norskman!"

"Thought you'd want to see this, sir," said Elphin. "The guards found it near the king's body. They figure it was used to kill him." He passed Madawc a cloth bundle, which Madawc unwrapped.

Madawc stared at a dark grey dagger, its hilt wrought like a dragon's head. "Norsk-made," he said. "I'll take it back to my cottage and study it further, though this is a common enough weapon, even in the Woodland."

Cahira tensed, then struggled to her feet. "I will kill them all!"

Shaen spotted Cahira, then bent tearfully to hug her. "I'm so sorry, my precious child. This is the most terrible thing that has happened to me, and to you. We will get through it together."

Eliana braced, disliking the woman despite her outpouring of grief. "Cahira will live with the elder Mage." She paused. "And a Norskman couldn't have murdered the king. Damir has shielded the palace, and the king certainly wouldn't have trusted a blond assailant."

Shaen looked sadly at Eliana. "Ever you defend the Norsk, Eliana, even after this. Why?"

"It seems reasonable," said Eliana. "It's a fairly obvious cheat to place a Norsk dagger near the king's body. But Damir's shield wouldn't have allowed a Norsk assassin into the forest, let alone into the king's palace."

"Nothing can be certain now, Eliana, not even Damir's shield," said Shaen miserably.

"You don't think anyone in Amrodel would have noticed a blond fellow ambling about?"

Shaen's eyes darkened, and Eliana wondered if anyone else noticed the contrast between the woman's grief and her thinly veiled anger. "I assume he was in hiding."

"But not from you."

Shaen turned to Madawc, her expression pleading. "I only caught a glimpse of him, from behind. I could be wrong. At the time, I thought his hair color might be a trick of the light, or he was an older man, with white hair like you."

Eliana frowned. "Then I hardly think you can say a Norskman killed the king."

"They have tried before," said Shaen. "Everyone knows that Bruin the Ruthless had a vial of your most deadly potion, and intended to use it against the king."

Eliana glanced at Damir. "Is this true?"

"It is true that he obtained a vial of a strong sleeping potion, and that you provided an antidote. But there is no proof he intended to use it on the king. And, in fairness, it is hardly the usual method of the Norsk. They prefer axes in battle, not potions."

"I can't explain it, either," said Shaen. "But I could tell the king was concerned."

"You seem to think you know what is on all our minds," said Eliana. "But if you knew mine, you'd run from here, screaming . . ."

Cahira came to Damir's side and tugged on the hem of his shirt. "I want to go with you, Damir. I have my bow, and I'm a good shot. I want to fight the Norsk."

"Eliana is right, Cahira," said Damir. "We don't know yet who killed your father. It is wrong to fight in anger. You must learn to develop your *ki,* and to find balance in yourself before you can direct your energy. Madawc will teach you, and your time will come."

She looked small and young, and he took her hand. "Your father loved you, Cahira, and he was very proud to have such a brave daughter. You will honor that, and one day, you will help to restore the balance of this land."

She nodded, but Eliana could see the shock of her loss was beginning to set in. Madawc placed his arm over her shoulder. "When the sun rises tomorrow, we will perform the ritual of release for the king's spirit. Then I will take the Mage Child to her stepmother and sisters. Then, when you're ready, we will commence with training."

Shaen reached to touch Cahira's hair. "I should go with her. She needs a woman's comfort."

Madawc eyed her doubtfully. "I think, considering the circumstances, it would be best if you did not, Shaen."

Shaen bit her lip as if she'd only just realized the potential trouble caused if the new mistress went to the home of the bereaved wife. "Perhaps you are right. But I would be happy to offer my help once Cahira is in your care."

"That is good of you, my dear," said Madawc, and Cahira seemed too stunned by the loss of her father to object. Madawc turned to Damir. "I'll take the Mage Child now, and I will keep her safe."

Damir knelt before Cahira, and he whispered a soft chant in his father's language, then looked into her eyes. "I have shielded you from all harm, but you must beware in whom you place your trust, for I cannot protect you from those you allow close of your own will."

"I trust no one, save you, the elder Mage, and Eliana. You have my word."

"You are a wise child," said Damir. Very gently, he kissed her forehead, and when she looked up, she was no longer free of the world's sadness, yet Eliana saw a strength that seemed beyond the reach of Cahira's years.

"You be careful, too, Damir. I know you will take care of Eliana, though. And she will take care of you." Her small face knit and her eyes burned. "When you find the person who killed my father, make him pay."

"I will," said Damir. "You have my word."

Madawc left with Cahira, and soon after, Shaen's friends led her away, presumably to stay with them rather than return to the palace. Damir went to Elphin and seated himself by the boy. Eliana started to follow, then decided to give them this time alone. She watched as Damir offered comfort, and she saw Elphin respond. She liked his kindness, with Cahira and now with Elphin. Yet where had that sensitivity been when she woke in his bed, alone and afraid, with no memory of herself?

True, she had, according to him, brought this fate on herself, and it did seem in character for the woman known as "The Fiend." But couldn't he have told her she was a chipmunk instead of his wife? Eliana considered this. He had intended to make love with her, then discovered her virginity, which he hadn't expected. For some reason, that had stopped him. So his vengeance had limits.

Alouard brought Elphin an overflowing tankard of ale, and Fareth delivered a bag of coins, which Elphin assessed with restored happiness. Damir slapped him on the back, and returned to Eliana as the boy counted his gold.

Eliana looked around at the tavern crowd, and for a moment, she seemed lost, like a stranger in a new land. "I do not understand this. Their king has died, yet they go on as if nothing had happened."

"They know what has happened. For Cahira, they will perform rituals in private, to give her strength and their support. And tomorrow at dawn, they will gather together as they honor the release of the king's spirit. If a person's life is cut short, that ritual takes place at dawn. If they have lived to the fullness of age, it commences with the sunset. For the Woodland people, death is not viewed as an ending, but as a transition to a form that allows freedom and peace. Though his ending was cruel, we know that Owain Daere is safe now. Even Cahira knows it. It is one of the great strengths of the Woodland that we do not fear death, but accept it, even as we accept life."

"What is the weakness, then?" asked Eliana.

"I think, in the end, our fear is greater. We fear ourselves."

The tavern patrons began to desert the bar, and the big stone fireplace burned low. Fareth the innkeeper yawned, and offered a pointed look at Damir. "It worries me to leave the two of you alone in my gathering room, considering what you've done to the Mage's tower."

Eliana looked at him in surprise, but Damir frowned. "As has been previously detailed, the fault of the Mage's tower wasn't ours." He glanced out the thick pane windows and saw that the rain still fell in heavy currents. "It's a long walk home."

Fareth eyed him doubtfully. "Didn't you bring that magnificent horse of yours? Sling The Fiend over his back, and head off home!"

"As it happens, I was in too great a hurry to . . ." Damir glanced at Eliana and felt an unexpected shyness, "to deal with the situation at the tower, and didn't have time to retrieve Llwyd."

Eliana's brow angled. "You mean, you were in a hurry to rescue me."

"That, too." He didn't look at her. He didn't have to. He knew exactly the expression on her little face.

Fareth dusted his large hands on his apron. "Well, then . . ." He paused and smacked his lips. "It *is* a darksome night, what with walking in the rain and all, and the two of you all bruised up from whatever you did to the tower. Might be you'd care to rent one of my guest rooms?"

Damir hesitated, then glanced at Eliana, who also appeared pensive. "What do you think?"

"Do you have a room for each of us?" she asked, and Damir's heart fell. It wasn't the answer he wanted to hear, though he wasn't sure what he'd expected.

"No, I do not," said Fareth. Damir didn't detect the slightest trace of deceit in his voice, but knew just as well that the innkeeper was lying. Fareth gestured at the rainy night. "Thanks to this here downpour, several folks already booked my rooms, and you two are lucky to get this offer at all." He paused. "Normally, I wouldn't cotton to The Fiend spending two minutes in one of my rooms, figuring on what she'd do to it, but in her current state, with you keeping such a close eye on her, I'll take the risk."

Eliana glared. "You do not have to speak as if I'm not here! And I recognize this as a trick, your perverse way of placing myself with Damir on behalf of what, presumably, is your own wager." Eliana marched to the tavern door and yanked it open. She looked up into the black sky, and rain pelted her face. She held the posture a moment longer, then retreated back into the inn. "Very well, we accept your offer, and will spend the night in your guest room. I assume it has two beds?"

"It has one. A small one."

"I knew that," said Eliana. "I shouldn't have bothered to ask." She paused. "Fine!"

Damir angled his head. "What makes you think I'll agree to this?"

"Take a step outside, and you'll see the wisdom of my decision."

Droplets fell from Eliana's hair and her cape was already wet. "I see your point. We'll take the room. It will be a good start on our journey—we'll have nights in the wilderness, anyway, so we might as well get used to it."

She bit her lip. "Are there taverns on the way to the Norskland?"

"A few," said Fareth. "Not many as good as The Hungry Cat, but you'll find passable fare if you head first to

Amon-dhen. Farther north, there are inns, of a sort, though you might want to skip those."

"Why?" asked Eliana. "Surely it's better to sleep in an inn than to make camp in the wilderness?"

"Clearly, you haven't seen, or don't remember, the taverns north of Amon-dhen," said Damir. "They're run mainly by Norsk traders and Guerdians, and if you can endure the drunken brawls, the noise, and the violence, the filth of the places should be enough to make the wilderness an appealing bed."

"We'll deal with that when we come to it, then," said Eliana. "For now, I am tired, and I'm sore, and I want to go to sleep."

He hadn't considered that she might be injured, and he looked at her more closely. "I didn't ask if you were injured. My shield should have kept you from all harm."

Her lips twisted to one side as she struggled against exaggeration. "I don't believe the tower's collapse injured me, in particular. But it has been a long day."

"It has," said Damir. "We will rise with the sun to bid the king farewell, and that leaves us only a few hours of sleep. And we're both exhausted." He added this with a pertinent glance Fareth's way, but the innkeeper didn't comment.

Fareth led them to a small room at the back of the inn, though Damir noticed they passed several that were clearly unoccupied—and equipped with several beds. Fareth pretended not to notice those, though he quickly closed the doors as they passed.

He directed them into their room, which indeed had a small bed, and also a low-burning fireplace. He administered a doubtful glance at Eliana, then turned to Damir. "See that she doesn't cause trouble. Never trust The Fiend, memory or not, I say!"

Fareth left, and Eliana glared at the closed door. "I haven't heard that I did anything in my past that warrants this hostility!"

"A man whose voice sounded like a woman's for a week is unlikely to be forgiving," said Damir.

"Was Fareth one of them?" she asked.

Damir smiled. "With his large frame, he was particularly unsuited to the sound."

"Did this potion of mine affect you, too?"

"As it happens, I escaped that particular brew. And for once, I don't believe it was aimed at me. One or other of them had offended you—stars knows why. Perhaps you'd learned of their penchant for betting."

"Then I had good reason," said Eliana, but she yawned. "It is good to have a bed, but I miss your pleasant bathing facilities."

"You always did covet my bathing area," he said, and he couldn't restrain the element of longing that crept into his voice.

"Did I?" Eliana seated herself on the bed, then pulled off her cape and tossed it over a nearby chair. "Why didn't I have something similar?"

"I'm not sure. You had a little bathing tub, quite big enough for you, and Madawc fixed it with hot water."

Eliana removed her overdress, adjusted her chemise, then crawled into the bed. She folded her arms behind her head and gazed thoughtfully at the ceiling as she pondered the matter. Then she nodded as if it had resolved itself to her satisfaction. "I suppose you gloated over yours."

He had, mercilessly. "Not at all."

Eliana smiled, her expression knowing, and her eyes drifted shut. Damir stood in the center of the guest room. He felt uncharacteristically uncomfortable, though he wasn't sure why. Even more strange, Eliana seemed completely at ease. He removed his own cape, folded it, then placed it first on a bench, then on a higher table. Eliana opened her eyes and watched him, her brow knit in confusion.

"What are you doing?" she asked.

"My cape is still damp—from the rain," he added, and he realized he offered unnecessary information because of his nervousness.

She eyed him doubtfully. "Then hang it—there's a hook on the door."

He nodded. "I didn't see that." Damir hung his cape, fiddled with it, then considered his shirt. He glanced back at Eliana, but her eyes were closed, and mercifully, she didn't seem aware of his discomfort.

This is ridiculous . . . Damir removed his shirt and hung it next to his cape. He patted his leggings, and found them also still damp. He couldn't very well take them off. He hesitated, then pulled back the quilt on the other side of the bed.

Eliana peeked at him. "You're not going to wear those into bed, are you? You'll get the bed wet!"

Damir puffed a breath of frustration. "Well, what would you suggest?"

She rolled her eyes, sat up, then reached to extinguish the lantern beside her bed. She flopped back into bed, then curled up on her side, facing away from him. "Now I won't see a thing—not that I haven't seen you naked before. Calm yourself, Damir ap Kora. I am too sleepy to ravage you tonight."

He stood beside the bed, holding the quilt elevated in his surprise, and he stared at her shadowy form in the darkness. He opened his mouth to speak, but no words came. Damir hesitated, then dropped his leggings and eased into bed beside her. He cleared his throat. "I wasn't worried about that." He paused, and he heard a small huff from her direction. Damir settled in, but couldn't make himself comfortable. "I just didn't want to make you uncomfortable."

"Then stop talking and go to sleep."

"Fine . . ." He paused. "Good night, Eliana."

She glanced over her shoulder. "Good night, Damir."

189

He lay beside her, listening to her breaths as they grew increasingly heavy and deep. He wondered if she felt any residual desire for him, then reasoned she was probably too tired to feel anything. She hadn't expressed as much anger as he'd feared, though her distrust was obvious. Yet she seemed to understand the nature of their past relationship, and accept that it had been almost a game between them.

This didn't satisfy Damir. He wanted more than what they'd known in the past. He wanted what they'd discovered, briefly, when she thought she was his wife. Damir rolled onto his side, away from her. He lasted a moment only, then flipped to his other side so he could watch her in the dim light of the low hearth.

The firelight cast a soft, warm glow on the waves of her hair, and he fought a desire to sift its tangled mass through his fingers. Only hours ago, they'd sat on his couch, her head on his shoulder, as he'd done exactly that. Until she grew jealous of herself and ran off into the night. Until a tower had crumbled over their heads. Until the King had died.

Damir closed his eyes. He didn't like to think of death, but he felt the bitter pang of remorse that his attention had focused on the woman he wished were his lover, and not on the loss of a kind man. Owain Daere had left life behind—as Cahira had said, he was with her mother now, the woman he had truly loved. Life went on, but for Owain, Damir knew there was contentment.

Loneliness was bitter—and though the king had known many lovers, he had always pined for that one. This was something Damir understood too well. He thought of Cahira, and his heart ached. The firelight faded almost to nothing as the darkness of the night moved in around him.

He had made many mistakes. He should have carried Eliana to Madawc and been honest about the effect of her "Wine of Truce."

But for a little while, he had tasted the life he wanted, with a woman he adored at his side, sharing his life, sharing hers. He squinted, and realized to his horror that tears stung his eyes. Damir swallowed to contain his emotion, but Eliana rolled over to face him. She drew a soft breath, then slipped her arm over his shoulder. To his astonishment, she moved close to him and gently kissed his cheek.

"You and I can resume our battle tomorrow," she whispered. "But you don't have to grieve alone tonight."

Damir lay stunned as she wrapped her arm around him, but he knew what she offered this night wasn't sexual. He drew her close and held her against his body, and he kissed her forehead. "Thank you." And in her arms, he let himself drift into sleep.

The sun broke over the eastern horizon, and the people of the Woodland chanted in one voice as its rays cut through the high tree branches. Damir stood beside Eliana in the wide glade before the palace, and he felt the power of the joined souls as they bade farewell to their king. Cahira clasped Eliana's hand and tears glistened on her cheeks, but her high voice rose above the others as the chant turned to song, and the Woodland minstrel played a harp, joined again by musicians with smaller lyres, and the bard, Rhys, added his aged but powerful voice to Cahira's.

A soft mist rose softly through the trees and surrounded the people, and Damir felt the spirit of their king among them. Cahira's stepmother and her older sisters had come to bid the king farewell. Shaen stood apart from them, though Damir had seen her greet them with surprising warmth.

Cahira stepped forward and held out her arms in farewell. "My father," she said, her voice trembling but strong, "I thank you for your time among us. I love you very much." She paused. "And I'm sorry I didn't protect you. I will never fail that way again."

There were no words to comfort her. Cahira would choose her own path, and Damir couldn't alter its course for her. But his heart ached at her grief, and at the remorse he recognized, for he had felt the same, long ago. Cahira lowered her arms, her vow complete, and the Woodland voices faded into a quiet chorus, *"Farewell, farewell . . . We shall meet again, across a distant sea, and live again in light . . . Farewell . . ."*

Damir closed his eyes, and in his mind, he saw the king, a delicate, young spirit as he rose up into the light, and then sailed into its midst. The king had gone on, and those remaining were left to follow their own paths. It was understood in Amrodel, as in no other land, that both life and death followed individual paths, but it didn't make the parting easier for those left behind.

The crowd dispersed quietly, but Madawc stayed behind with Damir and Eliana. "It is a path we all must take," he said quietly. "And each time, it is new." He looked between Eliana and Damir. "But you two, at least, will make the time on this side of the light interesting— for us all."

"I hope we will make it safe, at least," said Damir.

Madawc clasped his shoulder. "If anyone can, it's you, Damir ap Kora. You have a great power within you. You've never had to really use it before, and maybe it's never fully been tested. But don't rely on your strength as a warrior, only. It's your heart that takes you beyond."

Damir glanced at Eliana. She was looking up at him, her face pensive in the morning light. "I have not always listened to its wisdom," he said.

"I know that," said Madawc. "Don't let fear determine your fate, either of you. Go forward, and trust your hearts, and you'll find the wisdom to face Rodern and whatever he has planned. You'll find the wisdom to set the Norsk back where they belong."

192

"It would help if I had some idea of what Rodern intends," said Damir.

"Go first to the seaport of Amon-dhen," said Madawc. "Rodern went there more often than the rest of us, and its likely he found his Norsk contacts there first, and then reached the ear of Bruin. It's a good idea to go there for supplies, anyway, since you'll be needing more than the Woodland can offer in the way of warm clothing and traveling gear."

"The road, such as it is, strikes north from Amon-dhen, so that was my plan," said Damir. "But if Rodern had contacts there, we might learn even more of good use before we ride onward to the iceland of the Norsk."

"Bruin inhabits a village near the heart of the Norskland," said Madawc. "So assuming he's not off pillaging one of his neighbors, you should find him there."

"But what about my supposed 'ally'," asked Eliana. "How will we know where to find him? Can we be sure he's even with Bruin?"

"We can't be sure of anything, lass," said Madawc. "And with you not remembering, you'll have to rely on your instincts in this. But if you don't recognize this fellow, my guess is that he'll know you."

Damir frowned, which both Madawc and Eliana noticed. Eliana cocked her head to the side and placed her hand on her hip. "That is what we're hoping, isn't it?"

"On the hope this man is in some way trustworthy, yes," agreed Damir. "As I said last night, it is a risky plan."

"It seems wise to me," said Eliana. No, she wasn't going to make this easy for him. She had to keep reminding him, subtly, of this other man's presence in her life and her heart. It looked to be a very long journey ahead.

Cahira came out of the palace again, her bow over her shoulder, and she took Damir's hand. "I know I can't go with you," she said. "I wish I could. But Shaen says that is not my place, and I suppose she's right." Cahira paused. "I still don't like her much," she added, but it seemed to Damir that she had softened somewhat on the matter of her father's mistress. "But she has been very kind to my stepmother and my sisters, and I think they've forgiven her somewhat."

"Shaen is especially kind when others are suffering," said Madawc. "I believe your stepmother understands that her marriage wasn't as it should have been. Perhaps there need be no ill will over . . . other arrangements."

Cahira turned to Eliana. "Shaen asked me to apologize to you, Lady Eliana."

"No, Cahira . . . that is for me to do. I was wrong to ask you to speak for me." Shaen appeared behind them, her head bowed as if in shame. She faced Eliana, who looked stiff and uncomfortable as Shaen seized her hand. "And I was unfair to you, Eliana, but only after this long, terrible night, have I finally come to understand why."

Eliana's eyes shifted and she hesitated before answering. "Why?"

"You are only a few months younger than I am," said Shaen. "But when we were children, I so desperately wished I had your power. I used to imagine that I was a Mage, like you and Damir, and I even believed it for a while. But during my brief studies with the elder Mage, I came to realize I could never equal your power." She paused, and offered an embarrassed smile. "Perhaps that's why I've tried to dress like you. It was pure fantasy, nothing more. But I always did wish I could be like you, and I hoped I could be your friend. I hope you will forgive me if my words last night were harsh."

To Damir's surprise, Eliana patted Shaen's hand. "That is very brave of you to say, Shaen. And I am sorry if I wronged you in the past, by acts I no longer recall, and for my behavior last night. But I see this has been a difficult time for you."

Shaen seemed to blossom with Eliana's acceptance, and she hugged Eliana tight, tears on her cheek. "Thank you, Eliana. You are a truly loving, accepting person, underneath. As I'm sure everyone has guessed, the king and I had a . . . special relationship, but I know I wasn't truly in love with him. I just wanted to feel important, too."

Damir stared at her in amazement. "Such honesty honors you, and the king, Shaen," he said, and she smiled sadly at him.

"I had always hoped to win the heart of a man as powerful as yourself, Damir. But I can see your happiness lies elsewhere." As she spoke, Damir recognized an unfamiliar sensation that he had experienced before with Shaen—it was as if she looked through him, almost as if trying to see another who was standing behind him. Maybe he sensed she had wanted to attach herself to his power, and not to him, but it was a strange realization, and he wasn't entirely sure what it meant.

Shaen turned again to Eliana. "Thank you for your understanding, Eliana. I wish you luck against the Norsk, and I hope you will take care. They are very dangerous, and cruel. You will need all your power against them."

She kissed Eliana's cheek, then went with Cahira back into the palace. Eliana shifted her weight. "There's something I didn't expect."

Damir smiled. "Nor I, though I confess, it was your reaction that surprised me most."

Eliana frowned. "I couldn't very well refuse her apology, could I? And it seemed sincere enough."

"It did," he agreed. As he spoke, several dragonflies entered the clearing, darting and circling in the morning light. Eliana watched them, but then she closed her eyes and seemed to enter a trance. The dragonflies circled around her as Damir and Madawc watched in astonishment.

Eliana opened her eyes, and a strange light gleamed in her eyes. "I heard her voice—they brought her to me!"

"The dragonflies?" asked Damir.

"Whose voice?" asked Madawc, his expression ripe with suspicion.

"The spirit of the Woodland queen," guessed Damir.

Eliana nodded excitedly. "Yes, in a way—they carry her message. She says there is a greater power than yours, Damir, for it does not seek balance as you do, and in it, the light holds no sway. She speaks of *him*, and she says his power is greater than we know, and that we cannot fully understand his lure, for we have not given ourselves over to that darkness. But a person who seeks his power will stop at nothing to reach it, to attach to him. You and I stand in the way of this." Eliana paused, her eyes wide. "And she says we cannot stop it."

Madawc seized Eliana's shoulder. "It is a dark voice you hear, lass. Pay it no heed."

Eliana shook her head. "No . . . you don't understand. It wasn't dark, though the message was foreboding. She says there is hope, if we follow our course, and she says a path is laid before us, if we find balance in ourselves. But she warns that even our victory is not enough to stop his return. Yet in victory, we will win what is most valuable for the future of the Woodland, and for all."

"What is that?" asked Damir.

She looked up at him, her green eyes wide and shocked. "*Time*. Time for another to rise, the one who must face him. The one she speaks of, Damir, is the opposite force of the Arch Mage's energy. As the Arch Mage is pure darkness, this one is pure light."

A chill coursed through Damir. "No Mage has ever been pure light, even the Woodland queen herself. Among the youngest of the Mundanes, there is pure light, but no power, certainly not to balance the dark power of the Arch Mage. What other kind of 'pure light' is there?"

Madawc looked between them. "The Mage Child's *ki* is unlike any I've encountered before, and it will take time before she is old enough to direct its power. But in any case, a Mage's *ki* is formed from a balance between both darkness and light. Even the Arch Mage began with light. He was known once as 'Cheveyo,' which meant 'Spirit Warrior' in the tongue of his people. But when he turned to darkness, they called him 'Matchitehew Otaktay,' for 'Evil Heart that Kills Many.' Within all who have great power, is also the potential for great evil. For this reason, 'pure light' is not possible in any Mage—I doubt this prophecy refers to Cahira." Madawc paused, and his doubt echoed Damir's own. "But if neither of you who are strongest among us, are 'pure light,' then who is?"

Chapter Twelve

"So, this is my cottage?" Eliana looked around and felt a wave of sadness at the upturned chairs and broken table of what had once been her home.

"It was," said Damir. "Though it little resembles the neat—overly neat—dwelling that you kept so perfectly."

"Was I overly neat?" she asked.

He huffed. "Not when we were children, no. But when you claimed this little cottage as your own, you lost an element of sanity." Damir glanced at her. "Do you think the Woodland queen's spirit—or her dragonflies, or whatever spoke to you—was she referring to Rodern as the 'one who seeks power?'"

"I don't know," said Eliana. "Perhaps. But what I sensed was an element of . . ." She paused and fidgeted. "Well, of lust."

Damir grimaced. "I cannot think Rodern lusted for the Arch Mage."

"He did speak of the Mage in an odd way," said Eliana. "Something about *'Wake me, serve me.'* I thought he was mad when he said that."

"Still, I wouldn't term it as 'lust.'"

"My sense was of lust disguised as love."

"Even less likely," said Damir. "The Arch Mage was notorious in his exploits with women. And Rodern has dallied with females only, to my knowledge. I think you misunderstood the dragonflies, my lady."

Eliana angled her brow, wondering at Damir's reaction. "Or they didn't refer to Rodern. From what he said to me in the tower, I had the distinct impression he wasn't alone in his efforts to resurrect the darkness."

"I wonder who it is that the Arch Mage's soul is reaching for?"

"I am under the impression someone is reaching for him," said Eliana. "And yet, I sense from the queen's spirit that she expects him to return, that the darkness in some other person seeks him, and, in a sense, he is using that person's lust to bring about his resurrection."

"Such people are drawn to the darkness, because they are consumed with that darkness themselves, though they lack his power," added Damir. "Could it be Bruin the Ruthless? Though the people of Amrodel, and my father's homeland of Kora, have the Mage's *ki,* no Norskman has anything but the simplest energy. He might seek to supplant his own with dark power."

"I suppose so," said Eliana. "But it makes no difference now. We must follow our course as it is set before us."

"Prophetic words, my lady," said Damir. "I had not remembered you were so fateful of nature before." He paused. "I wonder how your Wine of Truce fits into all this, if indeed our paths are already set?"

Eliana pondered the matter. "Our natures were set, that is certain, so what I attempted to do to you, and what you did to me, were simply turns along the same river. So my loss of memory must be part of this course."

"You're accepting it better than I'd hoped."

Eliana shrugged. "It seems I brought it on myself. And

you did what was within your nature. However twisted."

Damir frowned. "I don't consider my actions particularly 'twisted.'"

"They weren't particularly light."

"Nor was trying to rob me of my memory!"

"If that's what I was really trying to do . . ." Eliana had inwardly accepted that it was, but she liked seeing Damir irked.

"What else?"

She had no idea, so she gestured around the room. "Didn't you want to look for items of value?"

"Indeed. We might find some devious potion to use upon the Norsk."

"I imagine it will take more than making their voices high," said Eliana. "But I'll see if I feel any reaction to anything."

Eliana picked through the scattered items on her floor. Occasionally, she spotted a vial or a bottle that drew her attention, and she stuffed each into her pack. Damir rifled through an overturned wardrobe closet and tossed everything that might be useful for traveling onto her tiny bed. Eliana eyed the little bed. "How did you ever imagine I had a vast assortment of lovers when I had only this small bed?"

"The size of your bed, my lady, only served to fire my fantasies."

Eliana shook her head. "I do not understand . . ." He started to speak, but she held up her hand. "I don't want to know." She spotted a well-worn pair of leggings, made of soft brown and green, matched with a fitted bodice. Eliana beamed. "Indeed, I had traveling clothes, and no foolish gown to hinder me!"

Damir eyed her doubtfully. "I don't recall any such garment." He paused. "Though it might be interesting to see you in it."

"And comfortable," added Eliana. She seized the leggings and bodice, as well as a full white shirt, then motioned for Damir to turn his back while she changed into them. "There! What do you think?"

He turned around, skeptical, but then his dark eyes widened and he swallowed. "No wonder you never wore that around Amrodel!"

"Why?" She felt deflated. "Do I look foolish?"

"You look . . . delectable," he responded, and his voice sounded hoarse. Damir shook his head. "It fits perfectly. There, around your little backside, especially."

Eliana blushed. "Maybe I should choose something else."

"No!" He cleared his throat. "This is most practical, since we'll be riding."

Eliana studied her reflection in a polished, oval mirror that seemed overlarge for her bedroom. "I think it makes me tougher, more formidable, don't you?"

He nodded eagerly. "Formidable, yes." He paused. "If we reach the taverns near Norskland, you might put a dress on over it."

"Why? That's when I'll need to appear most dangerous!"

Damir stuffed her red velvet dress into her pack. "Just in case."

Eliana frowned and pulled the dress out of the pack again. "It's heavy enough already. If you stuff this one in there, I won't have room for more important items."

Damir frowned, but Eliana had already turned her attention to a pair of leather boots with laces that crisscrossed nicely. She pulled those on instead of her light shoes. "I suppose we'll need to bring extra clothing for warmth?"

"Unfortunately, neither one of us has suitable clothes for the Norsk weather," said Damir. "But we'll go first to the seaport of Amon-dhen, and find wares from the Norsk trader shops. They raise sheep in the Norskland. That's one thing I envied of the Norsk—their great, heavy coats made of shearling. We'll find something there, and warmer boots, too."

"And mittens," said Eliana. "I would like a pair of fleece mittens."

Damir smiled, and she wondered at the change in his expression. "It is funny you should mention that," he said. "When you were small, you had a pair of fluffy mittens, which you wore even after the cold weather passed. You were very proud of them. I believe they were a gift from your parents."

Eliana felt sad, though she couldn't remember the time of which he spoke. "What happened to them?"

Damir fidgeted and looked extremely guilty. "I don't remember, exactly."

Eliana read his expression too easily. "Why would you destroy my mittens?"

"I didn't mean to!" He winced. "I threw you into a lake, and didn't realize your mittens were in your pack."

"What were you trying to do to me? Drown me?"

"No, just get you wet. But instead . . ." He stopped and sighed. "Instead, I destroyed the one thing you treasured."

"I see."

"I tried to fix them, after you'd gone. But the water had ruined them."

Eliana studied his face as their past together grew clearer. "Where did I go?"

"As I remember, you went screaming to Madawc. I was duly punished, by the way."

"Whipped?"

"Denied the pie he'd made for dinner," said Damir, and he sounded sheepish.

"What a sacrifice! I should have gotten something of yours!"

"Just what you said at the time." Damir paused, and he looked wistful. "I kept them for a long time, in secret, trying to use my *ki* to mend them. But instead, I dissolved them. I assumed you wouldn't understand that, so I gave up my efforts."

"Did I know you tried to fix them?" asked Eliana.

"No."

"Did you apologize?"

"Yes . . . under Madawc's orders, so I don't think it had much meaning to you."

"But you were sorry, weren't you?"

"I never meant to hurt you, Eliana. Drive you crazy, yes, but I would never have destroyed something that important to you."

"Then I forgive you now, Damir ap Kora."

He looked surprised, but a shy smile formed on his lips. "I have waited a long time for that."

"For the mittens only," she added. "I'm not sure yet about the wife business, and . . . other matters."

"The mittens issue is a good start," said Damir. He looked around her little cottage. "I'm sorry this happened to your home. When we return, I will help you set it to rights."

"Like my mittens." Eliana's heart warmed. "I hope you don't dissolve my cottage, too."

When they had searched through her cottage thoroughly, and found nothing else of use for their journey, Eliana followed Damir back out into the sun. "My cottage isn't as grand as yours," she said as she looked around. "I like that yours has a clearing, and a view, but this is very . . . protected. I must have felt safe here, in amongst the trees, with my herbs growing everywhere." She had planted several herb gardens in different shapes and lined with small rocks, and all seemed to have a theme and a purpose. "I see that, in fact, I didn't require my herbs to 'grow naturally,' as you told me."

Damir seized Llwyd, who was grazing from Eliana's

herb garden. "I hope you're not going to bring up every little distortion I might have told you."

Eliana led Selsig to a large rock that seemed placed just for the purpose of mounting. "I am trying to sort out what is true, and what you made up to confuse me."

Damir mounted and waited as Eliana climbed astride her mare. "Lies build upon each other, unfortunately," he said. "They became interwoven in an effort to explain the inconsistencies that arose with making you my 'wife.'"

Eliana sighed. "I expect marriage is never as easy as it sounds."

They rode off, down and away from her little cottage. Eliana looked back before they rounded a corner. Once, this had been her home, but she didn't remember it. She must have picked her way up this winding hill, walking or on her fat mare, alone, her thoughts bent on some scheme or plot against Damir. Or maybe she had been thinking of the mysterious Norskman with whom she had formed a secret alliance. *I wonder who he is.*

Had she really been in love with him, this stranger she couldn't remember? And if not, what could have mattered so much that she might have betrayed her own people for the sake of his? Eliana faced forward again, as they rode around the corner, cutting her cottage from view. Damir rode ahead, borne by Llwyd's long stride. Selsig jigged to catch up, but Eliana found the mare's gait even and soon got used to the light trot.

They rode in silence, and Damir also seemed deep in thought. Before going to her cottage, they had first returned to his cottage for his gear and the horses. He had selected a rolled-up map, and planned their journey accordingly. After this stop at her old home, they would make for Amon-dhen for further supplies. He had also provided her with a light dagger, which fit in a small sheath at her side. Eliana felt lonely, and she missed his conversation, so when the path widened, she urged her mare into a canter and rode up beside Llwyd.

Damir glanced down at her. "It's a long way, Eliana. Two days to Amon-dhen, and rest for our horses. Don't wear her out too early."

"Selsig is fine," said Eliana. "I expect she's much sturdier than your overly large horse, because her legs are shorter."

"But she's fatter, so she has more to carry."

Eliana frowned. "Never mind that." She fingered the dagger hilt. "You didn't tell me about my new weapon. Does it have magic, too, like your sword?"

"Not like the sword, no. But it should have power."

"Such as what?"

"When you want to reach something—or someone—it will give you added power to do so—if your heart directs. But I made it when I was mad at you—I don't remember why—so I expect it's filled with all the infuriating qualities you can muster."

Eliana urged Selsig forward, past him. "I find you infuriating, too."

Llwyd eased back up beside Selsig, but the little mare fixed her small ears forward in a determined stance and widened her stride, with what must have been great effort. "She's faster than she looks," said Damir.

"She's a creature of the Woodland, like me," replied Eliana, proud.

"Actually, she's a product of the frozen north, like the Norsk." Damir rode with one hand on his laced reins, and one on his hip. His white sword hung at his side, and he looked impressive. Eliana adjusted her cape so that her dagger showed, too. "All the Woodland ponies originated north of the Wilderness. They migrated southward ages ago, perhaps to escape the worsening climate and forage for greener food."

"Do the Norsk have such ponies now?"

"I believe they do, used mostly for pulling their sleds and carts. I have seen a few in Amon-dhen. But the ponies the Norsk use are larger, sturdy of build like Selsig, though not as well fed, and many are nearly as tall as Ll-wyd. Like the Norsk themselves, they are big boned and rough haired."

Eliana gazed along the pathway ahead. "So they're not a beautiful people?"

Damir glanced down at her and his full mouth twitched with a frown. "They are in no way 'beautiful.' Unless you like men of great bulk, with filthy blond hair, pale skin, and eerily light amber eyes."

"Not blue?"

"Some," said Damir, obviously annoyed by Eliana's line of conversation. "What struck me, however, were the men with pale amber eyes."

"That's different from the usual." Eliana peeked up at him. "It almost sounds beautiful to me."

His frown deepened. "The amber shade matches their filth perfectly." He paused. "And their pale skin tends to resemble weak cream with red splotches on their cheeks. The rest of their faces is covered with unkempt beards, and their dirty hair hangs past their shoulders."

"That is a disgusting rendition," said Eliana. "But you've only seen a few Norskmen, comparatively. I will withhold my opinion on their appearance until I've seen them in their homeland."

Damir urged Llwyd past Selsig and he took the lead, blocking the path in front of Eliana. "You'll find out soon enough."

They spent two nights sleeping in the Wilderness. Both nights passed uneventfully, though Damir discovered that when tired from a long day's ride, Eliana had a tendency to snore. It was just a light little rumble, but worth telling her about the next morning. Eliana had fallen into a dark silence after that, and since they were now riding across a barren, open heath, she rode a good distance apart from him.

In the distance ahead, the sky changed to a lighter shade of blue, and the horizon altered from the barren fields they'd seen for the past two days. Eliana halted her mare, who seized a quick bite of heather, then rode over to Damir. They stopped their horses and allowed them to graze. Eliana shaded her eyes and pointed to the southeastern horizon. "What is that land that I see?"

"There lies the causeway to the port town of Amondhen," said Damir. "The heath will soon give way to marshland, and the ride will be slower until we reach the developed areas of the city."

"I do not remember the geography of this land, but it seems familiar to me."

Damir pointed back at the distant grey-green haze of the fading forest. "The Woodland stretches south from the northern mountains, which are all but impassable, and then dwindles many leagues south of Amrodel. Near the south, few people now live, though in its fullness, many lived on all corners of the forest. At its ending, the land gives way to a vast desert, and endless leagues, more impassable than the northern mountain range, reach at last to my father's land of Kora."

"Have you ever seen that land?" asked Eliana.

"No, nor would it be safe for me to return. As I told you once, my father was in exile, and my return would be deemed a threat to the new prince, who, I believe, is about my age. The penalty for the return of any of my father's kin is death, so I do not think it would be particularly welcoming. But since I've never seen Kora, I consider Amrodel my true home."

"I would be curious to see it," said Eliana. "But not at that price."

"Indeed," agreed Damir. "Southeast of here begins the

shore of a great sea, and this is its most northern point. It is from this shore that ships travel, and where my father arrived when he escaped Kora. The ocean begins at about the midlevel range of the Woodland, and once, it was a great pilgrimage for the Mages of Amrodel, for they loved the sea. Now, they come here seldom."

"Because of the Norsk? But aren't Mages more powerful? Why do we fear them?"

"I am more powerful," said Damir, and he glanced at her. "As you are, and Madawc. But few remain now whose *ki* can be used for defense, or battle. Cahira may prove as powerful, one day. But most are like Serafina, who wove fabric with magical qualities, or Rodern, who crafted buildings that obeyed his commands."

"Wonderful," said Eliana. "Commands such as 'crash!'"

Damir smiled. "I could think of better directions for a building."

"I would direct it to warm itself in winter, or be cool in summer."

"Or to lower lights in the evening," added Damir. "I had done that for my own home, but Rodern took the art farther. Little did the rest of us know how, but that was the direction of his *ki*, anyway."

Eliana gazed westward and sighed. "What lies that way? I see only a grey haze."

"The mountains of the Guerdians," said Damir. "They are less formidable than those north of the Woodland, but far more dangerous."

"Why?"

"That is where the Arch Mage lies buried in darkness. Long ago, he left Kora, where he defied their prince, thinking by virtue of his greater power that he should rule. It is said that he single-handedly slaughtered the vast army the prince sent after him, but in his fury, he also killed many innocents—hence the name they gave him, 'Otaktay,' for 'Kills Many.' He sailed east across the sea and built a magnificent palace on a cliff where the eastern mountain range ends, overlooking the great southern mesas. It was more splendid than anything in his old homeland, and there, his power grew. Many who admired him came to live there. He created underground channels that reached north under the mountain, even to the realm of the Guerdians, who at first trusted him and then came to serve him. At some point during this time, he made contact with the Mages of Amrodel. And apparently, he fell in love with their queen, or she with him—that has never been certain, nor is it known if he really cared for her, or just sought her power. But when she realized he had betrayed her, she defied him. After her death, he was trapped in a great pit near the northern entrance to his palace, which lies opposite us now."

Eliana nodded, looking thoughtful. "I feel the energy from that place," she said quietly. "It is repellent, and yet . . ." Her voice trailed.

"What?"

She looked up at him. "It is also strangely compelling. Often my gaze turns in that direction. I do not know why."

"He is calling you, I think," said Damir. "Because you are the heir of the one he desired, and the one he needs to regain his life."

Eliana shuddered. "I wonder if Cahira feels the same pull?"

"I imagine she does, on some level, but it seems his energy is focused on you now."

"I feel it more now that we've left the Woodland," said Eliana. "Before, it was a shadow in my thoughts, with no shape. I also know that his energy does not want me with you, though I'm not sure why."

"Maybe his resurrection requires a virgin." He liked the thought. "If so, there is an easy solution."

Eliana ignored his reference. "Possibly, though I think it is more substantial than that."

Unfortunate. "In what way?"

Eliana's face puckered as she considered the matter. "A child . . . If I become a mother, I will be of no use to him. And I feel his fear that I am drawing close to that time."

Damir frowned, and he urged Llwyd forward again. "As you draw closer to the Norsk."

He thought—or imagined because of hope—that he heard her whisper, *"Or closer to you."*

They reached the long causeway to Amon-dhen, but Damir's thoughts still fixed on Eliana's proclamation. Pregnancy would render her useless to the Arch Mage's resurrection. And she was "drawing closer" to that point. The Arch Mage, even in a state of dark energy without form, would sense the currents of Eliana's fate. Like a river flowing, those currents weren't set until the spirit reached that time, but there was a path laid before her.

Damir intended to reach the Norsk, then do what was necessary to protect the Woodland and defeat Rodern's plans. But what if, in so doing, he delivered Eliana into the hands of this mysterious Norskman? That was part of his plan—to find this man who apparently had already acted against Bruin, and whose secret presence still terrified Rodern. But he hadn't fully considered what this might mean to Eliana. Maybe seeing this Norskman would trigger her memory. Maybe she would run into the arms of a pale-haired warrior, and be lost to Damir forever.

"You couldn't have known him very well."

Eliana rode alongside him, but at a distance as she gazed dreamily at the horizon. She looked over at him, confused, as if he'd drawn her back from a far-off place. "Who?"

Damir hesitated, embarrassed. "Your Norsk friend."

"Of course. How do you know how well I knew him, given that you knew nothing about it to begin with?"

"It's reasonable to assume," said Damir, and he tried to

seem both detached and careless. "You never left the Woodland, other than a few excursions to Amon-dhen with Madawc."

"You kept a close watch on my activities, then?"

She was smiling. The Fiend didn't need her memory to drive him crazy. "It was common knowledge to all," he replied, his voice even.

"But only of interest to you." She paused, her green eyes glittering. "Maybe I met him in this lovely seaside port that you and I are about to visit." Wonderful! Now every street and every ocean breeze would remind him of Eliana walking misty-eyed beside a towering, probably shirtless, Norskman.

He was glowering. He didn't mean to glower. "Madawc would have known. He certainly would have noticed if you were whiling your hours with some brawny warrior."

"Well, at least you're jealous of someone who, theoretically, exists."

"I'm not jealous."

Her brow angled. "Personally, I think you're insane with jealousy." She didn't let him interrupt. "I assume you're used to your position as 'most desirable male.'" He was used to it, though Eliana hadn't agreed in the past.

"Not at all."

She ignored his denial. "It must horrify you to think there's a strong, young, extremely handsome and mysterious man out there who is also capable of stealing women's hearts."

"For all you know, he was a father figure to you!" "Detached and careless" wasn't going well.

"Possibly." Her cheerful tone gave every indication that this was inconceivable, whether she remembered the Norskman or not.

Damir glared. "Let us not forget that you remain a virgin, despite this Norsk demon's 'extreme good looks and strength.'"

"But you're not jealous."

"No."

"Maybe he respected my innocence, and won my heart in other ways, such as with trust and honesty. Unlike yourself."

"No Norskman, ever, has respected a woman's innocence. If you met up with one of them, it's a wonder you're in one piece, let alone a virgin."

"That is disgusting. Your mind wanders to particularly dark fantasies."

It had been a dark thought. Damir kept his expression straight, but inside, he cringed. "I meant you were lucky he didn't hack you to bits with his war axe . . . not anything romantic."

"Oh, that's so much better! A thought almost glowing with light! 'Hack me to bits with his axe.' Lovely! You *are* related to the Arch Mage, whether you admit it or not."

"Even the Arch Mage wasn't tormented with a female as exasperating as yourself."

"We have no idea of the Woodland queen's temperament. I doubt very much she would have liked being called 'sweet,' either. Unless she was more like Shaen, and nothing like me, her descendent."

She had been exactly like Eliana. Proud and independent, and without question, completely infuriating. Damir didn't need a study of history to know that. "No wonder the Arch Mage turned to darkness."

"I hope you aren't sympathizing with Rodern's quest," said Eliana, her voice light and still cheerful. "But the lure of darkness must be particularly strong to you, given your distant but obvious relationship to a Mage who was, by all I've heard, the darkest individual the world has ever known."

For one brief instant, he imagined whipping out his sword, holding it at her lovely throat, and then . . . utterly giving himself to darkness, and taking her with him.

Instead, he urged Llwyd faster, and the big horse broke into a canter, and then a gallop. To his surprise, Selsig sped up and raced along beside him, her small head angled in determination. Eliana was laughing, and her dark hair flew in the wind, her cape fluttering behind her. Damir stopped short, and Selsig stopped beside him. Llwyd was breathless. Selsig grabbed a marsh flower and ate.

"As I said, 'insane.'" Eliana looked pert and happy. Damir twitched, then reached for her, seized her hair, and leaned down to kiss her.

Her mouth popped open in surprise, and no doubt with a ready comment, but he slid his tongue between her lips, and she gasped instead. She froze a moment only, then grabbed his shoulder to steady herself, and she leaned closer to kiss him back. Their kiss had all the fire of their first, but with a passion they had already learned together.

He broke the kiss, and she settled back on her saddle pad, breathless and appearing a little dizzy. Damir felt satisfied, but Llwyd sidestepped in confusion. Damir momentarily lost his own balance, which Eliana saw and commented upon with one delicately arched brow.

She puffed a quick breath. "Well. Clearly, this 'dark current' is taking its toll on you." She fanned herself with her hand. "And me." She popped her lips. Apparently, she'd run out of ways to provoke him—for now. She looked at him, tense, but polite. "Shall we go onward? I'd like to reach this fine city before sunset."

"Good idea," said Damir. And after sunset, he would select the most lavish inn that Amon-dhen had to offer, rent their best room, and his latest impulse, courtesy of the 'dark current' or not, would find its rightful solution.

Chapter Thirteen

As Eliana and Damir rode into the seaport town of Amondhen, Eliana stopped Selsig to stare at her surroundings. Every building was made of white brick, and the streets were crafted of the same material. Colorful awnings shaded shops along the street, filled with promising wares. Selsig eyed a stand of red and yellow fruit, and inched her way casually toward it before Eliana halted her progress.

Damir looked bored, as did Llwyd, but Eliana reasoned they had seen this glorious town before. "What a magnificent town! Why do we live in the Woodland at all, when such a place beckons?"

Damir shaded his eyes against the afternoon sun and seemed to be looking for something. "It becomes tiresome after a few visits. Clearly, your loss of memory has allowed renewed intrigue to something you had long ago foresworn."

"'Foresworn?' What are you talking about? And why would I 'foreswear' such an interesting spot?"

"Maybe it was too interesting . . . and too expensive,"

said Damir, but Eliana was already dismounting. She squeezed a red fruit, and Selsig leaned eagerly over her shoulder.

"We'll take two!" she announced to the shopkeeper, a tall, lanky woman with red hair and a friendly face. The woman looked at her a moment, then seemed to recognize her. She offered a broad smile.

"Lady Eliana! It has been many months since you visited Amon-dhen. It is good to see you. I assume you'll also be wanting a bag of your favorites?"

Eliana didn't hesitate. "I will, thank you."

The shopkeeper fished around in a deep basket behind the counter, then produced a bag filled with a wide variety of pleasant-looking edibles. Both Eliana and Selsig beamed. The woman waited a moment expectantly, and Eliana turned to Damir. "He has the money."

Damir frowned. "Which we need for our journey, I remind you."

"This won't cost much." Eliana glanced at the shopkeeper. "Will it?"

"Not at all," said the shopkeeper. "Only fourteen quid."

Eliana waited as Damir paid the woman, though he plainly considered her purchase overpriced. The shopkeeper smiled at Damir, then winked at Eliana. "Nice-looking fellow you've got carrying your gold, Lady. Looks like one of those from Kora. Don't see many of your kind here, sad to say," she added. "The seas have picked up, and few ships make the journey now."

"I am only half of Kora blood," said Damir. "I was born in Amrodel."

"Then you must be Damir ap Kora!" said the shopkeeper, and she clasped her hands together over her chest. "Others of my trade have spoken of you, those younger than myself." Her eyes widened, and Eliana eyed her suspiciously as Selsig seized one of the red fruits and ate it. "You are quite as handsome as they say, though I can't speak to the other attributes about which I've heard so much."

Damir's face flushed, and Eliana frowned. "You're legendary even here?"

"He is," said the shopkeeper. "If you have won this one, Lady, you will be the envy of many here."

"I have not won him," said Eliana, annoyed. "We are partners in a quest. That is all."

"From what I've heard, no woman comes within arm's reach of this man and could consider him a partner only."

"One has," replied Eliana. She tied the bag to Selsig's felt pad, then climbed up on a barrel to mount again. "Thank you for your time."

The shopkeeper waved, and Eliana started off ahead of Damir. He caught up with her, but she refused to look at him.

"My reputation overtakes reality," he said.

Eliana feigned a look of indifference. "Your sordid exploits, with women you barely know, are of no interest to me." She paused. "And something tells me that your reputation can't compete with the actual details."

Damir didn't respond, indicating her guess was accurate. Eliana frowned and shook her head. "It appears you wasted no time in frittering away your time despite your 'complicated' feelings for me."

"Considering that you were more interested in enslaving me with one of your devilish brews, I don't think that's too hard to understand."

"So as always, you chose the easier path."

"The path less painful!"

Eliana watched with misgivings as Damir forcibly altered his expression. He gestured down the white brick street. "There's a shop that may interest you, and might actually serve on our journey."

Distracted, Eliana spotted a large shop with great swathes of shearling items on display beneath a red awning. She hurried Selsig to the shop front, hopped off, and hitched her to a pole. "This is just as I imagined!" Eliana fingered large coats of soft suede and shearling, and Damir followed her into the store.

"Pick one, and let's go," he said, but Eliana barely heard him. She pressed a soft coat against her cheek, then spotted another, in a darker color, and tried that one. The shopkeeper took notice of her, and hurried to her assistance. Like the previous woman, the man appeared of mixed heritage, and in their height and light skin both hinted at blood from the pale-haired Norsk.

"May I help you, Lady?" he asked, and he bent slightly forward as if to encourage her.

"Yes, thank you," said Eliana. "I am planning a journey north, and I need a very warm, soft, but pretty coat to wear."

"We have just what you need!" The shopkeeper hesitated and his heavy brow furrowed. "You're a Mage of Amrodel, are you not?"

"How do you know that?" asked Eliana, her attention fixed on an especially fluffy coat.

"You have that way, mistress," said the shopkeeper. "Few Mages come to Amon-dhen now, more's the pity. Only Rodern, and he's always in such a hurry, never stops to talk. Came by one, two days ago, bought a coat, and didn't say two words."

"Do you know where he was headed?" asked Damir, though Eliana rolled her eyes.

"One supposes 'north,' " she cut in.

"I mean after this shop. It would be wise to learn of his purposes."

The shopkeeper looked between them. "Think he went to the armory, down the street, though I'm not sure what he bought there."

Eliana pulled out the fluffy coat and tried it on, then peered at herself in a large mirror.

"It looks lovely on you, mistress," said the shopkeeper, but Eliana shook her head.

"I look like a fat pillow." She glanced at Damir and he shrugged.

"You do, a bit."

Eliana put it back and looked around. The shopkeeper smacked his lip. "Now, I do have one coat you might find interesting. One of the best Norsk traders brought it in just this morning, and I couldn't imagine who would be both graceful and yet powerful enough to wear it properly. It's a bit . . . expensive . . ."

Damir sighed, but Eliana clapped her hands. "I'll take a look."

The shopkeeper brought out a mushroom-colored shearling coat, with a fine, wide hood and a long, rolled collar with a cream-colored, fluffy lining. Eliana caught her breath, snatched it out of his hands, and immersed herself within it. "I'll take this one!"

"How much is it?" asked Damir.

"Only two thousand quid, sir. A fair price for such a garment . . ." Damir's harsh gasp interrupted what Eliana considered a very reasonable argument, but the shopkeeper squeezed Damir's shoulder in a commiserating male fashion. "And for such an exquisite woman, can there be any price set on her happiness?"

Damir groaned, but shelled out the necessary gold. Eliana beamed. "Thank you!" She paused. "But you haven't picked a coat yet."

Damir's eyes narrowed to slits. "With the gold we have left, I can afford one mitten and a sock, assuming you intend to leave enough for renting rooms and buying food along the way."

Eliana squeezed her new coat around herself and eyed him dreamily. "Can't we sell something?"

The shopkeeper brightened, then fingered Damir's cape

without preamble. "Fine weave, this. You being a Mage, I expect it might have some other qualities, too."

Damir looked weary, but he appeared ready to haggle. "As a matter of fact, this cape is beyond price. It was woven by the Mage Serafina, of whom you have certainly heard . . ." He paused, and the shopkeeper smacked his lips.

"I haven't, by name, no. But a Mage, you say . . ."

"The finest seamstress in Amrodel," said Damir. "Special qualities . . . yes. For one thing, no stain ever mars the weave . . ." This didn't appear to interest the shopkeeper. "And it is said to attract wealth to its bearer, as well as other good fortune."

"I'll take it!"

"Two thousand quid," said Damir, his voice flat.

"One thousand, not a quid more," said the shopkeeper.

"Seventeen hundred."

"Thirteen!"

"Done."

Eliana looked back and forth between them, a bit dizzy, but she sensed Damir had gotten the better of the deal. By the light in his dark eyes, apparently, he thought so, too. The shopkeeper took the cape, and Damir selected a dark shearling coat that was both warm and light. He tried it on, and Eliana sighed.

"It fits perfectly," she said. It hugged his broad shoulders in just the right way, and hung even longer than his "magical" cape. He looked magnificent, and he quite obviously agreed.

Damir glanced at his reflection and Eliana sighed again. "You are extremely vain."

"I had to be sure it fits."

"And that it sets off your black hair, adds to the bronzed glow of your skin, brings out the warmth in your pretty brown eyes, and matches your boots, too!"

His gaze lingered on himself a bit longer, but then he looked around. "Speaking of which, we'll need boots."

The shopkeeper's footwear selection wasn't as vast as that of his coats, but he found tall sheepskin boots for both of them, and Eliana noticed that Damir, indeed, selected the pair that best matched his new coat.

Eliana aimed for the door as Damir paid the shopkeeper. Reluctantly, she removed her coat, since the evening was warm, and she rolled it carefully. Damir came out behind her. "You forgot something," he said.

Eliana turned, and he held out a pair of fleece mittens. She looked into his eyes and he smiled as she took the mittens. "Are these . . . like mine?"

"Somewhat," he said. "These are warmer, but the look is similar. Do you like them?"

Eliana beamed, then kissed his cheek. "It is you I like," she whispered. "And the mittens, too."

"I've waited a long time to return them to you."

"Thank you."

He looked romantic. She felt romantic, too. "Where do we go now? Do we find an inn for the night?"

His eyes glimmered, but he frowned as another thought struck him. "First, we should investigate the armory, and see if we can find out what Rodern did here."

"He probably bought a sword and a shield, and headed north to the home of Bruin the Ruthless! Let's find a inn."

Damir smiled. "We are on a 'quest,' my lady. Or had you forgotten?"

Eliana blushed. "It had temporarily slipped my mind." She looked up and down the bustling street. "Inns in Amon-dhen must serve fine food, don't you think?"

"If they have sufficient provisions to accommodate you, I'll be surprised," said Damir. "But yes, we will find a place to stay that will linger in your memory ever after."

Eliana issued an unexpected squeak as she caught his meaning, and she caught her breath. "Oh! Really? That will be nice." Her voice sounded high, and his smile widened.

"To the armory, Eliana."

They led the horses down the street, but Eliana's thoughts raced, and her pulse refused to ease. He meant to make love to her, tonight, here in some magical inn with the sound of the ocean outside their window. Eliana could find no fault in the plan. She peeked over at him as he walked beside her. He looked so tall and so beautiful, greater than anything she could imagine. *I want him, too.*

There were no lies between them now, and she felt no hesitation at the thought. Her memory hadn't returned. Perhaps it never would. But what could exist in her memory that would change what she felt for him?

They passed a store laden with salted meats, with two large men arguing outside its door. Damir started across the street to avoid them, but Eliana stopped and stared.

Here, surely, were two full-blooded Norskmen. As Damir had told her, they were extremely tall and large of build. Their hair fell below their shoulders, tangled and unkempt, and without question, unwashed. Both men appeared slightly drunk, and under no circumstances would either be termed "beautiful."

One struck the other, and he staggered back, but he was laughing as he swung at the first. They both noticed Eliana, and one called out in a language she didn't understand. The other laughed and grabbed at his lower region. Eliana blanched as they both came toward her.

Damir sighed heavily, then drew out his white sword as he hurried back for Eliana. "Come no closer."

Both Norskmen seemed to recognize Damir's greater power, and as surely, neither cared. They approached him with a lust for fighting that Eliana couldn't understand. Damir closed his eyes and mustered his *ki,* and the white sword glowed with a light that outshone even the setting sun. The Norskmen weren't afraid of battle, but obviously, magic terrified them. They shrank back, then disappeared down an alley, leaving unclaimed packages of salted meat behind, which Damir collected and put in his pack.

Eliana eyed Damir as he sheathed his sword. "They don't seem terribly formidable," she said.

"Those weren't Norsk warriors," said Damir. "They were puny traders, and not fighters."

"They were *puny?*"

Damir nodded. "Wait until you see their warriors. But because the Norsk have no magic of their own, they hold ours with utmost suspicion. This may explain why Rodern was able to sway Bruin's opinion, and gain his alliance. They fear us, yet sense our power. For a long time, that fear was all we needed to hold them at bay. Until Rodern interfered, it created its own balance, but if Bruin believes he has a Mage ally, his reservations about attacking us may lessen."

Eliana scratched her head and adjusted her hair. "I have to admit, your description of them seems remarkably accurate." She paused. "Are they all so . . . unclean?"

"From what I've seen, yes," said Damir, and he seemed to take a particular relish in confirming her impression. "Though as I said, the warriors are far more formidable of build, and have no similar lack in courage."

"It is hard to imagine why I might have befriended one of them."

"It is," agreed Damir.

"Of course, you haven't seen all of them," she added. "And perhaps I was able to look beneath surfaces to see warmth and kindness within."

"Tell me, my lady. Did you sense any 'warmth and kindness' in those two who just, in their language, termed you a 'lusty wench,' vowed to ravage you through a long night, sharing you between themselves . . . ?"

Eliana grimaced. "Is that what they said?" She shuddered. "How repulsive! And how do you know?"

"I know something of their language, crude though it is. There was more, but I expect you'd rather not hear it."

"Thank you for sparing me! How much worse can it get that what you've revealed already?"

"Frighteningly, quite a bit worse."

Eliana held up her hand. "I don't want to know." She looked around. "Where is this armory you mentioned?"

"Straight ahead, and around the corner," said Damir. "But next time I suggest we cross the street, I hope you'll follow."

Rodern hadn't purchased anything at the armory, a fact which seemed to annoy the smith greatly. "He's been one of my best customers in the past," the stout Guerdian informed Damir. "But this time, he came in here, demanded to see my wares, then passed on everything."

Eliana watched the small armorer with undisguised interest. She had certainly dealt with Guerdians in the past, but her loss of memory made the meeting new again. Damir remembered a trip they'd taken as children, when Madawc had led them from store to store, teaching them of this world. Then, as now, the little Guerdians had fascinated Eliana, and she had begged Madawc to let her take one home. The Guerdian had been offended, and Madawc had to ease her from the shop before the fellow lost his temper. By the look on her face, Damir guessed she was about to make a similar suggestion.

"Did you make all this?" she asked, and her voice suggested she was speaking to a child. Damir winced, aware of the Guerdian pride.

"The Guerdians design the greatest armor in any land," he told her. "Often, the Mages of Amrodel have worked with us, and created mail and helms that no weapon can breach."

Eliana beamed. "In different sizes? Some very small?"

She caught sight of a small but elaborate suit of light armor and her face contorted with happiness. "It's precious!"

The Guerdian stiffened and Damir seized Eliana's arm. "By precious, she means magnificent."

"She had better," said the Guerdian in a husky voice.

Eliana bit her lip and seemed to sense her error. "Yes, magnificent."

The Guerdian accepted this, and turned back to Damir. "The females of Amrodel, I see, are high-strung and flighty."

"They are," said Damir. "Especially this one."

Apparently, Eliana was too taken with the Guerdian to notice this slight. "What are your females like?" she asked.

"Strong," said the Guerdian with pride. "This armor that you've been admiring is made for one of them."

"They fight?" asked Eliana.

The Guerdian frowned and shook his head. "They wear it for dancing!"

Damir eased Eliana behind him with a look that he hoped suggested that her silence was wisest at this point. "Do you know what Rodern was looking for?" he asked.

"If I'd have known that, I'd have given it to him, and at a steep price after the way he stormed in here. Normally, he's not so rude, but the last few times he's visited my smithy, he's been brash and arrogant like he was the King of Amrodel. By the way, my sympathy for the loss of your king."

"How did you know that? Did Rodern tell you?"

"Word gets around," said the Guerdian. "We heard the news before Rodern came by."

"Had he bought anything recently?" asked Damir.

"Only a Norsk dagger," answered the Guerdian. "Don't know what he wanted something like that for—the ones we make are much better, and I told him so. But he said it was a gift, and took it anyway."

"A gift, indeed," said Eliana. "He used it to kill our king, and then implicate the Norsk in his murder."

The Guerdian huffed. "As if those brawny devils would bother with a dagger! They use those to pick their teeth!"

Eliana winced, but Damir smiled. "For a stealthful killing, a dagger might be useful."

The Guerdian's broad face squinched even more. "And when has a Norskman ever thought of being stealthful? They don't think—they just bust in wherever they want to go, and bash in heads along the way. 'Stealth!' Ha!"

"A fair point," agreed Damir. "Were you aware that Rodern had acquaintance with the Norsk?"

The Guerdian sighed. "There's no knowing why people take up with the allies they do. But I haven't seen him dealing with them at all. Just some other Mages, those I don't know by name, and a few of the local people here, and those are ones I don't care to know." He paused and his unfathomable eyes lightened. "But who would have thought Damir ap Kora and the witch Eliana would ever be strolling about the streets of Amon-dhen, practically hand in hand, and looking like lovers?"

Damir gaped, and Eliana's face flushed pink. "You know who we are?" she asked.

The Guerdian puffed himself up and looked taller. "As I said, word travels fast in the port of Amon-dhen."

Eliana peeked up at Damir. "I didn't realize I was so famous."

"Madame!" said the Guerdian. "Every shopkeeper in Amon-dhen knows you!"

"Why?" Damir and Eliana asked in unison.

"Because you buy so much," said the Guerdian.

Eliana deflated at this, but Damir took her hand. "Which is why we need to move along now. I don't like the way she's looking at that armor, and we only have a small amount of gold left."

"A shame," said the Guerdian. "But should you ever

225

have use of it, Lady, I'd be happy to do up a fine, feminine set of mail for you, and have Damir ap Kora set a spell on top of it. Can't beat that, I'd say. When you get more gold in hand, come by."

"I like that idea," said Eliana, and Damir eased her toward the door.

"You don't need armor."

"But it's shiny!"

Damir groaned and escorted her out onto the street. "I wonder if your Norsk friend was a trader? It would certainly explain how you met him."

Eliana's eyes brightened. "Perhaps he made jewelry, like my brooch!"

"All too likely," said Damir. He looked across the street, then spotted another roadway that led down toward the beach. "There's a very good inn down that way. I think you'll like it. If you're ready?"

She gazed up at him, and he knew the answer before it was given. "I am."

Damir held out his hand, and she took it. "Then, my lady, let us dine."

Damir found the inn he was looking for. The Sea Swan had the best food in Amon-dhen, and more important to Damir's mind, the most elaborate guest rooms. It was the perfect spot for seduction, and one he had enjoyed before, though never with the same passion he felt for Eliana. Despite his need to conserve their gold, he reserved the finest room the inn had to offer, complete with a balcony overlooking the sea. While Eliana was puttering about in a dress shop, he made certain the room had a large bed, and low lighting.

"I bought two dresses!" Eliana entered the inn holding up two long dresses, neither of which made any sense for their journey. Both looked expensive.

"How did you get those? I have all the money!"

Eliana looked happy and smug. "As it happens, I am known in Amon-dhen, Damir. I popped by the apothecary and discovered that I am her most esteemed supplier. She has a whole section of potions labeled 'The Witch of Amrodel.' Oddly, she had heard I lost my memory, but I gave her some of the herbs I've collected, and fetched a very good price, too."

"It occurs to me that the people of Amon-dhen pick up news with the same enthusiasm that those of the Woodland place wagers on the escapades of others," said Damir.

"They do seem newsy here." Eliana held one of her dresses up to the light. "Which one do you like better?"

"Neither makes any sense for a trip to the iceland of the Norsk." Damir paused. "I like the light purple one."

"The very sheer one?" Eliana nodded. "I thought you would. I will wear that tonight, for dinner."

"What about the other one?" asked Damir.

"I couldn't decide which I liked better, so I bought both." Before Damir could comment, she placed her delicate hand on his arm and smiled. "Did you get us a room?"

"I did. Follow me." Damir placed his hand over hers, and led her to the room he'd chosen. Eliana's reaction was everything he'd hoped.

"It's beautiful!" She pushed open the wide doors to the balcony and stepped outside, then leaned on the laced iron railing. The ocean breeze caught her long hair and tossed it behind her, and Damir sighed in admiration as he joined her. She looked up at him, and her eyes glittered in the fading sunset.

"You are beautiful, Lady Eliana."

"And you, Damir ap Kora."

He touched her cheek, then softly kissed her mouth. She closed her eyes, but he broke the kiss, then brushed his lips against her cheek. "Put on your new dress, my dear, and we will dine by candlelight in the parlor."

"There's a parlor?"

"It has an entire wall of glass overlooking the ocean, as a matter of fact."

Eliana beamed, then darted into their bedroom to change. Damir resisted the urge to watch her, though a quick glance told him she struggled with her snug leggings, stumbled, then leaned on the bed to remove them. His heart warmed with happiness. Here was the life he had dreamed—an adventure with the most interesting woman he knew, a woman so beautiful that no sunset compared.

"Damir! What's keeping you? I'm hungry!"

And whose appetite knew no rival.

"I'm coming."

Eliana waited eagerly by the door. She wound her hair into a twist, probably so as not to inconvenience her assault upon her meal, and shuffled from foot to foot as he changed his own shirt for dinner. "You look fine," she said. "Let's go! I am intrigued by the prospect of the best food in Amon-dhen."

She chattered on as they descended the stairs, but Damir's plan for the night extended well past dinner. "The night has just begun."

"Dessert!" She startled him with the thrill in her voice, but Eliana fixed her attention on a large platter of pastries and cakes that someone had cleverly positioned near the parlor's entrance. "I want two of those, and that one!"

Damir frowned. "If you eat all that, I'll have to carry you back to the room. Pace yourself."

She nodded, but he noticed that she licked her lips as they passed the platter.

The graceful hostess of The Sea Swan came forward to greet them. She held out her hands elegantly and Damir took them. "Damir ap Kora! You honor us with your presence. It has been too long since you visited The Sea Swan."

Eliana peeked up at him, her brow furrowed. "You've been here before?"

"A few times."

"More than a few," said Vanora with a light laugh. "There is no man, in Amon-dhen or beyond, who treats a woman with such care. Only the wealthiest traders and noblemen are able to make The Sea Swan their 'home away from home,' but not a one has the innate taste and sensitivity to select the finest like the legendary Mage of Amrodel!"

"*Legendary?*"

Damir cringed inwardly, but he maintained a gracious smile. "Lady Vanora flatters me with her praise."

Eliana nodded. "I see that."

Vanora took Eliana's arm and leaned toward her in a friendly, if contrived, posture. "You are a fortunate woman, but I can see you also share Damir's graciousness. I hope you're enjoying our 'Sea Swept' Suite?"

"Is that what it's called?" asked Eliana. Her voice sounded a little dry. Maybe if she understood how much he'd spent to gain that room, she'd appreciate his efforts on her behalf—unless Vanora let slip how often he'd rented this same grand room. Better to move on. . . .

"Do you have our table ready?" He hoped Vanora sensed that she should say no more about his previous visits to her inn.

She didn't run the finest inn in Amon-dhen for nothing—Vanora understood his meaning. "I have reserved the best table in our parlor for you. Come with me." She led them to a private table near the glass wall and placed a bottle of Koran wine between them. "Enjoy your dinner."

Damir opened the wine and poured a portion into Eliana's goblet.

"What's that?" she asked.

Damir smiled. "It is a rare, aged wine from the land of

my ancestry. You might call it my 'Wine of Truce.' This time, again, we will drink to our partnership . . . and each other."

Eliana waited as he filled his glass, then held the wine to her lips. Their gazes met and locked, and they drank together. Damir lowered his glass and then took her hand across the table. "We have a long and grueling journey before us. I would spend this night with you, and think of nothing else but what we can be together."

She smiled, and he thought she looked young. "I would like that, too," she answered, and her voice was shy.

They ate together, first a light but flavorful soup, then a mixture of rare greens and spice, followed by a dish of roasted shellfish freshly caught from the sea. By the time the dessert tray was presented to Eliana, she looked weak from feasting. Mercifully, her mood had softened since Vanora's somewhat awkward introduction. Damir sat forward, ready to forego the final course, but Eliana selected a flaky pastry, and dug into it as if she hadn't eaten in days.

Damir watched with misgivings as she finished the pastry, then took a last sip of tea. "You eat more than a Norsk warrior." He cringed before the words were out. This was not the way to compliment a lady he intended to seduce.

She peeked up at him, and appeared unoffended. "I must fill myself up for the journey!"

"Fill yourself up? At this rate, you'll climb astride Selsig, and the poor mare will crumple to her knees."

Eliana frowned, then delicately dabbed the corner of her mouth with a napkin. "I hope the stable you chose feeds our horses well."

"For Llwyd, I have no worry. But I'm not sure that barn has enough hay and grain for your mare."

"She needs to build sustenance, too."

He had to do something to change this line of conversation, or his sultry designs could be lost. Damir rose from the table and held out his hand. "What truly amazes me is how you can eat so much, and yet remain so utterly ravishing."

She eyed him doubtfully, as if wondering why he was so intent on flattering her. "Do you think we have enough provisions for the journey north?" she asked. "If the Norsk taverns are as bad as you say, we'll be on our own."

"We should have enough. If not, I can venture in alone and fetch what we need. There's no need to worry, my dear."

Eliana took his hand, and Damir led her from the parlor to a deck that overlooked the ocean. "Would you enjoy a walk along the shore?" he asked. Eliana nodded eagerly, and Damir felt satisfied. A fine dinner, a walk along the beach at sunset . . . They were the perfect first steps to seduction.

White gulls swooped over the crashing waves, and small boats tossed back and forth on their moorings as Damir and Eliana walked along. "The sea does appear rough, as the shopkeeper mentioned," she said. "Do you think it has anything to do with the dark current emanating from the Arch Mage?"

"I doubt it," said Damir. "No Mage has successfully altered the weather, even the Arch Mage. That is a power beyond us, and probably always will be. But the world has its cycles. For long years, the sea was calm, but in ages before that, rough like this. It's my guess we're simply entering another such cycle, which most likely ties into the increasing ferocity of the northern winters, too, and also explains why the Norsk have moved their villages southward."

Eliana shaded her eyes and gazed across the sea, and the sun turned its waves to gold as it faded beyond the horizon. "I suppose I knew all this before."

"It was common to our study with Madawc, yes." He didn't want to remind her of her lost memory now, especially as he considered his own part in the deed. He would have to divert their conversation to something more romantic. "But the ability to learn anew, that is a rare gift."

Her brow angled. "I would gladly exchange this 'gift' with you."

"And if you'd had your way . . ." Damir caught himself and forced a smile. "Then I would be deprived of your sweetness as you learn of the world again."

She didn't appear convinced, but mercifully, she didn't argue. They walked along in silence and Damir struggled for something more romantic to say. "The setting sun suits you, Eliana."

"Fading into darkness?"

Damir twitched. "No . . . its beauty and serenity."

"I suppose we won't be seeing much of the sun as we head north."

"Probably not." His face felt tight from forcing a pleasant expression. "So we should enjoy this warmth while it lasts."

She looked up at him, decidedly suspicious now. "Did you drink too much wine?" she asked.

"Only enough to savor its taste," he replied in a way that he hope suggested savoring each other, too. "Did you enjoy its flavor, my dear?"

She nodded, but she wasn't as impressed by the wine of Kora as he'd hoped. "It was pleasant. Very light." She said "very light" in a way that implied she would have preferred a drink of more substance.

"Well, it's not as heavy and lacks the froth of Norsk ale . . ." Again, he stopped himself. "But it is sweeter and more fragrant."

"Yes. Very pleasant." Eliana adjusted her cape as the wind from the sea increased. Better to end the walk now before he resorted to another verbal battle with a woman he intended to make his lover this night. She wasn't reacting as women usually did to his romantic overtures.

Rather than drawing closer in response, Eliana had stiffened and seemed to withdraw.

Here, in the most romantic city he knew, in a beautiful inn by the sea, he should be able to win her over easily. Eliana was a woman, and he was an accomplished lover. She obviously desired him, and he wanted her, too. Damir considered this. Maybe he wanted her too much. He wanted her before another man could claim her, and he had little time before that other man might seize his advantage.

"Shall we return to the inn?" he asked, and she nodded.

The wind blew hard against them as they walked back toward the inn, kicking up sand and salt spray into their faces. So much for a romantic walk. Eliana pulled her hood around her face, but because Damir had been forced to trade his for a warmer coat, he was left to endure the sand and salt without protection.

When they reached the shelter of the inn, Eliana turned to look at him, and she laughed as she pulled back her hood. "You look like you've been caught in a whirlwind! Your hair is going straight back."

Damir glared, then ran his fingers through his hair, which indeed felt stiff from the salt spray, and clearly harbored particles of sand. "Well, if I'd had a cape . . ." He bit his lip hard. "Then we'd have no reason to bathe."

"Bathe?"

Damir seized her hand, a bit too forcefully, then led her up to their guest room. As he'd requested, the inn's staff had readied a large tub of steaming water to their room, placed on a marble platform, with several pitchers for rinsing. Eliana eyed the tub, then Damir.

"You've planned this very well."

He smiled, pleased with himself. "No detail is too great to lavish upon you, my lady."

She nodded, but then she sighed heavily. "So. You intend to seduce me." She drew another long breath and shook her head. "I should have known."

"Is that so hard to understand?"

For a third time, she sighed. "No. It was predictable really." As if to further destroy his mood, she sighed again, then gazed wearily up at him. "Well, let's get it over with."

Damir felt like she'd slapped him.

"*Get it over with?* Do you know how hard I've worked to set this evening up right?"

"I have a fair idea, yes," said Eliana. "You've choreographed everything perfectly."

"Except for my choice in women, yes!"

"Maybe you'd prefer someone a bit easier," she replied. "You seem to have a fine reputation in this town as well as in Amrodel. It wouldn't be too hard to find a woman to replace me."

"Not hard at all." Damir spun around, but then he stopped and a dark fire seemed to burn within him as he approached her.

Eliana backed away. "What are you doing?"

"Ending this conversation." He picked her up and before she could react, he stripped away her dress. Eliana struggled, but she was too surprised to react more forcefully as he carried her to the tub of bathing water.

Damir paused, then dropped her unceremoniously into the water. Eliana sputtered, but before she could scramble out of the tub, he tore off his own clothing and climbed in beside her.

"This is *not* romantic, Damir ap Kora!" Her voice sounded very high, and she sank lower until everything below her neck was submerged in water.

" 'Romantic' hasn't been particularly effective, has it?"

They glared at each other. Eliana's breath came in swift, angry gasps. But suddenly, without any reason that he could tell, Eliana smiled, and then she laughed. "I suppose a bath wouldn't hurt you," she said, and before he knew what she intended, she dumped a large pitcher of water over his head. "Sorry. That was cold." She seized another, and dumped that over his head, too.

"That one," he said through clenched teeth, "was hot."

Eliana grabbed a small bar of fragrant soap, then rubbed it into his hair. He was too furious to stop her. She refilled the pitcher and rinsed his hair, then sat back, satisfied. "You look much better!"

His whole body trembled. "And now, my lady, it is your turn."

He scooped her up, pulled her onto his lap, then snatched the bar of soap from her hand. He pinned his gaze on her surprised face, then lathered her delicate body, one slow swirl at a time. He needed no other seduction. As soon as his hand grazed over her round breast, Eliana was his. Her eyes drifted shut, she bit her lip, and she arched her back as he used his skill on her warm skin. The peaks of her breasts drew taut, and he bent to taste her there. Eliana caught her breath and moaned, and he knew, despite the battle she waged, he had won.

His body throbbed. There was no resistance left in Eliana, and Damir lifted her out of the water, dried her with a fluffy, white towel, then carried her to the bed. He kissed her mouth, and she went limp in his arms. He lowered her to the bed, then knelt beside her. He ran his lips over her breast and she clutched his hair. He slid his hand along her side, over the flare of her hips, and to the soft skin of her inner thigh. She quivered when he teased his finger inward, and his whole body clenched when he found her slippery and wet to his touch.

"It is time we end this, Eliana," he said. "No matter what lies ahead, you are mine."

Eliana stiffened at his words, then shot up in bed, knocking Damir off balance. "What do you mean?"

He barely remembered what he'd said. "That it's time we . . ." He didn't remember what he meant.

"I know what you meant! I'm 'yours.'" He had no idea what offended her, but he didn't like the challenge.

"You will be tonight."

"That's it! That's what's wrong with this 'romantic evening' of yours. It's a ruse!" Eliana squirmed away from him, then hopped to the floor. "You aren't making love to me because you love me, or because you want to be with me. You're conquering me!"

Well, yes . . . "Not at all."

"Then tell me the truth. Is it because you want me, or because you want to keep me from another?"

Damir stared. "What?"

"You're seizing your advantage!"

Before another man could, yes . . . Eliana seized her discarded dress and wriggled into it, though it was backwards when she put it on. She ignored the state of her attire and pointed her finger at him. "This was just another battle in an ongoing war for you. You're always in control, aren't you?"

Damir rose from the bed, shocked by her fury, and just as determined to conquer it. "You are afraid to give yourself to me."

She nodded vigorously. "Yes, I am. I am terrified, because I do not believe you are truly giving yourself in return. You arranged this all so perfectly, it was so well planned. Even when I tried to . . . do whatever it was I meant to do to you with my potion, you had the upper hand. You were in control of me, but more, of yourself!"

Eliana stormed to the door, but Damir was too stunned to stop her. She turned back and her eyes glimmered with tears. "That is the problem. You are invulnerable, Damir ap Kora. There is no crack in your armor, and no weakness. Has it occurred to you that this man you hope to defeat by bedding me had the one thing you lack? The Norsk have no magical energy. Maybe that is why I cared for him. You are too strong."

He had no idea what to say or how to stop her. "Where are you going?"

"I am going to rent my own room." She held up a small bag of coins. "I made enough money on the sale of my herbs. I will not be dependent on you."

He watched her go, and he heard her determined footsteps as she headed down the stairs. Damir lay back on the wide bed, listening to the roar of the ocean outside the large window. His body ached from thwarted desire, but he had no will to ease its pressure alone. As much as he hated her argument, Eliana was right. He had meant to claim her irrevocably, before he risked losing her to her mysterious Norskman.

And now they would ride north, together but apart, and he would be forced to deliver her to this man whose vulnerability was the one thing he couldn't defeat.

Chapter Fourteen

For three days, they barely spoke to each other. For the first two, Eliana had harbored resentment and anger against Damir, and for the last, she had become too embedded with the silence to do anything to break it. He seemed just as miserable as she felt.

Trust would be hard won between them, if it was even possible after all that had happened. And Eliana wanted trust. Maybe The Fiend hadn't deserved Damir's trust. But without the protection of her memory—the sword and the shield of all she had learned during her lifetime—Eliana had come to realize that her faith and trust in others was all she really had.

Except her faith and trust in herself. Her instincts were clear. She knew her desires and those things that gave her joy. Clearly, The Fiend had enjoyed puttering in interesting shops, and Eliana liked it, too. She wasn't a different person, but she felt naked without the armor she had created for herself in a lifetime she couldn't remember.

And it had been armor. Eliana gazed at Damir as he rode along ahead of her. It had been armor she wore to protect herself from him, and perhaps, from what she had felt for him, even then. Her pride had been a wall between them, and it was threatening to become so again.

Yet his will to dominate her and his refusal to allow any vulnerability in himself, that was a wall, too, and probably built for the same reason. He didn't want her with a Norsk lover, so he'd tried to claim her for himself. If he had simply surrendered to his feelings for her, she would have answered him in full. But instead, she felt certain he had not wanted her for himself, but to keep her from someone else.

She couldn't fight the regret that she hadn't become his lover, and her own unabated desire had certainly affected her mood for the worse since they'd left Amon-dhen. But there was something more. She was waiting for something, not the restoration of her memory, but a sign that she could trust and love Damir.

A light snow began to fall, as it had in the afternoon for the last two days. It started earlier this day, and Eliana looked up miserably into the sky. Damir had made a quick shelter for them the past two nights, and she had been warm enough sleeping, but the wind had picked up all through this day, and even her fluffy shearling coat couldn't negate its bite.

They rode along an empty road, and the snow fell harder. Both Llwyd and Selsig bowed their heads, and Eliana pulled her hood up, then tucked it around her face. It wasn't even sunset yet, and the sky grew dark in the east, then slivered to an ominous dark blue in the west.

"It is going to be a long night," she muttered.

Damir glanced back over his shoulder and nodded. "And cold."

Their words felt strange and hollow, strained for lack of speech between them. "If you agree," he added, "we should ride on a while longer, despite the weather."

"I don't mind," she answered, but she sighed.

They rode on, and the snow fell in fat flakes until Selsig's neck and mane were covered in white. The land was flat, with only a few bare trees, but Eliana noticed a small fork in the road ahead. She urged her reluctant mare into a trot and caught up with Damir. "There is a sign beside that other road," she said. "But I cannot make out the words."

"It is written in the Norsk tongue," said Damir. "It reads, THE SIGN OF THE LUSTY BOAR." He groaned. "A tavern, and one notorious enough that I have heard tell of it."

Eliana looked up at him. Her teeth chattered and her lips were numb. "Damir, even if it's on fire, it will at least be warm. Please, let us go."

He eyed her doubtfully. "You've seen the Norsk, Eliana. At best, they'll be drunk and brawling. At worst . . ."

"You have your sword. Threaten them!"

"This far north, there are as likely to be Norsk warriors as traders."

"You can handle them, too. Can't you?"

"I can, yes, but I don't relish a night fighting to protect your virtue."

"If they're that drunk, you might be fighting to protect your own. But right now, I don't care. I can't feel my toes, my nose is frozen . . ."

"And your lips are blue." Damir sighed. "Very well. As cold as it is, I see no other way. If the battle begins now, so be it. At least we'll be warm."

The Lusty Boar was everything Damir had warned. Loud voices sounded even before they reached the front door, and the windows were covered in a haze that indicated the interior was both warm and filled with customers. Damir found a stable boy outside, and paid him a good sum to take the horses. The boy seemed pleased with the task, and Eliana relaxed when Selsig nuzzled him and he slipped her a carrot. He was more leery of Llwyd, who seemed embarrassed to be in such crude surroundings. Selsig took to the place with glee.

Damir stopped in the courtyard and turned to Eliana. "I'll try to get us a room, if there are any available, and if they'll rent one to us." He paused and seemed uncomfortable. "But I think it wise for us to pose as husband and wife, and share the same room."

The distance between them widened with his words, and it had begun to hurt more than Eliana could have imagined. She nodded, but she didn't meet his eyes. "Very well."

"And remember, the Norsk distrust Mages. Tonight, it will be wise for us to conceal our identity. I will protect you if the need arises, but if possible, we must both mask our *ki*."

Eliana steeled herself against what was certain to be an unpleasant night, with rank smells, fights, and even worse food. Beyond that, she dreaded another cold and awkward night with Damir. He climbed the stairs to the tavern entrance, and Eliana tucked herself in close behind him. He reached for the large brass door handle, but the door opened from inside and a huge man in a coat of rough hide and fur came tumbling out.

"And stay out!" A large blond woman thrust herself into the doorway and dusted her hands on her apron. Eliana peeked out from behind Damir to stare at her. The woman caught sight of them and laughed loudly.

"Two black-haired Woodland folk! And in the Wasteland in the middle of a snowstorm!" She didn't let them speak as she stood back in the door. "Don't mind him," the woman added as she gestured at the man at the bottom of the steps. "He's taken more than his share of ale, and the snow's a better bed for him, anyway."

She motioned for Damir and Eliana to enter. "We don't get many travelers from the Woodland." Her pleasant tone surprised Eliana. "I am Gudrid Jorund. Welcome to The Lusty Boar!"

Damir glanced at Eliana, and he shrugged. "Thank you. My wife and I are hoping to find a guest room for the night, and a meal."

Gudrid led them into a narrow front hall with a high desk in its midst. "We're pretty full up tonight, what with the storm delaying folks from moving on. I'm afraid I can't offer you much in the way of sleeping quarters. But I've got a room in the back still available." She paused. "It overlooks the stables. I can give you that."

"That is fine," said Damir. "We will be pleased to take it."

Gudrid furrowed her brow and studied him. "You're a polite one, aren't you? And handsome! Didn't know they bred 'em so big and tasty in Amrodel! Most of the Woodland folk are slight and weedy, like this little one beside you."

Eliana frowned. Weedy, indeed! "I am of above average height," she said, but the woman laughed.

"For one of our children, maybe. But even so, you'd best keep your wife close by. She's got a pretty face, and most of my customers aren't adverse to taking a sample of any female that passes." Gudrid flexed her arm. "Since I lost my mate, I've learned how to fend for myself, but a little sprite like this wouldn't stand a chance."

"I can take care of myself," said Eliana. She paused. "Where do we eat?"

Gudrid nodded toward a large and very loud room behind her. "We serve meals in the gathering hall, and all the ale you can drink. Mind yourselves, and you should have a good night of it. Our guests should find travelers from Amrodel interesting, just so long as you aren't Mages, of course."

"We are Mundane, traveling for purposes of trade," said Damir.

"What's wrong with Mages?" asked Eliana, but Gudrid shuddered.

"Now, you folks live with them in your midst, but there

ain't nothing that can freeze our blood like the threat of them whirling up their powers, secreting away with people's souls as they do. In the Norskland, we like to see our enemies coming, we like to see the axe that's swinging at us. With Mages, you never know what they've got up their sleeve—all slenderlike, they are, but they're known to place spells on a man that can make him think he's a hummingbird."

Eliana glanced at Damir, then mouthed the words, *"Did I do that?"*

Damir shrugged, then shook his head. "The Mages of Amrodel are unpredictable, and some few have been known to cast such afflictions," he said.

"The females are the worst," added Gudrid, but Eliana frowned when Damir nodded his agreement. "Nothing puts fear in the heart like the thought of a Woodland witch."

"I'm sure they're very dangerous," said Eliana in a flat tone. "But you mentioned food . . ."

"I did, at that, and I'm pleased to see one of your slight stature has such an interest! It will do you good—put meat on your little bones."

"So I take it no Mages come by this way?" asked Damir as Gudrid led them toward the gathering room.

"There's one, by the name of Rodern," said Gudrid. "I serve him well enough, but most of my customers clear out when he's here. He don't take to ale and salted meat—always brings his own wine, if you can believe it. But you must know of him."

"I know something of him," said Damir. "It is said he has dealings with Bruin the Ruthless."

"Can't imagine Bruin putting up with wine instead of his ale!" said Gudrid, and she laughed heartily at the image. "But maybe our chieftain has found a way to subvert the Mages. I hope so. We have enough to worry about without fear of an attack by them!"

Eliana held her breath in anticipation of the foul odor she expected, when Gudrid pushed open the door to the gathering room. Instead, she felt the warm glow of a large central fireplace against her face. She took a tentative breath, and smelled the pleasant scent of roasted meat and wood smoke, and an even more inviting aroma of freshly baked bread. She peeked around Gudrid and saw a large room filled to capacity with a variety of people. Most appeared Norsk, and as Damir had said, these men were larger and more powerful in appearance than those she had seen in Amon-dhen.

Some seemed to be warriors—they wore leather jerkins beneath cloaks, with heavy axes propped up against their chairs. Their low, sonorous conversation was broken often by hearty laughter and boisterous comments that Eliana didn't understand, and several appeared to be immersed in a type of game near the corner of the room.

Damir stood watching them with disgust, but when a pretty blond barmaid winked at him as she passed by carrying a plate of frothy mugs, he smiled in return. Gudrid shoved her way into the room, and shouted above the din. "We've got a couple of travelers from Amrodel among us tonight."

Her words silenced even the most drunken patrons, and they all turned to stare at Eliana and Damir. A few stiffened in their seats, and several warrior types took hold of their axes.

Damir stepped forward and bowed. "I am . . . Eldarian of Amrodel, and this is my wife, El . . . Ella. We are traders in simple herbs and carved wood."

One of the warriors rose somewhat unsteadily to his feet and came to face Damir. "Eldarian, eh? I am Aevar, son of Ketil, of the Eastfold in Norskland. And by trade . . ." He smiled and held up a battle axe ridged with many notches. "One day, maybe it will meet with a Mage's neck, but it won't be wasted on the simple folk of Amrodel." He eyed Damir more closely. "You have a strange look to you, not like any Woodlander I've ever seen."

"My father was a trader from Kora," Damir answered, and Eliana was impressed by his calm and the evenness of his voice. "He . . . lingered in the Woodland long enough to produce me, and moved on."

The warrior laughed. "He traded in more than Kora spice, I'd say!" He resumed his seat, then glanced at Damir.

"You're a fair size. But there's not a man in Amrodel, be he of Kora blood or not, that can take a Norskman at the table."

" 'Table?' "

The warrior pulled up the sleeve of his rough linen shirt and flexed massive muscles. Eliana grimaced, but Damir appeared unimpressed. "I'm not interested in a bout of strength."

Eliana began to sense the direction of the conversation. "A wise decision," she said. "But not to worry, husband. Your shirt is still much whiter than his."

"He is wise to refuse," added the Norskman. "Puny little fellow like him wouldn't stand a chance against a true Norsk warrior."

Damir fingered his sword, and Eliana sensed the power of his *ki* surging. She pulled him aside, then stood on tiptoes to whisper in his ear. "No magic, remember, *Eldarian?*"

Damir frowned darkly, but she felt his *ki* subside. Fortunately, the Norsk didn't appear sensitive to a rise in another's energy. Instead, they seemed to be the most earthy people imaginable. Yet Eliana didn't feel the fear she expected in their presence. "If you don't mind my asking, sir," she began, but the warrior looked at her in surprise, probably because of her polite manner.

"What is it, little fae?"

" 'Fae?' " she asked.

" 'Tis the term we use for female sprites such as your-self, for you resemble our myths of faerie creatures."

"He means 'little girl,' " added Damir, but Eliana pre-ferred the Norskman's description.

"When we met others of your kind in Amon-dhen, they were quite threatening, to me in particular. You are not. Why?"

Aevar laughed. "You met up with traders, no doubt. Their kind lolls about and if they see a woman they like, they've no choice but to win her by force. But a warrior like myself . . ." He stopped and slammed his fist into his extremely broad and hard chest. "I've only to wink, and I'll have them on my lap. A little sprite like yourself might be tempting to some, aye, but I like my women full-limbed and lusty."

Eliana eased back to Damir's side. "That is lucky, isn't it?"

Aevar cast a disparaging glance at Damir. "Looks like you've got a mate just suited for you. One of our women would leave him in a faint."

"Where's the table?" said Damir through clenched teeth, and the Norskman laughed as he guessed his chal-lenge had been accepted. He slapped his hand on a table-top and the others rose to give the challengers space. A crowd gathered around, and Eliana seized a portion of warm bread from the young tavern maid's platter. When another bulky warrior's attention focused on the upcom-ing match, Eliana added a slab of roasted meat to her plate, and a crisp chicken leg. She munched on her dinner as Damir seated himself opposite Aevar.

"Shirts off," commanded Gudrid. Eliana noticed that the other tavern maids gathered around, just outside the ring of Norskmen. Several Guerdians joined them from a separate corner of the room.

Aevar peeled off his rough linen shirt and flung it aside. His body rippled with almost unnatural muscles, and

Eliana cringed. There was such a thing as too much muscle, obviously. Several large scars dashed his skin, worn as proudly as medals of valor. Damir unbuttoned his own shirt, and Eliana fought the urge to giggle as he folded it, then set it carefully over the back of his chair.

Damir wasn't as massive as the Norskman, though until now, Eliana had considered his musculature formidable. He was certainly more beautiful. His dark skin, benefited first by being clean, glowed warm in the firelight. And in contrast to Aevar's overwhelming bulk, Damir's body seemed sculpted as if by the loving hand of a goddess who treasured the ultimate beauty of man.

Apparently, the tavern maid agreed, because she moved brazenly forward and swept her hand over Damir's skin. "It's soft like a baby's!" she exclaimed, and Eliana burst into laughter. "But he's got muscle, Aevar. Watch yourself."

Eliana caught Damir's dark look and she pressed her lips together hard. She held up her roast chicken leg and nodded. "Good luck, husband."

He turned back to Aevar. "Now what?"

"Now we test our strength," said Aevar and he placed his massive elbow on the table before Damir. He motioned for Damir to do likewise. Looking bored and annoyed, Damir did so. They clasped their fists, and Gudrid banged her hand on the table.

Before Eliana knew what happened, Aevar pinned Damir's wrist onto the table. "That was some test," she offered, but Damir glared.

"It was but the first."

If the night in The Sea Swan had been his greatest disappointment, this time spent at The Lusty Boar was likely to become his worst humiliation. Damir followed Aevar to another table, where the Norskman threw out four bone squares marked with ancient runes. He gave two to

Damir, and kept two for himself. "Fulthark," he said as if that might be an explanation for his latest challenge. "Highest wins."

Somehow, Damir managed to lose ten bouts of Fulthark, though he never felt certain of the rules. Whatever it was, it meant a lot to the Norsk, who howled with laughter each time he rolled the bone squares. With each round of the sport, he lost more gold. Worse still, Eliana stood behind his chair, and seemed to have gathered both the point of the game and its rules, and she agreed he had fared poorly each time.

Damir glanced back at her. She had finished her chicken leg and salted meat, and now nibbled on a corner of a hearty bread loaf. In her other hand, she held aloft a tankard of frothy ale, which she sipped as if sampling a rare wine—a wine such as the "weak brew" he'd given her in Amon-dhen.

"I see you're enjoying yourself," he said.

"Immensely," she replied. Damir gazed at her long enough to lose another round of Fulthark, but the sight was worth his latest defeat. Her dark hair hung long and loose around her face, and she had discarded her shearling coat so that she wore only her snug leather bodice and perfectly fitted leggings. She looked delicate and beautiful, and as at home in The Lusty Boar as he'd ever seen her.

To Damir's surprise, the Norskmen treated her with respect, and even affection. He had no idea why.

Aevar tired of the game, and he collected his winnings from Damir, then seized the pretty tavern maid and hauled her onto his lap. The woman didn't resist, and instead, snuggled up so that her full bosom rested on the warrior's bare chest. He took her mouth in a hungry kiss, but then motioned to Damir. "Watch this, Woodlander. You might learn something."

"Thank you, no," said Damir, and he rose to leave the

table. Three stout Guerdians awaited him, and he met the grim realization that they, too, had a challenge in mind.

"You've become a target," offered Eliana, speaking around a mouthful of bread. She passed him a chicken wing off another man's plate. "Eat this. You need the sustenance."

Damir ate the meat, then found himself seated with the Guerdians, engaged in another hopeless match of wits in a game they didn't bother to explain. But somehow, he ended up owing them all a round of ale. He treated himself this time, too, and one sip proved why Eliana enjoyed the brew so much. It was more filling, indeed, than any Woodland brew, and offered a heady delight. Damir finished his mug of ale, then engaged in another challenge.

As the night progressed, he had battled four Norskmen in the arm challenge, and won only once, when, as Eliana noted, the other man keeled over in a drunken stupor.

Damir replaced his shirt, but didn't bother with the buttons. It fit with his mood. Eliana seated herself at a table and motioned for him to sit opposite her. "What do you want?" he asked.

"A challenge," she replied, and she pulled back her sleeve. Her green eyes twinkled, and Damir's fury finally burst to the surface. "After what I've seen tonight, I think I'll win fairly handily."

He reached across the table, caught her beneath her outstretched arms, and lifted her high, then swung her over the table and into his arms. Eliana squealed in surprise, but she laughed, further inciting his complete loss of self-control. "A challenge? If you want a challenge . . . my beautiful Fiend . . . a challenge you will get."

The Guerdians eyed him doubtfully, then shook their heads and muttered amongst themselves, clear with the implication that they treated their women better than other races. The Norsk paid no attention whatsoever, intent on their own pursuits as they hoisted overflowing tankards of ale and engaged each other in rough combat. Aevar had partially disrobed the tavern maid, but the Norskman's crude design couldn't compare with the images in Damir's mind.

He carried Eliana through the gathering hall, paused near Gudrid, and she casually indicated a room down a long hall. Eliana squirmed and struggled, but Damir barely noticed as he stormed to the end of the hall and kicked open the door. He slammed it behind them, then dropped her to her feet.

She looked dizzy, but she pointed her finger at him. "This is it," she said, her voice broken with gasps. "You have gone too far."

"I haven't begun!"

Eliana stared at him with wide, fiery eyes, rose up on her tiptoes, seized his hair in a firm grip, then pulled him down to kiss her.

"What are . . . ?" Her tongue slipped into his mouth, and slid sensually against his. He intended to ravage her, beyond argument or battle. Instead, her little fingers worked feverishly as she pulled apart his open shirt. She kissed his neck, and tasted him, then sucked. Damir caught his breath, but she pressed her lips against his throat, then his chest. She tasted, and he felt the warmth of her wild breath against his skin.

"Eliana . . ." He clasped her shoulders, but she nipped him lightly, then pushed him back against the door. Her face knit in determination as she yanked off his shirt and flung it over her shoulder. Before he could speak again, she found the belt of his leggings and fiddled with the clasp, then lowered them past his hips. She wrapped her fingers tight around his arousal and leaned up to kiss him. Her tongue met his and she sucked, and her breath came in small gasps.

Damir was lost. His thoughts fled, and he gave himself over to the fire between them. He fumbled with her bodice, then untied its strings. He pushed it down until it pooled at her waist, then slid his hands beneath her closely fit leggings. Somehow, he lowered those, too, and she squirmed free of them, and kicked off her boots at the same time.

Their clothes dropped away, and they kissed wildly, not stopping. Eliana propped herself up on one foot, on her toes, and curled her other leg up around his. He cupped her firm bottom and lifted her off her feet. She wrapped her arms around his neck and twisted against him. She must have been frustrated by their height difference, because she slid back to her feet with an exasperated huff.

Damir leaned back against the door, truly weak this time. She stared at him with wild eyes, her hair ruffled around her face. She looked around as if taken with a fever, then fixed her fiery gaze on the low bed at the back of the little room. She seized his arms, then pushed him back toward it. Damir bumped against the bed, then flopped down backward.

Eliana didn't wait. She crawled onto him, resumed kissing him, and straddled him perfectly so that her bottom rested just above his length. She twisted around, then maneuvered herself so that she was poised just above him. He looked up at her. A low fire burned in a small hearth in the corner of their room, and it glowed on her warm skin, and sparkled in her long hair. He ran his hands up her sides, then cupped her round breasts. He grazed his thumbs over the little peaks and they pebbled to his touch. She caught her lower lip between her teeth, and her beautiful head tipped back as she leaned forward.

She reached down and took his length in her hands, then guided him to her feminine warmth. He felt her dampness against the heat of his arousal, and his whole body drew tight with desire. She moved up and down against him, pleasuring herself, but when she positioned herself above him, he caught her hips and held her still.

"Eliana, I can't stop this." He gulped and caught his breath. She looked down at him, dazed, as if she didn't understand. "Are you sure?"

She nodded, breathless. "Yes."

"It's not the ale?"

Her lips curved in a sensual smile as she lowered herself over him. "It's you."

He thought he would die of bliss. Her soft, inner folds met the blunt tip of him, then enveloped him until he ached from desire. But she stopped and took him no further, and he wondered if this was a last, dire scheme to rid him of sanity, concocted by The Fiend herself in an effort to destroy him. She moved back and forth, and his hips arched, but she didn't take him fully inside of her. "Do you want me?" she whispered.

A hoarse groan ripped from this throat, and his words came as if torn from deep within him. "I want you, Eliana. I want you before some Norsk devil can steal you from me. I want you so much that I'd kill to have you."

Everything he'd said echoed the words she hurled at him when she stormed from their room at The Sea Swan. He'd admitted his jealousy, his rage to possess her, and the madness of desire that consumed him. He steeled himself against the inevitable retort and another furious rejection. Her lips parted and she looked a little dizzy. Probably from the ale. She blinked once, slowly.

"Is that so? We will test it, shall we?"

Eliana's green eyes darkened, her lips curved in a sensual smile, and she fixed her gaze on his as she sank lower. He felt the barrier of her innocence, and it gave way to her own pressure as she took him deep inside her body. She tensed, then moaned softly as her inner walls squeezed tight around him.

She seemed uncertain, but he gripped her hips in his hands and he guided her, and she learned the rhythm as if she had craved its motion forever. Her head tipped back and she surrendered to their bliss. Damir arched and drove himself up inside her, then withdrew, and she met his thrust. Her legs curled on either side of him and she quivered as they joined. She trembled, and Damir clasped her waist, then rolled her over on her back.

He looked down into her face, then entered her slowly again. Eliana wrapped her legs around his, and her hips rose to meet him. He ached, and his pulse raged, but he held back his release until her breath came in harsh gasps, until every breath became a moan. She gripped his shoulders to steady herself and her body arched and twisted beneath his. He watched her face as the first waves of rapture crashed through her.

Damir's release claimed him with a force he'd never experienced. His whole body gave way and every portion of his energy surged and melded with hers. He moaned her name, and poured himself into her, not only his essence, but his heart and his spirit, and all that he was.

They crested together until the rapturous waves abated, and Eliana lay limp and gasping beneath him. He withdrew gently from her body and gathered her into his arms, then kissed her forehead. *We are one.*

He listened to the rapid pulse of her heartbeat, and felt her quick breaths against his skin as she rested her cheek on his chest. Her small hand found its way to his chest and her fingers curled as she lay sated beside him. He had no idea what to say, so his words came without thought. "What happened?"

She peered up at him with sleepy eyes and she smiled. "You made me yours."

"Three days ago, you left my bed in a fury for just such a claim."

"Of course." She kissed his shoulder. "You were so competent then. You had it all planned. Everything was going your way. It was so perfect."

Damir's brow furrowed as he considered this. "In contrast to this evening's progress, yes."

She gazed up at him dreamily, and almost, he thought, in love. "Tonight was a disaster. It's a wonder you could lift me at all after being so thoroughly stomped in every competition you engaged."

"Thank you for reminding me. I don't see how that would appeal to you."

"Don't you see?" She sounded wistful, and satisfied, so he could find no fault in her comment, however it reflected on him. "You weren't the strongest man in the room tonight. Even the little Guerdians made a complete pudding of you." She paused. "You know they were making up that game as they went along, don't you?"

No, he didn't know. Damir refused to answer, but she kissed him.

"True, you were masking your *ki*, but that's beside the point." She pressed her lips together adoringly.

"You like me because I'm weak?" He resisted the term, but Eliana smiled as if he'd offered her a bouquet of sweet flowers.

"Not weak. Vulnerable. And you did it, I think, for me."

He had wanted to impress her, indeed, by defeating the brawny, drunken Norskman, but he'd forgotten how much of his power involved the artful use of his superior energy. He was untrained at working without it. "If I'd had more time . . ."

"He would have beaten you twice!"

Damir frowned, but she eased closer and slid her leg over his. "Make love to me again," she whispered, and all thoughts of defeat fled his mind.

"I don't understand you. I admitted my wish to keep

you from your Norskman. Isn't that why you fled me in Amon-dhen?"

"Exactly. You admitted it, though you didn't want to. It's because you want me."

He wasn't sure of the distinction between his declaration tonight and the way he'd said it before, but Damir didn't argue. "When your memory returns, you may never forgive me."

"If that is the case, so be it," said Eliana. "But I would have this memory, no matter what, and for now, I speak for myself, and not The Fiend."

"If she returns and takes you from me . . ."

Eliana stopped him with a kiss. "Then give her a memory she will never, ever be able to forget."

Chapter Fifteen

Eliana floated upward from the depths of sleep, and the sound of distant horns blowing came to her thoughts. Great beauty accompanied the sound, as if her soul was called by something ancient and primal, and heroic beyond imagining. In her mind, she saw Damir facing an ocean of foes, and he stood alone. She couldn't reach him, but still, the distant horns called.

Her eyes snapped open, but the room was quiet. She lay snuggled close beside Damir, safe, with his arm over her as he slept. She breathed the warm masculine scent of his body, then pressed her lips against his shoulder. He stirred and opened his eyes, and his mouth formed a lazy smile.

"That was the best night of my life." Damir stretched, and his eyes darkened as he looked at her. "Shall we make the day its equal?"

Eliana kissed his neck. "It's better . . ."

He liked her suggestion—she felt him grow hard against her body. Damir gazed upward and seemed to be pondering something. "What is it?" she asked.

"We've made love . . ." He paused to count. "Three

times before sleep . . . Then twice when you woke me in the night. First, with you on top, then me."

"Then beside each other," she reminded him, and he nodded. "And when I was lying on my stomach . . ."

He gulped. "I liked that part, especially when you . . ."

Eliana blushed, then stopped his words with a quick kiss. "I liked it, too."

"Strange that I should feel so . . . ready, when by rights, we both should be sated."

"I was sated last night, and in the wee hours," said Eliana. "But now . . ."

He kissed her cheek, then her ear lobe, and his hand found its way to her breast. "I would not leave you unsatisfied, Lady."

"Nor I, you." He eased her onto her back, but a loud ruckus outside their window disrupted their intentions.

"What is that?" asked Eliana.

Damir sighed, then left the bed and looked out the narrow window that faced the stables. He glanced back at her. "I'm not sure. The Norskmen who entertained us last night appear to be leaving. After all they drank, I can't imagine rising at this early hour. The sun hasn't crested yet over the horizon." He looked out again. "But their axes are at the ready."

"Are the Guerdians leaving, too?"

"I think not," said Damir. He frowned. "Perhaps we should learn the reason, for I see only the warriors gathering, and their expressions are grim."

"From what they drank last night, do you think?" asked Eliana, but she, too, rose, and a heavy shadow set in around her heart. They looked at each other, and Damir shook his head.

"I would guess they have been summoned."

Eliana pulled on her bodice and leggings, and Damir dressed, then gathered their gear. She sat on the edge of the bed to replace her boots. "Before you woke, I thought, or dreamed, that I heard the sound of horns blowing in the distance. It was beautiful beyond measure, but still, my heart ached at the sound. But when I woke fully, I heard them no longer, so I thought it had been a dream."

"Then you heard the horns of the Norsk, and it is as I guessed. They are summoned to muster."

"That isn't a good sign," said Eliana. "Do they 'muster' often?"

"Only in times of war, but if they're summoning even their distant warriors, their intentions must be more vast than usual." Damir sighed heavily. "It would seem Rodern has reached his destination."

He held open the door, but Eliana paused to look one final time at the room where they had loved. It was small, the bed narrow, and the bedding crumpled and strewn. For a moment longer, she drew in the sight, the thick, rough wood of the wall, the small window, the primitive sconces, the heavy furniture. "For all I have seen of beauty, this room is most dear," she whispered, and Damir took her hand.

"We will bless many rooms such, Eliana," he said, but she heard the doubt in his voice.

"Once we, too, reach our destination," she replied, and he smiled, but she saw sorrow in his eyes. "You are afraid, aren't you?"

"I will not deceive you, my love. I do not know fully what we face. The Norsk legions are vast, and though I have great power, I do not know what Rodern has devised against me." He paused. "It may be that my *ki* is no longer enough, and I will fall." His expression hardened. "From here, we must ride hard and fast, and there may not be time for us to say all we need to say to each other. But I would know that you are safe, no matter what happens." Again, he paused, and she knew his next words came hard. "Whatever happens, if I cannot protect you . . . If I fall, my shield will fail, too. It may be that only your Norsk friend can save you."

Eliana shook her head, and tears filled her eyes. "No . . ."

Damir gripped both her hands. "Let him. I would have you live."

"Not without you."

"Eliana, give me your word in this. If you live, you carry me with you. Use all the power you have, and stay safe."

He needed her promise. She would give it. But she would hold a promise of her own, close in her own heart, that she would not let him fall without surrendering herself for him. "If you fall, I will do as you say."

He kissed her forehead, and mercifully, didn't guess the provision she had made for their fate. "Thank you. Our ride north will be easier for your vow."

"And to that vow, I hold."

The weather had cleared overnight, giving way to a bright sunrise and a clear day, but the snow was thick, and the ride north progressed slower than Damir had hoped. They followed in the tracks of the Norsk warriors, and by the tracks, it seemed they remained a fair distance behind. To Eliana's surprise, Selsig proved more than equipped for the task. Her thick coat proved ample protection against the cold. Even after Llwyd had tired and his energy flagged, the little mare plowed along. Llwyd seemed disgruntled, and Damir laid a blanket over the horse's back when they stopped at sundown.

Mercifully, only a few flakes of snow fell during the night, but both Damir and Eliana were too tired and too cold to make good use of their rest. He wrapped them together in their blankets, and they lay beneath the quick shelter he had readied, but the sorrow she had seen in him hadn't abated since they left The Lusty Boar.

"Damir . . ." She almost didn't want to ask. "Something weighs on your mind, and I'm afraid. What have you seen that troubles you this way?"

Damir sighed, and he didn't answer at once. "That night in The Lusty Boar, despite all the bliss we shared . . . maybe because of it . . . I dreamt, too." He fell silent again, but she didn't press him. "I saw myself alone, without power. I saw myself, as if in victory, yet without hope, without the ability to protect myself. And I knew, unless another comes forward, one whom I cannot see, that I would die, and be without you."

Eliana's heart chilled, but she wrapped her arms tighter around him. "It was only a dream. You told me once, dreams arise from our fears. They aren't real."

He smiled faintly at her reminder. "But at the time, I said that to appease you, lest your dreams remind you of who you really were, and who I was."

"Nonetheless, you were right. Go to sleep now, and dream of the time we return to Amrodel, together."

The iceland of the Norsk was even colder and grimmer than Eliana had feared. Snow drifts went on as far as sight reached, like frozen waves on an endless sea. Only tracks in the snow indicated that anyone lived in this bitter region of the world. Distant tendrils of smoke blended with softly blowing snow, but at last they seemed nearer to an inhabited area.

Damir stopped and shaded his eyes against the mid-morning sun. "There, to the north and just east, lies the village we seek. There, we will find Bruin the Ruthless, and no doubt, Rodern at his side. But how do we enter? I have pondered this as we rode, and I've come no nearer to a decision. I see no way for us to enter unseen, nor in disguise, with Rodern present. But appearing as ourselves seems likewise destined to failure."

"We could arrive as emissaries," suggested Eliana. "What was your plan when you advised we seek them out and meet them on their own ground?"

"To do just that," said Damir. "And for all its flaws, I can see no other way." He glanced back at her. "But remember your vow, Eliana. I will not ride farther unless I know you will take care for your safety."

"I will keep to my promise. You need not fear for me."

"Good." He paused. "I will shield us both when we come within sight of the village. They cannot harm us with weapons, though they might imprison us, if I do not fight at that time. It is my hope that we can reason with Bruin, or at least attempt to do so—he is not known as a reasonable man—but in so doing, we may attract the attention of your Norsk ally."

"But Damir, without my memory, how will I know him?"

"Let us hope he will know you."

They rode to the Norsk village and found that it was barred by a heavy iron gate. Two guards stood by the gate, taller than the men Eliana had seen at The Lusty Boar tavern, though smaller in build. Both wore long, pale braids and helmets, and they carried halberds that appeared dangerous as well as ceremonial.

Damir motioned for her to wait, and he road forward. The guards didn't move. "I am Damir ap Kora, Mage Protector of the Kingdom of Amrodel. I come to parlay with your leader."

Neither guard responded, nor seemed even to hear Damir, but they stepped back and the gate ground slowly open from within. Eliana held her breath, but Selsig stamped her small hooves, probably impatient for whatever fodder lay within the Norsk stables. Llwyd appeared tense but proud, and the large horse held his head high as Damir urged him forward.

Selsig, perhaps afraid Llwyd would find food before she did, trotted forward unexpectedly and positioned herself beside the larger animal.

Damir's energy focused intently, but Eliana shivered. He had shielded her. She felt the warmth of his *ki* around her. But his dream in the wilderness still haunted her, and she eased Selsig closer beside Llwyd. *I will protect you. Somehow, I will . . .*

Beyond the gate, a large crowd of Norsk had gathered. Warriors lined a rough, snow-covered roadway. Behind them, Eliana saw Norsk women and children watching curiously. She saw few old men, and they seemed to hang back farther than the children. A sense of shame emanated from them. With a cool thrill, she understood why. *They lived.* To the Norsk, a death in battle was the only honorable end for a man's life, and to live beyond its opportunity was to live in ignominy.

Eliana looked among them, but though several Norsk looked at her with suspicion, she saw no sign of recognition. If her mysterious ally was among the warriors, he gave no indication of his presence.

No warrior made a movement against Damir, but they held themselves tense and closed in behind after Eliana and Damir had passed. The long line of Norsk filed onward, then formed a wedge in front of a large wooden building. All the huts they passed had thatched roofs and roughly carved doorways, with runes Eliana guessed bore the name of the inhabitant's lineage. The door of the great hall was lined with such runes, but grander, and before the entrance stood two columns carved like tree trunks. Above the arched doorway, she saw images of battle and conquest etched deep in wood.

Damir stopped before the entrance, and the tall door swung open. A huge man appeared, and the guards at his side seemed dwarfed in comparison. Eliana required no introduction. Surely, this was the notorious "Bruin the Ruthless," and never was a man better named. Thick braids of unwashed blond hair hung low over his massive shoulders, and he wore a heavy leather jerkin laced with iron mail. In one hand, he carried an axe that looked so heavy, Eliana couldn't imagine lifting it, let along swinging it against an enemy.

Even the chieftain's legs looked like tree trunks, clad in leather greaves and boots that might have been shod in iron. Bruin exuded power, and without question, had no fear nor doubt. Eliana's gaze shifted to Damir. She knew he had fear. She knew he had doubt. But he dismounted and bowed before Bruin, and suddenly she understood those things had no power over him.

If ever a man could face this primitive leader, it was Damir. Eliana hopped off Selsig, and the little mare looked pleasantly around as if to question for facilities, and a good supply of grain. Selsig spotted a child holding an apple, and eased in that direction, but Eliana drew her back, and the little mare sighed.

"Damir ap Kora, '*Mage Protector of Amrodel,*'" said Bruin, and his deep voice matched his physique well. "It is indeed an unexpected pleasure to have the Woodland's 'greatest warrior' deliver himself upon my doorstep."

Damir stood at the foot of the wide stairs and faced Bruin. "I come to offer parlay on behalf of the Woodland, which I serve," said Damir.

"But not its king?" asked Bruin, and his voice held the ring of taunting.

Damir betrayed no emotion. "Our king is dead. But our land lives on, and its power remains undiminished. What quarrel has the chieftain of the Norsk with Amrodel? Tell me this, that I might end it."

Bruin laughed. "What quarrel? We will take your land, and bend it to our will!" He slammed his fist into his other hand. "Then we will harness what feeble power you have, and the greatness of the Norskland will stretch from here to the sea, and beyond!"

"Your aims are high," said Damir, his voice still low and quiet. "I will stop you."

Bruin waved at his guards. "Take the woman."

Eliana froze as a horde of guards moved in around her, but still, Damir didn't react. "The woman is shielded, and even were she not, she has great power in her own right."

"The chieftain knows the witch's power." Eliana startled at the mocking voice. It came from the darkness of the hall behind Bruin, but she recognized the voice even before Rodern stepped forward into the light. He looked small and weak beside the great Norsk chieftain, but Eliana sensed he had the greater power.

"Rodern," said Damir, and he didn't sound surprised. "You make great haste in the wake of murder. But you have not divulged much of your reasoning with the chieftain, I think, for the conquest of Amrodel is surely beneath your purposes. With me gone, with Eliana in your hands, you seek to wake the Arch Mage . . . and what? Share his power with your Norsk allies?"

"A great power awaits a land long held at bay by the Mages of Amrodel," answered Bruin. "It is right that I should harness it, and bend it to my command."

"I do not think you understand the nature of that which you seek," said Damir. "The Arch Mage is harnessed by no one—not you, and certainly not Rodern. Or will you do this dark wizard's bidding, and serve him like slaves, as he once commanded the Guerdians, so that only a few of their previous numbers remain?"

Bruin waved his hand dismissively. "There is no power greater than the will of the Norsk. I will command him, and it is he who will be my slave."

"Where did you get that idea?" asked Eliana, too surprised by Bruin's arrogance to feel fear. "Rodern may be persuasive, but that's just crazy."

"We have you, dark witch," answered Bruin. "Our Mage Servant, Rodern, will use you to call forth this great power, but he will answer to us for your sake."

"Or he will just take me, and destroy all of you in vengeance."

Bruin ignored her. "While your magic shield remains, we cannot destroy you. But Rodern, who serves the Norsk to the benefit of us all, has devised a method to keep you interred, and harmless while we determine your fate. But come," he added, his voice rich with his arrogance. "I would not have it said that the hospitality of my hall is lacking. Enter, Mage Protector, and bring your witch with you. Eat, and tell me what you would do against me." He laughed, but without awaiting a response, turned and entered his great hall.

Damir waited for Eliana to join him, and they followed. High torches lined the hall, and inside, Eliana saw the same columns carved like tree trunks. They led back past great tapestries that showed the battles of Norsk history, past guards standing like statues, and low fires that warmed the hall through its endless winter.

Bruin led them to the rear of the hall, where a large seat sat upon a platform. There, the light from the remote sun pierced high windows and sent its feeble rays down to those who waited.

Two women stood by the seat, and behind them, a tall, thin boy waited with his head bowed. He appeared to be a servant or a slave, but as they approached, the light of the cold sun glanced on his pale hair and it shone as if it had sought him out on purpose. Slowly, he lifted his head, and the light of his amber eyes fell upon Eliana. For one second only, their gazes met and held, and she knew him. But not from memory. She had seen him in a dream.

* * *

"You, boy, bring me bread and ale." Bruin waved his hand and the boy bowed, then retreated from the hall. Damir glanced at Eliana as she stood beside him, but her face looked pale and her eyes were wide with shock. Damir looked around, but he saw no man who fit his image of her Norsk ally. Instead, her attention appeared fixed on the servant boy who returned silently and poured ale into an overlarge tankard, which Bruin seized.

Damir eyed the Norsk boy. For a child, he was uncommonly handsome, his face more refined and sculpted than any Norskman Damir had seen. He appeared to be about fourteen years of age, in the midst of growth that promised great height. The boy didn't look at Damir, and he glanced only once at Eliana. Unlike the others in the hall, he showed little curiosity about the faces of his enemies up close. Perhaps his life was harsh enough as Bruin's slave to warrant little interest in the threat of others.

Bruin drank heartily of his ale, but his pale eyes remained focused on Damir, as a man assesses his challenger. "My Mage ally, Rodern here, tells me you have great power, and that by your magic, you have already defeated many of my warriors."

"I have done so," said Damir, "when they challenged me at the border of the land I am sworn to protect. But I do not desire battle."

Bruin huffed and wiped his chin with his sleeve. "From what I see, you are not fit to battle even the least of my warriors." He didn't wait for his taunt's effect as he absently waved his arm, indicating no one. "Here, prove yourself, Mage Protector! Battle the least of my warriors before me, and I will decide if you are worthy to treat with me."

Bruin turned in his chair and motioned to the boy behind him. "You, boy—defend the honor of my house! Your lord commands it." He spoke with deliberate mockery, but despite his attempt to belittle the boy, Damir sensed a penetrating anger—this was a boy he wanted humbled, not because he scorned the child, but because, impossible as it seemed, Bruin feared him.

The boy stepped forward to stand beside Bruin's chair. He revealed no emotion, no expression, and his amber eyes fixed straight ahead.

"Do as I bid, boy," said Bruin, and he drank again of his ale.

"I will not fight your slave," said Damir.

Bruin laughed. "If you cannot face even this, the least of my warriors, you are even weaker than I imagined!"

Eliana stepped forward and placed herself in front of Damir. "Damir will not fight with a child!"

Bruin laughed. "You have little faith in your 'Mage Protector,' witch. Be silent!" Bruin kicked at the boy. "Have you no courage, boy? Face him, or face the shame you have earned already!"

Silently, the boy descended the steps, seized an axe from the guard, and faced Damir. Tears welled in Eliana's eyes, and she looked desperately to Damir. He knew she expected him to prevent this, but he drew out his sword and took a step toward the child.

Eliana seized his arm, and her voice quavered. "No . . . you cannot."

Damir hesitated, but the boy raised his axe and swung without warning. Eliana's breath caught with a broken cry as Damir raised his sword. Damir focused his *ki* and it surrounded him, strong and impenetrable. The boy's axe did not ring against the sword, but impacted with Damir's own energy. In a flash, the light surged and enveloped the boy, then abated. Damir's *ki* wavered and he stared at the child. "*What are you?*" Damir murmured, but the boy stumbled back, then regained his position facing Damir.

The Norsk chieftain laughed, but Damir's attention fixed on the boy. The other warriors mocked the boy, but they could not know what Damir had felt in that one instant—that the lad himself owned the light, and Damir's energy was as nothing before it. It had lasted only a second, and then was lost, but the impact remained strong as Damir regained command of the dragonfly sword.

The Norsk boy stood motionless, his face set in grim determination, until he swung his weapon again. Again, the power of Damir's sword deflected the attack. This time, Damir's *ki* held without wavering. Maybe he had imagined the break, the strange surge of the boy's power. It was not present in his second advance.

The boy again lifted his axe, but Bruin stood up, bored. "Stop! As before, you have done me no honor, and cannot dent even a Mage's feeble sword."

"Would you like to try?" asked Damir. "You would fare no better."

Bruin's eyes gleamed as he fixed his attention on the white sword. "Without that sword, you would be powerless. With such a weapon, a true warrior would rule supreme over all."

Damir laughed, tossed his sword in the air, then lobbed it toward Bruin. "Any man who dares claim it, do so!"

Bruin grabbed at the sword, but it flashed with light and the Norskman howled with pain, then clutched his right hand. The sword clattered to the ground, and Damir retrieved it.

Rodern edged toward Bruin's side, his lips curled in a sneer. "The sword is charmed, my Lord Chieftain. It will accept no other hand but that of Damir ap Kora. It will sear any other, save those with a Mage's power to match Damir's. To hold that sword would be death—but no matter."

"The Mage Protector and his sword are not easily parted," agreed Damir.

"The weapon will do you no good," said Rodern. "I cannot devise an antidote to your shield, but my Norsk friends can hold you hostage. I knew, of course, that the fall of my tower wouldn't destroy you, Damir, but it served my purposes nonetheless. It gave me time to devise a more fitting end for the Mage Protector of Amrodel—and because of your foolishness, you've delivered the heir of the Woodland queen into our grasp."

"She is in your midst, yet she is safe with me," said Damir.

"For now," replied Rodern, and his tone was mocking. "For now."

"Guest quarters have been arranged for you," said Bruin, and the tone of his voice indicated that no "guest" would welcome these. "Either surrender the woman willingly, or remain trapped here by Rodern's magic while my legions annihilate your land."

"Neither is my choice," said Damir, and he guessed Rodern was far too intent on his scheme to risk invading Amrodel without purpose or chance of gain.

Eliana turned to Damir, but she seemed more distracted than afraid. "What do we do?" she asked.

Damir glanced at Eliana as the guards came forward to take them. He nodded, and mouthed the words, *"Let them."* They had to go along with Bruin's illusion of control until their unseen ally arrived. If he had been wrong, then indeed he would battle the Norsk legions—and win, unless Rodern had developed some tactic he couldn't foresee.

The guards led them from the great hall to a wooden hut lined with iron bars. Damir barely saw their direction. It wasn't the energy of a Mage he had perceived, but neither was it the brute force Damir knew from other Norskmen he had fought. *What is that child?*

The guards seemed wary of Eliana, perhaps more so than of Damir, but she offered no resistance when they manacled her wrists to a chain, then bound her to the wall. They bound Damir likewise, then hurried away, leaving them in darkness.

"Are you all right?" he asked.

"Damir . . . I think I have found my ally, but . . ."

"*No* . . . Not the boy . . ."

She started to answer, but a thin figure moved like a shadow from the back of their cell. " 'The boy,' " said a low, soft voice. "I am Aren, son of Arkyn." The Norsk slave hadn't spoken until now, but Damir didn't need to see the child's face to recognize him. Despite his youth, the voice came closer to the strange power Damir had sensed when the boy first wielded his primitive axe.

"I was afraid of this," said Damir, but the boy went to Eliana and unlocked her manacles, then freed her.

The boy's gentleness left no doubt as to the identity of her "ally," and Damir drew a long, miserable breath. "Wonderful." The valiant Norsk hero they sought was, instead, an infatuated youth.

"Your name is Aren?" asked Eliana.

"It is me, Lady," he answered. "I was afraid you wouldn't recognize me because I've grown so much since you last saw me."

Damir, still affixed to the cold stone wall, frowned. "How small were you before?"

Aren ignored Damir's slight, though Eliana cast him a reproachful glare.

"Fear not, Lady Eliana. I will take you from this place. But I do not understand . . ."

He helped her away from the wall but gave no indication that he intended to free Damir likewise. Aren gently wrapped her shearling coat over her—Damir spotted his own lying in a heap by the corner.

"What is it, Aren?" She fished around in her pockets, then pulled out her mittens and held them happily against her cheek. Apparently, she hadn't noticed that Damir was still bound to the wall.

For the first time, Aren turned his gaze to Damir. His eyes were the clear amber common to his people, but there was a strange depth and wisdom in his gaze. "Why did you let *The Demon* speak for you?"

Eliana's eyes widened. "The *what?*"

"Is this not he?" asked Aren. "The man you called *The Demon?*"

Of course! "The Fiend" would have chosen such a name for him. Damir frowned, but Eliana brightened and she smiled, too happy for their dire circumstances. "Is that what I called him? How fitting!"

"Yes," said Aren, confused. "Don't you know?"

"No, sadly, I do not. It is too much to explain now, but suffice to say I drank a potion that erased my memory."

Aren's breath caught like a hiss, and he turned to Damir, fury snapping in his eyes. "Had I known this, I would have slain you at the foot of the Great Hall!"

Damir's face felt etched with annoyance. "Is that so? I don't recall that you had much choice in that regard."

"Only because I restrained myself," said Aren.

Damir wanted to argue, but he knew now what he had felt in the skirmish with the child. Impossible as it was to believe, the boy had been restraining himself.

Eliana bit her lip and looked even happier. "It is good you didn't kill him, Aren. While it's true I drank the potion thanks to Damir—The Demon's—trickery, I am not without fault. It was I who called him to the truce, and I who attempted to administer the brew upon him."

"Of course," said Aren. "That means you finally perfected your potion." He paused and sighed. "I thought it was risky, given his treachery, but obviously you came close."

"Close to what?" asked Damir. His arms ached, and the term "Demon" was beginning to grate.

"Close to fulfilling her great plan," answered Aren. "When you first arrived, I assumed it had worked, and I guessed you spoke as she instructed. Had I known otherwise, I would have killed you then and there."

271

"You saw what happened when your chieftain touched my sword," said Damir, annoyed. "Your fate would have been no different."

"I don't know about that, *Demon,*" said Eliana.

Damir's teeth ground together. "He would have been seared to a crisp, and left in a puddle of blood."

Eliana winced. "Must you be so . . . blunt? Show him the hilt of your sword."

Damir flexed his—manacled—wrists. "And how would you suggest I do that?"

"Oh . . . yes. Aren, if you would please release The Demon, I promise he will do no harm."

"Don't count on it," said Damir.

"Don't mind him," said Eliana pleasantly. "He is testy from our long ride, little sleep, and less food."

Eliana gestured at the sword which hung at Damir's side. "Look at the hilt, Aren."

He leaned forward and held up his torch, but then his eyes widened. "The dragonfly stone!"

"I assume it was as gift from you?" asked Damir.

"It was," said Aren, but he still gazed in awe at the hilt. "The hilt of a sword is a far greater home for the jewel I made than adornment for woman's garb! But how does it come there?"

"Damir and I made the sword together, before I knew the truth of who I really am," answered Eliana. "The brooch seemed right, so I placed it there myself. So it has something of you in it, too."

Eliana sounded proud, like a mother. All his past jealousy of an imagined lover seemed foolish beyond measure, and Damir pressed the thought from his mind. "Since I used your jewel in my greatest creation, don't you think it fair to release me?"

"He is right, Aren," said Eliana. "Through this sword, we are all joined, and the bond between us is fated."

"As you wish, Lady," Aren started, reluctantly, to free

Damir, but he hesitated before he unhitched the manacle. "If he tricked you into taking this potion yourself, how can we trust him?"

"He didn't know its purpose then. He hasn't asked me to do anything . . . political." At last, she sounded embarrassed.

Aren's eyes narrowed. "What did he tell you, then? Not the truth, I'd wager."

Her eyes shifted and she shuffled her feet. She must have guessed the boy was infatuated with her. "Well . . . he told me I was his wife."

Aren whipped out his axe and elevated it to Damir's throat. "For this, I would kill you now. At her word, you die!"

Damir's irritation reached a pinnacle. "You cannot breach my shield, boy." Despite the youth's slight build, he appeared to have no trouble holding up the heavy axe, but Damir didn't care. "Put that primitive weapon down before your arms give out."

"Damir! There is no need for rudeness!"

"He is holding an axe at my throat, and *I'm* rude?"

Eliana tapped the boy's bony shoulder. "Please release him, Aren. He has not harmed me. And it's possible . . ." She paused and cast a mischievous glance Damir's way. "It's possible that my feelings for The Demon have always been . . ." She paused and tapped her lip thoughtfully. "*Complicated.*"

"I know that, Lady," said Aren, but rather than the jealousy Damir expected, he heard sympathy and compassion in the boy's voice. "It is for that reason that I feared for you, and do not trust him now."

"You know I cared for him?" asked Eliana, but then she paused. "Did I?"

"You never said so," said Aren. "And I never asked. But when we first met, you were weeping, and this man was the reason."

Wonderful. They'd probably both leave him there hanging. Damir had begun to lose feeling in his fingers, but neither Eliana nor Aren seemed likely to sympathize at this point.

"Can we save this until you've led us to safety?" He didn't like the way the conversation was going. It had been Eliana—a woman rightly known as "The Fiend"— who tormented him, and himself who suffered. A strange tightness began around his heart at the hint he might have been wrong.

"Perhaps that is best," said Eliana. Maybe she was afraid to hear the story, too. "Where are you taking us?"

Aren sighed with exaggerated heaviness, then released Damir's manacles. Damir rubbed his wrists, with more care than his pain actually warranted, then picked up his coat from its heap by the corner. Aren turned his back to Damir, and gestured toward the door. "To a place of safety, Lady. Follow me."

Chapter Sixteen

Aren led them from the dungeon, but Eliana froze at the sight of two guards standing by the door. There was no way to pass them without being seen. To her surprise, Aren simply went to them, spoke quietly, and the two Norskmen glanced up and down the snowy street, then motioned for Aren to pass.

He waved to Eliana and Damir. Damir shook his head. "That child has far more power than his size warrants."

"He's almost as tall as you . . ."

"He's a full head shorter."

Eliana hushed him, and they crept forward after Aren. He led them quickly across the street and into the darkness behind what appeared to be a noisy tavern. A light snow fell, and the lights from heavy lanterns blurred in the dark. He stopped and seemed to be waiting for something. "Why did the guards let us pass?" asked Eliana. "Do you have some sort of hypnotic power over others, Aren?"

He eyed her doubtfully. "I asked them, Lady."

"Of course," said Damir. "I remind you, Lady Witch,

that the Norsk do not have the *ki* of a Mage, even this boy."

"He has a power neither your nor I understand, Damir. Admit it!"

Damir frowned. "Maybe so—but it's not the *ki* of a Mage."

"Stubborn man."

Aren peered down a footpath that ran behind the tavern, then shaded his eyes against the falling snow. "This way, Lady." He ignored Damir, which pleased Eliana. For once, she was the trusted one.

Aren led them through deep snow. Neither he nor Damir seemed to mind, but Eliana was thankful for her new boots as she picked her way along. In the shadow of the snowy lamplights ahead, Eliana saw tall figures waiting, and beside them, three horses. She recognized Selsig, the smallest and fattest, and Llwyd, taller and lean, but the third looked like her mare's bigger brother. Rough-coated and heavy-limbed, Aren's pony was as large as a horse, but his build was stocky and his coat much heavier than that of either of the other two.

Aren greeted the waiting Norskmen, and Eliana saw a woman among them. She held Llwyd, and patted his neck before handing his reins to Damir. "This is a fine horse," she said. "Good for racing, but his hardiness is questionable. I added an extra blanket beneath his saddle, and we wrapped his legs to protect his delicate skin. You have chosen a horse suited for you, but not the north."

Damir frowned as he mounted. "We fare better in the frozen north than any of you or your fat ponies would do in the desert of Kora."

"The warmth would, indeed, be tiresome, and make for weak limbs, I think," said the woman. "Though in the darkness of winter, a visit to a desert might not be unwelcome."

Damir settled himself into his saddle. "Who are you people, and why do you dare defy Bruin the Ruthless?"

Aren turned to him. "We are those loyal to the land my brother has joined into one," he said. "We are loyal to the man he was before the Mage Rodern poisoned his mind with greed and desire for greater conquest, before darkness infected his soul."

Eliana stared at him, aghast. "Bruin the Ruthless is your brother?"

"We are sons of the same father, yes."

"Then how could he treat you as a slave?"

Aren took his horse from its handler, and his young face was grave. "I defied him, and in his anger, he made me his servant."

"Apparently, he didn't get the title 'Ruthless' for nothing," said Eliana. "It's a wonder he didn't kill you."

"He may yet," said Aren. "For such a betrayal as this tonight, the penalty is death. Bruin will know as soon as he discovers your escape that I am responsible." Aren turned to his followers. "The guards know what to do?"

"I have told them to leave signs of a struggle, and they will leave a trail eastward," answered a Norskman.

"It won't throw Bruin off our trail for long," said Aren. "But it will give us time to plan our defense, and give the Mage a chance to effect his plan."

Eliana glanced at Damir, but he gave no sign of doubt. "You risk yourself for us, Aren," she said. "Why do you have such faith we can help?"

Aren glanced at Damir, then mounted his stout horse. "You had faith in him, Lady. You said he could defend us, and bring my brother back to sanity. And I have faith in you."

Following Aren, they rode long into the night, but the boy seemed to know every path in the dark, and he never wavered. The snow ceased and the wind stilled, but the night grew bitterly cold and Eliana drew her coat tight around her. She had long ago lost feeling in her toes.

Aren glanced back at her. "You are chilled, Lady?"

"A bit, yes. Don't you feel the cold?"

He smiled and shook his head. "It is a pleasant evening to me. But in summer, we Norskmen suffer the heat as you do the cold."

"Do you have summer here?" asked Damir. He hadn't spoken much during their ride, and Eliana sensed something was troubling him.

"We do," said Aren, "and it is a time of great beauty, and great celebration for my people. The barren meadows spring to life with red and yellow flowers, springs burst forth into swift streams, and all that was frozen renews. In this season, the newborn animals come from their dens, and a short time of planting begins for us. It is said that our ancestors moved north and feared the winter, for they had struggled to live—and many fell. But when spring came, and then summer, they fell in love with this land, and we bonded ourselves to its soul. We fought to survive, and we came to love the battle. It made us what we are."

"I have heard a different description of your people," said Eliana, and she glanced over at Damir, who rode beside her.

"We knew little of the Norsk in Amrodel," said Damir. "Until your brother began assailing our borders, there was little contact between our races. The love of battle exceeds the desire for survival, it seems."

Aren sighed. "It has come to that, yes, and for this reason, I first defied my brother. He ordered me to lead an ambush against a Guerdian party traveling to Amondhen. There was no reason behind it. We have no quarrel with the Guerdians, so I refused."

"Why did he want you to attack them, then?" asked Eliana.

"I don't know. It is said, by other races who know us little, that we battle for sport, but that hasn't always been true. Our people place a high value on our warriors, and our legends and songs praise them above all others. To die in battle, that is a great honor, and one many seek. A man who lives to old age must have many scars, if he lives at all, or his life is deemed unworthy. But though battle has defined us, its goal has always been the good of our people, and our survival. Now, I fear, it has changed."

"Bruin's greed has changed it," said Damir.

"So it would seem," agreed Aren. "But it was not always so. Even before my birth, my brother dreamt of uniting our people, long sundered by warring clans with chieftains who saw nothing greater than their own little realms, their own fields and taverns. Bruin wanted more, and he believed we could be made whole."

"He seems impossibly arrogant," said Eliana. "It is hard to imagine he was acting for anything more than his own aggrandizement."

"Now, perhaps," said Aren. "But he was different then. The man you saw in the great hall is not the man he was. He was always proud, and his confidence in his abilities knew no shadow. But he was also good, and even kind. Though we were not of the same mother, he treated me well. He taught me to fight, with axe, club, and sword, as well as with my own hands. He was a patient tutor, and I admired him. I admire him still, but a darkness has descended upon him and many others, one I do not understand."

Eliana turned to Damir. "Could this be the same dark current that infects even those in the Woodland?"

"It could," said Damir. "This may be what brought Rodern and Bruin together, because they are caught in that same current. Their own vanity and desire for power makes them susceptible."

"That is true," agreed Aren. "When I first heard people whisper that Bruin had met with Mages of Amrodel, I didn't believe it. It was beneath him to seek out magic to further his ends, rather than to rely on his own valor and wits. And for a long time, I ignored the rumors. But when my brother began to speak of invading the Woodland, I knew it was true, though I didn't know with whom he met."

"How did you and I meet?" asked Eliana.

"I was on my Quest of the Warrior," said Aren, and he smiled at the memory. "That was five or six summers ago now."

"You came to the Woodland alone?" asked Eliana. "You must have been very young!"

"I was nine years. It is the age of testing for the warrior class of my people. This was before the darkness took hold of my brother, and I wanted to make him proud, so I took a greater quest upon myself."

"What was it?" asked Eliana.

"My task was to bring home evidence that I had encountered a Woodland witch."

"A witch? You mean a woman?" asked Eliana.

"The females are most fearsome to my people," said Aren. "Because they are slight of build, yet have power than can level the strongest among us. Your kind was rumored to be the most vicious."

"That much is certain," said Damir, but Eliana ignored him.

"What did you have to do for this quest?" she asked.

"I was to steal something from a witch's lair."

"Not unlike a quest to a dragon's lair," said Damir. "Though perhaps more dangerous."

Eliana frowned. "Let him speak!" She turned back to Aren. "So you entered Amrodel to steal from me?"

"Yes, Lady," he answered.

"Why didn't my shield bar your entrance?" asked Damir.

"It did, I think," said Aren. "No matter how I tried, I couldn't find my way into the forest. At first, I thought it was because I was unfamiliar with the growth of trees, but it seemed to me that they moved, and shifted. Even when I marked my trail, it disappeared when I attempted to retrace my steps. I then realized it was a Mage who barred my way."

"Good. Then it did work," said Damir. "Go on."

"I did not give up, but I was lost. I had run out of food, and I confess that I began to lose hope. I could not return to our land empty handed, but neither could I find any sign of what I sought, the trail of a witch. I couldn't move forward, and kept moving in circles instead, and soon I thought I would die there."

"Your shield confused him," said Eliana reproachfully.

Damir's expression darkened still more. "That's what it's supposed to do!"

"How did you get out?" she asked.

"I didn't, Lady. I wandered without hope, but a strange thing happened. An insect came to me . . ."

Damir nodded. "Let me guess. A dragonfly."

"It was," said Aren. "But larger and more beautiful than those that dart over our meadows in summer. Its wings were a pale violet color, and it hovered before me, then moved on through the forest. I followed, and the creature led me to that which I sought—a dark-haired woman wearing a grey, hooded cape passed by me."

"Me?" asked Eliana.

"You," said Aren.

"Were you afraid of me?"

"A little. But you didn't seem dangerous to me, despite all I had heard of the Witches of Amrodel and their power. Instead, you seemed . . . lonely. I followed you up a long, winding path, but just as I caught up with you, you turned and saw me, and for a reason I don't understand, I fainted, though I have never done such a thing before."

"It was the shield," said Damir. "It responded to Eliana's fear of you. If you acted in threat against one of us in the Woodland, the shield would claim your waking mind and leave you vulnerable—unless your victim trusted you."

"She had no reason to trust me, not then," said Aren. "But neither did she kill me as I thought a witch would. I woke and she was gone, but I followed her trail."

"I left a trail?" asked Eliana.

"One only a Norsk warrior could read, Lady. A broken twig, the soft impact of a shoe on fallen leaves—these are enough for a Norskman to track."

"I trust my shield prevented that," said Damir.

"It did not," said Aren, and he sounded proud. "But my intentions had changed, so your shield had no effect on me then. It was curiosity that drove me. Why didn't she kill me? Why was she so alone? So I followed her. Her path led northward, and even though I guessed she was seeking help against me, I followed."

"Where did I go?" asked Eliana.

"You went within sight of a cottage built into the mountainside, and there you stopped."

Eliana turned to Damir. "I went to you."

Damir looked uneasy, but Aren nodded. "I believe you intended to enlist this man's help or tell him about me, but when you arrived, he emerged from the dwelling with a woman." Aren paused and his amber eyes narrowed. "A woman who fawned over him, praised his 'magnificence,' and thanked him for the 'blessings of the night.'"

"I see," said Eliana. And she did, too well. "Go on."

Aren administered a scathing look upon Damir, then turned back to Eliana. "In my land, it is not this way. A woman does not pretend to admire a man's skill, or pretend to love him, if all she desires is his flesh."

"In your land, men take as many women as they wish," said Damir. "I had not heard that love entered into it at all."

"We love," said Aren, and his soft voice indicated that he considered the Norsk emotion far removed from the baseness of Woodland passion. "But we know that only a rare few share this bond, and for the rest, lust suffices as another matter entirely."

"Perhaps that was true for me, also," said Damir.

"But you had this bond already, and you denied it."

"She denied it first!"

"It is the man's duty to make the woman safe," said Aren. He sounded like a patient elder speaking with a miscreant youth.

"And he didn't give me reason to trust, it seems," Eliana added.

Damir huffed. "If I had, you would have . . ."

"Delivered a potion in your stew that would make you think you were a chicken, and had you pecking about your yard for worms! I'm sorry I missed the opportunity!"

"Only because I kept a close watch on you, woman!"

Aren interrupted them with a heavy sigh. "Things have not changed so much between you as I imagined."

Eliana's eyes filled with tears and her shoulders slumped. "No, I guess they haven't."

Aren reached from his pony and patted her knee. "For some, the journey is long, and there are many tests along the way. But the destination remains as long as you keep going."

She looked up at him and saw kindness and wisdom in his amber eyes. "I hope so."

"We all face a future. It is laid out before us as we enter life, like a map from a high mountain to a distant shore. Some points are set along the way. These things, we will do, and these events will happen whether we will them or not. How we get to those points, at what time of day or in what weather, that is uncertain, but the people we meet along the way, for good or for ill, that also, I believe, is destined, and so it was with you and me."

"How do you know this?" asked Eliana. "Is this the teaching of Norsk priests?"

Aren smiled, and for a moment he looked young. "I *am* a Norsk priest, Lady. I was born knowing these things that elude others. I do not know why. Few listen to me, and fewer still hear. But that is why I knew you were good."

"What do you see for me and Damir?" She held her breath for his answer.

"Only what I see for all who are bound as you are. That a time will come when you both must surrender, and when you both must choose. The journey onward from that point to the shore will be altered by that day. Our choices along the way determine our fate."

Eliana glanced at Damir, afraid of what she might see on his face, if it was scorn or disbelief. But his gaze shifted from Aren to her, and what she saw instead pierced her heart. It was fear, fear his choice was wrong, or that he would fail.

"But if it is set, Aren, how is there a choice at all?" she asked.

Aren smiled. "Because the wisdom of our souls determines the choice." He looked between them, and now, he looked almost ancient. "Have faith in yourselves! You doubt too much, I think."

"But he hurt me . . . And I think I hurt him."

"Because you fear each other, but see—you are still by his side, and he is with you. Your path is set, though maybe you do not see it. Long ago, you planned to steal his memory. You thought to set him on this path where he would defend my people, and save us from darkness, for indeed, only he can do that. Fate intervened—your intentions were good, but your faith in him was lacking. But here you are, by his will instead, doing the same thing."

"This was her plan, then," said Damir, and his voice was very quiet. "Not to 'turn me into a chicken' or her slave, but to bring me here, to prevent war, and save the good she saw in your people."

"I believe that is so," said Aren. "Mostly." He didn't say

what else Eliana had planned, but Eliana was beginning to understand the woman she had been when she was known as "The Fiend," and she had a fair guess.

She looked over at Damir. Snow moved in soft gusts around their horses, around Damir, and beyond. The night sky receded into a dark indigo. Somewhere above, the waning moon must have faded to a sliver, but its dim light reached the snow and reflected its way back into the sky. Strange that here in the Norskland, where the day sun lasted only a few hours, the night should be lighter than in the Woodland. Here, light was a treasure, and even beneath a cloudy sky, it found its way.

He is so beautiful. . . . Damir rode with his hood thrown back, and his black hair fell loose around his shoulders. She saw in him now the struggle between darkness and light, and she knew that he felt it, too. He was doubting everything he had chosen, what he had wanted, and what he wanted now. Eliana closed her eyes, and her mouth moved in a silent prayer, *"Please, when the time comes, let him want me."*

"Yonder lies the hamlet of Eddenmark," said Aren. "I have led us northeast in the night by a longer path than the usual road, lest Bruin send out scouts in this direction. Already, my riders will have come this way by the wider road, and will tell us what we will face. The hamlet is only a short ride this morning, and we make take our rest in The Snow Pony inn, which is my favorite because the wild ponies gather here in winter. My brother will expect us to ride southwest toward Amrodel, though he will soon learn of his error. But I chose this area for another reason."

Damir looked around. The hamlet was built on a high, wide mound, and from its vantage point, visibility would stretch far. Any attacker would be forced to climb that long slope, and prove a rare target for defenders. "The geography lends itself to battle, and a fair defense," said Damir.

Aren smiled. "You are a warrior, despite your appearance." Before Damir could comment, the boy nodded. "I thought my brother was wrong in his assessment of you. Though you lack the bulk of our strongest warriors, you appear quick. Lady Eliana informed me you had no equal in battle—though I sensed then that she favored you and might be biased."

Did she? She had never complimented his skill during their long past. "I can fight," Damir said. "But it is my *ki*, the energy of my spirit, which renders me powerful."

"Yes, she told me about that, though I didn't fully understand it until I battled you myself." Aren didn't seem as impressed as he should have been, but neither was he dismissive. "She said you had trained this *ki* since your childhood, and that you could direct it in battle. Because of this, she convinced me that you could defeat my brother—as no man ever has—and free him from the bonds the dark Mage has placed upon him."

"I do not believe Rodern has enslaved your brother with a spell, Aren," said Damir. "The force that controls him is greater than any living Mage."

"I know this, too," said Aren, and Damir repressed a breath of frustration. "Lady Eliana told me of your history, of an evil wizard who now lies buried but undead, beneath the Guerdian mountains. She said he called to her, so she knew it was his energy that rode the dark current, and that she feared it would infect all of us. Though I have not yet heard it myself, others among my people have reported something akin to this."

Damir turned to Eliana in wonder. "You knew this, even then?"

She shrugged. "Apparently. But why didn't I say anything?"

"You feared the other Mages, Lady. You knew one, at least, among them had treated with my brother and engaged him against your people. You spoke of a new darkness in the king, your uncle, and said that this man, Damir, was the only one you trusted."

Damir beamed and his heart filled with happiness. "Truly? She said that?"

"As a Mage," said Aren. "Not as a man."

"Still . . . you trusted me."

She looked at him and shook her head, but she was smiling. "If only you had felt the same." She paused. "But the king . . . could he have been in league with Rodern?"

"I doubt it," said Damir. "He spoke of a darkness growing within himself." He paused, hesitant to speak in front of Aren. Despite the boy's wisdom, he carried an air of innocence, too, that reminded Damir of Cahira. "At the time, I believed he meant . . . well, a carnal sort of darkness."

"Sexually," said Aren. "Darkness often reveals itself in that art, I believe."

Damir sighed. "How old are you, again?"

"Fourteen," said Aren, "though I do not have a mistress, yet. Many girls admire me, despite my lowered station as servant, but I find it hard to choose between them. Some are pretty, some flirtatious. And some say too obviously what they think I want to hear. At times, I find that irritating. I would prefer a more straightforward maiden. But as things stand now, no one close to me is safe. I must fight my brother's darkness, if I can. It is the only chance of saving him."

"Why do you want to save him, if he has become so dreadful?" asked Eliana, echoing Damir's thoughts.

"Because he is a good man," said Aren, "and because I love him, despite all that he has done. The darkness has claimed him, yes, but not fully. I see good in his eyes, occasionally, even now. If he is defeated, if he can see that this power he has wrapped himself in is not as great as he imagined, I believe the good man he was will return, and our people will be safe from the machinations of Rodern."

"Rodern speaks the will of the darkness, he seeks to resurrect the Arch Mage using me," said Eliana. "But he is not the only one."

"I suppose he knows that, too," said Damir, though he felt foolish feeling competitive with a child.

"No, I did not," said Aren, but his amber eyes glittered as if he recognized Damir's foolishness, and enjoyed it. "Once I learned the Mage's name, I was not able to return to Amrodel to warn you, Lady, and I feared greatly for your safety. But I was not aware that there were others in league with him."

"We think there may be Mundanes among our people involved, too," said Eliana. "Those that are susceptible to negative energy."

"Like my own people, then," said Aren. "There are those that lust for power, some on a grand scale like my brother. But others seek it in petty ways, and sometimes I think those are the more dangerous desires, for they are not easily detected, and so they are not so easily defeated. They grow, I think, like the creeping sickness that withers a man from within. And once it takes hold, no healer among us can conquer it."

"Did you speak this way when you first found Eliana?" asked Damir. No wonder the child had such a hold on her affection.

"I didn't speak at all when we met, though of course, I knew your language," said Aren. "After I followed her to your dwelling, I hid myself in the trees to watch what she would do. I didn't understand why at the time, but when you came out, Lady Eliana hid herself, too, until you rode away with your mistress. As you passed by, I heard you laugh about a woman you called 'The Fiend.' Lady Eliana bowed her head, and at first, I thought that was her name. 'Fiend.' Only later did I learn it was a name you called her for sport."

Damir cringed. He didn't remember the day Aren spoke of—there had been too many like it. How often had he denied his feeling for her, and made a joke of her wild nature to others? *She had come to him for help.* . . .

Aren seemed to know his words hit their mark, but he wasn't finished. "After you were gone, she made her way to a deep forest glade, and I followed her there. She sat on a large rock and cried, and my heart wept for her."

"I was crying?" Eliana asked, her voice small.

Aren nodded. "I went to you and I put my hand on your shoulder as comfort. This time, you didn't run from me. You just looked up at me. And never in my life, before or after, have I seen such a look of defeat, of an open heart torn asunder."

"I wasn't afraid of you?"

"No. I think you recognized . . . a friend." Aren smiled, but Damir's heart clenched. *A friend. What he had never been . . .* "You took me to your cottage and fed me. You said you had never seen anyone eat that way before."

"She'd never looked in a mirror during a meal then," said Damir, but his words felt hollow and he wished he hadn't spoken.

Aren ignored Damir's comment. "You told me of your people, and I told you of mine. You gave me herbs that healed me, and then took me in secret around your land. You let me ride your mare. You had just gotten her then, and you were very proud of her." Aren paused and glanced at Selsig. "She was somewhat thinner at that time."

"Is that when you told me about your brother's darkness?" asked Eliana.

"No, because it hadn't begun at that time, not that I knew of," answered Aren. "But we became friends, and you even helped me sneak into your uncle's palace, where the king of Amrodel was hosting some sort of party. You told me about The Demon—already, he was accompanied by yet another woman—and you said he played tricks on you, and tried to outdo you in all you attempted." Aren paused and administered a dark look upon Damir, which

Damir felt keenly. "You said he made you feel small and stupid, and though you didn't confess it to me, I knew it was because you admired him."

"I never meant to make you feel small or stupid," said Damir, but his heart sank low and heavy, because he had seen a look on her face that said as much. "But I never thought you admired me, either."

"Then you missed the obvious," said Aren. "She pretended not to care, but somehow, that made it all the more painful to witness. But even so, as you reveled with yet another female, Lady Eliana led me on an adventure all through the palace. Its wonders linger still in my mind—we have nothing like that in the Norskland. But the greatest wonder came when a little girl spotted me. Lady Eliana shushed her as if to enlist her in a conspiracy between us, and she said nothing about my presence." Aren paused and sighed. "She was the most beautiful girl I'd ever seen, with black hair and eyes like the sky above. I suppose she doesn't remember me now."

"Cahira," said Damir. He shook his head. "So she knew about this, too."

"I expect she remembers you," said Eliana. "But even after her father was killed, and a Norsk weapon found by his body, she said nothing about you."

"I had heard the king was killed," said Aren. "I am sorry, for he seemed a kind, if ineffective, person."

"He was a good man," said Damir. "But his daughter, I fear, will carry the weight of guilt for a long while, though she bears no responsibility for his death."

"If she believes it is so, then she must release that shame on her own," said Aren. "She will find her own path."

Eliana smiled at the boy. "You give me hope, Aren."

"As you gave hope to me, Lady," he replied. "When I left the Woodland, I knew I had your friendship. You even gave me a token so that I could prove my quest fulfilled—

which it was, in that I had found a witch and though I hadn't actually stolen from her, I had a part of her treasure. You gave me a potion and a scroll, which you said could make a man think he was a spider, though I don't possess the necessary *ki* to manifest such a spell myself."

"The old bards of Norskland will thank you for that," said Damir. "Did you give her the brooch in exchange for this treasure?"

"That gift was later," said Aren. "When the darkness came, and I saw it replacing the light in my brother's eyes, I returned to Amrodel in secret, when my brother believed I had ventured to Amon-dhen on an errand. I told Lady Eliana of his affliction in hopes she could create a potion to save him, and she shared with me her fear of the darkness in her own land. She told me about the Arch Mage, and that is when she devised a plan to transform her sleeping potion into something that could instead steal memory, and use it to enlist you."

"But how did Bruin get hold of Eliana's sleeping potion?" asked Damir. "Before offering me her 'Wine of Truce,' she admitted she had been responsible."

"She gave it to me, to use as I saw fit," said Aren. "And when my brother ordered the ambush on the Guerdians, I almost gave in to the desire to use it, not to kill him, but to confine him to sleep. But he found it, instead." Aren paused, and a faraway look came into his eyes. "Before I realized what had happened, a guard loyal to me took it upon himself to 'confess,' and he was slain as a traitor. It was then I realized my brother was mad, no longer himself, and I knew only Eliana's plan could save us."

"That is why I remembered crying when I saw the brooch you gave me," said Eliana. "I must have been afraid for you when you left."

"I gave it to you so you'd have a part of me, forever. You didn't want me to return," said Aren. "But we all have our paths. Mine lies beside my brother's."

"But he would kill you, Aren," said Eliana. "Surely you know that?"

Aren smiled. "I know that, Lady. But he has not. I know there is good in him, buried deep perhaps, but it is there. I would see that renewed. That is the only gift that I ask, and one only the two of you can give me."

A weight settled around Damir's heart. "Your hope is a noble one, and I will do what I can. But there are limits to all energy, both negative and positive, and against this new tide of darkness, I have not been tested. The time may come when the power of my *ki* alone is not enough."

Aren looked at him, and his young face was kind. "But you are not alone, Damir. Didn't you know?"

Aren led them to the hamlet of Eddenmark, and the Norsk there greeted him with affection and admiration. They seemed to know that he had brought battle upon them, yet they appeared eager to do his bidding. Strange that one so young could inspire such confidence in his followers. Damir had studied the boy as they rode together, but had come no closer to understanding his mystery.

As Damir assessed Aren's unnatural maturity, the boy's eyes widened and he clapped his hands with the glee of a child. He rose up in his stirrups and pointed excitedly at a herd of extremely fuzzy large ponies. "See, there! The wild ponies of Norskland gather! The people of Eddenmark feed them, though we think they gathered here long before the hamlet was founded, because the snow on the mound is less deep, and tall grasses sometimes poke through the ice. Are they not beautiful?"

"They're certainly fat," said Damir. "With very heavy coats. How do they move?"

"Like the wind!" answered Aren and his eyes lit with challenge. "On the desert sand, perhaps your horse is faster. But here . . ." He shot away toward the hamlet, and his stout pony bounded through the snow. Llwyd met the challenge before Damir recognized it, and took off after Aren.

For the first strides, Llwyd was the pony's match, and then some. His longer legs made good work of the snow, and he edged past Aren's smaller mount. The wild ponies startled and scattered, then galloped through the drifts, pitching up clouds of blowing snow as they ran. The snow was deep, and Llwyd tired despite Damir's urging. As they approached the gates, Aren's sturdy pony pulled ahead. The gates swung open, directed by startled guards, and the two horses swept through.

Aren drew his pony to a halt, laughing as he held up his skinny arm in victory. "The steed of the north surpasses yours, Mage! I win!"

He was a boy, after all. Damir dismounted and bowed. "If ever we meet again, perhaps we can repeat this test on a field of grass rather than snow."

Aren laughed again and swung his leg forward over his pony's neck, then hopped down. "I don't think so. I know my mount's limits. In snow, I am your better. But on the flat ground, I would give you no challenge at all."

Still a boy—but a modest one, and honest. Despite himself, Damir was growing fond of Aren, and he understood now why the boy had meant so much to Eliana. Aren had accepted her without question, seen into her heart, and given her compassion. He hadn't teased her or tried to better her, as Damir had. He had been her only real friend—when Damir had been her nemesis. Damir envied Aren this closeness, and Eliana's trust, but he knew the boy had earned it—when he himself never had.

Why couldn't I give you that? Wasn't that what you wanted, desperately? Instead, I fought you at every turn. The realization had haunted Damir more intensely since they left Bruin's village. For all these years shared between them, he had never offered Eliana friendship nor tried to win her trust. Instead, he had played with her, and waited for her to come to him, to surrender to him, to be lured by his sexuality and power, all the while expecting her to ask nothing of him in return. He had taunted her with his lovers, while imagining she did the same—and she had encouraged him to think so. But now he was forced to admit she had manufactured those romances in response to his own. Instead, she had been alone, and lonely, until a Norsk warrior-child had befriended her as she wept—because of Damir.

It wasn't like him to feel guilty. She had brought it on herself. Eliana was quick-tempered, highly emotional, too imaginative, stubborn, and extremely impulsive. But now he knew what he had never understood before. Eliana was also kind. He should have known—she was a sensitive creature, like a dragonfly, responsive to each breath of the wind. He should have known her heart was the same.

He wanted to make it up to her, to change their past with what he knew now. They had become lovers—but it was not enough. And because of his trickery with the Wine of Truce, he couldn't win her true forgiveness because the part of her he had wounded most deeply was lost. He could have helped her retrieve that part of herself—the scroll Elphin had found revealed the method. Eliana had found all the herbs she needed—except one. Eliana had told him the final herb needed was one found only at night during the full moon, and Damir had known exactly which plant she meant. The moon was not yet full—but the time was coming soon. But he hadn't told her, because he was afraid of what would happen if The Fiend returned. If all Eliana's memories came back, could he still convince her that he was good for her, that he could love her like no other? Would she forget how he'd hurt her, and lied to her? Even now, the risk seemed too great.

He had made a choice. It was a poor one—and one he might never have the chance to reverse.

Eliana rode up behind them. While Llwyd and Aren's pony puffed heavy clouds into the cold air, Selsig looked calm, rested, even a little bored. Eliana had the same expression on her little face. She hopped off Selsig, and handed the mare a small apple. "At least you didn't humiliate yourself this time, Demon."

She had taken to calling him that. Odd that she'd never used the term in his presence before—"The Fiend" was certainly a title she had known well before her memory loss. Aren patted Llwyd's damp neck. "He is a magnificent horse, and one I confess I would like to have myself. In a year or two here, I think he would adjust to the cold and grow a thicker coat. His foals would much improve our stock."

A guard interrupted them. "Welcome back to Eddenmark, Aren son of Arkyn," he said. "A rider arrived in the earliest hours before dawn and sends word to you that your brother rides west with a great party. They are fitted for battle, and the Mage rides beside Bruin."

Aren sighed. "This, I expected, but it appears my brother was misled by our allies, and that is to our benefit. He will soon learn his error, and he will guess I brought you here instead. But the delay will give us a day and a night to prepare." Aren turned to Eliana and Damir. "I will direct you to The Snow Pony inn, and there you can rest, and eat—and bathe, I suggest—as you wish. My scouts will report on my brother's progress during the day, but I do not expect him here before midday tomorrow."

Aren led them down a central street, then pointed to a large sign with a white pony, its mane and tail blowing in a blue wind. "Go there—the innkeeper knows your purpose and will give you quarters, and stable your horses as well. I must gather my friends together, and make such a plan of defense as seems best, but we will trust you to direct us when the time comes. Farewell."

Damir watched him go, then sighed. "He has too much faith in me."

Eliana held up her hand and wiggled her fingers inside her new mittens. "And you, I think, have too little."

Chapter Seventeen

The Snow Pony tavern was cleaner and quieter than The Lusty Boar, and not as extravagant as the place they'd stayed in Amon-dhen. It reminded Eliana more of The Hungry Cat in Amrodel—warm and friendly, with patrons who seemed to consider the inn their home. Indeed, the Norsk people she saw there appeared as normal and familiar as those in the Woodland. She wouldn't have been surprised to find them wagering on each other's romantic escapades, but instead, they seemed to be engaged in the game of Fulthark that had defeated Damir so thoroughly.

Eliana tapped his shoulder. "I suggest you avoid entering a tournament this time."

He looked at her and smiled, but he seemed sad. "I find no temptation to the sport."

Eliana took his hand. "Let's get a guest room—preferably one that doesn't overlook the stables this time. You are tired, I think."

"Yes." He said nothing more, and Eliana's concern grew. *I will protect you.*

A portly innkeeper approached them. He closely resembled a blond, red-cheeked version of The Hungry Cat's proprietor, Fareth. He clapped his large hands together and smiled. "Welcome, Mage! I am Ranveig, son of Eirik the Fat, and likely to inherit my father's title too soon. Aren son of Arkyn has told me to give you our finest guest room. He says you will save us, and need rest before battling our chieftain."

"Young Aren is optimistic," said Damir. "But we appreciate your kindness. A room is most welcome."

"And food, if you please," added Eliana. She looked around. Everyone seemed to be drinking ale, despite the early hour. "Do you have anything to drink besides ale?"

Ranveig looked mystified. "What else would you want, Lady Witch?"

He spoke the title pleasantly, but Eliana sighed. "My name is Eliana. I would like tea, if you have it."

Ranveig paused. "I'm not sure . . . what is it?"

"Herbs steeped in boiled water," said Eliana.

Ranveig cringed. "Why would anyone want that?"

"Because it has a pleasant taste, and relaxes the nerves—especially for warriors."

Ranveig appeared dubious, but he shrugged. "I can boil water, but we have no herbs, save those for cooking. None, I think, would be flavorful in boiled water."

Eliana fished around in her pack and drew out a small bag of herbs. "Use these. First boil the water, then let this bag soak in it for a bit. Honey would be nice, too, if you have it."

"Honey, we have," said Ranveig. "I will bring it to your room with bread and cheese."

"Thank you," said Eliana, and she felt satisfied. She glanced at Damir, but his expression was faraway, and he didn't seem to notice her success. "Where is our room?"

"This way, Lady."

Ranveig led them up a short staircase, then to a large guest room that faced east. "I have prepared a basin of hot water so that you may wash before your meal." He bowed, and left them to fetch their breakfast.

A warm fire burned on a small stone hearth, and the room was filled with the new morning light. Eliana pulled off her heavy coat and hung it on a hook, and Damir did likewise, though he seemed distracted. Eliana splashed off her face and fluffed her hair, then found the dress she'd purchased in Amon-dhen in her pack. "I will wear this today." She peeked at Damir. He stood before the large window and looked out over the snow-covered fields. Eliana laid the dress on a chair and went to him. "Are you all right, Damir?"

He looked down at her and he smiled, but his eyes were sad. "I'm fine." He touched her cheek, then bent to kiss her forehead. "I'm sorry, Eliana. I wish things had been different between us. I wish . . ." He turned his gaze back to the endless, rolling drifts of snow, and his voice trailed into silence.

"You have my heart." She paused. "Do I not have yours?"

He turned back to her and the emotion written on his face told her all she needed to know. "You have always had my heart, Eliana. Always, from the moment I first saw you."

Her heart lifted and happiness surged inside her, but his face remained grave. "But I tell you that too late, when the woman you were is lost, and can no longer hear me. You accept me now because you don't remember—you don't remember how I hurt you, you don't remember the tears you wept because of me. You don't remember feeling small and stupid. If you did—you would hate me, Eliana. And you would be right to do so."

Her happiness evaporated. "I am the same person inside."

"I know you are." He cupped her face in his hands. "All this time, I had thought I had made you into something sweet, someone who would love me. You were that woman all along. I called you 'The Fiend.' You were an angel, instead, and I didn't see. I stripped away your memory, and saw you for what you really are, but I didn't see myself. I thought I had captured you. You had captured me."

"According to Aren, that was my intention! Damir, you are not alone in fault between us. I'm the one who tried to steal your memory, for my own purposes. You stole mine by accident."

"But your intentions were far more honorable than mine."

Eliana shook her head. "I was wrong to try to force you. I should have just told you the truth, and asked for your help."

"No, Eliana. You were right. I would not have listened, and I would not have heard you. I would have thought your pity for a child endangered us all, and I would have advised the Council against your plan."

"Why?"

"I was a fool." A faint smile touched his lips. "I have always thought your heart was closed against me. But I see now that it was mine that was closed to you. I was so busy trying to prove I was your equal, that I was worth your attention, that I couldn't see how far above me you really were."

Eliana backed away from him and stared. "'Above you?' I cannot come close to you! You are so strong, and so beautiful, and you always seem to know what you're doing."

He laughed, but the sound lacked joy. "Then I have convinced you well, my lady. I am none of those things."

Eliana seized his hand and led him to a chair by a small, round table. "You are overtired and the dark current is affecting you." She paused and shook her head. "Damir, we did what we did. Maybe we could have done better. I'm sure that is true for me, even since I lost my memory. Maybe your heart wasn't open. I doubt very much mine was, either." Eliana knelt before him and placed her hands on his knees. "But we are here, together. Please, don't let this darkness come between us."

"It is my own darkness that came between us, Eliana." He touched her hair. "I cannot blame some villain from the past for that."

Eliana gripped his hand. "It was fear that infected us both. We are not perfect. But, Damir, we don't have to be. I want to be with you, and I think you want to be with me, too. Isn't that enough?"

"I don't know. What if I can't give you what you deserve. What if I can't protect you when the time comes?"

"Then I will protect you!"

"I will not fail you, Eliana. Whatever happens, know that."

"Nor I, you," she whispered, but tears filled her eyes. "There is a promise between us, whether we speak it or not. I know you will hold to yours. I will hold to mine, too."

His eyes narrowed in suspicion at her meaning, but the door opened, and Ranveig entered carrying a large tray of food. The innkeeper spotted Eliana on her knees before Damir, and he hesitated. "Begging your pardon . . ." He cleared his throat, but Eliana rose and examined the tray.

"Mages talk in this position, Ranveig."

"If you say so, Lady."

"I do." Eliana lifted the top off a little pot of steaming liquid, and she sniffed the vapors. "Very good! Even better than I hoped. You should try some."

Ranveig cringed and shook his head. "No, thank you, Lady. I prefer warmed ale in the early hours."

Eliana grimaced. "That is disgusting! Tea would serve you better."

"Might cause any number of complaints to my innards," argued Ranveig, and Eliana saw that he would not easily be swayed.

"Well, offer it to your customers, and see what they say." She gave him another bag of herbs and pressed them into his hand. "Try it!"

Ranveig sighed. "As you say, Lady." He placed the tray on the round wooden table, then bowed and left them alone.

Damir sat quietly as Eliana reached for a portion of warm bread and stuffed it into her mouth. "This is very good. Try some."

"I wouldn't want to deprive you." He was teasing her, but the sorrow in his voice remained. Eliana broke off another piece of bread, then handed it to him.

"Eat!"

Damir smiled and took the bread she offered. He ate absentmindedly, and she poured tea in a mug for him. "Maybe you should have ale, after all."

Eliana finished her bread, and ate a little cheese, but her appetite waned with Damir's dark mood. She had felt it growing in him, and it began to shadow her heart, too. She didn't remember her past, but she knew what it felt like to be alone and lonely. She didn't have to remember her past to know what it felt like to hurt, and to ache with a love unreturned.

Maybe this was what the shadow woman in her dream had warned of. *Don't let me feel that way again.* When she met Aren, she had recognized the angelic boy, but now she knew the shadow woman was herself, "The Fiend," and her fear was for her own heart.

Damir finished his breakfast, then washed himself in the basin. He undressed and lay on the bed staring at the ceiling. His brow furrowed and he seemed deep in thought. Eliana sipped her tea and watched him. He needed to think, to plan for his upcoming encounter with

Bruin. Or did he? Maybe thought was the last thing he needed right now.

Eliana went to the basin and refilled it with warm water. She sprinkled herbs on its surface, and a soft fragrance wafted across the room. Damir didn't notice. She studied him a moment, then slowly and casually removed her clothing. She stole a furtive glance his way, then frowned. He didn't look at her. His gaze remained on the wooden beams above, and his mind, she guessed, was farther still.

Eliana folded her soft leather bodice and supple leggings, then, idly, crossed the room to a chair. She hesitated. His expression hadn't changed, and he hadn't seen her. She drew a determined breath, then deliberately dropped her bodice to the floor. She allowed an instant for him to react to the sound, then bent slowly to pick them up. He had mentioned that he liked the sight of her bottom—she would test how much.

She heard a sharp breath, and she smiled, but she pretended not to notice as she placed her clothes on the chair, then walked back to the basin. She dampened a soft cloth and, with painstaking ease and care, laved herself with the scented water, her back facing him. She turned slightly, as if to look out the window, and allowed the water to trickle down her breast. She felt quite sure he wasn't breathing at all now. She dampened her lips, as if savoring an imagined taste, then dragged the cloth lightly and sensually down her stomach, then between her thighs, inward. Her eyelids lowered, and a soft warmth filled her. She knew she had his attention now, and the thought aroused her as much as the touch.

Eliana held her breath—this had to be perfect—then bent to lave her legs, her ankles, then her feet, which she curved as delicately as possible.

Suddenly he was behind her, taking her hips in his hands. She startled and the cloth flew out of her hands.

Apparently, she had won his attention. She straightened, but he picked up the cloth and slid her hair over her shoulder, then kissed her neck. Eliana leaned back against him. Her heart pounded—there was something incredibly alluring about seduction, when it worked so well as this.

"You are a temptation I cannot resist," he whispered, and as he spoke, he soaked the cloth in water again, then swirled it over her breasts. He dragged back and forth over the tips until each pebbled, until her breath came swift as desire flowed within her. Eliana turned her face toward him, and he kissed her. His tongue teased the corner of her mouth, and she slid her own over his. The cloth dropped, and he replaced it with his fingers. He ran his hand down her side, then over her stomach to the apex of her thighs. Her pulse raced as he teased inward until he found her tiny, feminine bud. He teased her until the ache became unendurable, until she sucked his tongue with wanton abandon, and her back arched against him.

She felt him hard and hot against her back and she shifted to increase the pressure. He moved against her and her breath caught on a moan. He slipped his finger into her warmth, and he moaned, too. Her legs felt weak and tiny licks of fire sped through her as he circled her small bud until she trembled with pleasure.

She murmured his name and squirmed against him, but he laughed against her neck and increased the pressure.

He teased her until every breath was a gasp, until she whimpered a demand for release. Just when she thought she would die of it, he stopped. She bit back a cry of frustration, but he laughed again, bent her forward, and drove himself deep inside her. Eliana caught her breath with a hot wave of pleasure and surprise. He moved inside her, and she gripped the basin table hard as he made love to her this way. He thrust as if he had no choice, and she heard the ragged groans of his pleasure. She tipped her head back, and he bent forward to kiss her neck. She rose

303

up on her toes to take him deeper and he gripped her bottom and drove himself hard within her.

Their passion crashed like violent waves against the shore. His rapture came with a shivering breath, a ragged moan, and Eliana's rose to match him. Every muscle in her body drew tight, she quaked as he gripped her, and she leaned back against him and gave herself over to ecstasy.

Damir withdrew from her body, and Eliana went limp against him, her energy spent in a wild pinnacle of rapture. He gathered her into his arms and carried her to their bed. He lay down beside her and still, she didn't move. She just lay there, on her back, her eyes wide, her lips parted. Damir hesitated, then touched her cheek. "Are you all right, Eliana? It wasn't . . . too much, was it?"

Only her eyes moved as she shifted her attention to him. For a moment, she just stared. Then her lips curved in the most sensual smile he'd ever seen. "You . . . are a god."

His concern gave way to utter masculine delight. "From a goddess, that is praise indeed." He kissed her cheek and she stretched her arms into a languid posture, then yawned.

"My body is full and ripe, like the soil in spring after a soft rain." She paused. "I am a goddess."

"We returned to our earliest origin, together," said Damir. "This is how we began, you and I. I am sure of it. In a burst of energy, joined and rent asunder, and joined again, when light is all we were, and love is all we knew."

"Yes," she said. "Exactly. Two, but one, joined, and apart, and joined."

"I feel like I've been searching for this forever, and never found more than its shadow."

Eliana rolled onto her side to face him. "Your mood has improved, I see."

"My mood has been transformed by perfection."

"It was so raw!" Her eyes closed and her teeth sank into

her lips. "So primal." She paused to shudder. "And it felt so good!"

"Wonderful." Little aftershocks of pleasure still coursed through his body. "I have dreamt of you this way for all the years of my adulthood. But this day exceeded even my most ardent fantasies."

Eliana snuggled against him and kissed his shoulder in a leisurely fashion. "I expect I had fantasies of you, too." She paused and yawned, and her eyes drifted shut. "I wonder what they were?"

Eliana drifted to sleep beside him, but Damir lay awake for a while. Outside their window, the morning sun rose in the east, brighter on the snow than any light he'd ever seen. It would be a beautiful day in the Northland. As much as he'd dreaded this land of ice and snow, today he had found more beauty than he'd ever witnessed before. He had found it in Eliana, and in himself, and for a while, at last, he was content.

They woke after noon, and made love at their leisure, slow and sensual, tasting each other, lingering over every touch. Damir felt sated as he never had in his life. Eliana splashed water on her face and fiddled with her hair, now tangled from their wild passion. She separated it with her fingers, then braided a few strands into the dark mass. She looked like a Woodland elf standing naked before him. Damir watched her as if he could draw the image of her into his soul, and protect it there forever.

Eliana pulled on one of the dresses she had bought in Amon-dhen. It fit snugly over her bust, then hung loose to her little feet. She looked beautiful and feminine as she turned to him, smiling. "What are you going to wear?"

Damir smiled, too. "A tunic of velvet? Or would you prefer leather?"

Her eyes glittered. "Or nothing."

"Even among the Norsk, that might be unexpected."

Eliana sat beside him on the bed, and he sat up to kiss her cheek. "They do seem uninhibited, don't they? I'm not sure about Aren, but he's young still."

"And I doubt very much he represents the Norsk as a whole," added Damir. "He's a strange young man."

"Yet they love him—that is clear. And I can see why. He has no thought of himself, he never asserts his self-importance, but he's so strong. I feel calm when he is near. I wonder why he's so different?"

"I have no idea," said Damir. "His true fate awaits him, I think."

"I wish we could help him." Eliana passed Damir his shirt and he put it on. "But I fear when his time comes, he will stand alone."

Damir rose and went to the window, and he sighed. "Maybe that is true for us all."

"You are not alone, Damir. You have me. Whatever happens, I am with you."

He turned to her and he held out his hand. She came to him and placed her hand in his. "Then come with me, and we'll find something to eat."

"I hope they have something for drink besides ale."

Damir angled his brow. "I think the Norsk bathe in ale."

He dressed, and Eliana waited by the door. He felt sure he heard her stomach churn. "You have a long fast to make up for. I am flattered to be the reason you delayed."

"And I am all the hungrier because of it." She took his hand and pulled him down the hall and into the Norsk parlor. Outside the thick windows, snow fell, and a fire burned in a stone hearth near the back of the room.

Ranveig greeted them at the parlor's entrance. "An odd thing, mistress!" Ranveig gestured to a group of Norskmen seated around the table.

"What is it, Ranveig?" asked Eliana.

"Your 'tea.' I poured it into mugs this morning—thought to do it as a joke, if you'll pardon me for using your herbs for sport. But—and who would have thought it? It's gone over well, and they're on their third cups."

Eliana seated herself at the end of a long table. "*I* would have thought it, of course. After all the ale you've immersed yourselves in, tea will clean your hearts and spirits." She paused. "You can use it to scent bathing water, too."

"Haven't tried it myself, but I might offer it for sale as a novelty for my guests."

"Good idea. You can collect the necessary plants in spring and summer, and dry them to use in winter."

Damir watched as Eliana drew little pictures on a Norsk parchment, indicating the herbs required for tea. The whole room seemed to recede from his view. Their voices faded so that he no longer heard what they said. He watched as if from a great distance as she waved her hands this way and that in explanation. Across the room, Norsk warriors sipped tea, and a tall blond woman sharpened an axe's blade with a whetting stone. A boy even younger than Aren fiddled with a helm, found it too large, then added cloth to better the fit.

They would stand behind him—these people who loved their Chieftain's youngest brother. They would trust Damir to defeat Bruin—but if Damir failed, they would fight, and fall, without fear or regret.

"They will stand behind you." Aren spoke quietly beside Damir, and the boy's presence restored Damir's sense of the room, and his place within. The voices seemed close again. Aren placed his hand on Damir's shoulder.

"A dark tide rises around us, you and me, and those we love. Maybe it will sweep over us, and take us all with it. You are the only one who can stop its advance." Aren paused. "I know, in my heart, that this tide will return again, on a shore I can't foretell. But if you can't stop it now and turn it back, the darkness will be inescapable forever after. Why is that?"

Damir looked at Aren. He spoke like an angel whose vision stretched beyond the veils of the living. But he still looked like a boy—Damir saw confusion in his amber eyes, and even the quiet chill of fear. "When our time comes, we can either hide or go out to meet it. I would meet it."

Aren smiled. "You are a warrior, just as Lady Eliana said."

"I . . . doubt." Damir's voice faded. "I don't know why. I can defeat Bruin. But Rodern knows this, too, yet he presses for a confrontation."

"My brother is no longer a Norsk warrior. He is a man possessed of some other force, the Darkness. Rodern has infected him with its force, and he will fight with that power when you meet in battle." Aren paused, and the light in his amber eyes seemed to burn. "That force has carried him faster and farther than I expected."

"What do you mean?"

"My scouts returned early this morning. Bruin rode through the night, and his forces approach. They will be here in the hour before sunset."

Damir's heart chilled. "Why didn't you wake me?"

Aren's smile returned, both sad and kind. "He will be here whether you wake early or not. What would you do, had you known? Practice the swing of your sword? No, you had what you needed, my friend. You had your lady, and you had to be within your own heart. I think you are. From what better place could you face the darkness?" Aren didn't wait for an answer. "Those who can fight will make ready. And I will stand with you. But what would you have us do?"

"Clear the village of those who cannot fight," said Damir, but Aren shook his head.

"If we fail, my brother will hunt them down and kill every one who followed me. They have no need to leave. They know this."

"Then ride out and meet them."

"Our horses are ready," said Aren. "Though Bruin rides from the west, he will circle around and approach from the east. You will stand with the sun at your back, as it fades into night, and we will stand with you."

Damir turned his attention back to Eliana. She slapped butter onto a large section of bread, took a bite, and continued her instruction of Ranveig. They seemed to be arguing, but Ranveig sighed heavily, then lifted a mug to his lips. He hesitated, then took a tentative sip. Damir watched as the innkeeper's expression changed, and he took a bigger gulp. Eliana sat back, folded her arms over her chest and looked proud. She glanced at Damir to see if he'd witnessed her victory, and he nodded.

I love you.

"I would send her from this place," said Damir.

"And she would not go. You know this," answered Aren. "But even if she would, they would hunt her down and find her. They need her. She is the reason they're here. She's the reason Rodern wants you destroyed."

"I know." And if he failed . . .

"You protect her. You have protected her all along. They want her to bring forth the great power that seeks her. But you have kept them at bay. So they will direct all the darkness Rodern has harnessed—and they will direct it at you."

"It is Rodern I should fight, not your brother."

"True enough," said Aren. "And Rodern knows you would win, so he puts another before him. The darkness claimed the wizard long ago, I think. He answers to it. But my brother has strength of another kind. I do not know why Rodern believes Bruin can be a sword and a shield against you, but it's apparent he does."

"Every person's *ki* is different. It can happen that a weaker energy, by the cleverness of its direction, can disrupt a more powerful force. Rodern believes he has accomplished this, though I don't know how."

"We will learn the answer soon," said Aren. He paused. "If there is anything you would ask of us, now is the time. We can give you mail, a shield, if you require it."

Damir shook his head. "I need nothing but what I have." He placed his hand on the hilt of his sword. "If this isn't enough, nothing is."

"Then I go to ready myself," said Aren. "I will meet you by the gate when the horns of battle are raised."

Damir watched Aren leave the tavern. A black puppy met him at the door and jumped at Aren's knee. Aren laughed and patted the dog's head, then headed off down the snow-covered roadway. A soft dusting of snow swirled along the road, and then curled upward and spiraled into the wind. Damir turned back to the inn, and through the shadows, he saw Eliana engaged in the game of Fulthark with a brawny Norskman. She held up her fist in victory, and the man took a swig of tea as if it were ale.

Damir moved to close the tavern door, but a haunting call met his ears, and he stopped, frozen by its beauty— and by the doom in its echo. Horns blew in the west. They echoed over the snow, accompanied by distant drumbeats, the sound of horses galloping over the dunes.

Bruin the Ruthless had arrived.

Chapter Eighteen

The sound of distant horns reached Eliana, and she moved as if in a dream. "It is too soon." She caught Damir's gaze across the room, and she knew it was true. The battle had come.

Norsk warriors set aside their tea. A tall woman pulled on a helm. Eliana stared, dazed, as they gathered their gear and moved to the doorway of the inn. Ranveig removed his dirty apron, then emerged from his pantry wearing a dented shirt of mail. A boy tucked a long shirt into his leggings, then fastened on a thick leather belt. He gripped a short axe, then took his place beside Ranveig. They spoke in low voices, betraying no fear, nor hurry.

Eliana didn't wait. She darted to her room and changed into her leather bodice and leggings. Her hands shook so much that she could barely tie the laces. She found the dagger Damir had given her, which she had almost forgotten she had. She fixed it to her belt, then turned.

Damir met her at the door. "If I asked, would you stay here?"

"You know the answer to that," she said. "I belong by your side."

He nodded, but she saw tears in his eyes. "This day may not go as it should, Eliana. I feel a power before me that I cannot overcome. It shouldn't be . . ."

She touched his face. "It is the darkness that speaks this way. It clouds your thoughts and your heart, because it fears you. You will meet it head on, Damir, and you will defeat it."

Damir drew her into his arms and he kissed her forehead. "Whatever happens, my heart is with you." He drew back to face her. "I love you, Eliana. I have not told you that before, but it has always been true. If I had been honest, maybe we wouldn't have reached this point where all will be won or lost by my sword. But I love you."

Tears misted her vision. "I cannot speak for the woman I was before—and if I did, I doubt you'd believe me. But I know my heart, and it belongs to you. I love you, too."

"If we hold to that, maybe I will find the strength to defeat this force."

"That is what helped create the dragonfly sword. It will help us now."

Horns blew in a battle call outside their window. Damir looked out and he sighed. "Aren has mustered the Norsk. They await us. And there in the distance, I see a cloud of dust and snow."

Eliana looked out, too. "It is Bruin, and he rides from the east."

"Aren said that would be his direction." He took her hand and squeezed it. "Let us ride out and meet them."

Eliana followed Damir from the tavern. Their horses were waiting. The Norsk stable boy had given Llwyd a red blanket beneath his saddle. He looked like the horse of a warrior. In contrast, someone had affixed a dried flower to

Selsig's bridle, and it had flopped to the side. Eliana adjusted it, then mounted.

The streets were empty, but Aren waited by the city gates. He wore a light shirt of mail and no helm. His pale hair sparkled in the sun. He mounted his horse as they drew near, then led them silently from the city. His Norsk followers awaited them outside the gates. Eliana saw a few warriors, those she had met in the tavern, but most of the gathering were townspeople, young and old, and she felt a strange relief to see other women among them. A few even wore mail and carried axes, though others bore staves and short swords. One old man held a club.

Aren positioned his horse before them. "We are not the strongest warriors of the Norskland. Nonetheless, a soul is not judged only by his might, but by the might of his heart. Our hearts burn with the same fire as our fathers, and we will fight for the future of this land. My brother has called upon the power of a Mage, and that Mage has enslaved him. I ask that the Mage Damir take back what is ours and return it to our people. We are one people, and for that people, we fight!"

The Norsk lifted their weapons and clashed them against their round shields. Aren rode out in front of them. "Ride as one!" he cried, and they leapt forward and galloped across the snow. Eliana tried to keep up. The little mare did her best to keep pace with the bigger ponies, but lagged behind despite her efforts. The Norsk rode in front of her, and the snow from their horse's hooves made a white cloud. Eliana closed her eyes and clung to her pony's mane. "Just stop when they do," Eliana whispered, hoping Selsig understood.

Eliana had no idea how long they had raced through the snow, nor how much ground they had covered. But eventually Selsig slowed her pace, then came to a walk. Eliana opened her eyes and found herself beside Damir. He shaded his eyes against the sun as it reflected off the snow.

"What if they just charge into us?" asked Eliana. She was shivering, but not from cold.

He looked down at her and he smiled. "I will prevent that," he answered. "Whatever happens, I will protect you, Eliana. I will not let them take you."

"If I lose you, I don't care what happens to me!"

She hadn't thought of this much. What Rodern and Bruin really wanted was her—they wanted her as bait, because of the energy born into her soul, inherited from a distant queen. Eliana closed her eyes. Bruin, and even Rodern, were just tools for a far greater power. The dark being once known as "Cheveyo the Spirit Warrior" wished to live again, to feed off her energy, to regain that power. *I feel him.* Eliana opened her eyes. "He is here."

As she spoke, a gust of cold wind stung her face and swirled around Aren's followers. The afternoon sun was already low on the western horizon, but the day was bright still. With the wind, clouds rose in the east and moved toward them like an advancing army.

Bruin's army appeared on the horizon, a line of charging horsemen. The western sun glittered on their shields and on their axes. Aren rode out before his people, and Damir rode to join him. They waited together, the tall dark Mage with his magical white sword, and the boy, with his light mail and his axe. Eliana's heart ached with a pain so strong and so sudden that she thought she might faint. She squeezed her heels into Selsig's side, and the little mare cantered out behind them.

She positioned herself beside Damir. He looked over at her, and to her surprise, he smiled. "What took you so long?"

"I was frozen with fear," she answered. *"By your side . . ."*

"By my side . . ."

Damir rode out a few steps, then turned Llwyd back to face them. "I will go forward and meet them. I must confront them alone. The two of you must stay here." His gaze locked with Aren's. "Keep her back, and keep her safe."

"I will do that," said Aren.

Eliana watched as Damir dismounted. He sent Llwyd back, and the horse obeyed. Aren and Eliana got off their horses, too. Aren kissed his pony's nose, then pulled off the bridle, and slapped the horse's rump. Tears welled in Eliana's eyes as she removed Selsig's bridle and pad. She fished around in her pocket and gave the mare a dried apple, which Selsig ate. "Go now," she whispered. "If this doesn't go well for us, I would like to know you will be free, and I think you'll find these Norsk ponies good company. But take good care of Llwyd, will you? He's strong, but he's also vulnerable, and he needs you."

Selsig nudged Eliana, then followed the other horses away. Only Llwyd remained. The little mare turned back, stomped over to him, bit him soundly, and drove him away with the others. *I will protect you* . . . Eliana's heart felt swollen in her chest. The snow swirled on the horizon, kicked up by Bruin's charge.

Damir drew his white sword, even as Bruin and his men charged over the great dunes of snow in their approach. Eliana trembled, but Damir showed no reaction to their approach. He held up his sword before his body, and slowly, it came to life in his hands. The white metal blade gleamed, and soon it outshone the sun. It formed a great arch, then a circle, and its light wrapped around him.

From the orb surrounding Damir, another arc extended, then bent back until it formed a barrier in front of Aren and his followers. He had shielded them. As long as his power held, they were protected, and Bruin would not pass.

Eliana's heart held its beat. To reach her, to break through, they would have to destroy that barrier—and to do that, they would have to kill Damir.

Bruin's horsemen faltered. The horses turned their heads as if the light of the sword pained them. The wind whipped around them, and around Aren's group, and snow dusted upward like a cloud. Bruin and the Mage Rodern rode forward ahead of their warriors and they came to stand before Damir. Still, he gave no reaction that he had even seen them. Eliana guessed that he was summoning his *ki,* drawing the power of his inherent energy. What she saw exceeded her wildest imaginings.

The wind tossed Damir's black hair, his long coat whipped in its gusts. He stood motionless amidst chaos, and he glowed with power. The sword protected him, but what came from within his body stunned Eliana. It swirled around him, within him, then formed a center of calm that seemed unfathomable in this wild place. It centered around his heart, then burst outward, and when it did, Damir looked up and faced Bruin. He walked forward to meet his enemy, and the snow itself seemed to part for him.

He will not be defeated. . . .

Aren spoke beside her, and she heard the awe in the boy's voice. "Bruin cannot stand against him. No one can."

Bruin moved to face Damir, but how could he dare match the young Mage's power? No light glowed around Bruin, yet he held up his axe and he laughed. Behind him, Rodern came forward. He was dressed in a black cape lined in red, which seemed to absorb the sunlight reflecting off the snow and turn it to darkness.

"Dare you face me, Mage?" said Bruin. "Give us the woman, and I may let you live."

"A man who lies down to live isn't worth the hours he has won," said Damir. "If you want her, you'll have to get through me."

Bruin's gaze flicked to his brother. "To cleave my traitorous brother's head in two, I'll gladly go through both of you."

316

"Your brother is all that remains of your own good, Bruin," said Damir.

"When his blood stains the blade of my axe, when it seeps into the snow to feed the ground beneath—I'll call that 'good'! You stand between the greatest Norsk warrior who ever lived and his prey."

"So be it." Damir moved forward toward Bruin and the wind howled as if struck itself by an unseen weapon. Bruin's warriors turned to look behind them.

Rodern held up his arms and spoke strange words that Eliana didn't understand. He waved a red staff over his head in a circle backward over his head. As he moaned and called, a dark tide crept from the east. It moved faster than the wind, then swept past Rodern and burned into Bruin's back.

Bruin howled, and his voice groaned like the wind, but the dark tide swirled around him, as if in opposition to the light that arose within Damir. The dark tide found its mark.

Rodern stumbled forward, then lowered his arms. He panted like a man who had run many miles, but his eyes glowed. "Fight this, Damir ap Kora! A greater power than you have ever known takes seed in the 'greatest Norsk warrior who ever lived.' Ha! Before this moment, Bruin was nothing. Do you feel the true warrior, Damir? It is *him*. The Arch Mage's *ki* now burns within this fool. You stand between a god and his prey . . ."

"You have used this man," said Damir. "Does he know his fate?"

Rodern laughed. "Bruin? He knows blood lust. He knows power. That is all he needs to know to be of service."

As he spoke, Eliana saw that it was true. Bruin saw nothing, no one. He had gained the power he sought, but he had lost what remained of himself.

This was the power Damir had foreseen—the power he feared he could not defeat. Not Bruin's power, but a strange force Rodern had summoned. The dark *ki* of the Arch Mage buried in the eastern mountains had risen.

Damir held the dragonfly sword in front of his heart, and for one moment, he bowed his head. Then he looked back to Eliana and smiled. He turned, then swung to meet Bruin. They fought like giants, and the clash of their weapons sounded like thunder over the snow-covered dunes.

Aren's people gathered together, and Bruin's warriors backed away. No warriors had ever fought this way. Damir held his own, but Bruin raged, driven without fear, his axe red and black as if fire burned within it. The white sword did not fail—but neither did it penetrate the darkness of Bruin's enchanted weapon. Damir slashed and drove against his opponent, and to Eliana's eyes, he seemed to have the better of the fight. Damir was as tall as Bruin, and quicker, and when his *ki* focused outward, his strength was tenfold what it had been.

But the fight went on, and Bruin didn't flag or waver. Damir pierced the Norsk chieftain's shoulder, but Bruin didn't react. He just swung his giant axe. It crashed against the white sword, and Damir stumbled back. Again, Damir lunged forward, and again, drove Bruin's axe aside. But there was no yielding. Eliana felt his energy, because they were connected. It was focused—but not focused enough. Something held him back, and suddenly, she understood what it was. It was her.

"Give up the shield." Eliana's voice came like a whisper, and no one heard her. She grabbed Aren's shoulder, and he turned, his young face drawn with fear. "Aren, give up the shield! He needs all his power."

"If we do that, Lady, they will take you."

"If Damir falls, they will take me, anyway! Please . . ."

Aren looked back at the fight, and then again at Eliana. "I don't know how to release the shield he put around us."

"It is possible. Rodern told me he had done this with

his own tower. We just . . . don't accept it." She closed her eyes. "To do this, we must release our own fear, for ourselves, for each other. Give up the shield he has placed on us."

Aren turned to his people. "The Mage Damir has placed a shield around us." He paused and smiled. "But we are warriors, and Norskmen. We fight for ourselves, and need no protection."

Aren's followers looked confused. "How?" asked Ranveig.

"Lift your weapons, deny the fear, release the shield. And fight!" As he spoke, Aren stepped forward and he held up his axe. "Fight!"

Eliana fixed her gaze on Damir. "I love you so . . ." She closed her eyes, and she let him go. The shield he had placed around her faded, and was gone. For one instant, she saw him turn. He knew what she had done. The power he had given her and to Aren's people returned to him, but he shook his head, and she heard him cry, 'No!'

Rodern saw what they had done, and he cried out above the battle. "Fight them, you fools! Take the woman!"

Bruin's warriors seemed confused, but they brandished their weapons and charged toward Aren's group. But Aren laughed and charged forward to meet them. Eliana drew her dagger as the onslaught began. Aren swung his axe and defeated one warrior, then spun to fight another. He was so young, and so fearless. Eliana drew her dagger and lunged through the snow to help him. Aren kept Eliana behind him, but a huge Norsk warrior leapt toward him. The warrior swung his axe, and Aren had no time to deflect the blow. Eliana's heart directed her dagger—she dove at the warrior and pierced the heavy gauntlet above his wrist. The Norskman howled and dropped his axe in surprise, and Aren knocked him aside.

"Stay behind me, Lady!" His amber eyes glowed, and he was smiling. "But I didn't know you were a warrior, too."

I'm not . . .

Bruin crashed toward Damir. He swung his axe with brutal force, and Damir leapt aside. The power restored to him was enough. He bounded back, swung the white sword, and it severed Bruin's axe. The Norsk chieftain fell stunned at his feet.

Victory . . .

Eliana heard a high scream of wild hatred and fury, almost as if a woman had shrieked from a great distance—or maybe she heard it on the waves of darkness that seeped inward around her. Eliana's senses blurred. *What is happening to me? Aren . . .* She tried to call to him, but the boy was fighting beside her and didn't hear—or maybe she hadn't uttered any sound. She felt as if the darkness lifted her and imprisoned her.

"Come to me . . . Wake me, serve me . . ."

"No!" Eliana heard her own voice, but it seemed muffled and far away. "I love Damir."

"Your lover will fall, and your ki will be mine. In you, I will regain her power, she will be mine. All the world will be mine!"

Eliana fought the dark voice in her head, and she closed her eyes tight. There, within her mind, she saw the dragonfly amidst the light. *My love is stronger than all else.* She summoned an energy from deep inside her body and her soul. It burned inside her, and she resisted the dark force with all her power.

Darkness encircled her. Eliana opened her eyes and she saw Damir turning toward her. His expression turned to horror as he saw what had happened to her. Rodern screamed behind them. "Get up, you fool! Kill him! Now is your chance!"

Moving as if half alive, Bruin struggled to his feet. Aren and the others slowed their battle and turned, too, stunned, as the broken man rose and moved toward Damir. Damir hesitated, his gaze still on Eliana, but then he lifted his sword again.

"You cannot defeat me. This is not your battle, Bruin. They have robbed you, and deceived you, and they have stolen your power. Would you let them?"

Where weapons failed, Damir's words finally penetrated the armor of Bruin's pride. Bruin hesitated, then sank to his knees and groaned like a man ravaged by deathly illness, though Damir's sword had done him only light injury. Rodern cursed the Norsk chieftain, then bounded forward. He whipped out a red dagger and plunged it into Bruin's back.

"Rise!" he screamed, and to Eliana's wonder, the broken Norsk chieftain rose up like a puppet to Rodern's command.

"What horror is this?" whispered Aren. The Norsk, both Aren's followers and Bruin's, recoiled, horrified by the magic that controlled the great warrior. Bruin walked toward Damir with no light in his eyes, no life, but only movement. Rodern laughed, then directed his own dark energy toward Eliana. She fell to the ground as darkness obliterated her sight.

"What will you do, Damir ap Kora?" Rodern laughed. "I have your woman. *He* has her. And he will take her when you fall. Will you let her go to defeat me?" Rodern laughed. "You have a choice. If you save her, you die."

A dark cloud had encircled Eliana as if a storm had sought her out and now claimed her. She had collapsed in its midst, and Bruin lumbered again toward Damir. If he fought the Norskman now, he would win. But in that moment, Rodern would claim Eliana fully.

Damir lifted his sword and it shone white before him. Bruin's eyes rolled back in his head, and he lifted a fresh axe as if another's hand directed him. Eliana screamed.

Damir gave up his *ki* and wrapped it around Eliana. Rodern howled, then directed the blackness at Damir instead. But Damir's shield held, and Eliana struggled to her feet. He kept his eyes focused on her, and nothing else, but his own life ebbed from him like the tide from the shore.

Bruin bared his axe and crashed it down upon Damir. The white sword held off the blow, but slowly, it lowered. In the midst of the howling wind, Rodern laughed. "Your power reaches its limits, Damir ap Kora! You cannot wield it against me and protect the woman at the same time. What will you do now? That sword answers to our 'Mage Protector' alone. No other hand but yours. And none but you can save your woman."

Huge, lifeless, and powered from beyond, Bruin bore down upon Damir, and Damir fell back. *None but you.* Life slipped from his body, and still, he held her. *I love you so.* Light faded, and Damir's eyes drifted shut, even as he held the sword over his head to ward off the next blow. Shapes swirled in the darkness, and he saw a dragonfly in his mind, and behind it . . . light.

Damir opened his eyes. Aren bounded through the snow and placed himself before Eliana, wielding a broken axe like a club. And then Damir knew what he had to do. "Aren!" The boy turned, and the dark wind gusted around him, hating the boy, yet unable to touch him. "The sword!"

Again Rodern laughed, a sound filled with hate and the lust for power and domination—not his own, but the fury of another. The Arch Mage's dark *ki* fueled everything. "A fool's choice! That sword will sear the flesh off any man who tries to wield it, lest he bears the *ki* of a Mage. Do it! Kill the boy—he has already lived too long."

Damir shoved Bruin, and the great Norskman stepped back once. It was enough. With his final strength, Damir flung the sword upward into the sky. It flew high above them and the evil wind coiled around it as if to obliterate its power. Aren leapt and caught the white sword by the hilt—and he did not fall. A white light burst around the blade like a star and the tall boy held the sword over his head. Then he spun around, and he hurtled it like a spear. It cut through the darkness and buried itself in Rodern's empty heart.

As if released from a noose, Bruin fell before Damir and lay still in the snow. The darkness shattered, and Rodern reeled back with a broken scream. In the echoes of the wind, Damir heard another scream, higher, more furious—a woman's scream. The sound lingered, then faded as if contained from within. It ebbed like the darkness, like a thwarted lover, and the wind stilled.

Eliana stumbled to Damir and knelt beside him. She was sobbing as she hugged him. "Damir . . ." Weak, but alive, Damir gathered her into his arms and held her. "I'm sorry," she whispered. "I could not let you fall."

He kissed her forehead. "I couldn't let them take you."

They looked out over the snow. For an instant, the dark tide seemed to swell over Rodern, but then it lifted and curled back on itself. "It looks like a snake," said Eliana.

"A snake that has struck at its prey, and failed, and now retreats."

"We drove it away," she whispered. "As we were meant to do. We defeated it."

"The tide is gone, but the promise I made also is broken," said Damir. "I couldn't bring the chieftain back to the light."

The sun lowered over the white snow and cast a red light over the dunes. As if spellbound, Aren walked to Rodern and retrieved the sword. He stared down at the dead Mage, his young face blank as he wiped the blade clean in the snow. Then he went to his brother and knelt beside him. He removed the red dagger from Bruin's back and cast it aside. Gently, he lifted Bruin's head into his lap.

Bruin opened his eyes, though his face was pale with oncoming death. He looked into Aren's face and his lips cracked toward a smile. He tried to reach for Aren, but his arms hung limp. "When all other lights went dim, I saw you, undimmed and untarnished . . . my brother . . ."

Tears fell down Aren's face. "I could not save you." He sounded like a child, at last. "I could wield the Mage's sword, but I couldn't help you."

With all his effort, Bruin gripped Aren's arm. "The Mage's sword . . . I name you my heir, and chieftain of our people. Take them where I could not."

"We are one people, because of you," said Aren, and his voice cracked. "I will not fail you again."

"One people . . ." whispered Bruin, and a smile softened his scarred and rugged face as he slipped into death. "Forgive me . . ."

Eliana and Damir went to Aren, and he wept silently beside his brother. Eliana put her arm around his shoulders, and all the bright fire Damir had seen in the young man's soul seemed to mute itself, to recede and abate, even as the dark tide had done. Aren had touched a moment of glory, and now he tried to refuse it, because it had failed to do the one thing he wanted—to save his brother.

Damir knelt beside Aren. "Your brother has passed as man, and not a slave. You gave him this, Aren. He died as a warrior, and he died with light on his face, not darkness. Don't blame yourself for the choices of another."

Aren handed the sword back to Damir. "It is done, and our people are saved from a far greater darkness. Under the Mage Rodern's control, Bruin would have led us to the cavern of the evil force we witnessed here, and we would have become its slaves. I understand that now. But it was you who saved my brother, Damir ap Kora. You gave of yourself for us, and gave him back himself. I thank you."

"We all thank you." Ranveig the innkeeper pulled off

his helmet, leaned back, and drew a shuddering breath. "I could use some tea."

They rode back to The Snow Pony, both Aren's followers and those that remained of Bruin's men. In the center of Eddenmark, they built a pyre and committed the dead to memory, and Aren spoke quiet words in the Norsk tongue that sent their spirits to the hall of warriors. There was no celebration of victory—the Norsk had seen a different enemy, and one they didn't understand.

"This power you own, Damir ap Kora, it is beyond us," said Aren. They sat around a table, bread and cheese uneaten before them. Ranveig brought salted meat, and seated himself beside them. The tall woman who had fought, removed her mail and helmet and returned to serving ale.

"Never have I seen such a battle," said Ranveig. "The wind itself seemed to rage and to throw itself against you. But it wasn't really the wind . . ." He stopped and shook his head. "Don't know what it was."

"It was the energy from an ancient Mage," said Eliana. "I'm not sure I understand it myself. But somehow Rodern harnessed his power, and directed it into your chieftain."

"It's as we've always said," added Ranveig. "Stay clear of wizards." He paused and cast a deferential glance at Damir. "Save this one here. If you've got to fight a wizard, enlist another one, I'd say."

"Do you think the evil will return?" asked Aren.

"I'm not sure," said Damir. "Not soon. Rodern found an apt target in your brother, because he had great strength and a simplicity within him that we lack in the Woodland. Bruin had no idea what Rodern intended, so he was vulnerable to the power Rodern seemed to offer. But you are warned now. It will not be so easy after this to turn a Norskman to the Arch Mage's uses."

"We are not so innocent now, you mean," said Aren, and he sighed. "We are raw, and we are primitive. Maybe we are violent. I felt the thrill of battle, and I liked it. But it comes from our own souls, our own hearts, for our own purposes. We do not wish to be used for another's lust."

"You are our chieftain now," said Ranveig. "Many of us have wanted this for a long while, and our people will follow you. It is the same in other villages. But what do we do now?"

Aren gazed out the tavern window, and again, snow fell outside. "We will move north again, as our people did in ages past. We will return to what we were, and seek no outward expansion. We will trade with the Guerdians, and they, with those in Amon-dhen. And I will protect our people, and keep us from the grasp of the darkness that too easily found its mark in my brother."

"I believe the darkness will return, one day," said Damir. "Such a power will seek its release. Because the Arch Mage was trapped undead, his energy has never been resolved. Maybe the light Mages made a mistake, after all. They put off the inevitable confrontation to a later generation—but at the time, they perceived no better solution."

"What will you do, the two of you?" asked Aren.

Damir turned to Eliana. "We will go home," he answered. "And then . . ." He would have given up everything for her, to save her. But he had taken something from her, and until that was returned, there would be no rest, and no peace. "We will go home."

Chapter Nineteen

Eliana and Damir spent a week with Aren and his followers, then they rode back to Amrodel a roundabout way, in the shadows of the northern mountains. Aren sent scouts to accompany them, but the Norsk turned back when they came within sight of the forest. The Norsk might have accepted Eliana and Damir as friendly Mages, but their suspicion of magic had been solidified by Rodern's treachery. In the spring, the Norsk would move their villages north, far from the danger they perceived in those more powerful than themselves.

Damir looked back as their Norsk allies rode away. He smiled as Eliana waved. "They had tea in their flagons," she said, and she felt proud.

"At least they'll ride straight," said Damir.

He had been so quiet throughout the ride. He had watched as Eliana played Fulthark in the snow with the Norsk scouts, but he hadn't joined in. She suspected his reason was more than the certainty he'd lose.

She felt safe, but she also felt a strange sense of loss. Damir's battle with Bruin lingered in her mind. She had seen his power unveiled, had seen his true greatness. What power she had herself was buried with her memory, though the moment she surrendered his shield, and gave it back to him, had filled her with another kind of strength.

If Damir had held her, if he had made love with her . . . but instead, they lay quiet beside each other through the cold nights on the journey home. They rode from the flat wasteland into a long strip of rolling hills that stretched the length of the forest. Here, fruit trees grew, and a few Mundanes tilled the fields beyond the trees. They spent their last night of the journey on the edge of the forest, but Damir seemed restless and didn't sleep well. Eliana woke briefly and saw him walking around in the light of full moon as if he were searching for something. She had meant to ask him what he was looking for, but she had fallen asleep, and dreamt of him flying over the grass like a dark dragonfly.

Eliana woke early and found him already awake, the horses bridled and ready for the last ride home. "Why were you wandering around last night?" she asked as she mounted Selsig.

"I couldn't sleep," he said, but he gave no further answer. "Our ride is less than an hour this morning."

"You are changing the subject," said Eliana, but he smiled and said no more. His smile seemed sorrowful, and she had no idea why.

Damir found a path through the woods, and they rode into the forest. Its warmth surrounded Eliana, and she closed her eyes, then breathed deeply of the fragrant air.

"It is good to be home," she said, but Damir didn't answer. "Are you all right, Damir? What is troubling you?"

"We've been through a lot, you and I," said Damir. "But for me, the real challenge, the true test, is now."

"What do you mean?" *No* . . . They had faced their

challenge, and they had won. They were free, and together. But Damir didn't look free.

Damir shook his head, and gestured at the path ahead. "Later, I think. We have company."

From the woods beyond, Woodlanders emerged, one by one, and then many. Eliana saw Fareth the innkeeper, and Madawc with Cahira at his side, and Elphin. Others came, and they surrounded Eliana and Damir, their faces eager, yet with an emotion Eliana couldn't read.

Madawc came forward, and tears glimmered in his clear, blue eyes. "You've done well, the two of you. The dark tide has receded."

Damir dismounted, and he bowed. "It will return one day, Elder. You know that."

Madawc nodded. "It comes from one who does not die. Yes, I know he will return. But you've taught him, and all those who clutch onto him, that his return won't be without a battle. And it's a battle he's not guaranteed to win. You've taught him we are strong."

"Maybe he knows now that he must fight his own battles," said Eliana, and she dismounted, too. "It was cruel and wrong to use the Norsk that way. But they have a new leader now, and though he's young, he has great wisdom."

"I take it you found your 'lover'?" asked Madawc, but his lips twitched with a smile as if he'd always known the truth.

Damir frowned. "The Norskman in question was a young man of fourteen. As it happens, his true admiration seems to be for a very pretty girl he saw once in our own palace, when he was the 'special guest' of The Fiend . . ." Damir's gaze shifted to Cahira and she blushed. "I do not think we need fear the Norsk again, but the Arch Mage's spirit has seen them. If he returns, they will not escape his wrath, for it was Aren, the new chieftain, who wielded my sword against Rodern."

Madawc's mouth dropped open. "A *Norskman* laid hands on your sword—and lived? How is that possible?"

"I don't know," said Damir. "One day, you may get the opportunity to study this boy—his energy is unlike anything I've ever encountered, though I sense no sign of a Mage's *ki* within him. What he has, instead, is something else entirely."

"He was a pretty boy," said Cahira, too casually. "But I sensed he could be trouble."

"He said you told no one about his presence in Amrodel," said Eliana.

"You seemed to like him," said Cahira. "But he winked at me, and I have not forgotten how annoying that was." She paused. "But if he avenged my father's murder, then I owe him my allegiance."

"If he's a strange lad, this one is stranger still," said Madawc. "Her *ki* hops around like a spring toad. I can't get a handle on it. One moment, it's as elemental as fire—and could burn as high. Then it flutters away. But she's a young lass—there's time to bring her power to fruition."

"So the Norsk are in hand," said Fareth, and the innkeeper sounded impatient. A few other Woodlanders nodded and muttered. "That's all well and fine—and the elder Mage here had reported as much, anyway. What we really want to know . . ."

Damir interrupted with a groan, but Eliana folded her arms over her chest and faced them. "Damir and I have become lovers, though I have not regained my memory." She paused. "Did anyone have a bet on that?"

"I did!" Everyone turned in surprise to see Cahira waving her hand, and then she snapped her fingers as if demanding gold.

Madawc's eyes narrowed to slits. "The Mage Child should not be betting, and certainly not on such subjects as these."

"*You* wager! I don't see why I shouldn't, and since I was right . . ."

"Fair enough," said Fareth, and he handed Cahira a small bag of gold.

Madawc seized the bag before she could grasp it. "As it happens, I bet on the same outcome, Mage Child, and that gold is half mine." Cahira frowned as the elder Mage divided their winnings.

Elphin sighed heavily. "I bet they'd be lovers, all right, but I thought she'd get her memory back and kill him."

"That was the nature of my wager, too," said Fareth. "Though I thought Damir ap Kora would bring The Fiend home on the back of his horse, kicking and screaming."

Eliana straightened. "Indeed! I will have you all know that *The Demon* and I have straightened out our various differences, and have been cordial as well as passionate ever since." She paused and glanced at Damir. "Haven't we?"

He smiled, but he still looked sad to her. "Before it can be truly 'straightened out' between us, I have some work to do. I'll meet you at your cottage later."

Madawc looked between them and he nodded as if he understood Damir's intentions. "We've cleaned it up for you, lass—Elphin, Cahira and myself. It's back to its old self, and better."

"Thank you," said Eliana, but she couldn't look away from Damir. "Aren't we going together?"

He didn't answer, but he touched her cheek, then kissed her forehead. "I will come to you later, but I will need Madawc's help at my own cottage."

He said no more about his purpose, and Eliana's heart sank as he mounted. He looked back at her, then rode away in the direction of the mountains. Madawc and Cahira left with him, and Elphin stayed with Eliana.

"What are they doing?" asked Eliana.

"I'm not sure," said Elphin. "But they'll be a while, it

seems. If you'd like, Lady, we can stop by The Hungry Cat on the ride back to your cottage. You must be feeling peckish after eating Norsk food."

Eliana sighed, but she climbed back onto Selsig. "You might find Norsk taverns to your liking, Elphin. Have you ever played the game of Fulthark?"

"Some Norsk battle game?" asked Elphin, suspicious.

"In a way . . . I'll teach you."

Eliana amused herself teaching the patrons of The Hungry Cat how to play Fulthark, and winning until Elphin caught on to the sport. The Norsk innkeeper, Ranveig, had given her a bag of Fulthark rune stones as a parting gift, and she had to turn down several offers from Fareth's customers to purchase her stones. "They can't be that hard to make," she suggested, but the Woodlanders seemed to feel Norsk craft beyond them.

"I wonder if both people might benefit from greater contact," said Eliana, but the Woodlanders reacted much as the Norsk had done at the same suggestion. "One day, you will have to, I think," she added, but no one listened.

Eliana looked around at the tavern patrons. "Where is Shaen? She wasn't among those who greeted us."

Elphin devoured a sausage as if he'd been the one on the long journey. "The lady fell ill a week or so back. She was screaming and delirious—had a high burning fever. Madawc tended her, and for a while, it looked like we'd lose her. Odd, she was, but she's recovering now, and she's as nice as she ever was."

"Was a sickness affecting people in the forest?" asked Eliana.

"Seems as if," said Elphin as he seized a large portion of bread and added cheese to it. "It looked like an epidemic was starting, but in the end, only a few came down with it. One or two Mages, lesser ones, and Shaen. But they all got better, and no one else came down with it."

332

"That's lucky," said Eliana. "It must have happened about the same time as Damir's battle with Bruin the Ruthless. I wonder if there was any connection?"

"Don't know," said Elphin. "I didn't sense anything myself, but Madawc came into the tavern on the same night they fell ill and told us you had fulfilled your quest."

"Did Shaen fall ill right then?"

"I think it was a little before—at least, before Madawc gave us the news. He didn't seem to think there was any connection."

"No, I don't suppose there's any reason for it to be of interest. Perhaps the more sensitive types picked up the energy of the battle—how much was at stake in that moment. I guess that could have made them ill." Eliana sighed. The dark tide had abated. She had watched it sink back into the eastern mountains and disappear. But it wasn't gone. The dark and light of all *ki* would never resolve its battle—it was the nature of existence. At least it had returned to balance once again. Why, then, did her own heart still feel heavy?

She ate a small meal with Elphin, and then they rode on to her cottage. The path to her little home seemed lonely, but to her surprise, Damir was waiting there by her door. Her heart rose, but something in his expression told her the meeting was not what she hoped.

"You were quick with your task," she said. She released Selsig into a small paddock, and the little mare rolled and kicked her hooves in the air. She whinnied and seemed happy to be home.

"It proved easier than I imagined," said Damir. He held open her door, and she went in. Elphin followed. He seemed depressed, too, as if he knew what was coming next.

Eliana looked around her small house. Madawc had set it to rights, and everything looked cheerful. He'd even put a small vase of herbs on her table. She was expected to stay there now, as she had before, alone. Eliana swallowed hard and looked up at Damir. "What were you doing?"

He drew a breath and presented her with a vial of amber liquid. She took it, then shook her head. "What is it?"

"You might call it my 'Wine of Surrender.'" He paused, as if the words came hard. "Do you remember the scroll Elphin found on the first morning you spent in my cottage?"

"I remember the scroll," said Eliana. "But I didn't realize Elphin was the one who found it."

"It was a lucky find. It showed your methods of distilling herbs into potions by sunlight. Your own instincts told me the rest. The herbs you gathered made a potion that will restore your memory."

"But another plant was necessary . . ."

He nodded. "I found that herb the night before we entered the Woodland." He paused, and she saw pain in his dark eyes. "I knew I would. I knew what plant it was the moment you spoke of it. It is called Moonlark, a plant that blooms only on the full of the moon. It grows near the forest's edge. I could have told you when I first realized, but I was so afraid of losing you . . ."

Eliana seized his hand. "And the moon still wouldn't have been full . . . Damir, everything comes in its own time, on its own place in our path." She eyed the potion. "This will restore my memory?"

"It will. I tested it on Madawc this morning. I wanted to test it on myself, but he said I wasn't old enough to have forgotten anything."

"It worked?" She felt hesitant, but her heart beat in odd little jerks.

"Yes." A faint smile curved his lips. "Madawc remembered a boy called something like 'Pickle' who stole one of Madawc's first girlfriends. He's still stewing about it. He and Cahira went on to The Hungry Cat with the intention of hunting down this 'Pickle.'"

"Then it does work!" Eliana pulled the cork from the

vial and held it to her lips, but Damir placed his hand over hers. "Wait . . ."

"Don't you want me to take it?"

"It is right that you do," he answered. "I would return what I took from you. But . . ." Damir's voice broke and he bowed his head before looking at her again. "This moment is for you alone."

"Damir . . ."

He held his fingers to her lips, then bent to kiss her. "I love you, Eliana. I have always loved you. But I would have you whole, in the fullness of your life. You are a great spirit, a woman with courage and wisdom, I think, beyond even the ancient Woodland queen. You saw good in our enemies when I thought only to defend against them. You enlisted them, and gave of yourself, and made them our friends. I fought the battle against Bruin, but it was you who set me free. You gave up yourself for me, and that came from the core of what you truly are. Let me do this for you, that I can at least honor your courage, and your sacrifice."

She wanted to tell him she loved him, too, but she knew he wouldn't hear her, not really. He would hear only this shadow she had become, a loving shadow, but a woman who couldn't speak for her whole life. Eliana rose up on tiptoes and kissed his cheek, then touched his hair. "Thank you."

He went to the door and looked back once. She knew he committed her face, and the love in her eyes, to his own memory. His gaze lingered a moment longer, and then he walked away. Eliana watched him go, then held up the potion he had given her. Elphin stood tense beside her.

"Don't take it, Lady. There's no need, really—is there? What's a memory but a long road you've already walked? Why go back, when the good lies ahead?"

Eliana looked at him, and she smiled. "A long road in shadow—even if it isn't seen, is still there, isn't it?"

Elphin clutched her arm. "You can go onward—you can go to him. Tell him you don't want to go back. Tell him this is where you want to be. Tell him that other woman you used to be is gone."

Eliana held the potion up to the sunlight as it streamed golden through her western window. And then she turned away.

A long night went slowly by, but Damir slept only fitfully. He rose at dawn and looked out his window. Llwyd stood sleeping in his paddock. The horse looked lonely. He must have grown used to Selsig's determined companionship—as Damir had grown used to having Eliana by his side.

He turned from the window, then went into his kitchen and made tea, though the warmed ale of the Norsk might serve him better this morning. He sat at his heavy wooden table and stared into the amber tea, watching the steam rise and disappear.

A knock on his door startled Damir, and he spilled the tea. His legs felt weak as he went to the door and opened it. Elphin stood there, and Damir's heart crashed in his chest. The boy's shoulders slumped and he drew a long, heavy breath before speaking. He looked up at Damir, and the dismal expression on his face told Damir everything he didn't want to know.

"The lady has sent me . . ." Elphin paused to sigh . . . "With this message: She 'requests' that you meet her in the Mage's Glade . . ."

Elphin's words trailed, but Damir's heart clenched. *Where they met for her "Wine of Truce"* . . .

Damir drew a cape from a hook by the door, but Elphin took his arm and looked up at him, eyes beseeching. "Don't go, sir. She's back . . ."

Damir smiled, and he placed his hand over Elphin's, but he said nothing as he left his cottage.

Elphin sighed again, then shook his head as he stood in the doorway. "I'll be at The Hungry Cat if you need an ale later, sir. Some steep wagers will be resolved today. 'Fraid mine's going down."

Damir caught Llwyd and bridled him. For a saddle, he used only the Norsk blanket that Aren had given him. He rode south along the long road, then turned eastward along the secret path that led to the Mage's Glade.

She was standing there already, her little mare grazing freely near the Mage's Rock. Damir entered the clearing, and his heart labored at the sight of her. She wore the same long red gown he had left in her cottage when they had departed for the Norskland—the dress that framed her lovely body and set her green eyes to a woodland fire. A gossamer headdress glittered in the new morning light, with pale green jewels sewn in, and silver chains that dangled amidst the loose strands of her hair.

Upon the rock sat a decanter, and beside it, a goblet. Damir dismounted, and left Llwyd free. The horse joined Selsig. They sniffed noses, then commenced grazing together like old friends. Damir bowed his head, then met her gaze across the clearing. He read nothing in her expression, except that she was waiting.

He walked to the Mage's Rock and stared at the decanter and the goblet, already filled with a clear and fragrant brew. He drew a breath, then lifted the goblet to his lips and drank until the glass was empty. The taste was crisp and light. He set it down and looked at her. Still, she showed no reaction. She just waited.

Damir sat on the flat stone on the north end of the Mage's Rock, and at last, he looked up at her. "Will it make me forget?"

Her black lashes lowered over her green eyes, and she looked like a goddess. All her memory glittered there—all he had ever known of her, and all she had ever been.

Eliana, "The Fiend"—the greatest, most beautiful, and wisest woman, stood before him, wholly herself once more.

Slowly, moving like a soft breeze through the leaves, she knelt before him. She looked up at him, and her unfathomable eyes shone. "Do you wish to forget?"

Tears sprang to Damir's eyes. "No."

"Then you shall not forget."

He wanted to touch her, he wanted to fall to his knees before her and beg her forgiveness, but instead, Eliana bent and kissed his knee.

"Eliana . . . You drank the potion . . . You know who I am, and what I've done to you. You know who you are."

"I am the woman who loves you, who has always loved you. Damir . . ." She took his hands and held them in hers. "Don't you know? It is true that I came up with my 'Wine of Truce' with the intention of bringing you to Aren—I knew you could help them, and in doing so, save us, too. But I didn't think you would listen to me."

He felt shy. He had known her all his life, and then they had become lovers. But now, in her presence, with all her memory intact, he felt shy. Eliana kissed his hand and her bright eyes glowed. "Can you not guess what else I intended with the brew I tried to give you?"

He smiled, but a tear fell to his face. "I can't imagine you would have sent a chipmunk or a hopping frog to Aren's aid."

"No," she said, her voice a whisper. "*A husband.*"

Damir stared. His gaze shifted, and then he looked back at her. "A husband?"

Eliana smiled and then pressed her lips together. "*My husband*—who adored me, and worshipped me, and had loved me always. A husband who was very sweet, and docile, and liked to cook, too."

Damir's mouth slid open and stayed there. "You were going to tell me . . . ?"

She nodded. "The same thing you told me."

Happiness flooded through him so fast and so strong that he couldn't move. "How were you going to explain your virginity?"

"I had planned to tell you it was our wedding day, of course."

"I wish I'd thought of that!"

"I even meant to say that you were injured in a fall. I couldn't come up with something better than a fall—and I'm pleased you didn't, either. I spent quite a while considering that, actually."

Damir sank to his knees and caught her in his arms. "If I had known that, I wouldn't have switched the goblets!"

He kissed her, and she wrapped her arms around his neck. Eliana laughed, and the sound poured from her heart. It was pure happiness. "That was not our fate, Damir ap Kora. Our path was never the straight road, but the winding path with many unexpected turns. But we are here, together, and I love you. I love with all that I am, and all that I ever will be."

He drew back and looked into her eyes. "You love me?"

"Do you doubt it?"

"I would hear you say it again."

"I love you." She kissed his face, then his mouth. "I love you. The Fiend loves you."

He smiled. "Does she forgive me?"

"If you forgive her . . ."

"Eliana, there is nothing to forgive."

"We will forgive each other, and accept what we are, shall we? We can't change what we were, or the choices we made. They brought us to this place. But from now on, I would walk by your side, and forever after, open my heart to you, rather than hide it in shadow and in fear."

"By my side . . ." Damir closed his eyes and all he had dreamed took shape before him. "Then would you wed with me, Eliana Daere, and live at my side, as well?"

Eliana glowed with happiness and she kissed his face. "I would, I would!"

Damir gestured at Llwyd and Selsig. "Those two will find the change for the better, I think." He paused. "Incidentally, I believe your mare is in foal."

Eliana clasped her hands. "Really? We must send the firstborn to Aren, as a gift. It should be a magnificent and sturdy animal—the start of a new breed!"

"An evolution," said Damir. "Like us."

Eliana hugged him tight, but then drew back. "Where will we live?"

"Your cottage is charming, but mine is larger . . ."

"Another abode awaits the two of you . . ." Madawc spoke across the glade, almost as if he'd appeared there out of thin air. Eliana startled and hopped into Damir's lap, knocking him backward. Madawc strode across the clearing and shook his head. "Straighten yourselves! The others of Amrodel are picking their way here now, and they can't see you wrapped together in a heap!"

Damir rose and helped Eliana to her feet. He straightened her disheveled headdress and they looked around in amazement as the Woodlanders entered the Mage's Glade. "What are you people doing here?" asked Damir, but then he groaned and clasped his hand to his forehead. "Don't tell me! You're here to find the results of your latest wager! *Fine!* Eliana's memory has been restored, she still loves me, and I've asked her to marry me. Did anyone place a bet on that?"

Fareth the innkeeper shook his head. "No point in that—we all knew the outcome. Elphin here reported on your doings, but there weren't no surprise in that."

Damir glared at the boy, who grinned. "Then why did you arrive at my cottage this morning looking as if your mother had died?"

Elphin shrugged. "Didn't want to spoil the lady's moment."

Damir turned to Eliana. "You told him to terrify me?"

"No. I just asked him to invite you here," said Eliana.

Elphin grinned. "Figured I'd set you up just right. But as Fareth says, it weren't worth betting on, since we all had it figured the same way by now."

Damir sighed and shook his head. "Then why are you here?"

Madawc crossed his arms over his chest and looked triumphant. "We're here on the matter of your abode, as it were, lad."

"What about it? Is there a bet about whether we'll settle at Eliana's cottage or mine?"

"Give us more credit than that!" said Madawc. "There's no interest there, now that you've admitted you're in love with each other, and will set to producing little ones soon."

Eliana uttered a small, happy gasp. "We will! Damir, we will have babies!"

Damir put his arm around her shoulder. "We will."

"Not in one of your little cottages, you won't," said Madawc.

"Well, where would you suggest?" asked Damir. He didn't wait for an answer. "We'll wed tonight, as the moon rises. Then we'll lie together under the stars. . . ."

Madawc interrupted with a loud cough. "You can arrange your wedded itinerary later. For now, the people of Amrodel have a proposition for you."

Damir gazed into Eliana's eyes and she sighed happily. "What is it?" Damir asked, though he wasn't really listening or in the mood to consider propositions.

Madawc came forward and laid his hand on Damir's shoulder. "Take your place as King of Amrodel, and if she can pry her eyes off you, Eliana will be our queen."

Damir shifted his gaze to Madawc. "I am only half a Woodlander . . ."

Madawc rolled his eyes. "By the word of the people,

you will be king. And you've got the heir of our greatest Mage to be your queen. You're both fit for the duty. And a duty it will be, lad. You know that. We all do. The world has changed, even in the air and in the water. And though the dark tide has receded, we all know it will come again, to a higher mark than before. We need a real leader. We need both of you, who defended us when the danger came, who risked everything for us."

Madawc turned to the Woodlanders while Damir and Eliana stared in amazement. "Will you have this man and this woman as your king and your queen?"

The Woodlanders called out, one by one, and the sound echoed through the trees, and softened in the morning mist. "Aye, we will, we will . . ."

The chorus ended, and Madawc turned back to Damir and Eliana. "Will you take this role, and live in the palace of Amrodel, and serve our people as our king and queen?"

Damir turned to Eliana and he took her hands in his. She gazed up at him and all the love he had longed for now shone in her eyes. She was his—the woman he had adored since he first beheld her, who had made his life a whirlwind and a torment, who had given him the greatest bliss. She was his. "Aye," he said, and his voice came soft. "We will."

CELTIC
FIRE
JOY NASH

In the wilds of Britannia, a fierce battle rages. Rhiannon, rightful ruler of the Celts, longs to see the invading Romans driven from her land. But when she is taken by the enemy, she can't deny her reaction to their compelling leader.

Having to look upon the ghost of his murdered brother every day is torture for Commander Lucius Aquila. But the strangely fascinating woman he captured has the power to make the visions disappear, and Lucius knows she can help him solve the mystery of Aulus's death. Even as he questions her loyalty, her courage and beauty hold him spellbound, and Lucius can only dream of the day he might succumb to her *CELTIC FIRE*.